W9-BVG-560

UNRELIABLE

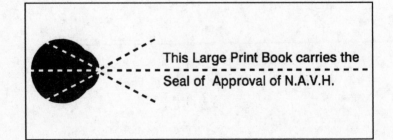

This Large Print Book carries the
Seal of Approval of N.A.V.H.

UNRELIABLE

LEE IRBY

THORNDIKE PRESS
A part of Gale, a Cengage Company

Farmington Hills, Mich • San Francisco • New York • Waterville, Maine
Meriden, Conn • Mason, Ohio • Chicago

LIBRARY OF CONGRESS CATALOGING-IN-PUBLICATION DATA

Names: Irby, Lee, author.
Title: Unreliable / Lee Irby.
Description: Waterville, Maine : Thorndike Press Large Print, 2017. | Series: Thorndike Press large print thriller
Identifiers: LCCN 2017027205| ISBN 9781432842659 (hardback) | ISBN 143284265X (hardcover)
Subjects: LCSH: College teachers—Fiction. | Homecoming—Fiction. | Truthfulness and falsehood—Fiction. | Richmond (Va.)—Fiction. | New York (State)—Fiction. | Psychological fiction. | Large type books. | BISAC: FICTION / Suspense.
Classification: LCC PS3609.R47 U5 2017b | DDC 813/.6—dc23
LC record available at https://lccn.loc.gov/2017027205

Published in 2017 by arrangement with Doubleday, a division of Penguin Random House LLC

Printed in the United States of America
1 2 3 4 5 6 7 21 20 19 18 17

UNRELIABLE

DAY ONE — JULY 1

1

Here's the first clue: the dead will die again.

Not possible, you grumble. But a coward dies a thousand times and a brave man just once, and honestly I'm a bit of both. So is our narrator (that would be me) dead or alive? It doesn't much matter, because my job is to deliver some blood on the very first page. Mine, hers, his. You want a body and I want to give you one.

This should be easy, since I'm on a killing spree. Actually, I'm just a college professor who drives a four-door Honda . . . but it happens to be midnight in Gettysburg, Pennsylvania, the witching hour, when darkness hisses with spooky noises and creepy strangers contemplate unspeakable acts, such as luring a waitress into a fatal trap. Here comes one now, emerging from the Dumpster-shadowed rear of a TGI Fridays.

Even though I'm sitting in the Honda, she glances over in my direction, not suspiciously, more of a cursory assessment of her surroundings. There is a cell phone in my hand and you might want to know what I'm doing with it. I'll divulge only that I was checking on the operating hours of the aforementioned TGI Fridays and just learned that it closes at midnight, which has just struck. So for a late dinner, I'll have to rummage through a nearby convenience store. But first let me work up an appetite.

The waitress continues walking toward her car, which is parked not far from mine. Something tells me that she is unhappy with not just her life but all lives. Her work shift probably demeaned her in a million ways, from fussy manager to rude customers, and now she heads home to a cramped apartment and an aging cat whose vet bills she can ill afford. She isn't scowling but more bemoaning in silence all that accosts her, and with grace and mercy I'll end her troubles with a single shot to the head.

I jest. I don't even own a gun! I understand I need to deliver a corpse, and I take this task seriously. It's all I have left to live for. My goal? My ultimate purpose? I want you to *disentangle*. As the great Edgar Allan Poe tells us, the analyst "glories in that moral activity." In the end what will we discover? That the dead never actually die?

Or that the living never really live? In the city of Richmond, Virginia, the distinction between the living and the dead can get blurry, on account of the Confederate ghosts who haunt the cobblestone streets. And who is Richmond's most celebrated literary son? Why, none other than Edgar A. Poe himself. Where did Poe spend the last few months of his life before he mysteriously died? Some say he was murdered, and if he was indeed targeted, his killers were to be found in, yes, Richmond, the RVA.

And me? Well, I'm driving to Richmond, as fate would have it, returning to my hometown for the first time in many years for my mother's wedding, but you'll have to wait for the details because I hate it when hack authors dump the backstory like a load of mulch.

The waitress is passing about fifteen feet in front of me. Time to pounce. I hop out of my car. "Can I ask you a question?" I call out to her just as she pushes a button to unlock her Soul (made by Kia). Butterflies flutter away in my empty stomach that churns with tumult. I adore women who teeter on the brink of collapse and I often dream of rescuing trapped damsels from bad boyfriends or crushing solitude.

"Sure," she replies after some hesitation.

She must've concluded that I pose little risk and thus has the uncanny ability to see right through me. Or she has a blind spot that will be her undoing.

"Is there a place nearby where I can get some decent food?"

She mulls over this question asked by someone she thinks is harmless. In her defense, it's true that I appear to be an unlikely murderer. After all, my current occupation is Instructor of Composition, Notting College, a leafy liberal arts school in Ithaca, New York, a town better known for being the home of Cornell University, where the great Nabokov taught. My rented flat on North Plain Street sits across from the ballet academy whose prima ballerina was said to be the real-life inspiration for Lolita. The crone is over eighty now and can be found in the lobby of the YMCA, perched in a wheelchair while chain-smoking Lucky Strikes. I've been too ashamed to ask her about Vlad, and anyway talking to strangers makes my stomach cramp. And she's probably a liar, like the rest of us.

But the salient question is: could I kill someone? Well, obviously. Under the right circumstances, anyone is capable of homicide. My closest friends, who number in the low single digits, would describe me as mild-mannered. My ex-wife would contend that I lacked the blind ambition to kill, and what great killer ever lacked the atavistic drive to dominate? My students have evaluated me as effective, somewhat bland, slow to return graded papers, but genial. So where is the red flag, the dark side, the demonic urge?

It is located in the bedroom, where it always resides, so let's delve deeper into my primal cave. Do I possess a deviant sex life, perversions powerful enough to impel me to impulsive acts? Hey, remember that casual reference to my ex-wife? Of all people she'd be in the best position to offer credence to the Twisted Killer hypothesis now under discussion. Usually she'd love to tell you all about my major issues and hang-ups, but these days she's too busy being in love with her new boyfriend. Yes, I'm insanely jealous. But I wish only the best for Bev and want very much for us to renew our friendship that has been strained the last two years.

I feel your finger quivering at me. He's killed her! And now he's on the run, headed back to Richmond to escape the long arm of the law. But wouldn't the police first go to my mother's house? A calm and collected killer would abscond to a foreign land where it's far easier to live under an assumed name. Who would be foolish enough to hide in plain sight? To act as if nothing untoward has happened? To follow established routines and then feign surprise when the handcuffs are clapped on? Such an audacious plan sounds like it comes directly from the pen of Edgar Allan Poe . . . so is this my homage to the master?

"I think everything around here is closed," the waitress finally replies.

A raucous group of young men stumbles out of the restaurant, cocksure and crowing, eager to raze all that stands before them. Their loud voices rule the night, virile squawks that send chills down my spine. I hate them, one and all.

"I haven't eaten all day," I say elegiacally. This personal admission borders on TMI and causes the waitress to scurry to her car. It's not like I'm going to chase after her, for Pete's sake. I stand and watch her hop into her Soul, not angry that she's rebuffed me, that she finds me heinous, or that she'd rather be alone than speak with a well-educated stranger.

I check my phone again. From whom do I expect a call? What message do I hope to get? Something, anything, but there's the usual nothing from nobody. This is the worst, to be hungry at midnight at an outlet mall in Gettysburg, Pennsylvania, site of the most pivotal battle in the Civil War, which began because exhausted Southerners came here looking for shoes.

Shoes! Oh crap!

I dive into the backseat of the Honda and begin pawing through my luggage, gripped by the sudden fear that, yes, I've forgotten to pack the shoes that I'd purchased especially for the wedding. My mother won't be happy with me. She's become obsessed with the smallest detail of her nuptials, as if she is a blushing bride in her early twenties and not a mature woman who's just turned sixty. But all weddings have an element of fantasy to them, not to mention stress and strain. This one will be no different. On Saturday afternoon, my mother will become Mrs. Mead George, and here's what I know about her future husband and my step-father: not much. He is forty-three, which makes him exactly five years older than *moi*. He has two children from a previous marriage, he owns a business of some sort, and he's really friendly, according to my mother, who can't speak about her new man without her voice lilting in exultation. She wants this wedding to be perfect, and thus we'll all be attired in white, virginal and pure, which

15

required me to buy a pair of white oxfords currently sitting in a Zappos box on my kitchen table.

Your hot glare falls on me. You detect my obvious displeasure at the wedding, and since I've promised you mayhem, you infer that I'm on my way to Richmond to kill the groom and thus exact a Hamlet-like revenge. But at the moment I'm just very upset that I've forgotten my shoes, and I actually stagger away from the burgundy Honda, walk over to the plate-glass window of Famous Footwear, and stare into the empty and darkened store.

Here's a thought. Did I leave my shoes for the wedding in Ithaca because I was in a hurry to flee? Was I in some kind of panic? Sure, I'll admit to being highly agitated. Fragile even. Last night I drove past the apartment Bev shares with her new man, named Igor, an artist no less, whose work consisted almost entirely of ceramics he'd spun on a potter's wheel that drooped and gyrated into amorphous contortions he called "shoshin," or "beginner's mind," which is a term from Zen Buddhism, whose self-denying strictures Igor pretended to follow. He had a shaved head and a severe manner of forced asceticism, and basically he looked like a gangling wraith of misplaced spirituality. But I didn't see Bev last night, or Igor, or them together making sweet love, which in all honesty is something I'd pay to watch.

Forget I said that. I don't want you thinking less of me too soon.

Until Bev took up with that fraud, she'd never displayed poor aesthetic taste in any medium. As for books, she read only the literary canon. Her taste in film tended to the absurdist but she also appreciated French New Wave, though often we disagreed about Truffaut's early work. One weekend we stayed in bed for thirty straight hours gorging on *Breaking Bad.* And music . . . I might start to cry. Music united us, literally created us. Our first date was to see Snorting Herzog at The Dock, and those crazy bastards just killed it — distortion, hammers beating on steel drums, amped feedback, and the onstage ingestion of a Brazilian hallucinogen. It was some pretty harsh sludge metal, but Bev never flinched. She found the show as exhilarating as I did, and during the twenty-six-minute drum solo, when my quivering hand found the small of her perspiring back, I hoped that we'd never spend a night apart for the rest of our lives.

The waitress still hasn't driven away. The

car is running and its lights are on, but she remains. How now? Is she inviting me to join her in an automotive version of hide-and-go-seek? Casually, hands stuffed in pockets, I ramble back to the Honda and get in. Not unexpectedly, the waitress backs up, slowly, giving me ample time to see her Soul in retreat. I thought she was afraid of strangers, but apparently not. The thrill of danger must animate her in ways nothing else can. A poet once told us: "Life, friends, is boring." Here is living proof.

I follow her. She turns left onto U.S. 15 and so do I. We're headed south, which may or may not be a coincidence. I could be resuming my drive to Richmond or in pursuit of my next victim. But how do you know there are any previous victims? No dead bodies have been produced. I've got no animus toward that waitress, just empathy and deep concern. It's not like she left me for another man. Plus, I'm going to my mother's wedding. From my car stereo blasts the boppy riffs of Le Mort Joyeux, a Grateful Dead cover band from Montreal whose lead singer sounds like a bizarre amalgam of Edith Piaf and Bob Weir. Has any serial killer in history ever listened to such an obscure band in prelude to murder? I highly doubt it, and so should you.

18

We drive past the entrance to the great battlefield, the gate to which has been festooned with banners to honor the festivities of yet another anniversary that will be under way in just a few hours. Lincoln said that the living cannot consecrate the dead of Gettysburg, and I tend to agree. Thousands of brave souls perished here, yet we trundle along just fine, engrossed by the odd and trivial.

Case in point: I speed up so that I'm a car length behind the waitress's vehicle, close enough so that I can count the hairs on her pretty little head. In turn she accelerates down a lonely stretch of highway, exceeding the speed limit by a considerable margin, the naughty girl. So she likes to play rough.

My car's engine, however, is making the kinds of desperate groans emitted from terminal patients in the last throes of decline. The tires are bald and dangerous to drive on — but the balding doesn't stop there. I too am shedding hair with the robust regularity of an October maple tree. An irrational part of me blames Bev's departure on my male-pattern misery, but as a scholar of rhetoric, I realize that my hairline is a metaphor that stands for a multitude of emotional and psychological sheddings.

I can barely see the taillights of her Soul off in the distance . . .

I need new music! What band can leaven the licorice sky that conceals the forces of ruin afoot in the roadside woods? Any second a herd of deer could leap out in front of me and then I'd crash into one and be stuck here, left to confront my fate alone. Not that Bev ever enjoyed going to Richmond. She loathed the city and all it stood for, and atop her list of repugnant offenses were the marble statues that lined fabled Monument Avenue — Stonewall Jackson, Jefferson Davis, and the largest of them all, Major General Robert E. Lee, astride his trusty steed Traveller, towering some sixty feet over the genteel environs of one of Richmond's most prestigious neighborhoods. (She didn't mind the statue of tennis hero Arthur Ashe, but I didn't have the heart to explain how much trauma was involved to get it placed there, next to the Confederate pantheon.)

"It makes me sick to my stomach" were her exact words upon seeing the parade of marble men for the first time. "How can a culture celebrate virulent racists and pro-slavery sympathizers?"

"I don't think General Lee owned any slaves."

Then came the Look of Disgust — Bev had the singular ability to eviscerate me with one stabbing glance.

"General Lee? You mean the car on *The Dukes of Hazzard*? You're defending this rubbish?"

"No! Look at it as a bizarre form of ancestor worship, like the Oracle of the Bones in ancient China."

"So I guess Berlin should erect a few monuments to Adolf, huh, in the name of ancestor worship?"

It was at this point that I decided she had to die and then spent the next three years of my life planning the perfect crime, which I'm in the middle of executing. As if! You hunger greedily for blood, and I'm trying my best to explain, but I don't even know myself what's happened. Things can become a blur and even the most steadfast among us can buckle from the g-force. Let's stick to the established facts. I'm in a car driving to Richmond. I need music that will allow my mind to clear and my spirits to lift. Nu disco, perhaps? Something fast and pounding that will speed up the passage of time and perhaps shorten the mental distance remaining in my journey. At my current pace, I won't be arriving to my mother's house until around four a.m.

Betty Crocker.

Not the cookbook but a trio from Stockholm who, in the name of full disclosure, Bev turned me on to. I crank up the volume and settle back for a long ride through the midnight dreary. My nerves are so on edge that the approach of headlights from the opposite direction sends me spiraling into a panic, because I don't trust myself that I won't step on the accelerator and speed into the blinding light coming at me. An admission of guilt? Is this a "Tell-Tale Heart" moment, when you expect me to confess that I killed Bev because her hideous eyes reminded me of a vulture? Hardly. Bev's eyes were her most attractive feature. They were verdantly green, feline and alert, beaming out an incorrigible energy unafraid to be different from the crowd. Bev's eyes were as brave and tough as she was. She worked as a case manager with hard-core juvenile offenders, the ones who'd sexually abused infants or set fires to homes. The irredeemable, the truly forsaken. The horrors she encountered on her job never dimmed the lustrous shine of her vivid eyes, yet when those same eyes danced and darted like fireflies, avoiding me, withdrawing, withholding, condemning me to oblivion, I knew then that our love had vanished — no, not vanished, because she said she'd love me forever and always, and so maybe the right way to phrase it is to claim our love had curdled. Cottage-cheese love, so to speak. It took her three months to find the words to end it, three weeks for her to move out, and three days for me to shower after she was gone.

I'm going to call her. The cell phone is in my trembling hand and I know she stays up late. But what would I tell her? The unvarnished truth. That I'm in serious trouble. That I'm on the verge of ruin. That I'm headed to Richmond to attend the wedding of my mother to a deadbeat who's my age. Bev would've appreciated the absurdity of the insipid spectacle that will unfold this weekend, as Bev and my mother didn't see eye to eye on most matters. This tawdry affair would've pushed Bev past the brink. Needless to say, my mother isn't unhappy in the least that Bev and I are kaput, and she insists that one day I'll find the person who's right for me.

If I were to call Bev now, when homicide detectives searched through my cell phone records, they'd find that I'd attempted to reach her, which could mean 1) I didn't know she was dead or 2) I was trying to cover my tracks by pretending I didn't know she was dead. These matters aren't easy to write about.

Just know this: It is now 12:36 a.m. I have yet to reach Maryland, morbid thoughts ransack my brain, and I've forgotten my shoes. I don't call Bev.

I drive and drive, until, at 2:07 a.m. when I approach the Maryland–Virginia border, I receive a text:

I miss u already! Hurry home! U mean everything to me.

It's not from Bev. Make of that what you will.

2

At 4:02 a.m. the first exit signs for Richmond appear, and soon I'll be driving through a subdivision called Traylor Estates nestled on the southern bank of the historic James River. This development sprang up in the latter stages of the 1960s so frightened middle-class white families could escape the turmoil of inner-city Richmond undergoing the fitful spasms of racial desegregation. Like most of Richmond's suburbs, the architectural styles of the houses in Traylor Estates harken back to the Colonial era, a comforting epoch when slavery and tobacco fueled the economy. These suburbanites, perhaps without realizing it, welcome the illusion of going back in time to an antebellum gentility suggested by brick walls and manicured lawns.

Will the police be waiting for me?

I can imagine our house surrounded by squad cars, possibly a SWAT team. The neighbors would be standing in robes and slippers, gawking at the spectacle of my undoing. Few saw it coming. As a child I didn't torture small animals. No one abused me. There's really no excuse . . . and there are no cops, either. Just a light on downstairs, a sweet glow in the darkness, indicating that my mother is expecting me. Hopefully she hasn't waited up. I already know that I'm to sleep on a pullout sofa in the basement, since Mead's adult children occupy the two other bedrooms upstairs. I don't mind at all because that basement has long been my refuge, and I need its succor now more than ever. Maybe the paneled walls will whisper to me and offer nurturing words of encouragement. I could definitely use some.

In the long driveway I count three parked cars. I recognize the white Acura as belonging to my mother, but there's also a sleek 1960s sports car — a Corvette, I'd later learn — along with a battered Isuzu pickup. The first issue I must confront is where to park. I don't want to block anyone in, and clearly there isn't room for my Honda unless I park in the front yard, a redneck move my mother wouldn't approve of. By default I'm left with parking on the street, which no one in Traylor Estates ever does except during a Super Bowl party. Isn't this week-end like a big football game? I position my car so that as little of it as possible protrudes onto Traylor Drive, and the two wheels on the passenger side are in a ditch, causing the car to list vertiginously at an angle. When I open my door to get out, it slams back into my leg. I can't say that the visit is off to a smooth start. Little do I know what other obstacles await me, but soon enough I'll find out.

I crave a hot shower and some time to decompress from the long drive, which was murder, let me tell you. What my mother has planned for tomorrow as far as a wedding rehearsal, I'm still unsure of, but I'd like to be somewhat rested. I trudge across the dry and brittle grass of the front yard, and I notice that the weeping willow my mother loved so much is gone. That tree in many ways captured the distilled essence of her personality — gentle, a hint of the tragic, exceedingly vulnerable. No wonder she shared such affinity with it. There were times when I was growing up that I'd find her standing at a window and staring out, and she'd say she was just watching the tree, but now I wonder if she wasn't looking for something within her that was gone. My father had left her, and she was alone. She'd vowed to move to France (of all places), but I had no desire to leave Richmond — that's right, I couldn't imagine a life for myself anywhere else. If only I'd agreed! The funny part is, not three years later I was ready to live on the Moon rather than stay here, as my hatred of Richmond had reached code-red levels. But the window of opportunity had closed. Moving to France was never discussed again.

Friable blades of grass literally crumble beneath my feet as I walk. The summer rains haven't come yet, and the drought is so severe that there's talk of canceling the Fourth of July fireworks due to worries about setting off a conflagration. Richmond has burned before, back in 1865, when the Yankees torched it . . . will history repeat itself, in a city stuck in the past tense?

Duffel bag and retro valise in hand, I veer over to the driveway after remembering that I'm to enter the house through the basement. A side door is unlocked, the same side door thieves smashed in to rob us in the 1980s, which led to the installation of dead-bolt locks. Take that, forces of anarchy!

At this ungodly hour I'm not expecting to encounter anyone. But immediately a figure emerges from the indigo darkness. This movement causes a floodlight to illuminate the gravel drive, and the intruder is positioned so that his elongated shadow reaches my feet. We wordlessly stare at each other, two aliens mesmerized by the otherness of our shared existence.

Have I just laid eyes on my future killer? I was kind of hoping for more of a dramatic flair, a slayer with robust manliness and Cro-Magnon features. This guy is short and stocky, more akin to a grocery store clerk than a homicidal maniac. Not to suggest a nondescript nobody is incapable of being a killer. For all I know he's already butchered my entire family and next he'll whip out a .44 and blow my brains out. Fear grips me by the throat, and I'm about to drop my luggage to charge him.

Okay, that's an overstatement. I'd turn and run first. But I am scared. Until he speaks.

"Hey," he grunts in welcome, his voice calm and even shy. Then he begins to walk toward me, his sensible shoes kicking up gravel as he goes.

"See you tomorrow," someone else calls out. My eyes dart to the side door and in the threshold light stands another young man, taller and leaner, attired in cargo shorts and Hollister T-shirt, with his hair neatly combed and his baby face smooth as polished silver.

The stocky guy hops into the pickup truck, and seconds later the engine sputters a few times as it turns over. Then the Isuzu backs up to where I'm standing, and I have to step out of the way to avoid becoming a holiday traffic fatality. The taller guy comes toward me with his hand outstretched in greeting.

"Hey there! You must be Edwin! He's back!"

There was a smidge of a Nicholson impression in his voice, but nothing too annoying. We shake hands. His grip is firm and manly, and his smile is bright.

"Yes, I'm Edwin."

"I've heard a ton about you from your mom. Pretty sure I know your whole life story."

"Wow, you must be bored to death," I say.

"Not at all!"

His outward appearance hints at nothing untoward, and he comes across as downright pleasant. I notice, though, that he has the habit of sucking in his cheeks, and, considering his face is shaped a bit like a shovel, his bland features contort into a fishlike pucker for a fleeting moment before returning to normal.

"I'm guessing you're Mead's son?" I ask.

30

"That would be correct! I'm Graves."

Graves: the name doesn't match his personality, which is as far from funereal as you could get. Looks can be deceiving, though. Many a time at Notting College I've been bamboozled by well-heeled con artists expert in pretending to be what they're not. The nice clothes, the sincere eyes, the excellent manners: no way they could be buying research papers from the Internet! So I'm reserving judgment.

We step into the basement together, with him leading the way. I don't ask about the guy who just departed in the pickup truck or why he was here at this ungodly hour. It's not my place to butt in, and besides, an unsettling scene greets me in the basement. There are boxes everywhere, of every size and description. Cardboard, wooden crates, plastic tubs, metal canisters, and imposing trunks stamped with ominous Cyrillic lettering. I can faintly make out the old workbench my father had left behind, a relic of my boyhood with its rusty vise, dog holes, and built-in tool tray.

"What's all this?" I inquire as genially as possible, not wanting to jump to a false conclusion. These boxes could be filled with aid to Haiti. Or Google stock.

"You're looking at the family jewels."

31

"I am?"

His laugh grates like medium-grade sand-paper and when he smiles, I see that his teeth have become bronzed, as if he wants them to be tanned, whereas his skin looks about as pale as a flock of laughing gulls. He obviously doesn't spend a great deal of time outside or flossing.

"These boxes are all that's left of my father's business," Graves explains cheer-fully, patting one of the Russian trunks.

"Which is?"

"Vietnam War memorabilia."

Not the answer I expected, and so I try to clarify. "Like guns?"

"Guns? Not just guns. You name it and if it's related to Nam, you can probably find it in here somewhere. Ammo, uniforms, maps. Anything. Everything."

All it would take is one spark from a lighter and my house would get blown to smithereens. But think of it! The trove of potential murder weapons right at our fingertips — literally enough weaponry to lay waste to an entire subdivision. If I don't have reason enough to harbor suspicions about my future stepfather, now I have an entire basement's worth. Still, I don't want to be overly alarmed, because there are hob-byists who collect such martial hardware.

Perhaps the business is lucrative. Or maybe the man is a lunatic. There's no reason both statements can't be true. I guess we'll have to wait to see.

"Was he in the military?" I ask innocently. Graves snorts in derision, lips puckering as beads of sweat roll down his angular face.

"Not that I know of."

"He used to own a store, right?"

"Ah, the store, yes. It was called Westmoreland's Closet, but most of his customers found him on the website."

A few details my mother has told me during our phone calls come back to me. The store went belly-up, and about eighteen months ago he met my mother, who is the office manager at a midsize law firm. Apparently Mead George had to retain counsel for a legal matter and hired the firm my mother works for. I can imagine polite conversations by the watercooler, a shared interest in — see, that's what I can't figure out, the attractive force that spawned their love. My mother enjoys making her own jewelry and serves on the board of a community theater, the Southside Playhouse, which each season puts on a gaudy musical and a Neil Simon comedy. She has a brood of "gal pals" with whom she dines out on a regular basis, a stable job, no major health problems, and no need of the aggravations that attend matrimony. Without doubt she doesn't need two young adults in her house, not to mention a basement full of artillery.

Most vexing of all, however, is the financial arrangement involved. Upon the death of a spinster aunt who lived in Fort Myers, my mother recently has come into a considerable sum of money, in excess of a half a million dollars. I haven't had the courage to ask her if she's planning on getting Mead to sign a prenup, and manners prevent me from ever asking. Something tells me no. My mother is a hopeless romantic who'd never allow a prenup to sully the dreamlike purity of Love, and unless I'm to take desperate measures, Mead stands to claim my birthright. A motive? People have killed for far less. But I'd never kill anyone over money. Love? That's a different question.

"I'm pretty tired from the drive," I say, barely suppressing a yawn. My head throbs as a migraine beckons, and I can't help but recall how Bev accused me of being a hypochondriac, insisting that I actually enjoyed feeling bad, strong words from a spouse who allegedly loves you. But my suffering now is legit. It's amazing I can even stand.

"Man, you shouldn't have to crash in the

basement," Graves says, impersonating a highly efficient concierge. "You take your old bed and I'll stay down here."

"No, it's fine. I love this basement. I used to hang out down here and just chill out, listening to music and dreaming of fame and fortune."

"I told your mom that I don't care where I sleep. I can sleep on the hard ground, no problem. I've done it before. I like to test my endurance."

"No need for that this weekend. I'm very happy in the basement."

"Well, if you insist," he chirps as we troop into the little den I called the Cavern. It's not large, about ten by ten, windowless, a drop ceiling of off-white tile, and the walnut wood paneling that adds even more cool darkness. Thankfully there aren't any boxes crammed in here. Just the same pullout sofa, two end tables, and the old family TV, cathode ray, still wired to a Sony VCR.

I drop my bags and fall into the bed my mother has made for me. The thin blanket has been turned back, revealing the sheets from my childhood, and the coarse fabric feels familiar against my skin. It was in this basement that all my dreams were born. I planned on taking Manhattan by storm one way or another. Playwright, singer-songwriter, actor. Perhaps all three. I just needed to get out of Richmond, and then nothing could stop me.

"Are you hungry?" Graves asks, hovering by the stairs. He doesn't seem eager to leave, as if he has something he wants to tell me but can't find the words.

"No, I stopped along the way." Did I ever! Had myself a great time, too. Ate my fill, went back for sloppy seconds. Gotcha again! When will you ever learn that you can't believe one word I say? That waitress is alive and well — maybe not well per se, but mostly alive. At least she was the last time I saw her.

Graves takes a step up and then pauses, gazing down on me.

"The rehearsal dinner is tomorrow," he announces, more like he's talking to himself or issuing a press release. Still, this is useful information because the details for the weekend remain sketchy in my mind.

"Do you know what the plan is?"

"They made reservations at the Tobacco Company."

"Well, well, how chic." This restaurant is located in Shockoe Slip, a gentrified portion of downtown along the river, and has long been revered as a symbol of the city's rebirth. A tobacco warehouse where slaves once toiled has become an upscale eatery where rich white people feast. The New South, in a nutshell.

"I've never eaten there."

"You're in for a real treat. The food isn't bad. Decent atmosphere. Lots of history, which depending on your viewpoint is either edifying or stultifying. Maybe a little of both."

"You don't like Richmond, do you?"

I chuckle to hide my trepidation, unsure of how much I can trust this earnest young person who again appears to be of similar temperament to my students. I'm pretty sure Graves attends college but I forget which one. My mother complains more about the girl, whose name I can't recall. I'll become an expert on both soon enough. "Richmond is a complex place," I reply warily. "I'd say I have a love-hate relationship, as I do with many things."

"My sister hates it here. I mean, despises it."

"Oh, right. What's her name again?"

"Gibson."

"I guess I'll meet her tomorrow. We can compare notes. Not that I despise Richmond."

Like many young people I work with, he's not listening as I talk. When I finish, he pounces. "Can you do me a favor?"

"Sure."

"You know that guy who was here earlier?"

"The one who almost ran me over?"

"Yeah, him. Can you just keep that between us?"

This request catches me by surprise. In so many words, Graves is asking me to lie, and normally I would do no such thing unless it meant protecting my own behind. In this case, I can't refuse him, under the banner of getting the weekend off to a good start. Not that I like it. "I mean, I will because you're asking me to. What's the deal? Why do you have to keep it under wraps?"

"Technically he's not allowed to be here."

"Why not?"

"It's stupid. My dad doesn't like him. They argue about everything and Avery won't back down, ever, which pisses off my dad because he always has to be right."

Ah, family drama! Nothing beats it for pure slaughter value. What cauldron has my poor mother been boiling in? By any ethical standard, I should tell the kid to get lost. If only I had! So here's my first major blunder. We'll blame it on fatigue and vexation.

"I'm not feeling so great," I say, yawning loudly, drawing my participation to a close. Graves sucks his cheeks in with nervous vehemence, watching me with eyes bugged. He's enlisted me as an ally, and there's nothing more frightening in this world than trusting another human being not to destroy you.

"Good night," he says before scurrying upstairs like a gerbil. Somehow I manage to fall asleep, which should rank among the greatest feats in the history of somnolence.

3

A dull thud awakens me, and then I hear footfalls down the stairs. My eyes blink open in time to see a young woman descending to the basement. I catch a quick glimpse. Something about her hair reminds me of a knotted tangle of forsythia, wild yellow curls that sprayed from her head in a sunny profusion. She stops when she sees that I'm awake and stands perfectly still on the last step.

"I didn't mean to wake you up," she whispers. "I just need something from the dryer."

"No problem," I groggily reply.

"Did you wake him up?" I hear my mother yell from the top of the stairs. "I'm sorry, Eddie! I told her not to wake you up!"

"It's fine! I need to get up anyway."

My mother's small feet plop down the stairs and, like a deer fleeing a ravenous bear, the blond girl scurries off to the laundry room. She is clad in a white T-shirt that barely covers her round and supple body. She might just be the most exquisite creature I've ever laid eyes on. I literally can't wait to kill her.

"So now you've met Gibson!" my mother sings, arms outstretched. I sit up in bed so that we can embrace. It's been two years since I've seen her, and she looks fleshier, ten pounds heavier, but her face is radiant. Her thistle-colored eyes sparkle as she gazes at me. Maybe all brides glow on the eve of their wedding, even those who've begun their seventh decade. "What time did you get in?"

"Around four. Graves made sure I had everything I needed."

"He was still up, I take it?" She frowns disapprovingly, glancing over at Gibson, who's pawing through a clothes hamper by the dryer.

"Yes. And he was a gracious host. He offered me food, in fact."

"He's a good egg, deep down. One day he'll figure it out. This one?" My mother nods toward Gibson. "She'll end up in jail."

"A lost cause, huh?"

"You don't know the half of it. I told her to get her laundry last night and she swore she'd do it. But she's just so lazy, it drives

41

me crazy."

Gibson, having found what she's looking for, rushes back toward us. Mother detains her for a quick intro, during which Gibson barely looks at me and seems to be in pain, as if I'm gnawing on her leg instead of waving.

"Gibson, this is my son Edwin," my mother explains. "He lives in New York and teaches college."

Suddenly the girl perks up. "New York City?"

"Sadly, no. I live upstate, in Ithaca."

Her beauty is almost palpable, an exotic force that emanates from her in pulsing waves. The wild yellow hair frames a face classically delineated by high cheekbones, oval-shaped eyes, and sun-kissed skin the color of golden honey. A thin, slightly upturned nose hovers above full, pouting lips that contrast so starkly with her brother's odd puckering. She exudes an untamed quality, whose beauty comes to her so naturally that even in her attempt to downplay it, she only adds to her own luster.

"Hurry up and get dressed!" Mother shoos Gibson, who dutifully floats away, her bare feet lightly touching the ground as she ascends the stairs. Then reality begins to sink in and my mother sighs plaintively.

"I've got so much on my plate today, and I don't know how it's all going to get done."

"Can I help?" I offer, glad to be of service.

My mother has a way of smiling that makes Mona Lisa seem like an open book. This upturn of the lips, is it a grimace? A mocking gesture to me, her wayward son? Or perhaps she's genuinely thankful for the assistance? "Don't you need more sleep?" she asks in an equally opaque tone.

"Not if you need me to pitch in."

"The big thing is that Gibson needs a ride to school because she's not allowed to drive since her conviction."

"Conviction?"

"DUI." Each letter spits out of my mother's mouth with venom. When feeling betrayed, the woman could coil into a viper, and her bite was meant to maim. "I could ask Graves, but his car was recently totaled when he got hit by an uninsured driver. Hey, I really want you to talk to Graves while you're home. He says he's not going back to VCU in the fall. He says he wants to take some time off and I don't think that's a great idea. He's a good student, though. Maybe he'll listen to you."

"I'm a trained professional, so he should listen to every word I say." No laugh. She can't think I'm being serious, and so I quickly add, "Just kidding!"

"Thanks, Eddie. He's a good kid but he seems confused."

Immediately I think of the person visiting Graves late last night, and begin to suspect that the two of them were up to no good, a surmise based on no evidence beyond my mother's own direful warning. Should I mention something to her? I promised Graves I wouldn't, and anyway, my mother seems on edge enough already. I see no need to add to her load of stress — and there's no way I'm bringing up my lack of white shoes.

"And I'll be glad to give Gibson a ride to school," I offer in a voice so sugary-sweet that I could've provided the candy for a toddler's birthday party.

"That would save me an hour! Oh, you're a real Johnny-on-the-spot! But look how tired you are! Circles under your eyes! Eddie, you worry me so much."

She never buys my bland assurances of well-being and leans forward as if inspecting my scalp for lice. "Of course there's plenty to worry about! How are you doing anyway? Have you been getting enough sleep?"

"Sleep is for weaklings."

"Stop it, you're being ridiculous. Tell me

you're dating someone."

"I'm dating someone."

"Really? Who?"

"One of my students. She just turned twenty and she's amazing."

"Eddie, can't you ever just answer my questions? Not everything is a joke."

"My love life happens to be a joke. A crude, offensive joke."

"We'll talk about that later. But the caterer has apparently lost her mind and on Saturday I don't know what we'll be eating. So I've got that to deal with." She falls silent and then slaps herself on her forehead, one of her more peculiar mannerisms that reminds me of my childhood, which was mostly spent waiting for her to get organized — keys, wallet, shopping lists, phone numbers — all of which eluded her at crucial times. "Oh my gosh, it just hit me. You haven't met Mead yet."

"No, I haven't."

"He's not here. He had business to look after."

"Another time then. I'm looking forward to it." A true statement, but not honest. I want to lay eyes on this miscreant the way an abnormal psychologist would desire an interview with a convicted pedophile. There's little pleasure in it but much data to be gleaned.

"I hope you like him. He's quirky but in a good way, and very, very smart. He's a real history buff. You guys have that in common."

Do we now? I'm a highly educated college professor, and he's a gold-digging arms dealer. How I want to defend myself! It's so easy for people to take shots at me, considering how little my life has amounted to. But my goal for the weekend is simple: to cause no upset, be a good sport. So I bite my tongue and lie through my teeth. "I'm sure I'll like him, don't be ridiculous."

She giggles in delight and flashes a bright smile. "Not everyone does, mind you." Then her voice drops like a fallen sparrow. "Some people who shall remain nameless think I'm making a big mistake and they haven't been shy about telling me so. Needless to say, they didn't get a wedding invitation. The caterer! I have to call her! You're taking Gibson, right?"

"Yes, of course. Whatever you need."

"And I promise we'll catch up. I want to hear all about what's new with you. Gibson needs to go. She's probably not even dressed. For the last year I've had to stay on top of that girl every minute or else she'll spin out of control like a tornado."

With that last lament she turns and minces up the stairs as fast as her short and stumpy legs will carry her. I too need to get dressed and hopefully grab some coffee before the car pool commences. To be honest, I'm more than a little disoriented. Five hours of fitful sleep isn't enough to clear my addled brain, and now I have to spend time alone with Gibson, who seems to have sprung from some deep and vast subterranean vault where the world's secrets are stored. She's the sort of Norma Jean who becomes a Marilyn, meaning that she's in the process of burning through her beauty, and the conflagration threatens to consume not just her but everyone in the vicinity. She was unabashed to parade in front of me nearly naked, and I can't fathom what that portends, if anything. Nothing good, for her or me.

I just need to get dressed and discharge this duty. Since it's blazing hot out, I pull on cargo shorts and one of my favorite T-shirts, a fake-vintage Wham! Bev gave me for my birthday two years ago, knowing how much I appreciated cheesy 1980s memorabilia. I've been debating whether I should bother to wear it anymore, as I've vowed to put Bev out of my mind, but then, I don't know, a flood of emotion overtook me a few weeks ago and I started wondering whether I couldn't win her back. Which was nuts, because we were officially divorced, but look at Richard Burton and Elizabeth Taylor. Reconciliation isn't impossible. Under some circumstances it plainly is, such as in the case when one of them dies. Or is killed.

There are scratches on my upper arm, and as I lie there, I examine the reddish stripes with odd detachment, like my skin is a canvas on which an artist has scrawled ravening lines that express . . . disgust?

Just get dressed, I tell myself.

Black socks. Black Chuck Taylors. And now for the part I most enjoy, the selection of a hat. My affinity for hats definitely comes from my mother, who also has a vast collection of headgear. I've personally given her a hat for every birthday and Christmas for the past fifteen years, thirty hats, to go with the fifty she's acquired. I'm not nearly that obsessed, but I possess around twenty-five hats, most of them of the "trucker" variety, meaning thick polyester on the lid and mesh in back. I packed four of my current favorites, and for this errand I select the one with "I Have Issues" stenciled in white letters across black fabric. This motto does seem appropriate for the goings-on this weekend, where issues of every variety will bloom in a field of dysfunction.

I wish that my thinning hair didn't require a hat, but I'm very good at concealing my flaws — especially from those who know me best. Yet women have paid me compliments, especially my boy-next-door dimples, and some have even described me as devilishly handsome, which might be, um, overkill. But am I the subject of schoolgirl fantasy? Bev said yes back when she still laughed at my jokes . . .

"Ready?" Gibson calls down. I'd categorize her voice as syrupy and modulated. Feminine, with a hint of huskiness.

"Let's go!" I eagerly reply, grabbing my mirrored sunglasses, *Miami Vice* knockoffs that really border on the tasteless, where I'm most comfortable, aesthetically speaking. My belief in cheesiness is a vehicle for me to express grave distrust with current social constructs and allows me to poke fun at my privileged position as a white male. Or something.

I need a steaming cup of coffee to jolt my brain into action, not to mention my lower extremities that have trouble climbing the stairs. I feel dizzy and nervous, with Gibson watching me with a backpack slung over a shoulder. Then she smiles, dazzlingly, a thousand watts that burn my eyes.

"Nice hat," she quips. A real compliment? I'll pretend it is.

"A gift from my ex-wife. It's the nicest thing she ever did for me."

"Besides marry you?"

"She didn't have a choice. I'm ready. Lead the way."

I follow her through the kitchen, which looks the same as I remember it, blue tile countertop, knotty-wood cabinets with hammered-copper handles and drawer pulls, round Formica breakfast table topped with a lazy Susan, a bright window looking into the backyard (where a vegetable garden is withering), and then we proceed to cross the dining room, which also has the same long table with the blue embroidered runner and eight high-back chairs flanking it, familiar, comforting signposts in an otherwise alien landscape. I'm trying not to stare at Gibson as she walks in front of me. I don't want to reach a sickly state of arousal by the sight of her long, tanned legs and perfectly sculpted ass that her jean shorts outline with frightening precision. She is to be my stepsister, and is basically a stranger, and yet I feel the haunting tug of desire.

Ever since the divorce, I've developed the unfortunate habit of falling for almost every woman I come into contact with, and in the world of higher education, you have contact with many women. At my college the ratio of female-to-male is around sixty-forty, meaning there is a preponderance of absolutely lovely young women for whom no date will ever come calling, and they seek solace, affirmation, confidence from male faculty members who have excellent listening but limited coping skills. This isn't a confession. I'm not going to touch Gibson, lay one crooked finger on her lovely golden locks, just as I've never engaged in inappropriate sexual conduct with any of my students, at least seven of whom in the past eight years have made overtures that would've enticed other, less ethical males to mount them right there in the office, right on top of the L-shaped desk made of cheap vinyl-laminated particleboard.

Do you find my vociferous denials credible? My college, for your information, has an Amorous Relationship Policy that expressly forbids sexual contact between a faculty member and a student, but this same policy is silent about romantic entanglement, about developing genuine feelings of human attachment to an unsullied and eager young woman who adores lyric poetry and Leonard Cohen — speaking purely in the hypothetical, of course, by way of illustration. No such person exists, and even if she did exist, I never defiled her.

Should I just make something up for prurience's sake? I can invent salacious details of a torrid and illicit affair, how she used to hang around after class so that we could repair to my office to discuss some utterly invented literary issue, such as the overuse of passive voice, while we actively groped each other with my door closed and locked — yes, locked from the inside! The college gave us all-new doors with this feature so that in the event of a mass killing by an armed maniac, some of us could survive by locking ourselves in our offices, but it turns out that these same sturdy doors created the required privacy where love could bloom, as only in secret does true affection burst forth like a tender bulb of a hydrangea. More? What more is there? There's nothing more. She was tall and willowy, with hair she dyed various colors, and largish breasts she vowed to reduce to B-cups one day, against my whimpering protests. A sliver of pubic hair the color of rust, which abutted a tattoo of a small butterfly. She was double-jointed. The boyfriend of a favorite babysitter had exposed himself to her when she was ten and for that reason she both abhorred and was fascinated by the male organ.

Get a grip on yourself! None of this is true. There is no girl named Lola who was once my student. Please, check my class rosters for the past ten years. You'll see I'm in the clear. I haven't developed a fondness for coed flesh the way some alligators become habituated to humans and then endeavor to devour one, and so you don't need to fret about Gibson as we make our way out to the car. I'm no registered sex offender. Get on a computer and scroll through the DOJ databases. Your appetite for depravity is limitless. Do you think I'm unable to control myself? That the mere sight of such a beautiful young woman is enough to send me into a sex-crazed tailspin? I really must object here. For the sake of argument, let's assume that I had an amorous relationship with someone named Lola (which I didn't). Do you think I'd risk my career, my marriage, my entire existence, just so I could see how unbelievably luscious and round her firm breasts were? No! If I were ever to risk it all with a student, it would be because I was in love. Let's not confuse the issues. There are other more pressing problems that will overwhelm us and cause considerable damage. The dead will die again, and so don't get caught up in what I might do to seduce Gibson.

As for the young lady in question, we know next to nothing. Gibson might be a nymphomaniac or an exhibitionist or a sadist or all three (which is your dream). And I'm sure she isn't the least bit attracted to me. But what if it's an attraction of a different variety? Perhaps Gibson is not my victim, but my killer? Now that is a real stretch, preposterous even. What motive would Gibson possibly have for killing me — unless of course she doesn't have one beyond the simple enjoyment of murder. Would my position as the natural heir to my mother's new fortune entice her? No, that is an unfortunate stereotype, and I refuse to be killed by a stereotype.

As for Gibson, let's remain skeptical. Let's watch her closely. It's blazing hot outside, and sweat is dripping down our bodies. The earth literally feels like it will burn, that rubber will melt. Gibson fumbles through the zippered pockets of her backpack and eventually produces a crumpled ball of cigarettes, ironically the same brand my father worked for. Richmond at its core is a tobacco city, and its riches derive from that "noxious weed," as King James labeled it. My father didn't actually handle the leaf but instead labored in HR, where at his desk and then in designated areas he was a loyal smoker of his company's product, which of course killed him. Gibson, being young and impetuous, lights up and inhales with relish, blowing smoke into the stifling air with a dramatic flourish, even though her fag is bent and deformed.

"Can we stop at a store on the way?" she asks me in a Lauren Bacall contralto.

"What kind of store?"

"The kind that sells cigs."

"Sure thing. I could really use some coffee."

She lopes past me and reaches my car before I do, as my ankles feel leaden and plodding. I don't want her smoking in my Honda, although I don't know that I have the courage to tell her so. But thankfully she takes a few last heroic puffs of her smoke, flicks it imperiously to the turf, and then crushes the butt with the toe of her canvas sneakers. I unlock the car and we hop in, and her tobacco breath reminds me of my father. She might smell like death, but she looks like an extra from a Van Halen video and suddenly I fear I've become a ghost forced to roam the land of the living in search of his intended grave.

"Get me out of here," she mumbles as I start the engine. The car then lurches backward even though I thought I was in drive, and I nearly get us stuck in the ditch. I step hard on the gas and the spinning tires kick up dust from the dying grass, leaving behind us a murky cloud of particulate matter. I'm so nervous I feel like I'm sixteen again and on my first official date, with Hannah Anderson, JV cheerleader and fellow virgin, who now resides in Deltaville and heads up the local La Leche League chapter. These days she might be an advocate for public exposure of breasts, but I assure you in high school she kept her perky little boobies wrapped up tight.

Gibson has taken off her shoes and has her bare feet propped up on the dashboard, a rather intimate gesture that assumes a level of trust between us that doesn't yet exist. But she does have exceedingly lovely feet, perfectly shaped, sinewy yet delicate, with toenails painted bright red.

"So where am I taking you?" I ask as we head north on Traylor Drive.

"Um, Manhattan?"

What if I reply with a resounding *Sure*? What a different sort of book this would be, the two of us renegades rolling north up I-95 toward Gotham, ready to throw our lives away for a weekend of debauchery. But of course I say no such thing, for many reasons. The wedding for starters, but also because I'm too chicken. Not spontaneous enough, according to Bev. Too careful. But these same attributes can come in handy in certain delicate situations that require extensive planning, e.g., a criminal enterprise.

"As enticing as that sounds, I would hate to miss the weekend festivities."

Gibson erupts in mordant laughter. "Yeah, whatever. My dad is totally whack. You know that, right?"

"I've actually never met him."

"See? Don't you think that's f-ed up? It's so stupid. I like your mom and all, but she's making a huge mistake."

"It's really not my place to pass judgment." We're now at the intersection of Traylor and Cherokee, a winding lane that follows the river that stretches out before us, the brown James, where America was born. We must go either left or right. "Seriously, where am I taking you?"

A forlorn sigh. "J. Sarge." A local community college, named after J. Sargent Reynolds, scion of a prominent Richmond family whose fortune came from cellophane and aluminum foil, commonly used to prevent spoilage. In other words, to thwart the passage of time, Richmond's real genius.

"Which campus?"

"Henrico."

"Which is where exactly?"

She gets out her phone and taps on the GPS app, and a second later I'm being told to turn right by a caviling metallic voice. I'd much rather know the actual location of the campus, but Gibson is already pissy enough and I'm sure I'll figure it out. I vaguely recall a J. Sarge campus out on Parham Road somewhere, in the heart of the suburban sprawl that is Henrico County, which I detest with my entire being. But at least I can stop at a mall and procure some white shoes.

It's obvious that we need some music to brighten the mood. I fish out my own phone and plug it into the car stereo, but then comes the hard part — what to pick?

"What kinds of stuff are you listening to these days?"

Her answer surprises, even enchants me. "Old-school."

"Old-school what?"

"Old-school anything."

"Give me the name of a band."

"The Fuggs."

"Seriously? I love them, they were bad-asses, but I don't think I have any. So you like early to mid-sixties? The Kinks? At some point I might've downloaded a few songs."

"No, it's cool. Just pick something. I'm pretty open to suggestion." Ha! In one phrase Gibson disclosed the core of her existence, and yet I didn't know enough about her at the time to understand she was revealing her authentic self. Throwaway lines often teem with truth, but few of us pick up on them. We cast our hooks in deep water in hopes of landing a big fish, neglecting the shallows where we can see the bottom.

"Bright Eyes?" I suggest in a near whisper, so as not to offend.

"Go for it."

Go for it. How I would like to, Gibson! Just once in my life I want to be the one who grabs the gusto, tosses care overboard, and steams into port to plunder and pillage. Maybe I'll release my inner pirate, possibly this weekend if not in a few agonizing minutes. Because really, what else do I have to lose? If I'm going down, why not with my hands caressing her shapely body? Admit it, you want me to. The honest among you will freely cop to the dark urge. Just hold on, these things take time.

I get the playlist cued up, still flummoxed by her appreciation for the Fuggs, an obscure band started by a poet. It makes me think better of her. The tunes come on, and Conor Oberst croons that it's the first day of his life. Speak the truth, C.O.! I actually feel relieved that I've managed to keep my hands to myself, just like a normal person, which is a trick harder than it looks. I'm at my best when sharing music with like-minded enthusiasts, as Gibson appears to be. In a different world I would've been a DJ or a producer, not a teacher of composition who makes the young eat their intellectual vegetables.

But the positive vibes quickly end when Gibson makes a request that complicates matters in an unexpectedly unpleasant way.

"Can I borrow forty bucks? I'm totally broke and I really need the cash."

"Sure, okay."

"I'll pay you back, I promise. Just until I get my driver's license back and then I can get a job. Two more months and it'll all be over, unless the judge hoses me like he did before. Because I wasn't even drunk when I got pulled over. I blew a bullshit .09, which is barely buzzed."

"I try never to drive when I've been drinking." Sage advice from the wise head who knows a thing or two about evading the long arm of the law.

"I wasn't even drinking that much. Like three beers, no biggie. But thanks for helping me out. You're awesome."

She lightly pats my shoulder, and even through my retro Wham! T-shirt I can feel the heat her body emanates, as though her beauty acts as a furnace whose fire she can summon whenever she wants. She asked for the money because she damn well knew I'd fork it over, that I'd be unable to say no. I wish I could summon the strength to refuse her, so that she might learn the limits of being gorgeous, except there really aren't any when you're eighteen, reckless, and breathtaking.

"I'm not awesome," I croak helplessly as we wind along Cherokee Road, past waterfront compounds behind which sit riverfront monstrosities, although a few are more modest and belong to a time in the 1970s when the rich were just rich and not engorged with ill-gotten gains. Many of those humble abodes have been bulldozed to make way for overstated mansions, but the one that my friend John Graziano grew up in remains, defiant in its Brady Bunch trilevelness, a dwarf relic in a city that has a chokehold on history. Remember that name: John Graziano. He'll become a very important person in this tale.

"I really don't feel like going to this class," Gibson sighs.

"What class is it?"

"Retard math. Sorry, remedial math. It's just me and this posse of dumb rednecks from Ashland, and the teacher is Romanian or Lithuanian and honestly no one can understand a word he says. And it lasts for three horrible hours!"

"Poor kid! Three whole hours of learning!"

"Seriously, it's the worst. You sit in there and see how you like it."

"No thanks. I hear enough complaining from my own students."

"You're a teacher, right? I'd bet you'd be chill in class." Her compliment perks me up, but she quickly stops flattering me to address what's foremost on her mind. "Don't forget to stop for smokes."

"Is there a place near campus?"

"Yeah, for sure. Just don't forget. I can't handle retard math without a pack of cigarettes." That I'll be buying, apparently, with the "loan" I'm extending to her based on the collateral of a harried promise of future employment. Why do I always get myself into these situations? Am I powerless to say no? Am I that weak of a man? Of course not! I haven't propositioned her yet, have I?

Or made an indecent remark. The battle must be fought one skirmish at a time.

"Don't worry, we'll stop. I'd hate for you to suffer unjustly."

"Your mom wants me to quit smoking. I know she's right."

"She is most of the time about most things."

"Not about my dad she isn't."

"Well, she might have a blind spot there, but usually she reads people well. She didn't like the woman I married and right now I sort of wish I'd listened to her."

"I didn't mean to sound harsh about your mom."

Her apology actually seems genuine, not crafted from a trove of fake emotion. She even touches me again, with her fingertips on my forearm, grazing my skin the way a lover might tickle with a downy feather. Of course she's not my lover — nor will she ever be. I promise, for the moment. There are websites you can visit if you want real action.

"No, it's fine," I grandly assure her. "She really wants what's best for you. She has a good heart, which usually ensures disappointment in this world."

"I don't know, your mom is so sweet and she tries and all. Are you going to say anything to her?"

"About her wedding? Not on your life! I came down here to be supportive, wear a white suit, say cheese when told, drink too much at the reception, and then exit stage left as soon as possible. How she lives her life is her business. There's no logic for why people fall in love, and so logic is never sufficient to argue against it." What am I referring to here, my mother's romantic situation or my own? It feels like I'm in my office on campus, meeting with an adventurous coed who's come to me for advice, and yet beneath the polite veneer of academic jargon seethes the bursting sexuality of a young woman eager for experience. Just when I thought I could escape the craziness for a few days, it's found me all over again.

"I'm never getting married," Gibson announces as we make our way across the river, on a bridge named for Harry F. Byrd, one of Virginia's most ardent segregationists, architect of the "massive resistance" to fight against integration. In other words, a hero. Bev has crawled into my head! It's like she's sitting right next to me, pontificating in her sharpest voice, the one that extracted my heart in a few deft cuts.

"It's not for everyone," I reply.

"Because it's total crap."

"You won't get an argument from me. I certainly failed at it."

"Do you know how many guys have already proposed to me? Seriously, I'm not lying. They've gotten on their knees, had a ring, begged me to say yes — three! The first time I was sixteen."

I gulp down some much-needed air. "How old was the guy?"

"Tommy? I don't know. Like twenty."

Her first victim. I conjure an image of a lanky skateboarder with blindingly white teeth, taut muscles, a wispy mustache, omnipresent boner, meager life skills, poor impulse control, vague plans for the future, and the taker of her virginity. In the backseat of his decrepit Dodge, atop burrito wrappers and crushed cans of cheap lager, and afterward he thinks he's in love with her, this angelic nihilist whose fleshy thighs slap together more or less keeping beat to the music.

"You turned him down, I take it?"

"Heck yeah! He was so dumb. Oh my God, he couldn't remember his own phone number. But he was gorgeous."

"Dumb and gorgeous," I repeat absently.

"Then he got some skank pregnant and skipped town. He was such a slut and I was so stupid to fall for his lame game. I thought

65

he was so cool because he'd gone to jail for selling weed."

We've now entered Henrico County and the traffic on Parham Road slows to a crawl. It seems like every vehicle is a bulky SUV being driven by a woman between the ages of thirty and fifty-five. They've dropped off the kids at school and now it's time to shop or work out, and all have cell phones affixed to their ears, as if each awaits final instructions from some unseen deity.

"There's a 7-Eleven," Gibson points out. I put on my turn signal and change lanes. I'm quite happy to stop because I need coffee, among other items. A well-regarded therapist, possibly a silver-tongued attorney. We all could use one or the other, am I right? Especially if we're prone to confessing to crimes we never committed, the opposite of Kafka's Josef K., the dumb bastard who keeps insisting he's innocent while showing us how guilty he is! I am, on the other hand, a bundle of guilt searching out my offense, high and low, if only someone would charge me.

I pull into the pothole-pocked parking lot and squeeze into a spot between a lawn maintenance truck and a Hummer. Gibson falls still, making no move to get out of the car.

"Is everything okay?" I ask, pulling up hard on the parking brake. I constantly fear that my unoccupied car will roll down a hill, propelled by gravity, with me helplessly watching from afar.

"Can I get the money?"

The money! It had completely slipped my mind, and now the poor girl is having to beg all over again. "Oh, sure thing! I'm sorry, here you go." I reach for my wallet and finger two twenties. She takes the bills like it's the most natural act in the world, and I surmise that she's had plenty of mooching practice in her short life. The money acts as an instant tonic and revives her from the doldrums. She launches herself out of the car with such force that I worry she's going to damage the Hummer, whose owner has just come out of the store and stands slack-jawed with a steaming cup of coffee and one imagines a gathering erection somewhere in his seersucker pants as Gibson glides on by. Directly next to the 7-Eleven in this strip mall is a business aptly named Puritan Cleaners, and I wonder with much sardonic musing whether I can hire them to wash out and disinfect my libido. Because I'm enjoying myself a little too much, watching Gibson prance around. Just get the coffee, I tell myself.

Dark roast, probably seven hours old, who cares. I fill up a large cup, take it to the front counter, and place it by the register. But something feels wrong. A chill passes over me, a fleeting sensation some equate with the arrival of paranormal activity. I hand the clerk a five and start to look around. Where's Gibson? Behind me in line stands the lawn maintenance worker, attired in ratty clothes, skin dark and leathery. The clerk lets the change drop into my waiting paw but I'm still craning my neck. No sign of Gibson. Did she go to the restroom? Is that even possible in 7-Eleven, which has always been an excretion-free zone?

Like a lost child I drift aimlessly, from register to candy aisle to the parking lot. She isn't outside smoking. She isn't in my Honda. She's vanished into thin air.

4

Consider the following question: is Gibson dead?

Here's the thing. I've already expressed my desire to confess, that I long for the chance to face my accusers, and that I demand to be held accountable for my actions, but confess to what? Face down which accusations? Let's back up a little. I claim that Gibson just up and vanished from 7-Eleven, but how likely is that? Not very, I'll submit. A more realistic scenario might involve me driving Gibson to Pony Pasture Park, where she could earn her forty dollars by fellating me beneath a towering sweet gum tree, and while her head was nestled on my lap, I put my hands around her neck and strangled the life out of her. Afterward, basking in the glow of homicide, I listened to Bright Eyes as I drove across the same river where I'd just dumped Gibson's lifeless body, finally stopping at a 7-Eleven to buy a cup of coffee and hastily concoct an alibi.

Authorities can try to track down the driver of the Hummer who perhaps saw Gibson at the 7-Eleven, but good luck with no name or plate number to go on. So now you need to analyze my next maneuvers set against the backdrop that I'm possibly covering my tracks. Gibson is missing, that much is established fact.

Still don't think I killed her? So when I call my mother to tell her that Gibson has absconded, you take me at face value, just a dutiful son reporting the grim news? But wait till you hear my mother's reaction! These words literally come out of her mouth:

"I'm going to kill her!"

So much irony gets dropped on our heads it's a wonder we don't collapse from the constant impact.

"She's always pulling stunts like this," she continues. "She keeps saying she's changed, but I don't buy it, not for one minute. If it was up to me, I'd throw her on the street. Listen, I have to go. Call me if she turns up. Sorry about this. And thanks."

"Don't mention it. I actually was growing fond of her. She's not a bad kid."

"Who told you that?"

"We were having a nice discussion, and then she just took off without saying good-bye."

"She's been conning people her entire life, according to her father. Oh, it's my turn. Bye!"

I should look for Gibson. Not because I think I'll find her, but because a decent person would take the effort to help out a family member, and I'm a decent person. Or I was until not that long ago. Bev and I both thought that we could make the world a better place, but here I am, pulling into the parking lot of a strip mall just so I can go through the motions of looking for Gibson so that when her body is found, I can assert with moral vigor that I tried to locate her.

Gibson, Gibson, where are you? Hiding behind the boxwood hedge that surrounds a usurious bank? In back of that closed Chinese diner? Come out, come out, wherever you are!

Somebody does, much to my surprise. From behind a large trash bin, a homeless guy jumps out and waves at me. "You lose something?" he yells as he squats on his haunches in front of a shopping cart that contains his meager possessions. Maybe he lives inside the defunct restaurant, though it's not obvious how he gets in and out.

"No, just looking for someone."

"Who?"

"A girl."

"I just seen a girl go by. Nice looking! She belong to you?"

"No."

"What's her name?"

"It probably wasn't her."

"How do you know?"

A great question, and one that I can't logically answer without incriminating myself. Maybe it was Gibson skipping by this homeless man. But think about it. This is a very busy road, with all kinds of traffic and congestion, and maybe a dozen people have already walked past during this brief interlude. So am I confessing to being Gibson's killer? No way. She never meant to harm me. She never tried to ruin my career. The only possible motive was that I made an untoward sexual advance that she rebuffed . . . and normally I'd never do something so stupid . . . normally I know how to behave around women . . . normally I'm extremely normal.

"Thanks for your help."

"She went that way." He points in the general direction of Regency Square Mall, which would be a likely destination for a truant with forty bucks in her pocket. I'll have to go there then, though I do have another reason for stopping by. Shoes. Specifically white shoes for the wedding, since I left mine behind. If I happen to see Gibson at the mall, all the better. No one will be more surprised or relieved.

Regency Square was once Richmond's most fashionable high-end shopping mecca, with its glass elevator and assortment of eateries, the best known of which was O'Briensteins, which billed itself as an Irish-Jewish bagel pub. But it's long gone, and so are the upscale boutiques, now replaced with cheap discount chains, which in all honesty suits me fine because I don't feel like shelling out another eighty dollars for shoes I won't wear again. In and out, that's my goal. Park, buy the shoes, and get out of a place that even in high school sickened me. Yes, I'm actually at Regency Square Mall, which feels surreal because the last time I was here had been during high school, when confidence oozed from every blocked pore and I swaggered up and down the concourses with a disdainful sneer. Prom time was just around the corner, though I had no date . . . just like I have no wife . . . or lover. At least, not anymore.

While I'm still sitting in my car, however,

I get a text.

I was in a 3some last night it was fantastic

Now who would send me such a text? For the sake of argument, let's say it's from Lola, the willowy double-jointed temptress who is possibly a student of mine. The real question becomes: how should a sane person respond? I could offer congratulations, in which case I'd cease to be a sane person. I could also beg her to stop bothering me, which would validate my probity and possibly redeem me in your eyes.

What to do, what to do?

If Lola exists, then she isn't respecting any boundaries. She knows I'm helpless, powerless even, her captive, which apparently gives her the right to intrude at will, burst through the closed doors of my soul like an aggressive encyclopedia salesman, "sharing" the latest with me, the tales of her wanton excursions with men, women, men and women, sometimes lots of men and women. There are also potentially complex legal reasons why she shouldn't be telling me about a threesome or any other integer-based sexual dalliance.

It's safe to say I should consider this text the ultimate bad omen and begin to disengage from her as quickly as possible. But I don't do that. At some point I've embraced what Poe called "the spirit of PERVERSE-NESS," when one is drawn to behavior known to be wrong, repugnant, possibly criminal, simply because it's wrong, repugnant, and possibly criminal. As Poe put it, "It was this unfathomable longing of the soul to vex itself."

Hence, my reply: *Who was the guy?*

I send the text and almost vomit, right there in the nearly empty parking lot, next to a minivan dotted with anti-Obama bumper stickers. My reply text has to rank among the dumbest questions ever asked in the history of wireless communications. It's not necessarily germane to the story for me to recount the larger context of this bizarre exchange of texts, but I offer this glimpse into my gestalt as evidence of the kinds of pressure I was under at that moment. Otherwise nothing else makes sense, how I let myself get duped and put in the precarious position I'll soon find myself.

A quick review. I'm at a mall, shopping for white shoes. My almost-sister is missing, and perhaps I killed her (and the waitress in Gettysburg, not to mention my ex-wife). My mother's house has become a weapons depot. In my hands is a smartphone and I'm waiting for it to buzz. For her reply. Waiting in vain, as her reply never comes because she's cruel. Or merciful. It's some-times hard to tell the difference, and besides, I control my destiny, not her.

I wish I believed that. Lola controls my destiny and she can be a heartless taskmas-ter . . . I'm under her thrall and have become her minion, and if I just stop there, there's nothing to worry about. But we're just scratching the surface . . .

I slip the phone into a pocket, and some might congratulate me for showing strength. A man in my position can't get waylaid by some extremely promiscuous nymph who delights in hurting intellectuals. So she had a threesome. Big deal. What she does on her time is her business and she can spend it any way she wants, no matter how sala-ciously.

I'm almost at the entrance to Macy's when my phone buzzes again. I know it's her, based solely on the vibration. She has a way of forcing her personality into my electronics, just as she's managed to pene-trate the darker recesses of my mind and implant her noxious brand of sweet poison. I ignore the buzzing in the vicinity of my groin, again showing fortitude and restraint in abstaining from checking my phone, qualities often associated with virtue, ex-tolled by Aristotle and countless other seekers of wisdom.

But America is a land surfeited with traps and I walk right into one. Inside the department store, I'm accosted by the overwhelming stench of perfume that smells as if it's being blown through the AC ducts. My senses besieged, next I encounter two mannequins, lithe male figures perched on a pedestal, both attired in pastel-colored beachwear, their skin a dusky shade of ochre, their facial features bland, with chiseled cheeks and slightly upturned mouths, but eyes that survey the horizon with caution, the way a sentry at a lonely outpost might scan the night for any sign of the enemy, as I should've been. Something about the mannequins triggers in me a memory of one of Lola's former lovers, a sullen journalism major who earned spare money posing nude for a drawing class in our art department. At one point she regarded him with sickening reverence, until I was able to convince her of his numerous foibles.

In a flash my resolve melts away and I take out my phone. It's all so wrong, so horribly wrong. I know what awaits me. A photo.

Here he is.

Because there's always a photo, since she's a diligent documentarian of her misdeeds, a careful curator of her crassness, and a trained assassin who shoots only for the head, seldom missing.

The image that appears on my phone is clearly of a man, and clearly he's naked and standing in front of a mirror in his bathroom, holding his phone up next to his face as he snaps off a selfie. She always picks the same kinds of men — feckless, hairless breeds with scant muscle tone, buzz cuts, and a penis of Priapus, the Greek god of fertility and livestock, and this one looks to be part donkey.

Wait a second. I know this one. Had him in class last year. Biggest pain in the ass ever, always nagging me about the assignments and how hard I graded. Him? Of all the guys she might have coupled — or tripled — with, she has to select a suitor she knows I dislike, intensely so, as I grunted angrily when she claimed he was "super-cute," and honestly there's just one way to interpret her action here — she was out to maim in a deeply personal way.

I'm just about to finger a retort on the small keyboard when I hear a voice.

"Eddie? Is that you?"

I look up from my phone, my face panic-stricken, because I know that voice, even if I can't place it right away. One glance at the woman standing across from me instantly generates a name: Leigh Rose Wardell. We share a warm embrace, my phone still in hand, but the digital image of Loverboy fades to black.

"Fancy running into you here," I quip, falling into my Richmond persona, the disgruntled aesthete with a compassionate core. It's like learning to ride a bike: one never forgets how.

"I was just about to say the same thing! How are you?"

"Oh, fine. I just figured I'd wander aimlessly around Regency Square and buy a Led Zeppelin poster from Spencer's."

No wedding ring. Hair in pigtails. Expensive but tasteful workout clothes, but she does look plumper than the girl I knew in high school. Not unpleasantly so. In fact she's damn attractive in a kind of earth-motherly way, her flawless skin free of makeup, giving her a natural, unmediated appearance. Real, in other words. Mature, adult, confident. No bra straps showing. No random piercings. No acne, no garish fingernail polish. A grown woman.

"That sounds like you," she chuckles, eyes brightening in delight, animated by my eternal goofiness. "Are you living in Richmond? Of course you're not! Why would I even ask that question? You're in New York, right?"

"Upstate."

"Not the city?"

"I take the train down as much as possible."

"Are you still writing?"

"I teach writing, but I guess that's not the same thing. You look fabulous, by the way."

"So do you! Hey, you feel like getting some coffee? I was just on my way to Starbucks. I have this routine. I pretend to work out at the gym and then go stuff my face with chocolate croissants."

"Sure, I could use a new routine and yours sounds perfect. No pain, all gain."

"Eddie! I can't believe you're here! I was thinking about you last night, as a matter of fact."

Let me add at this juncture one salient point about Leigh Rose Wardell. She is rich. Filthy, stinking rich. The kind of rich that can buy private islands, make a politician bark like a seal, and cause Mercedes dealers to weep uncontrollably. Her family eats money for breakfast instead of cereal. But I never cared about that element of her life, one of the reasons we still have a connection after all these years, despite losing touch. It seems like a connection anyway, not that I can discern true human emotion anymore.

My phone buzzes again. Another text from Lola. A thin, pained smile forms on my face.

"Thinking of me? Why? Were you suffering indigestion?"

"No! Oh gosh, it was just a weird dream. Come on, let's go."

She grabs me by the arm and we skip off like Hansel and Gretel. She genuinely appears to relish being with me, because in her mind I'm the same dashing and fearless lad from 1993 who had goals and aspirations, but if she ever got ahold of my phone and scrolled through the texts contained therein, her opinion of me would change. What's the all-time record for living a lie? And once she discovers the truth about me, she can tell the world of my fetid secret life, unless I eliminate her first. There's a motive for you! I kill only to protect myself . . . but the truth is I'm the one who's in grave danger. This might look innocent to you, long-lost high school lovers who've serendipitously reunited in a major department store, but the reality is far different. It's like I've strapped dynamite to my back and, though the fuse is long, it's lit. Chekhov advises that, if a playwright intends to explode a bomb onstage, then it's best if this bomb gets passed around so that every character can handle it, thereby pushing the audience to the edge of their seats, waiting for the big *ka-boom!* Is your pulse pounding yet? The dead will die again, don't forget.

Just as we're about to exit Macy's, I see that off to my right is the shoe department. I screech to a halt.

"What's wrong?" Leigh Rose asks me.

"I need shoes."

"Shoes?"

"For a wedding. Come on, a detour."

"I love shopping for shoes! Whose wedding is it?"

"My mother's."

"Get out! Good for her."

"Not quite."

"No?"

"Long story. I need white oxfords."

So we veer off, still arm in arm. What's eerily coincidental is our reunion echoes our first meeting, which was also happenstance and at a store, although a very different venue, Plan 9 Records on Cary Street. I was combing through the New Wave bin when this totally grunged-out girl came in, ripped jeans, ratty flannel shirt, reeking of freshly smoked pot, and she started chatting up the clerk, who played in bands, and I inched closer to eavesdrop on their conversation, because I'd overheard mention of Domino's Dog House, a crazy bar at Shockoe Bottom I'd wanted to check out. I was wearing retro Converse sneakers, the same kind that Kurt Cobain wears in the "Smells Like Teen Spirit" video, and she called me on it. "Hey, Cobain" were her first words to me, and my reply elicited her first laugh: "Can you call me Kurt?"

Everything about our relationship was accidental. We didn't go to the same high school. She lived in an enormous mansion in Windsor Farms, the stately neighborhood of Richmond's wealthiest and most powerful, while we dwelled in decidedly middle-class Traylor Estates. We had no common friends. But we were both high school seniors who wanted out of Richmond, and for three months we were inseparable, exploring the clubs and dives of the city's old quarters that were beginning to be gentrified. She was the black sheep of her prominent family, and I was a kid whose father had just died. But she was headed off to Tulane and I was matriculating to William and Mary, and as random as our meeting was, so too was our drifting apart. There was never acrimony, no bad blood, but just an understanding that we were moving in different directions.

When we get to the shoe department, Leigh Rose shoves me into a chair and instantly takes charge, one of my favorite traits of hers. Many of the Richmond girls I knew were afflicted with a fatal case of Scarlett-O'Hara-itis, which caused them to act coquettish and overly helpless, forgetting that Scarlett was a fierce tigress and not an indolent wallflower. Leigh Rose had been raised to be a Southern belle but had rejected the premise, much to the consternation of her parents. She spoke her mind. She defied stereotype.

One look from her is all it takes to get a drowsy "sales associate" over to us. She's already selected three different styles for me to consider and orders him to fetch them. After he trundles off, she sits down next to me as we wait for his return.

"I actually bought a pair of wedding shoes but forgot to pack them," I explain, somewhat sheepishly, reluctant to speak to her of my life in Ithaca, which suddenly seems to belong to another solar system.

"I do that kind of thing all the time. My mind wanders. I forget things I don't want to, and remember stuff I don't want to. If I could just reverse the order, you know? So anyway! Who is your mother marrying?"

"I haven't met the groom, to be honest.

His name is Mead George. He is roughly our age."

She repeats the name to herself and gazes down at her lap as if she stores her address book there, and then she looks up at me with a startled expression. "Our age?"

"So I've been told. I don't want to impugn the man's motives, and perhaps he loves her, but an impartial observer might conclude that he's after her money, which she came into last year when an aunt died, which is when he moved in with her. So his timing is pretty much perfect."

She winces and recoils her head, her body stiffening ever so slightly, straightening her arms like she's trying to push herself up off the seat. "That's terrible," she says in a very somber tone, the way one begins a eulogy. "I can't believe she's falling for it."

"Should I say something? I wasn't planning to. I just don't think it's my place." Twenty feet away a group of young children, who don't seem to be supervised by an adult, begin groping a male mannequin who's outfitted in a pair of snug-fitting briefs. Each in turn squeals in delight when a small hand makes contact with the contoured groin, until a harried mother toting a newborn shoos them away. Almost on cue, my phone buzzes. What torment has Lola

85

visited upon me now? What photo has she sent spiraling to my blackened heart?

"No, you can't say anything. It's her life, and ultimately her money, and she can do what she wants."

"So my initial reticence is the way to go?"

"It has to be."

I've forgotten how alluring Leigh Rose's eyes are — a bewitching tone of fern green, deeply set, with flat brows and porcelain skin that contrasts with the luminous color of her pupils. Sure, wrinkles have begun to sprout here and there, but I also can still discern the girl she was. But we see in our lovers what we want to see, not who they really are. For thirty years the French artist Pierre Bonnard painted the same woman, who was his mistress, and not in a single painting did he age her. Even when she was in her sixties, Bonnard envisioned only the brash and bounteous young beauty he'd first fallen in love with, not the harping crone she later became.

The sales associate brings out three boxes of shoes and plops them down in front of us. Each pair costs around $100, money I really can't afford to spend on an item that will get worn maybe twice. I kind of wish Leigh Rose had perused the sales rack, where white shoes often languish, but she really isn't a sales rack kind of girl. I'm certainly not going to alert her to my depleted bank account, and so I dutifully try on each pair that she picked out. But one really stands out: a moc-toe slip-on with a decorative silver strap that screams 1977 pimp.

I perform a stilted version of John Travolta from *Saturday Night Fever,* complete with a strut and an arm extended at a jaunty angle. "Studio 54, anyone?" I rasp.

"So cheesy! I adore those shoes! You have to get them, especially for this wedding."

"I'll be straight-up hustling in these bad boys."

"I thought you needed oxfords?"

"Nah, white is right. Isn't that what people say in Henrico County?"

"You're so bad, Eddie."

"Sold!" I exclaim to the sales associate, who's been watching us with a blank expression, as if the hours of retail toil had robbed him of any ability to appreciate mirth. With a solemn nod he begins to sort out the boxes and then, kneeling down, gestures to me, indicating that he wants to put the pimp shoes back into their box.

"No, I'm good to go," I say manfully, admiring my new kicks, which are deliciously hideous. "I think I'll wear them out."

"Now there's a real brave heart for you!" Leigh Rose sings in delight, clapping her hands while egging me on to make a fool of myself, something I'm only too happy to oblige.

"I need to break them in, right?"

"Of course you do!"

"And these go with shorts."

"I think so."

In the blink of an eye, we're eighteen again, mercurial and undaunted, ready to sally forth like a couple of oddballs in weird clothes, impervious to disapproval, our inner punk rockers arising from dormant ashes. It feels like we're on our way to slam-dance at Hard Times and hop on the table-tops at Domino's, but I also realize that I know nothing about her current situation. There's no wedding ring, but who knows what that means. I'm sure she'll fill me in at Starbucks, yet the person I want to ask about, but am afraid to, is her older brother, named Jeb. Even better, his full name is Jeb Stuart Wardell, in honor of the Confederate cavalry hero.

Jeb hated my guts. One presumes he still hates my guts, despite the fact that we haven't laid eyes on each other since high school. Normally if a person hates me, I try to smooth the troubled waters between us, and consequently most people don't hate me for very long. But not only did Jeb hate me, he'd warned me to stay away from his sister or else. At the time he was a sophomore at some party school like Elon, and he'd been kicked off the football team for breaking the starting quarterback's leg in a scrimmage (not to mention the horrible grades and other off-the-field issues), and so he was someone I rightfully feared because not only was he capable of violence, he seemed to enjoy inflicting it. Nothing in his background indicated that he felt remorse. He was large, beefy, and rash. He told me that I had no business being with Leigh Rose and suggested I "get a clue" before "it was too late."

So after I reported his threat to Leigh Rose, brother and sister got into a huge fight, she wrecked a Mercedes on her way to Casablanca, and her parents grounded her for a month, which had the indirect effect of separating us, and a few weeks later she ended it, perhaps because of pressure she was getting from her parents or she just got bored. I was ready for college to begin anyway, so I just wished her well and moved on. But something tells me that Jeb has never forgotten, and here I am, again with his sister.

Is Jeb Wardell the man in the black hat, my nemesis, my killer?

"You're just what the doctor ordered," Leigh Rose gushes as we make our way to the register. "All the people I've been hanging out with are just so uptight and prim and proper. I actually joined the Junior League. I really did."

"I haven't exactly set the world on fire, either."

"You're a college professor."

"Meaning what?"

"You touch the lives of young people."

Oh, I touch them! There's no doubt about that. Or is there? What is true and what is false in my tawdry tale? I'm confessing, but I'm also conflating, confusing, and contorting reality, because who would want to read a book about a college professor who goes home for a wedding? Yawn! On my phone is a photograph of a former student standing in front of a mirror admiring his massive erection. Is it really there? Or if you looked, would you just find the ordinary sorts of texts that a lonely man might get? Married friends checking in, college chums too busy to call, my cell phone provider updating my minimal data usage . . . you recognize this life, because it's yours, which is why you want my story to drag you away from the banality that enshrouds you.

So guess what? This is delicious and you'll love it. As we're standing in line to pay, Leigh Rose gets a call on her cell phone. I'm a little surprised that she answers it, but she does say "Excuse me" before turning away. I take this moment to check my own phone, and find an unread text from Lola. It includes another photograph, this time of her and her roommate, a pinch-faced though chubby vixen named Dahlia, both of whom are naked and in a bed, with arms around feckless Priapus. Lola is gripping the swollen mandrake of this otherwise nondescript nobody as if she's just captured a snake and holds its head so it can't bite her.

The caption reads:

he calls it thor

The Norse god of thunder and lightning, from which we derive our English word "Thursday," and so one day a week for the rest of my life I'll have to think about this venereal pervert who fouled Lola (and her roommate). She'll grow out of it, I ardently believe that. She's just in an experimental phase and indulging every whim, and next year she'll graduate and we won't have to hide our affection, assuming any remains, because right now what I'm feeling is disgust. Disgust mixed with a tremendous desire to cry in her lap. Leigh Rose, get off the phone! Look what happens when you separate from me! My mind boggles, my id becomes hideous, and my desire for life ebbs with the neap tide . . .

She hangs up and rejoins me in line. "Sorry about that. My kids are at camp and I go get them on Sunday. My daughter is pretty sure I'm leaving her there." A sardonic laugh. "Which isn't a bad idea."

"You have kids?"

"Two. A boy and a girl."

But any further explanation will have to wait because it's my turn to pay. The sales associate at the register scans my item with the alacrity of a lobotomized simian, and I reach for my wallet, slowly and surely, like the sheriff in a Western movie readying for a shoot-out, but in this fight I'm woefully outgunned. The quite interesting question is: will my credit card even work? Count me as someone who's eager to see the result of this experiment in creative finance. Will I be mortified if my card were to be declined right in front of my ex-flame? Then again, what's one more emasculating indignity? The more, the merrier! There's no shame left for me to give to the world, and at this point the best I can do is grudgingly accept my pitiable plight. I swipe my credit card with rococo certainty and then hold my breath. In less than a second, Leigh Rose will learn that my life is one big lie, artlessly constructed, a ramshackle dwelling for pent-up hostilities and warped sexuality (which Lola undeniably adores, much to my chagrin).

Miraculously the transaction goes through. I'm thrilled, but really had my credit card been denied, my story might have turned out very differently. Poe would appreciate the macabre irony of desiring that which ultimately will prove to be your undoing. From a banking standpoint, there's no logical reason why I was able to buy the shoes, but I don't quibble. I quickly scrawl my name on the electronic pad, grab a big, billowing bag (containing the sneakers I'd worn), and now I'm free to go.

"I'm proud of you, Eddie," Leigh Rose prods me as we scud out of Macy's. "You haven't lost your sense of humor."

"In my line of work, you need a sense of humor."

"Please. I bet all the girls are secretly in love with you."

"Right." A nervous giggle, straight from the Lee Harvey Oswald School of Charm. Maybe I should confess everything, and I mean everything. It'll feel great to unburden myself, to lift the onerous weight from my sagging shoulders. How much guilt can one person lug around? I thought I had the right build for it, but my knees are starting to buckle.

"At Tulane there was this English professor and I thought he was so handsome and debonair. I tried flirting with him but he wouldn't give me the time of day."

"I bet he was gay."

"That's sweet, Eddie. But he wasn't. He was sleeping with half of our class."

"Really?"

"So I heard."

Starbucks abuts the Macy's, and as we walk to it, I feel strangely liberated from the years-long embargo Bev waged against spending money at Starbucks, which at times forced us to drink coffee from convenience stores whose labor practices were far worse. "It's been a long time since I've indulged in a biscotti," I say with gusto.

"Why's that?"

"My ex-wife hated Starbucks and so I kind of picked up her feelings and made them my own, which is one reason she's my ex-wife. But I know lots of students who work at Starbucks and they all like it." Take that, Bev! Empirical evidence that Starbucks isn't the corporate criminals you made them out to be, a charge you based on highly subjective rants from the leftist bloggers who fueled your almost-but-not-quite Marxism. Occupy Ithaca lasted how long? Barely a week?

"It's a guilty pleasure of mine," she concurs.

"Those are the best kind."

"You are so bad!"

My insouciance has quickly become her oxygen. She's beaming joyfully as we head off for coffee. My new white shoes make a funny clacking sound, almost musical, and my feet feel light in them, like any second I could break into a rousing tap routine, Gene Kelly to her Debbie Reynolds, but instead of singing in the rain, we'll be confessing at the mall.

Or not.

Why do I need to let Leigh Rose see Ithaca Eddie in all his tattered glory? Ithaca Eddie is gone forever. New shoes, new attitude, new identity. Leigh Rose doesn't need to know about Lola and Thor and the letter from the dean I got last week requesting to meet with me. Deans in academia love meetings, and so now it's my turn to sit in the hot seat. It's not like I've been having sexually inappropriate relationships with six (or more) of my current students, no matter what you think. I disclose to you what you need to know and nothing more.

"This is my treat," Leigh Rose informs me once we get in line.

"But I'm the man. I wear the pants in this relationship."

"I like you so much better without pants." She delivers this line in a whisper, and I can't tell whether she's playing with me or inviting me to seduce her. I don't mean to suggest that our high school fling was an epic adolescent fuck-fest, because we spent most of our time together going to shows and groping in parked cars. We enjoyed each other in the informal way of teens, but mostly for her I was a sort of rebellious outlet, a kindred spirit, a fellow traveler, and not a Lothario with a pocket full of condoms. But we have had sexual inter-course, which could mean myriad different things depending on the situation.

"Well, I guess you're paying then." I chuckle lightheartedly.

"Thanks. I only feel alive if I'm spending money."

"At least something makes you feel alive."

We're at the counter now, and I'm struck by how openly quirky Leigh Rose still is. The suburbs haven't yet eroded her, though solitude clings to her the way a smoky smell can persist in the kitchen despite opening all the windows to air out the burnt odor — because just the fact that she's even at this mall makes me wonder about her life, her two kids, her lack of a wedding ring. I'm enjoying myself, maybe a little too much, considering the dire straits I'm in.

I order a double espresso (and biscotti), and she opts for a mocha latte. "We'd better grab a table," she suggests, surveying the interior with an expert gaze. "I see one in back."

"You get it and I'll wait for the coffees."

As I stand there alone, out of habit my cell phone finds its way into my hand, as if it were tethered to my palm by an invisible string. Lola has sent me yet another text, and I really don't feel like looking at it. There's so much about our relationship that doesn't work. My weakness is just another symptom of a more virulent disease that threatens my very existence. Her latest missive:

9 inches

I close my eyes and then with a puritanical rapidity begin deleting her texts, one at a time, but I'll never get through them all. I've fallen into a pit of quicksand and struggling to get out only makes it worse. I have to endure photo after photo, her rogues' gallery of conquests, and her pithy commentary on each.

But then our coffees are ready and my purging comes to a halt. I shove the biscuits into a pocket, along with my phone, and carry the cups over to a table in back, scooting around a hirsute technophile who's typing on a laptop with a Bluetooth earpiece affixed to a lobe. Leigh Rose puts her phone down and shoots me a wan smile.

"Of all the gin joints in all the world," I growl in my best Bogart imitation, which is actually decent. Even Bev thought so, and she pretty much detested all my celebrity imitations.

"We'll always have Paris," Leigh Rose replies right on cue.

"I took you to see that film, if you recall, at the Biograph on Grace Street."

"I do recall. We smoked dope in my dad's old Mercedes and when he smelled the interior in the morning, he made me scrub the seats."

"You were such a troublemaker."

"Some things never change."

We each take a prolonged sip of our coffee. I see no point in beating around the bush, and so I make the first foray into personal disclosure. Perhaps I'm being inspired by the enlarged photograph on the wall opposite me, of a sturdy Central American farmer hoisting a load of coffee beans, grown organically, of course, just the sort of corporate propaganda that used to drive Bev batty. But who's to say that the brown-faced peasant isn't deliriously happy? Well, if he can shoulder a burden, so can I.

"So let me guess," I venture in my nasally ironic tone. "You married a doctor."

Her placid face betrays no emotion. We could've been talking about cloud formations or cookie recipes. "No, he was a lawyer."

She delivers this clarification in the past tense, which might explain the lack of a wedding ring. The idea of her availability motivates me to wade farther in, an intrepid explorer roving across the hostile landscape of adult failure. "I don't mean to pry. Okay, I do mean to pry. I'm totally prying right now because I'm a terrible person. Are you divorced? Do we share the stigma of botched matrimony?"

"You can definitely say that we screwed up our marriage, but we didn't get divorced. He died two years ago."

"I'm so sorry! Now I feel like a jerk."

"You were trying to be funny, and that's something I've always liked about you. So don't apologize. Trust me, widows get tired of being the object of pity."

"I can imagine."

"Everybody makes the assumption that I'm too frail to walk down the street or cook pot roast. This might sound cold, but I wasn't exactly torn to pieces when Trevor died. The kids were obviously very hurt, but my husband was a mean person, cruel even."

"To you?"

She leans forward like she wants to tell me a secret. "When I was pregnant with my second, I went to the ob-gyn for a normal checkup and it turned out I'd contracted an STD. Hmm, how did I get that? Trevor was the only person I was having sex with. It was a miracle I didn't miscarry. I actually started to hate him after that little faux pas." She shakes her head in disbelief, eyes fixed on a point far, far away from us. "I haven't told anybody that story. Not even Trevor."

"You didn't confront him?"

"He would've just lied or blamed me. There was no point."

A gaggle of pregnant women takes up a large round table and their confident voices form a kind of singsong counterpoint to the sotto voce dirge of Leigh Rose's tale of woe. We actually sit back and observe the surreal scene unfolding: these all-white women in the throes of baby-making reverie, radiant in displaying the fruits of their successful mating strategies, with belly bumps perfectly framed in trendy expecting-mommy attire, smiling, laughing, oblivious to the ravages of marriage, the incipience of disharmony, the very real possibility that one day they will hate their husbands. Perhaps a decade ago Leigh Rose had belonged to their ranks, but now she's on the outside looking in, a stranger in a strange land, a widow who's run into an old flame — little old me, who just might be a tragedy in the making.

I've got no reason to harm Leigh Rose. None. I won't even insult your intelligence by contorting the plot in such a way as to make it seem possible that I'll choke her with my bare hands. The real issue here is her brother, the one who hates me. He's lurking in the background, a ticking bomb. He's the one to keep an eye on.

Now, there are certain novelists who strain credulity on every mediocre page they produce, the worst offense being the amazing coincidence that advances the threadbare plot but leaves a lingering odor of artlessness wafting in the stale air. I will never stoop to that banality, mostly because I'm dedicated to delivering you the Truth, without concern for the niceties involved.

But sometimes in life, in ways impossible to predict, surprising tangents arise, two vectors intersect, and we're left shivering in the vast cold blackness of a universe we'll never understand. If I were composing a work of fiction, I'd never allow this scene to play out in the manner I'm about to delineate. But this isn't fiction.

Against all odds, at that very moment, Jeb Wardell, Leigh Rose's brother, comes storming into the Starbucks like he's been fired from a cannon, eyes ablaze, hulking physique padded by a layer of fat that makes him resemble an inflamed walrus, with a bushy mustache that seems to have belonged to a Halloween costume. Judging from his attire, he's been golfing. Judging from the gold chains around his flabby neck, his taste is still poor. He'll forever remain malevolent-looking enough to belong in a Bosch painting, and I certainly don't want this greedy trust-fund demon to be my executioner. Anybody but him!

"What's he doing here?" mutters Leigh Rose, straightening up in her chair as if she's prepared to launch a counterattack. Maybe I should ready myself for combat as well. Jeb looks awfully pissed. For a second I worry that he's going to steamroll the pregnant women, but he does dodge them, thereby avoiding senseless tragedy. For now.

"Can I talk to you?" he blandly asks Leigh Rose, in the manner of an angry customer returning a defective item, though he remains oblivious of my existence.

"No, you cannot" is her curt reply.

I turn to face him, to confront him, to declare myself on the side of goodness. Perhaps I should've remained invisible, but his voice, dripping with Southern frat boy cockiness, drew me in and caused me to don my Superman cape.

Our eyes meet, and he studies me with a strange fixed gaze, seemingly mesmerized by my trucker's hat. "Didn't mean to interrupt," he stammers, trying to remain polite but obviously straining against the social graces that hold him back.

"Do you remember Eddie Stith?" Leigh Rose asks in a casual tone. "He's a friend of mine from high school."

"I thought you looked kind of familiar." He extends a beefy hand and we shake, with him attempting to crush all my metacarpals. "Nice seeing you again. Do you still live in Richmond?"

"No, not anymore."

"He escaped." Leigh Rose is relishing this moment, which confuses me. I'm shaking in my boots but she's lapping it up, an odd incongruity I'll soon enough fathom. "He's one of the smart ones."

"I just need five minutes," Jeb tries again, with a bit more tact. But his softening only makes Leigh Rose stiffer in her denial.

"I don't want to discuss it with you."

There ensues an awkward pause, during which I fully expect Jeb to reach down my throat and pull out my intestines. Nonplussed, I sip at my coffee like we've all met at the Café du Monde following a night of revelry on Bourbon Street, but even I know that this performance is stilted. It takes him no time to strike first, which he does by making an accusation I don't altogether understand.

"Oh, I get it now," he says with anger that borders on glee, which has the same purity as newly minted gold. "It's crystal clear what's going on."

"Think what you want, Jeb," Leigh Rose replies nonchalantly.

"This is ridiculous."

Leigh Rose's hand finds mine and she grips it tightly, and I can feel within her skin a pulsing heat that reminds me of being at the beach. But this display of affection isn't intended to soothe me but to ruffle Jeb, who's already on the verge of snapping, and her taking hold of my hand only exacerbates his already frayed nerves. I can hear him snorting in derision above me, a disgruntled god glowering down upon a recalcitrant humanity. "Go ahead and throw your life away," he hisses. "You've lost your mind. You realize that, right?"

She doesn't answer, because now she's leaning over and nibbling on my earlobe. Her breath reeks of Colombian coffee and the effect it has on me is almost stimulating. I'd love for a woman to dump a tepid pot of java over my head and then lick it off my naked body (just so long as the lights were off). I understand that she's putting on a show for Jeb, and what the hell, I join in with some gusto, reaching around her midriff for a loving hug. At that point I really don't know much about the turbulent waters into which I've waded, but my caresses seem to be causing Jeb to grow even more agitated. Murderously so? With him, that's entirely possible.

"Fine," he says. "Whatever works for you. I thought you had my back on this, little sis. Guess I was wrong."

"Oh, please. Don't be so dramatic. And anyway I don't owe you or anybody else an explanation."

He ignores her and instead stares at me with the intensity of the middle linebacker he once was. "See you around, Eddie" are his parting words before he turns away and marches out, his topsiders slapping against the floor and causing the entire store to shake. Even after he's gone, however, Leigh Rose is still holding my hand and my arm continues to loop across her chest. Our coffee sits on the table, growing cold. The pregnant women chat away in voices that sound like a murder of crows.

Leigh Rose's mouth finds mine and we kiss.

5

The sex scene.

I've got a thesaurus handy so that I can regale you with interesting phrases that will better describe the passionate lovemaking that ensues. If I were stronger, more in control of myself, I'd just leave the dirty bits out of my tale. Does it really matter what I do to Leigh Rose and what she does to me behind closed doors? Will our coupling in any way alter the fundamental course of my fate? Isn't it enough that I'm going to her house, thereby risking life and limb to reconnect with her? That alone should send alarm bells clanging.

This won't be easy for me to write about, even when armed with a dizzying array of titillating descriptors. Because as I'm following Leigh Rose's behemoth Chevy Tahoe, dread and fear quickly fill up all the interstitial space in my putrid soul. Now, most erotic sex scenes require a male lover who is chomping at the bit to stick his bulging shaft into some willing pudenda, but at this point I must reveal to you a rather delicate detail about myself. You see, my schlong has proven to be rather complex, if not downright elusive, a sort of shy and retreating creature afraid of being seen or venturing too far out of its shell. The "long and short" of it is, my member has developed an aversion to standing at attention, and the sight of a vulva often heralds a sudden loss of vigor. Lola has exploited my enervation for her own perverse enjoyment, evidenced by the numerous photos she texts me of her absurdly aroused lovers as a way of grinding my confidence to nothing, which is precisely and illogically what I want from her. But when ordered by a physician to wear a Velcro strip around my manhood while I sleep, lo and behold I reach such a nocturnal state of arousal that my wood bursts out of the strap like a veritable porn star's, yet in my waking hours this turgidity vanishes and I become a ninety-nine-pound weakling. Thus, there's no physical reason I can't attain an erection, and I've been told that it's quite rare for a man my age to experience what is commonly known as "erectile dysfunction," a term too technocratic for my taste, as I prefer a condition known as "anhedonia," or the inability to feel pleasure. Bev lovingly referred to my condition as the Fall of Man, as there would be engorgement, but achingly, fitfully evanescent, despite Bev's heroic ministrations and cooing words of encouragement, as if she were nursing a very ill patient to sit up and eat. *Come on, you can do it, just relax.* But nothing she did could reverse my downward spiral toward oblivion.

A limp dick: nothing hints at extinction quite like that. If called upon to propagate the human race, I'd fail. Now it might make more sense why Bev ended up in the lanky arms of a highly unoriginal ceramicist, because she did take my "Mr. E.D." personally, despite my futile protestations that I found her sexy and desirable, in body and soul. Basically, she went from blaming herself to blaming me, a fierce calculation I couldn't fault as the problems in our connubial bed were of my making, and doubtless the talentless sculptor for whom she left me could get a hard-on, which only proved Bev's theory that I should shoulder the blame for the increasingly comical misfires in the boudoir. Even now I can't explain what went wrong. In bed Bev was always fervent, sensual, and satisfying. So what has defeated my groin? Worse, how in the world could I explain any of this to Leigh Rose, who doesn't live far from the mall and at whose house we'll be arriving any second? Then what?

Down River Road we zoom, past the Collegiate School from which Leigh Rose had been expelled in seventh grade, for repeatedly smoking on the leafy campus. A wild child even then. Took her first lover at fourteen. A senior whom she described as a "great ape" without getting into details. Other boyfriends followed, and then me. We had some good sex back in the day. Didn't we? Or was I just a rebellious aside? As her left-hand turn signal flashes, I debate whether I should continue on with this farce.

Have I mentioned yet that Leigh Rose is rich?

Don't judge me too harshly. I'm not after her money, even though I'm essentially penniless and perhaps soon will be unemployed, if not arrested — I don't know what's taking the authorities in Ithaca so long to charge me with something; just accuse me of a crime so I can confess to all my misdeeds and end the agony of waiting. Until then, I've got to suffer with my private guilt, and apparently I'll do so in a house that's around the size of a small airport.

Leigh Rose pulls into a circular drive and parks. I roll to a stop behind her, my mouth agog from the sheer enormity of her palatial residence. From where I sit in the front seat of my Honda, I can see basketball and tennis courts, between which sits a pool roughly akin to Lake Superior. The house itself is really a series of buildings that have been crunched together at an odd L-shaped angle, and each section appears to be the size of my house on Traylor Drive — I count four sections. The architectural style is of course the trite neo-Colonial mansion (is there any other kind around here?), and the lawns (yes, plural) are immaculate, and in fact a grounds crew is tending to the various gardens and grooming the grass with old-fashioned reel mowers.

Only when I get out of my car do I notice a FOR SALE sign.

"Home sweet home," she chirps. "At least until I sell it."

"How many people live here?" I ask, still stupefied by the sheer gigantism of the dwelling. "A hundred?"

"Trevor liked everything to be the biggest and the best. This is his house all the way. Whatever, time for a fresh start. I'm moving downtown. Get over here."

I shut the car door and follow my legs over

to her, where she's standing by a flagpole that seems to reach the heavens, an obvious phallic symbol that does nothing to quell my unease. I trip over a slate paving stone and fall into her waiting arms, a dork move direct from a B movie.

"Careful." She laughs, hoisting me up with surprising strength. She must spend a good amount of time in the gym, and now I wish I'd stuck to my vow to get in the best shape of my life, an unfulfilled goal that is going on twenty years old.

"You're buff," I tell her, and her eyes glisten as she arches her head back. We kiss again, our bodies pulled close together, though the stifling heat is making us sweat. Little beads of perspiration dot her forehead, and the relentless sun dogs us from above.

"Let's go cool off," she suggests, taking my hand and leading me to the front door. She has to deactivate a complex security system by pushing an assortment of buttons, which she does with practiced dexterity. "Something else about this house I hate," she grouses. "My husband loved gadgets and stuffed all kinds of crap in here. I can't tell you how many times I've set off this alarm. But did it stop the maid from stealing my jewelry?"

"I'm guessing no."

"Of course it didn't! If it was up to me, I wouldn't even put locks on the doors! Locks only keep out the honest."

We're inside now, and the first thing I notice is the dramatic staircase that sweeps upward, looking like an exact replica of the one Scarlett O'Hara gets pushed down in *Gone with the Wind*. A huge chandelier drops from the high ceiling, its crystals shining like a torrent of diamonds. Beneath my feet is an expansive Persian rug of exquisite quality, with a paisley motif of red and green. On a wall is an enormous portrait of a regal-looking man with a mane of snowy white hair sitting atop a chestnut Arabian horse, and he looks like he's about to send out the hounds.

"And that is?" I ask, nodding at the garish gilt-framed monstrosity.

"Trevor's grandfather, who didn't even own any horses. The man was a dolt who made a fortune in latex. Condoms, actually. But then it turns out they were defective, just like Trevor. Oh, that's too mean. We were happy, I think, after we got married and before the children came. My adorable daughter used to cry all night. Why are we still sober? I want a drink, and I hate to drink alone."

"I guess one won't kill me."

"Depends on the bartender. Come on, this way!"

She takes me through the dining room, past a landing strip of a table that seats twenty, and into the "Smoking Room," a term Leigh Rose delivers with a devilish chuckle. "It's a man cave, but he was so pretentious he hated it when anyone called it that," she explains as we step inside. There is a bar of burnished teak, a flat-screen TV mounted over a fireplace, posters of various football heroes, and a Kappa Alpha fraternity paddle (from Tulane University). Leigh Rose ducks behind the bar and quickly produces two tumblers. I take a seat in a high-backed stool, feeling slightly voyeuristic, a little like a cannibal, for relaxing in the sanctum sanctorum of a dead man's personal space.

"Pick your poison," she calls out with dramatic flair. "I'm drinking vodka."

Pick your poison. Are you paying attention? Aren't you even slightly curious how Trevor, her badly behaved hubby, met his untimely demise? At that point I don't even know or much care. I've entered a woozy, fuzzy state of mind, and giddiness has dulled my usually sharp critical faculties. A drink before noon? Not since college for

114

this forthright academic, this toiling intellectual. A role model. A shaper of young
minds. A caresser of young bodies.

"I'd venture to guess that Trevor liked a
nice bottle of scotch," I surmise with elbows
propped up on the bar, thinking that some
music might be in order. It's what brought
us together in the 1990s, after all.

"I know just the thing."

She reaches into a cabinet and pulls out a
wooden case about the size of a shoe box.
In it, much to my delight, is an unopened
bottle of Glenfarclas 1955, which I'm guessing retails somewhere north of eight grand.
"He got this at a charity auction and was
saving it for a special occasion, and I don't
like scotch at all. What the hell, Eddie. Let's
live a little. I'm officially calling this a
special occasion."

"Are you sure? That costs an arm and a
leg."

"I'm so tired of money, you have no idea.
Here's mud in your eye."

She replaces one of the tumblers with a
snifter emblazoned with a family crest, pops
the cork, and releases a beautiful stream of
nectar whose amber tone hints at the oaky
taste that awaits me. I could get used to this
lifestyle, but hovering above me is the
disembodied voice of my own former

spouse, and Bev is telling me that this sybaritic excess is obscene given the income disparity that roils our nation. How many hungry children could that bottle feed?

"Inshallah," I toast, lifting the glass to my lips. The first sip causes my entire body to glow like a white-hot brick of charcoal. Only one thing can elevate my mood even higher. "We need some tunes! I see speakers over there. What are you into these days?"

Leigh Rose is slurping down a huge gulp of straight vodka on the rocks but stops when I mention music and her entire face lights up like a Christmas tree. "I am totally consumed by Neko Case! I love her voice! Oh my God!" She bounces up and down excitedly, grabbing her phone to cue up the album. Her phone is synched to the speakers, and seconds later come the first twangy chords of a guitar. Then Neko Case asks: *What drug will keep night from coming?* Leigh Rose closes her eyes and melts into the song.

"She's really talented," I say cheerfully. "Great sound. Reminds me of Lucinda Williams."

"Did you see her on *Letterman*?" Does she honestly think that I watch network television as the clock approaches midnight? Lola would never allow such mundane media to reach her screen, as we invented our own form of adult entertainment.

"No, I missed that."

"She killed it. Oh my God, she was amazing."

Leigh Rose appears to be deliriously happy, drink in hand, favorite jam blasting, and it reminds me of the time we listened to Portishead's first album together, in the very same basement confines where I'm currently bedded down, and we screwed to some funky trip-hop, and now she mistakenly thinks that I'm still that impetuous, strong-willed boy, just like she once saw rebellion in my ripped jeans and Cobain sneakers. She's probably also thinking that I can still get it up, which she will soon learn is incorrect, and in time she'll come to see that all her impressions of me are as illusory as a Disney hologram. But the scotch is going down smoothly and I really don't care what comes next.

"Let's go make ourselves comfortable," she purrs, reaching across the bar and stroking my forearm.

"Are you sure?"

"Trevor told me before he died that he wanted me to be happy." Then she groans in mock despair. "Listen to me, I'm such a bitch. He did say that, though. Where have you been all my life?"

117

"That's a great question. Didn't you break up with me?"

"Did I? Well, I think I know how I can say I'm sorry. I'll kiss it and make it feel better."

She fetchingly traipses over to the largest of the sofas, which looks soft and plush, with puffy throw pillows, and she launches herself onto it like a swimmer diving into a pool. Most red-blooded men would have dropped trousers right then and used their protruding boners like a divining rod, but instead I gulp down one last swig of the best drink of my life and tell myself: *If you can get hard, dude, all this will be yours.*

"Aren't you coming?" she asks, after noticing that I haven't moved.

"I hope so!"

A girlish giggle bursts forth as I carefully slither to where she waits for me. I'm hopeful that the Glenfarclas will magically repair my stubborn penis, which even after fifty lashes won't perform the usual tricks. There are remedies for my condition, purple pills and such, but my problem apparently goes deeper than that (my urologist wants to write a paper about my case for a medical journal). And what did Bev say? *I don't care about sex that much anyway. Don't do anything to jeopardize your health. Our love means more than that.* Not four months later, our marriage was over.

"I'm so sick of the men in this city," Leigh Rose whispers as I position myself next to her, with the studied determination of a student driver learning how to parallel park. "You're like a breath of fresh air, just what the doctor ordered."

"Luckily for you, I do house calls."

"What procedure are you going to perform on me?"

"You'll need to show me where it hurts first."

"Oh, Eddie, I thought I was going crazy! Nobody understands what it's like, the pressure, the stupid games. But you're different."

Deviant might be the correct word, but I don't quibble. She rests her head on my shoulder and buries her face into the nape of my neck. I feel tenderness surge within me, the desire to protect her from the forces that torment her, even if I'm powerless to do so. For a brief second I entertain the notion of Destiny, that pathetic construct we drag out to explain the random, but I can't help wonder about the vagaries of life that have brought me here, next to this woman who actually seems to need me, who seems to appreciate the very gifts of mine that the world has soundly rejected, who craves my attention, who derives energy from the things I care about. Is this, gulp, the handiwork of Destiny, that I'd be plucked from the depths of hell and deposited on a sofa in a dead man's mansion to console the widow whose wounds are still raw?

I kiss her — not because we're going to have intercourse, which is a physical and/or emotional impossibility, but because I feel gratitude and in her lips reside the last vestiges of the person I was, as if somehow she has come to possess the secret elixir that will restore me to my former grandeur. Her skin reminds me of the Atlantic Ocean — there is a salty flavor, marine in texture, warm and sun-dappled, and I try to summon my inner Rimbaud, the Jim Morrison I know still lives in me, the buried hedonist ready to burn for pleasure — but can only Lola and her depravity truly touch my deepest, darkest places? Is that impetuous coed the symptom of my disease or its sinister source? Out of sheer desperation, knowing it's the polite thing to do, and in an effort to rid myself of the onus of Lola, I begin to knead Leigh Rose's breasts, still firm as ever, breasts most men would eat nails to nuzzle against. My touch causes her to stir and squirm, and her hands roam from my chest down to my midsection, as though on a trip south toward my groin. My body tenses and she pulls back from me, her puzzled expression radiating concern.

"You okay?" she asks.

"Yeah, of course. Maybe this is a little overwhelming for my delicate senses."

"I want to be overwhelmed. Overwhelm me, Eddie."

"I'll see what I can do."

Such bravado! It's John Wayne on that sofa, getting ready to pull out his six-shooter and mow down a helpless tribe of Injuns. The American male can admit to no weakness. Dutifully I unzip her workout jacket, somehow convinced that this time will be different, that I'll become Priapus, and so I lift up her microfiber T-shirt and wedge my hand beneath her jogging bra. She inhales sharply, arching her back ever so slightly, while running her hands through my thinning hair, knocking off my trucker's hat. It tumbles to the carpeted floor behind us.

"Take me, Eddie. I'm all yours."

"You are so sexy. I forgot how hot you are."

"You don't think I'm old and washed-up?"

"No way in hell!"

"You're so sweet. I've always liked that about you."

She sits up and removes her warm-up jacket and shirt, and her breasts flop out when the jogging bra comes off. They are rugged-looking, with oval-shaped areolae the color of uncooked flank roast, and heavily freckled near the cleavage. Lola's jut out with porcelain precision and her nipples protrude like two bullets poised to execute me, but Leigh Rose's sag under the weight of childbirth, death, gravity, confusion. And yet they are quite welcoming, not imperious like a young woman in the bloom of unblemished beauty, not haughty in the knowledge of their perfection, but honest and friendly, almost neighborly, as if saying, *You can stop by anytime!*

She crawls onto my lap, sits on her haunches, and then leans forward to press her chest against my face, though there is something robotic and perfunctory in this gesture, and just as suddenly as she arrives, she tumbles off me as if she'd been knocked over by a gale-force blast of wind. The horrible thought occurs to me that she's suffering a heart attack, but then she curls into a ball on the sofa and covers her face with her hands as sobs erupt from her. Her crying makes my throat constrict — and I blame myself for this lamentable outcome. My lack of ardor has hurt her feelings and I curse myself for being such a lying scumbag, because Leigh Rose has done nothing to deserve my lame attempt at romance. Except that I actually do want her. At least I'm pretty sure I do. It's hard to tell anymore.

"What's wrong?" I ask, petting her shoulder as softly as I can.

"I'm so sorry," she sniffles, her face now blotchy and tearstained, a picture of exquisite agony. "I'm just a total mess and I don't know what the hell I'm doing. It's not fair to you."

"What isn't?"

"You make me feel free, Eddie. But I'll never be free. I'll never be the person I was before. That's impossible." She sits up and hurriedly begins to pull her clothes back on, now ashamed to be undressed in front of me. Far from being insulted, I feel a huge weight lifted from my shoulders. "I know you think I'm crazy, and it's not you. It really isn't. Seeing you today, it sent shock waves through my body. I felt alive for the first time in a long time. But here's the thing. I'm just going to tell you because I know you won't judge me and I trust you. The whole idea of sex, it makes me sick. Like physically ill. I want to puke right now."

"Let me get you some water."

"That's sweet, thanks."

I hop up from the sofa and hurry to the bar, where there's a small rinsing sink. I fill a glass from the tap and bring it back to Leigh Rose, who gulps down the water as if she'd been wandering the Sahara for a year. She seems to take comfort in my small gesture of kindness, and her face relaxes as she leans back and gives me a weary smile. "How long has this been happening?" I ask in a clinical voice, the one I use with students who come to me with stories of sorrow to explain why an assignment will be late.

"Oh, gosh. It's gotten worse lately, that's for sure."

"Why do you think that is?"

"I hate to use the expression 'it's complicated,' but it's complicated. Really stupid and complicated. Eddie, I'm so sick of everything. Not my kids. I love them with all my heart. But everything else, I could do without. Including sex. Especially sex." She pauses for me to register an emotion, but I can maintain a detached facade for hours. I've heard it all from my students, which is an understatement of epic proportions.

"You're moving downtown, so that's a positive step."

"It's paltry compared to what needs to

happen. You're not mad at me, are you, for being such a tease? Because I feel like a huge loser for freaking out on you."

My chance to be the Sensitive Guy! You might remember this stereotype from the 1970s, with the turtleneck sweater, suede jacket, and bell-bottom jeans, who was hip to feminism and had an open mind. We gave him a Viking funeral in the Reagan Years. But in my case, I don't even have to pretend. I abhor intercourse as much as she does, possibly more. "You're a beautiful and sexy lady, and I just like spending time with you. Maybe not getting puked on, but I'm down with just hanging out and listening to music."

She appears stunned by this assertion and shakes her head in small, disbelieving circles. "Seeing you is a sign, that's exactly what it is. Me running into you was no accident. It was meant to happen."

"I usually don't like to attribute things to fate, but now I'm starting to wonder."

"Yeah, I was meant to find you, today of all days. To keep me strong."

I infer that Jeb's sudden intrusion at Starbucks relates in some way to her newfound adherence to our shared destiny, but at that point I'm not sure how the dim-witted walrus factors in. Remember that Jeb

Wardell is but one of my possible killers and/or victims, as I'll soon find out. Very soon, by the looks of it, because a loud buzzing interrupts the music and Leigh Rose's face becomes stricken with sudden anguish.

"Someone's here," she gasps, bolting up from the sofa. I assume it's Jeb, who's come to resume whatever argument with Leigh Rose he'd tried to start earlier. At this point I still don't know the extent of the situation into which I've unwittingly stumbled. Jeb is an idiot, for sure, but even an idiot must realize that I pose no threat to Leigh Rose, and I don't see why he'd hold a grudge against me, to the point of twice barging in on us like a ferocious house mother at a sorority sleepover. But there is much about Jeb's life that remains hidden from me, and a plausible motive will emerge in time.

"Maybe I should go," I suggest, but Leigh Rose pushes me back down when I try to stand up.

"No way! Not unless you've got somewhere else to be. I'm not letting them shove me around anymore. And we haven't finished our drinks."

Them. A plural pronoun and the first intimation that my adversary isn't only Jeb Wardell, but another unnamed coconspirator. This is indeed getting heavy. I gaze down at my white shoes, the proximate cause of my current dilemma. I could end this entire standoff in one second by simply showing Leigh Rose the remaining texts from the Promiscuous One back in Ithaca, and all her illusions about me would shatter. But Leigh Rose seems to need me for emotional support and I don't intend to bail on her just to save my own skin. What Richmond gallant would ever retreat on the first day of Gettysburg, when it still seemed as if General Lee could march our brave boys to victory?

"I do like this scotch," I say with a Tom Selleck flair, "and Glenfarclas is probably worth dying for. So I'll stay until I hear from my mother."

Another clamorous buzz of the doorbell. Leigh Rose's mouth grimly sets into a disapproving frown. "Great. Pour another drink. I'll be right back."

Alone in a dead man's man cave, drinking his scotch, coveting his spouse, and checking the smartphone for a new message from Lola, the only person in the world who truly understands me. She has vowed to write a book one day, a tell-all, the kind of confessional sob story that Americans crave. But I've beaten her to the punch, haven't I? You can push a liar only so far before he begins to worship the truth like a sadhu. Hail all liars who vow one day to divulge the depths of their secret depravity! Lies form the volcanoes from which truth erupts in great spurting spasms of hellacious lava, and I do apologize for the sexual overtones of that imagery.

Nothing from Lola. Perhaps she and Thor and the feral roommate Dahlia are off cavorting again, and maybe today is the day I'll finally summon the courage to ask Lola to send me no more of those photos, those texts, that thrill me to the deepest parts of my soul. Why do I even like it? That's what I'll never understand. Sometimes I compare my morbid curiosity about Lola's sex life to the process of desertification, when once-fertile areas undergo profound environmental degradation and then turn into barren wastelands. Trees are removed, soil erodes, and streams dry up. I grew limp, Bev left me, and Lola took up the space in my brain once devoted to love, to scholarship, to being happy.

If my inner life is a desert, then Leigh Rose represents the first nourishing drops of rain that can reclaim the blasted lands of my soul and turn them once again into a garden, not of Eden, but perhaps of Nod, where Abel was sent to live out his days.

At that point Leigh Rose returns, alone, no Jeb clamoring for my head on a platter. She breezes in and heads right to the bar and her vodka. "That was one of the lawn guys," she informs me, hoisting herself onto a stool. "He thought he saw someone snooping around."

"Really? Is everything okay?"

"Yeah. I'm pretty sure I know who it was."

"Jeb?"

"He'd just kick the front door down. No, it's a man I've been seeing. A man who wants to marry me. A man I really don't like very much." This series of disclosures makes my chest tighten, since each tidbit contains its own unique surprise. She has a boyfriend? He's proposed? She doesn't like him?

"Is he gone?" I actually crane my neck to scope out my blind side.

"Yeah, he's gone. The lawn guy saw him run and jump into a car and take off."

"I don't know this person obviously, but aren't you worried? This isn't normal."

"It bothers me a ton, which is why I don't want to marry him. Trust me, if he does it again, I'll call the police."

"Stalking someone is against the law, and I think you're being too charitable. Even one time isn't acceptable." I know plenty about the stalking laws in the state of New York, so I'm speaking as an expert.

"He's just pissed. He proposed to me last night and I said I didn't know what I wanted. But I do now, thanks to you."

I appreciate the compliment but I don't let it go to my head. There are still too many unanswered questions that linger. "Is that why Jeb chased you down at Starbucks?"

"Yeah, he's ticked at me because it's his best friend. Norris Mumford."

I try to place the name but can't, as I've been gone from Richmond too long and I never moved in the same social circle as Leigh Rose anyway. "He proposed to you?"

"He did, but he doesn't love me. He's a jerk. He just wants my money and I was too feeble to call him on it. See, Eddie? That's the kind of person I've become. I can't even stand up for myself anymore. But as soon as I saw you, it's like my entire personality changed like that!" She snaps her fingers for emphasis, and then rushes over and jumps into my arms, and I cradle her as if I've just rescued her from a burning building. "Your white shoes saved me. I was so lost, and now I just can't even describe how strong I feel. Norris doesn't even like music! I mean, come on. Who doesn't like music?"

A good question, but an even better one is: "Why were you with him to begin with?"

She summons the answer from a plaintive sigh that floats out of her mouth as her body slumps low, tranquilized by confusion. "I don't know, why do I do anything? There's no good reason. He's a spoiled brat from St. Chris who emotionally never left high school and I just went with it because he was Jeb's buddy and I was lonely. He's good-looking, I guess, in a plastic sort of way. He can be funny in small doses. But he is so incredibly boring and predictable! Not like you at all!"

She kisses me on the cheek and then lets her head rest on my shoulder. So now I realize what I'm up against. Jeb Wardell thinks I've broken up the relationship between his sister and his best friend, and Jeb Wardell isn't the kind of person who just forgives and forgets. If Norris Mumford is anything like Jeb, then I've got double the trouble to deal with. But Leigh Rose doesn't seem concerned about my safety (or hers), perhaps because she can't admit the worst about her brother and can't entertain the possibility that I'm even in danger. Or are they the ones in danger, Jeb and Norris, the dynamic duo of my undoing?

At that point my phone rings. My mother

131

is calling, and thus I have to take it. Leigh Rose eases off me as I answer.

"I can't move," my poor mother rasps in a voice as rocky as a celebrity marriage.

"Where are you?"

"In my car."

"Are you driving?"

"No. I can't drive. My body won't work." Then she sniffles, as heartrending a sound as I've ever heard.

"Are you having chest pains?"

"No. It's a panic attack."

"I didn't know you got those."

Leigh Rose is looking on with an expression of concern, which is touching. My mother's plight matters to her. Not that Bev was cold or lacked compassion, but she at times kept a distance from my problems. I reach over and squeeze her hand in gratitude.

"My wedding dress doesn't fit," my mother explains, still sounding weak and breathless. "I was at the shop speaking with the seamstress and we were debating what to do with the sleeves. I hate the sleeves. This dress makes me look so ugly, so old and ugly."

"I'm sure that's not true."

"I don't know who I'm kidding. I'm going to be the ugliest bride in history."

"Don't say that. You look great."

"I look sixty years old. No, ninety! My arms are so fat. They didn't used to be. Is it too late for liposuction?"

"Have you called Mead?"

"Of course I haven't called him. Why would I do that?" Sarcasm drips from her tremulous voice in thick, mordant gobs, and it's apparent that this "panic attack" is related somehow to him. He's done something to make her question and doubt.

"Because he's going to be your husband." I roll my eyes and shake my head, and Leigh Rose sighs in commiseration.

My mother clears her throat as a way of gathering her strength. "He's too busy today. I don't want to upset him. He gets very emotional when he thinks I need help. He feels things very deeply."

"I'll come get you then. Where are you?"

She doesn't reply right away, but instead inhales sharply before emitting a cleansing sigh. "I'm starting to feel better," she offers without much conviction. "I'm pretty sure I can drive."

"Mom, come on. I want to help you and you shouldn't drive when you're having a panic attack. You might get in an accident."

"You can't tell anyone. Promise me, Eddie. This is between me and you. No one can know." She sounds panicked now, and for reasons I don't understand. Why does she want to hide her condition from her loved ones? Or is it just Mead who can't know? I can't say that I like the dynamics of their relationship, in which she can't count on him when she's in trouble and he isn't allowed to learn of the inner workings of her psyche.

"Fine. This is our secret. Where are you? You haven't even told me that."

"I'm in the parking lot of O'Bloom's on Forest Hill. I'll be fine, Eddie, I promise. We're supposed to meet up for lunch at one o'clock back at the house. Mead really wants to meet you. You can make it, right? One o'clock?" All of a sudden she's morphed back into her old self, yet I can't fathom the reason for her original call. Was this her way of letting me know that not all is well in the House of Mead, an indirect method of communication where she tacitly admits that this marriage is a mistake while continuing to rush headlong into it?

"Of course I can make it. But I'm worried about you. You sure you can drive?"

"I'm sure I'm sure. I don't know what got into me." A nervous laugh that does nothing to assuage my unease, followed by an equally misleading stab at an explanation:

"I guess I'm just a little nervous!"

"Nerves are one thing, panic attacks are something else."

Then she starts chirping like a merry bird without a care in the world. "Oh, it's nothing to worry about, Eddie! I've had so much on my mind recently, and sometimes those kids of his can be aggravating. Once this weekend is all over, I'm sure life will settle back down."

Meanwhile Leigh Rose takes a call on her cell and heads out of the man cave, leaving me alone on the sofa.

"Speaking of his kids, any word from Gibson?" I actually keep a straight face. It staggers me at times to consider just how amorally I can behave.

"Nope. She won't answer her phone. I just don't know what gets into people sometimes. I'm sure she'll show up eventually. She usually does, with her tail between her legs."

Look closely at my face — notice that my mouth ever so slightly curls into a knowing grin. What do I find amusing? My mother's colorful language? Or the fact that she can't imagine me ever hurting another human being? The thing is, I liked Gibson. But I liked them all, every last one, especially their bright smiles and eagerness for adventure of all kinds. Their willingness to open up to me. Their desire for my approval.

"Well, I'll be home by one for lunch," I say. "Call me if you need anything."

"I will, honey. Bye! I love you!"

I'm tempted to go look for Leigh Rose, who's wandered off somewhere to talk in private. Much of her world remains shrouded by fog banks of mystery, not the least of which is the immediate trust she's placed in me. I'm essentially a stranger to her, yet she's convinced herself that I'm the ordained answer to her prayers. I want to invite her to lunch as my date — I don't want her out of my sight, in fact, because in just a few hours she's already made me feel better about myself than anyone else has in many years.

As an indication of how seriously I'm taking my relationship with Leigh Rose, I start to text Lola, and I tap out these words: *We really need to stop this. I've found somebody else and I just need to get my head together. I need space and time and distance. I hope you understand.*

When Leigh Rose comes back, I triumphantly hit Send, rejoicing at the congratulatory beep as I slip the phone back into my pocket. If nothing else, this small act of "courage" shows how determined I've become to change my ways. Having made an utter mess of my life, I'm handed that rarest of finds, the second chance, and I won't blow it. I hope.

"You should go," she tells me in a stricken voice. "I don't want you to, but Norris is coming over and we need to talk. I owe him that much."

I swallow back the familiar bile and beg myself to remain impassive, a statue made of white marble. "You don't owe him anything."

"I didn't mean to drag you into the middle of this. I saw you at the mall and I let myself go, for the first time in a long time."

"My mother is making lunch and I was hoping you could join me."

"I'm sorry. I really am, Eddie, but I need to deal with this. Everybody's freaking out and I can't handle another situation like last night where everybody's hating on me."

I pull myself up off the sofa and unsteadily step toward her. Twenty minutes ago we were going to have sex, and now she's banishing me from her sight. "Maybe we can hook up later," I offer without much conviction. "We can see a show or something." Little did I know that I'd be seeing her again, and under much different circumstances.

"I have to get up at the crack of dawn and go get the kids from camp. And besides I won't be good company. Not the mood I'm in."

Suddenly I feel very stupid wearing my white shoes. As soon as I get to the car, I'll switch back to my sneakers.

"Norris is on the way," she continues, tears welling in her eyes that glint like flecks of mica. She obviously feels something for me, as otherwise she wouldn't weep at my departure. But she's hemming herself in, building her own fence, and leaving me to puzzle over her sudden change of heart.

"I'll get out of your hair."

"Eddie, don't be mad at me, too. I can't take that."

"I'm not mad, I just thought . . ." But I don't finish my sentence because I don't know what I'm thinking. Or I can't articulate the hazy outline of my hopes that have just been dashed, in the same way a shy student can't respond to a simple question in class. The look of terror when I call on them! They'll wear scant clothing that reveals all but can't bring themselves to expose their innermost thoughts for fear of being ridiculed.

"Thought what?"

"Nothing." Then, out of the blue, that vast

138

sweeping expanse of repression, sallies forth a confession of sorts, whose appearance causes my heart to skip a beat. Because one confession can beget another, and another, until there's a swarm of guilty locusts buzzing around . . . "I'm kinda seeing someone anyway. But she's young. Too young."

Leigh Rose's face shines brightly as she sniffs back the tears and laughs at my stilted admission. "How young?"

"Twenty."

"Eddie, wow. She's a baby. Robbing the cradle, huh?"

"She seduced me, as a matter of fact." True! Don't even dispute it! Try resisting a young woman who doesn't care about convention and is eager to explore new sexual dimensions. Weak, yes, so very weak . . .

"Is she a student?"

"On advice of counsel, I will neither confirm nor deny the allegation."

Leigh Rose nearly swoons like a heroine in a Victorian novel overcome by the vapors of sexuality. "I wish I could be you, Eddie! And just do whatever I want and not care!"

"I think the pool boy is outside."

"Stop it! He's gross. And too skinny."

"Call the company and tell them to send over a real man next time. With a big pole,

139

you know, to clean the pool."

"Great advice. I'll have to do that."

Perhaps it's my imagination, but methinks the lady doth enjoy this ribald banter, as talk of Norris stopping by has ceased and we're being playful again, light and feathery, just when it seemed that she was on the verge of saying good-bye to me for good. At least now I can leave with my head held high, knowing Norris bores her and that I can still keep 'em rolling in the aisles.

"I'd better get home to check on my mother," I say, glad I can get in the last word. Leigh Rose isn't pushing me out; I'm leaving. A distinction without a difference? I'll take a small victory at this point.

"Is she okay?"

"Just some pre-wedding jitters."

Her phone rings again. She checks the caller ID and groans with guttural displeasure. "It's Norris."

"Bye!" I wave, feeling no longer like John Wayne but more like Cary Grant, the debonair cracker of jokes, the urbane sophisticate in control of himself, a man comfortable in his own skin. I saunter out to my car with a skip in my step, my white shoes tapping against the walkway and my arms swinging like I'm off to see the wizard.

6

Now what? That's what you're asking your-self, with me behind the wheel of my Honda whistling a tune, happy, downright giddy, and seemingly far, far away from an attack or ambush — nor do I seem in the right mood for mayhem. But don't let my cheer-fulness fool you! I did not stick around to kill Norris Mumford — my story is more complex than that, and I am a more elegant storyteller.

You groan in disappointment, but let me fill you in on a little-known fact about me.

I had a literary agent at one point in my life.

A real one, a very accomplished gentle-man, and something of a legend in the industry. He gave me some sage mystery/thriller advice, before he stopped taking or returning my calls, namely that I should, whenever possible, *use violence to propel the plot.*

You seem unconvinced. Let me assert that I wasn't always the person who stands before you today, bereft of spouse and real adult accomplishment. Perhaps we should go back in time — flashbacks show considerable literary skill, after all — to the period I like to call the Golden Age, around ten years ago, when I first started dating Bev, when I first started teaching at Ithaca, and when I had a book being shopped around to publishers in Gotham, all of whom passed on it, sadly, even though in turning it down, many — or some — a few — editors praised my snappy prose and realistic dialogue. *Use violence to propel the plot.* I vowed to! I swore up and down to this literary agent, whose office was in Greenwich Village, that I would turn my future books into veritable orgies of blood, awash in gore, the kinds of smart thrillers that top the bestseller lists, and my agent — how I loved uttering those two words! — eagerly awaited my next masterpiece, which I churned out with fiendish devotion in six months. I had a dead body on the first page, clues galore, an amazing conspiracy that had been kept quiet for hundreds of years, the exposure of which threatened world peace . . .

Bev hated it. Said I was wasting my talent to churn out garbage. But I didn't care what my fiancée thought, only what *my agent* thought, my Greenwich Village New York City agent, who doubtlessly would convert this so-called "garbage" into gold — a movie with Tom Hanks, a *Today Show* appearance during which Matt Lauer would fawn over me, and a book tour that would be part liberal arts colloquium, part Replacements *Let It Be* tour. I imagined myself getting drunk à la Bukowski and tearing up a suburban Borders in a whiskey-fueled rant. I saw myself on the cover of *Rolling Stone.* But, as you probably have guessed by now, my agent also hated this book, and I never spoke to the man again. Or finished another book.

But his advice still haunts me. Whenever a writer gets stuck, as we seem to be now, always *use violence to propel the plot.* But I'm driving in my car down River Road, getting ready to retrace my footsteps over the Harry F. Byrd Segregationist Bridge, and violence seems to be nowhere in sight. I put on my left-turn blinker, still buoyant, proud of myself in fact, when I see a blond woman with her thumb out. A beautiful hitchhiker, but one whose flawless face and curvaceous body I instantly recognize.

It's Gibson.

Gibson's appearance on the side of the

road might reassure you that I didn't kill her, though I'll point out that this vision could be just a feverish dream I'm having in the middle of a killing spree, which, if you're keeping score, is up to three by now — or four, depending on whether you add Leigh Rose. If you were privy to my life in Ithaca, the total could exceed even that of the enraged Odysseus, who had all the maids of his house strung up to pay for their sins of screwing the suitors, which an astute reader would link to my motivation for killing Norris Mumford.

Ha-ha! I haven't killed anyone and I don't plan on it. But I must *use violence to propel the plot.* No, the truth is I refuse to play that game anymore. Look at what that agent did to me! Up to that point, I'd in no way betrayed the love of my life, Literature, and the person Bev fell in love with was an aspiring artist, one willing to suffer neglect for the higher calling of producing genius, and certainly not the groveling hack who was hell-bent *on using violence to propel the plot,* instead of following Kafka's advice to write a book that is an ax which will shatter the frozen sea inside of us. That agent, in other words, ended up ruining my marriage.

I pull over to pick up Gibson, to take her straight home so that my mother can have the second wedding of her dreams. But get this! When Gibson hops into my car, she doesn't recognize me. She treats me like I'm just an average Joe, a Good Samaritan offering a helping hand. Of course, she barely even looks over at me, and she sort of smells like reefer and is probably on drugs, which, when added to the fact that we don't really know each other, explains her inability to place my face. My "I Have Issues" hat is also gone, since I'd left it back at Leigh Rose's (no, I'm not reprising a *Seinfeld* episode).

"Thanks for stopping," she says nervously, trying to act cool but appearing even younger than her tender eighteen years.

At first I almost erupt in anger. This is the young woman who conned me out of forty bucks and then ran off without even muttering an insincere thanks. She has caused my mother endless grief and her reckless ways still might spoil the weekend. If anyone deserved a dressing-down, it's Gibson. Yet for some unknown reason, I decide to play along. At least for a few minutes, just to observe Gibson in her natural habitat, which admittedly takes on a voyeuristic overtone, and it's safe to say that I enjoy watching (don't I, Lola?). So the bubbling anger quickly gives way to a quivering

145

intoxication that can come only from true anonymity, the delirium of Gyges whose ring makes him invisible and thus absolutely free.

"Where you headed?" I ask in a sappy, Colonel Sanders drawl.

"If you can get me close to Chesterfield Mall, that would be awesome."

"Yeah, no problem. I was going by there anyway."

"Cool."

I keep thinking that the interior of the car, or my precious dimples, something will trigger her to remember me, and then I'll have some fessing up to do. But Gibson doesn't occupy the moral high ground here, and her actions to date cry out for closer scrutiny. As do mine. Looking back now, I was wrong to hide my identity from her. But once I took that first fateful step, I didn't see how to backtrack, and so the deception just rolled on under its own momentum . . .

We fall silent. I'm frankly too scared to say much, feeling both guilty and remorseless at once. I keep my eyes fixed on the road ahead, with sweat rolling down my temples as though I'm sitting in a sauna despite the AC blowing full blast into my face. But I need to be doused with ice-cold water and maybe punched in the chin, because suddenly it feels like the first time with Lola all over again, yet another instance when I lapsed into silence instead of removing myself from danger. With Lola, all I needed to do was pretend I had a meeting and then get up and leave, not let her ramble on about this crazy ex of hers, which is normally a conversation that doesn't venture too far afield in the confines of academia. In Lola's case, however, she loved dissecting every element of her life and fancied herself a burgeoning poet, who needed the approval of a real writer (that would be yours truly) — and before I realized it, we'd jumped off the cliff together. The first photo she showed me was an "accident," and she pretended to be sorry. But it was a test shot to gauge my reaction, and when I chuckled at her "mistake," it allowed her to describe in more detail the kinds of sex she preferred and with whom, salacious tidbits I lapped up with the frenzied gusto of a famished hunting dog, even knowing that ultimately there would be no sexual arousal, just morbid curiosity, which only fueled Lola's desire to send her experiences cascading down upon my addled head, text by hideous text.

But this situation is far different because Gibson is hiding from her family the truth of her travails, and I alone can glimpse into her secret life. So in a sense I am a rogue agent who's working undercover on a dangerous case, and if my cover gets blown, I could pay the ultimate price.

"People are such assholes," she sighs, leaning her head back against the seat. "It took forever to get a ride."

"That's hard to believe."

"Yeah? Why's that?"

Now I start to wonder if Gibson isn't playing the same game, toying with me for saying something stupid, pinning me like a novice wrestler going up against the state champ. I snort an aw-shucks chuckle but don't reply, and I'm thinking I should probably tap out before she breaks me in half. I can't keep making the same stupid mistakes, treading down the same dead ends, all because I need to feed this beastly sense of irony. So the ring of Gyges comes off and I reveal myself as the masquerading fraud I am.

"Gibson, it's me, Edwin."

"I know."

"Why didn't you say something?"

"Why didn't you?"

With the gloves now off, I see no reason to hold back and the words burst out in a staccato of wounded pride. "Why did you just bolt this morning? You blew off class and everyone was worried sick about you. You can't pull that kind of stunt anymore. I don't want my mother getting upset this weekend. Come on, that was bush league."

She glares at me, and out of the corner of my eye I can see her pink lips twist into a derisive grin. "You don't know me or my situation."

"That's true, but I think I deserved a little more respect than that. You hit me up for cash and I gave it to you, no strings attached."

We're nearing the exit for Stony Point and I put on my blinker, but she bolts upright and nearly grabs the steering wheel from me in a panic. "Are you going home?" she asks breathlessly.

"Yeah, for lunch."

"No, I need to run an errand. You said you'd take me."

"Whoa, I was messing around since you didn't recognize me."

"Seriously, I really need to stop by and see somebody."

"And then what, you'll run out the back door?"

"No! It's this guy I've been seeing — please? I just need to give him something. It'll just take a second."

She's totally lying to my face and we both know it, but I also get the impression that she'll hop out of the car at the next stoplight, whereas if I accede to her demands, I'll at least be able to return her home in time for the festivities. This dilemma really boils down to a Hobson's choice of sorts, because she's holding all the cards and so it's her way or she vanishes again. Since it's just dumb luck that I ever found her on the side of the road, I should consider her request a small price to pay.

"Fine," I blurt out, pressing down on the accelerator to zoom past the exit, "but tell me this. Who's the guy you want to see and why didn't he come pick you up? What man makes his chick walk all over town with her thumb out, which is freaking dangerous?"

"His car's in the shop."

"He doesn't work? It's the middle of the day."

"You're not at work."

"I'm a college professor. We never stop working."

"Well, he works, kinda sorta."

"Which means what, he slings a little weed?"

"Whatever, you don't care anyway, so don't pretend like you do."

"I don't care what you do on your own

time, but this weekend is my mom's time, and so you can't do anything to screw it up for her. Agreed?"

"You need to talk to Graves, not me. I'm chill."

"Why do I need to talk to Graves?"

"He's the one you should be worried about."

"Because?"

"I don't know, get off at Forest Hills."

I long to be back with Leigh Rose and laughing in the lap of her luxury, not running some fool's errand with a troubled teen so that she might find her benighted paramour. Yet I might be blowing this all out of proportion, because Gibson is guilty only of skipping a class (compared with my crimes). She's probably high as a kite, but when I was her age, I inhaled and snorted whatever substances I could get my hands on. How far removed from Leigh Rose is Gibson anyway — or Lola, who would walk over hot coals to cuddle with Thor? Still, I'm entitled to more answers than she's provided thus far.

"Where did you go this morning after you took off?" I ask, waiting at a red light.

"Band practice."

"Seriously? Why didn't you tell me? I was in a band back in the day." Not technically true, but enough that it avoids being an outright lie. I jammed a few times with various musicians but never made the plunge to join an organized band.

"I don't know. I was just in the mood to flex and that campus brings me down so much. I hate saying good-bye to people. It's so fake." Then she points, giving me directions. "Keep going straight. He lives like five minutes from here."

Oddly enough, we're approaching the parking lot of O'Bloom's, where my mother called me during her panic attack. Again, nothing overly remarkable in that, as O'Bloom's is an Irish pub that has been open at that location for several decades. But Gibson adds an interesting twist that I couldn't anticipate or fully comprehend. "Oh, my mom works there."

"Your mom?"

"She's the bar manager."

"At O'Bloom's?"

"Yeah. I don't see her car, though. She must be off. Wait, no, she's there."

"Do you want to stop in and say hi?"

"No thanks. She hates me."

"I doubt that."

"She seriously does."

But then I begin to wonder whether my mother's panic attack in the parking lot of the restaurant where her future husband's ex-wife works wasn't purely coincidental, that the poor woman had come here on a stakeout — but why would she do that? I debate whether to ask Gibson if she's privy to any insider information, but the kid seems poised on a knife's edge already and doesn't need one more issue to handle. I don't want to make a mountain out of a molehill, and I am curious about this band of hers, so I change the subject.

"So what's the name of your group?" I ask, trying to mask my enthusiasm so that I don't come off like an aging hipster.

"Hazzie Mattie."

"I like it."

"I think it's lame but Dog won't change it."

"Who's Dog?"

"This guy. He started the band like a year ago. He's a total dirty-foot hippie, and he has this friend of his named Trey who thinks he's a great guitarist but he basically sucks. I tell Dog all the time we need to boot him out, but Dog is lazy. Drives me nuts."

"What do you play?"

"I sing."

"Awesome. Have you had any gigs yet?"

"Like at parties and stuff. Nothing that pays."

"That could change, though. The only way you lose in life is to quit." And I should know, being an expert in the field of failure.

"That's why I need to drop a demo off. This guy I've been hanging out with, he can get us booked at the National."

"The National? Whoa, that's a big-time venue." The National has hosted a wide array of acts, from Juicy J to Ted Nugent. It would be a coup for an unknown group to get within a hundred miles of that stage. Somehow, though, Gibson seems capable of pulling off miracles. Or have I just invested her with special powers?

"I know, right? That would be huge."

"I'm speechless. Way to go, kid."

So it appears that I've totally misread Gibson, whose truancy wasn't fueled by antisocial hostility but by a desire to make music. Not only that, she was willing to walk across the city of Richmond to deliver a demo on the vague and unrealistic hope of getting onstage at one of the best venues south of D.C. But outlandish fortune can aim her slings and arrows at strange targets, and with her badass look, Gibson will generate interest from the slimeballs in the talent agencies. I admire her pluckiness, her determination. She doesn't seem to have a fallback plan, no contingency to attend college for four years. So in that way, she isn't like Leigh Rose or Lola at all. Or me.

"I'm glad I can help you," I offer with true fondness. "I'd love to hear some of the demo. Is it on a CD?"

"Yeah, but you need to turn right at the next block. We're almost there."

Forest Hill Avenue has become Semmes Avenue, named after Admiral Raphael Semmes, who headed up the Confederate Navy during the Civil War. Ghosts are everywhere you turn in this city. The neighborhood has taken a few steps down the socioeconomic ladder, and soon enough we're driving down a street populated with little ramshackle houses and small apartment complexes constructed of dull red brick. We pull up in front of a neatly maintained one-story home that stands in contrast to the other downtrodden dwellings surrounding it, and once again I feel as if I owe Gibson an apology. Even if this guy does sell dope, he keeps his lawn trimmed and presentable.

"I'll be right back," she tells me. "This won't take long."

I watch her skip off with her backpack slung over her shoulder, and I feel like a proud parent dropping a kid off on the first day of school. But I'm totally unprepared for what comes next. Life often lulls us to sleep, makes us drowsy with the promise of unbroken tranquillity, only to stir us from our peaceful slumber with thunderous claps of doom that at first sound like the gentle drops of an afternoon shower, quickly growing in intensity until we can hear nothing else but the thud of dread. I'm sitting in my car, window rolled down so that I don't waste gas, getting hot, but feeling good about my prospects. I even decide to check my messages to see how Lola has responded to my very brave plea for her to leave me alone.

Her reply: *Do you love her?*

Love is something Lola knows precious little about, evidenced by the fact that she's convinced herself that we are in love, that our relationship has a future, that we're perfect for each other. She can sleep with whomever she wants and I will sit in stony silence while she describes for me every vivid detail of her wanton lust. But just because Lola's concept of love is stunted and badly deformed doesn't mean that she can't feel the pain of rejection, and so I must take care not to injure her. One day she'll realize that we both ventured into insanity and she'll never speak of or to me again.

I care for her very much.
I don't want to lose you!!!!!!!!!
I'm not going anywhere.

Except perhaps to prison. And prison is where I belong. While in his Rome jail cell, the radical theorist Antonio Gramsci urged us intellectuals to remain in "permanent revolution," to use our hallowed positions to jolt the masses into insurrection. Though I preach the gospel of critical theory to my students, and fulminate against the oppressors who enslave us, I've done almost nothing to advance the cause of freedom. In my private life, I've perpetuated sexually demeaning stereotypes and indulged in utterly bourgeois perversions (without getting an erection, mind you).

I hear the approach of a car and glance into the rearview mirror. To my great surprise I spot a police cruiser. Here's my unexpected chance to become ideologically pure! The Hegemon has arrived, the embodiment of Foucault's "carceral state," and by all accounts I should waste that pig.

What tough talk from a lowly writing instructor! But isn't becoming a cop killer the ultimate union of Theory and Practice? The white-and-blue cruiser rolls to a stop and parks in front of my Honda. My chest tightens and my mouth gapes in terror.

Sweat is now literally dripping from the end of my nose, and I grip the steering wheel as though the car is careening down the side of a mountain.

Get ready for the curveball.

A female cop gets out of the police car, and she is extremely attractive, so pretty and sexy, with straight blond hair and a lithe body, that I wonder if she doesn't work for an agency that sends out strippers to remote locations for birthday and bachelor parties. But she has a very real service revolver clipped to her side, and instead of killing her in the name of a proletarian revolt, I want her to slap handcuffs on me and begin an aggressive interrogation. So much for my ideological purity! When the Hegemon is a hottie, all bets are off.

But she pays no attention to me and instead makes her way directly to the house where Gibson is dropping off the demo. She's the one who's going to get busted? Not me? How is that even possible? And what about the permanent revolution?

A hundred different panicky images simultaneously blow up in my brain, and I struggle mightily to formulate a contingency plan — knowing full well that it's a felony to interfere with official police business or obstruct justice. A lawyer — Leigh Rose must know one. I have her number but I decide to wait just in case I'm totally misreading this situation, which it turns out I am, and by a considerable margin. The first anomaly arises quickly. The cop doesn't knock on the front door, but opens it and proceeds inside, which from my extensive knowledge of TV police dramas I know is highly irregular. Don't they usually need a warrant?

Then, nothing. No backup arrives, no one comes out of the house. Several minutes lapse by, during which I become confused and filled with mounting anxiety. Do I have the right to ask if my almost-stepsister is okay? Asking a question isn't the same as harboring a fugitive or helping a suspect escape. But I don't want to get caught up in this dragnet, no matter how badly I desire to confess to a beautiful woman in a uniform. They say patience is a virtue, which I lack in abundance, but in this situation I force myself to sit tight, even if I understand almost nothing of what's going on.

More minutes drag by. Nothing reveals the paucity of imagination like an unforeseen crisis. We frequently encounter unscripted moments that defy our expectations, and most of us fumble for an adequate response, often trotting out the same tired clichés our taxed brains depend on for solace. I continue to assume that Gibson is in legal trouble of some kind and hence construct my view of this situation around that hypothesis without ever entertaining alternatives. I can't fathom that a female police officer would show up for any other reason than making an arrest.

Lola's genius lies in seeing past the surface and getting to the substrate, the grainy truth we missed because its texture is too coarse for our delicate hands. She might think: a man and a woman, joined by another woman, equals threesome.

My jaw drops to the floor of my Honda. No, I say to myself. This can't be. But think of it. The cop didn't knock! She proceeded directly inside the house as if her arrival was expected. Her gun wasn't drawn. No backup has been summoned.

I still refuse to buy this version of events, despite the fact that observational data support it. Lola has clearly infected my ability to think rationally and now I find perversions in the least likely places. I cling to the belief that any second now, Gibson will walk out of that house and we'll drive home. What happened inside will remain hidden from me, and perhaps that's for the best.

But they really need to wrap it up because

it's getting on toward one o'clock. I don't want to intrude on Gibson's private business, but she promised this errand wouldn't take long. If she indeed is inside having an orgy, then she is an even bigger liar than I am. I'd leave her here save for the emotional trauma her absence would cause . . . let's be clear . . . I don't go to the house motivated by prurience. I'm no peeping Tom. I'm a dutiful son doing his level best to stitch together a family torn and frayed by death and divorce, not to mention drug use and mental illness. I could have knocked on the door first without peering through a window, but there is a cop involved and I want to ascertain the full extent of the unfolding situation before interjecting.

Nervously, but with the skilled precision of a jeweler, I press my face against a pane of glass that looks into a den of sorts. But I see no one inside, so I walk along the east-facing side of the humble home, with its cracked paint blistering in the sun, and reach another vantage point. But a blind has been drawn over this window, and I can see only through a sliver at the very bottom, roughly an inch wide. I can make out a bed, and a nude female figure reclining — or is that what I crave to see? Lola invited me to hide in a closet while she worked her charm on some witless sperm bank of a boy, but I never agreed to that, to make our relationship come alive in the real world, which like the Monster in *Frankenstein* might threaten to overwhelm the master.

Through the window I can hear a man's voice. "Put the gun down, Theresa."

Those words push me back as if I'd been shoved by a drunk at a bar. I stagger, regain my balance, and then lean in again for one more view, which reveals the same truncated tableau.

"Let the girl go," the man says. "She's got nothing to do with this."

"You were fucking her in our bed!"

"Let her go."

"I hear something. Somebody's outside."

I duck down beneath the window, my knees planted in the dry grass and my eyes turned heavenward. I try to remain as motionless as possible and become a lifeless statue, which in Richmond is the default setting for most Southerners and thus comes easily to me. I'm hiding in plain sight! Nothing conceals me and I'm a sitting — no, squatting — duck. And I'm ready to die, for the bullet to buzz through my septic brain and drain it of all the accumulated soilage. But from my new position I can't hear what the others are saying and wait in agonizing ignorance. What if gunshots start blasting and none are for me? I'm spared but Gibson dies? I who have nothing left to live for and she whose whole adulthood sparkles before her? I can't even call 911 because the person with the gun, this Theresa, is a cop.

I creep along the ground like a sloth foraging for fallen fruit, with the vague plan of getting back to the Honda. I literally can do nothing to alter the outcome, and in this helplessness I find surprising strength. What's stopping me from going in there? Or at least knocking on the door? Perhaps just the pounding of my fists on the wood will knock some sense into this Theresa, who must've found Gibson in bed with her man and then promptly lost it. Not that I blame her! No, I'm the last person who can look askance at those consumed by jealousy, even to the point of homicide. Under different circumstances, I might've been able to help Theresa work through the dark, swirling storms of emotional upheaval. One might dream of revenge, but exacting it? Actually snuffing out the life of a person you once loved because they love another? So not worth it, Theresa.

Emboldened by impotence — on so many levels — I stand up and walk directly to the front porch, fully expecting confrontation, conflict, Man vs. Man — or in this case, Man vs. Woman Who Is a Law Enforcement Officer and Armed. Talk about *use violence to propel the plot.* I've arrived at the verge of a bloodbath, the kind of cinematic shoot-out that Hollywood execs swoon for, and the question is: how high will the body count go? Or will Theresa order me at gunpoint inside, where she'll force her cheating boyfriend/husband to watch as she makes love to me out of pure spite? Will the cold barrel of a gun finally make my erection obey? I don't mean to diminish the danger I'm in. But honestly, the thought does cross my mind.

I'm not even at the front porch when the door swings open and I see the female cop, who I'm guessing is named Theresa, standing there with a fierce scowl on her tearstained face and the pistol hanging limply at her side.

"Get in here," she barks at me, pulling on my arm.

"Can you explain to me what's going on?"

She shuts the door behind me and I'm standing in the den, darkened and reeking of pot. I see no sign of Gibson or the man, and that worries me. Has she killed them? Am I next on the hit list?

"You drove that little bitch here?"

"She said she had to drop something off."

"Here's what's gonna go down. You're gonna get in your car and drive away. Understand? This never happened. You need to tell that whore to stay away from my house or there's gonna be even more trouble."

"Where is she?"

As if on cue, Gibson emerges, dressed and looking terrified. She's obviously been crying. Behind her is the man, who is very tall and broad shouldered, chiseled in the way of a natural athlete, long limbed and irate, judging by his brooding, hooded eyes. He's wearing no shirt, revealing a ripped abdomen covered with ink. In short, your typical stud. I'm guessing erectile dysfunction isn't one of his issues.

"Get out of my sight!" Theresa screams at us. Gibson hurries to me and out of brotherly instinct I reach out for her and she puts her head on my shoulder, where it comes to rest as if it's been filled with lead. We share a very brief but touching moment of sanctuary, forged from a bond of terror, before we scurry out of that house, two lucky rats fleeing a sinking ship. But wait, because even though it seems as if we've escaped danger, there comes yet another twist of the knife, this in the form of a text from Lola. I check my phone really quickly once I'm in the car, just to see if my mother has contacted me. Nothing from her, but ominous words from the Wild Child, Lola:

I'm driving down there. Should take 10 hrs. We really need to talk because I love you and I don't want to live without you and I won't live without you.

7

"He told me he lived with his sister."

This sentence hovers between Gibson and me as if the words are spinning in a crazy cyclone, and after speaking, Gibson literally grabs an armrest to keep from pitching forward in shock. I'm reeling too. Not only did I nearly get my head blown off by a woman scorned, but my own scorned femme, Lola the Huntress, claims to be on her way to Richmond to "talk," which can mean many things. Talk? About what? I made myself perfectly clear. No more. It's done. Yet she won't be sated until she has my head on a platter.

Wait a second. Did I hear Gibson correctly?

"His sister?"

"Yeah! I saw pictures of them together and that's what he told me. I don't mess around with married guys. That's one of my rules."

Gibson has rules, good to know. But I

have a few rules of my own, a major one of which is not to get shot by a police officer. I'm steaming mad at this beautiful creature, in the same way I grew irate at Lola not that long ago, when she too acted stupidly . . . and tried to deceive me, though not as blatantly. Why is she even coming down here? There's really no excuse for her behavior, just as Gibson should know when men are taking complete advantage of her. And who gets caught in the middle?

"I think it's safe to say that we're both lucky to be alive." I abhor the patronizing tone in my voice, but at that moment I'm not in control of my inner life.

"That bitch was crazy! And a cop! But check this out: he's the biggest drug dealer I know. How f-ed up is that?" Admiration oozes from every pore of her glistening skin. She couldn't love him more now if she tried, despite the fact that his gutless lies nearly got us both killed.

"Extremely. He's a piece of garbage and you should stay away from him. Does he even know anybody at the National? Or was that just another game he was running?"

"Said he did. And I bet he does, knowing him."

"I promise you he doesn't. He was just taking advantage of you."

"No he wasn't."

"How can you say that?"

"I wanted him, too. I just thought he was single."

Oh, this is a perilous conversation! When these lovely young women speak to me of their libidinous lechery, it sends me spiraling to the nether reaches of joy, which is located in Hell. I hate myself for how ardently I crave every detail. I've vowed countless times never again to become the dumping ground of their sexual escapades. Yet one innocent comment is all it takes for me to crumble like a five o'clock sand castle, and Lola is descending on me unless I can concoct a way to stop her. She might be lying just to torture me, which is one of her favorite hobbies. I never should have rattled her cage from afar, as my text only fueled her desire for dramatic gestures. But what else would you expect from the only child of two theater professors?

Haven't I mentioned that Lola is the daughter of two of my colleagues at Notting College, soon to be ex-colleagues when my perfidy is exposed?

"I feel like you haven't been honest with me from the start," I say, waiting to take a left onto Semmes Avenue. "You said you were just dropping the CD off. I was waiting in the car! I was doing you a favor."

"I didn't know he was married."

"That's not the point. I was trying to help out your band, not be a taxi service for a random hookup."

"It wasn't random."

She's just a kid, I have to remind myself, and prone to make mistakes. She assumed she could get in a quickie, and under different circumstances she might've and I would've known nothing, if not for the unlucky arrival of Police Woman.

"So you like him then?"

"Yeah, we have some real chemistry. It's hard to explain."

Lola would've had no problem explaining, and it's difficult to say what she liked more, the act itself or the reporting of it, especially when Dahlia got involved, Dahlia the pinch-faced corrupter, who promised never to tell anyone — maybe she's the one I killed, to keep her quiet. Just go check the Dumpster behind the Public Works hut at South Hill Town Park. You might find a body in there. Dahlia let it be known that she considered me a creep, that she didn't approve of Lola's relationship with me, and nothing, nothing, drives a person to homicidal rage quicker than the unvarnished truth.

"You don't have to explain," I add nervously, secretly wishing she would divulge all. "And I don't have room to talk. I've done some pretty stupid things before, especially when I was a little younger." Or last week. And last night.

Gibson calls my bluff. "Like what?"

I inhale sharply and my lungs fill with boning knives. Her limpid eyes fall on me and her feet are once again on my dashboard, her legs raised up and knees bent like they had been when her brawny lover had been on top of her — I really hope that prison will rehabilitate me. "Oh boy." I cough, hitting the brakes to avoid slamming into a postal truck stopped in the middle of Semmes Avenue. "That's a hard one to answer because there's so much to choose from."

She rolls her eyes dismissively and picks at one of her lovely toes. "I bet you've never done anything too bad. You're a college professor."

"Egging me on, huh? I know a thing or two about reverse psychology. Let's just say I've had my moments."

The postal truck lurches forward and I press gently on the accelerator. "Have you ever messed around with one of your students?" she asks.

"Too risky." Notice I don't directly answer the question — I can evade like a World War One fighter pilot.

"I bet they've come on to you, though."

"Nope. I'm too ugly."

"You're not ugly."

This is clearly entrapment. But the truth is, I am ugly, hideously ugly on the inside, a monstrosity unfit to inhabit the planet. "That's kind of you to say," I announce with great fanfare, as though I'm about to call out the winning number for the lottery, "but the sad fact is, unless you want me to make something up, my life is pretty damn boring."

"Do you get high?"

"Not so much anymore."

"I have some weed if you want to smoke while you're here."

"I thought you were supposed to be sober."

"Weed doesn't count."

"I'm pretty sure it does."

"Whatever, it helps me calm down."

At least my forty dollars was well spent. There's no reason for me to hector her about her substance abuse issues, given all we've endured up to this point. I'm bringing Gibson home more or less in one piece, not totally sober, no better at math, not chastened by her brush with death at the hands of a maniac cop, but alive and kicking. "Music helps me calm down," I say, handing her my phone. "Pick something out. Something snappy."

She groans and starts scrolling through my playlists. So we're right back where we started, babbling about music again with such vigorous excitement that Gibson never gets around to picking a song before we return home. And we won't even be late for lunch, at which my mother has planned for me to meet her betrothed, Mead George, which will happen in a matter of minutes. As we pull into Traylor Estates, I feel fear rising in my throat.

"I haven't met your father yet, you realize."

"I hope he's in a good mood. He's been so stressed recently. He keeps saying he's going to kick me out of the house. You can't tell anybody that I skipped class today."

"I already told my mother."

"You did? Why?"

"Because I didn't know what the hell you were doing! I was worried about you."

"I'm screwed." She sinks down low in the seat, like she wants to melt into the fake leather. "They're going to kill me."

"They're getting married. They've got

other things to worry about."

Then she brightens. "I'll just say I went to class. I mean, maybe I did. I walked over from 7-Eleven."

I cringe at the prospect of being swept up in another deception being perpetrated by one of my siblings, but in the name of keeping my mother happy, I agree to go along with Gibson's ruse. One never grows numb to lying. Each untruth carries away a small part of the soul, the way a river ceaselessly erodes a fraction of the muddy bank that contains it and in time the river changes course and thereby becomes unrecognizable.

"Maybe you did."

"There's always a solution to every problem."

I park in the same spot on the side of the road in front of the house. I notice right away that the Corvette is gone, meaning Mead is running late, possibly AWOL with his ex. With Clint Eastwood as my witness, I swear I won't let my poor mother get hurt by a scheming gigolo. But right when my ire reaches its apex, who doesn't show up but Mead George himself, wheeling his vintage sports car down Traylor Drive at seventy-five miles an hour like he's speeding for the finish line at Daytona.

"He drives like a maniac!" blurts Gibson. "He's gonna die in that car one day. Or kill somebody with it."

Foreshadowing? A red herring? There's a prophetic quality to Gibson that is quite alluring — a blend of youthful innocence and jaded adulthood, allowing her to speak her mind freely without fear of reprisal. At the same time, she spews lies like confetti on New Year's Eve. Can a liar also be a prophet? We'll see, we'll see.

Mead's Corvette kicks up gravel as he swings into the driveway, sending a plume of dust spinning into the air. The front yard now resembles a battlefield; just add in some bloated, rotting corpses and this tableau could be a Mathew Brady daguerreotype. Then the man hops out of his car. My first impression: he reminds me of Ed O'Neill from *Married . . . with Children,* as Mead is beefy, even fleshy, with a soft chin that seems to be retracting into his face, a widow's peak shaped in an arrowhead, and the heavy-lidded eyes of someone who is perpetually sleep deprived. He gives us a friendly wave and bounds over with the long, purposeful strides of a determined letter carrier.

"It is so awesome to finally meet you!" he booms at me with an arm extended for a

175

manly shake. His grip is strong and sure, but dare I say that he comes across as a wee bit insincere — I might as well be shopping for a used car. Tsk, tsk, I need to reserve judgment, because I make a very positive first impression that belies my hideousness.

"Hi, Daddy."

"Hey! How was class?"

"Boring."

Then Mead turns his attention back to me, and I quickly remove the smirk that Gibson's fib brought on. "So, Edwin, how's your morning been so far? Did you visit your old stomping grounds?"

"You could say that."

"It's been a while since you've been in Richmond, right?"

Gibson saunters off to the house and like lemmings we fall in behind her. My throat is parched, the scotch is wearing off, and I'm sticky from the oppressive heat that actually seems to take on a physical dimension, a heaviness that clogs the air. I don't know how much more I can take. Why am I speaking to this man about my existence? I have a smile plastered on my heat-reddened face. But the strain is catching up with me. The floorboards of my soul groan in agony from the weight of my anxiety, the brown grass crackles beneath my plodding feet.

"Yeah," I manage to spit out, "it's been a few years. Too long. I don't really have a good excuse."

"And you're a writer?"

"I teach writing."

"I thought you wrote books."

"Not so much lately, but I might have a good idea for a new one."

"Really? I'd love to hear it."

Well, it's about a college professor who may (or may not) be on a killing spree . . . never mind. My mother bursts out of the front door with arms outstretched to greet us, displaying energy uncommon to victims of panic attacks. I deduce that she must be feeling better, and she's so intent on us that Gibson breezes right past with nary a word. "Come on in!" she erupts joyously, making me think that my mother has ingested a euphoria-inducing pill. Wonder where she keeps her stash . . . "I was just making lunch. I hope you two boys are hungry."

Perhaps a poor choice of words, given our close proximity in ages. But Mead doesn't seem to mind. "Edwin here was just telling me that he has a new idea for a book."

"That's wonderful, honey! You'll have to fill us in."

"It's kind of hard to explain."

A cool blast of AC brings immediate

relief. I close my eyes and revel in the comfort. Even cooler is the basement, where I long to retreat so that I can call Lola, which might be futile since she seldom answers her phone, placing me in a bit of a bind. I absolutely must convince her not to come, but it would have to be by text, and given my lack of digital dexterity, these texts take me a long time to compose and don't convey the true meaning of my intentions. In short, there's probably no way I can convince her not to come and my next step should be planning on what to do once she hits town. She must remain hidden. My family can't know of her.

"I read somewhere that publishers are looking for books that have something called a high concept," Mead says. "That's where the title and the story are the same and so the readers can figure out what the book is about without really thinking about it."

"I don't write those kinds of books."

Mead looks at me with a puzzled expression. "What do you mean?"

My mother jumps in, sensing danger. She knows I can't talk rationally about my non-existent writing career without my engine overheating. "Eddie has had bad luck when it comes to publishing, but he's a great writer and one day the world will know it."

Yes, Mother, one day the entire world will know the name Edwin Stith, but not for the reasons that you imagine. The walls are already closing in, the noose I've placed around my neck is tightening. "Do you mind if I go take a shower?" I ask, but it sounds more like I'm pleading. Mead has his phone out and studies a text or e-mail carefully.

"Lunch will be ready in ten minutes," my mother replies. "Is that enough time?"

"I'll be quick. I just feel very gross right now."

"You look tired." She places her hand against my forehead just as she used to do when I was a kid. "Do you feel okay?"

"Yeah. I'm just dirty and need to clean up."

Mead heads off upstairs. Once we are alone, my mother pulls me into the living room, where no one is allowed to sit down because the furniture cost too much money back in 1984 when it was purchased. "How did you find Gibson?" she whispers.

Cover for her or not? A promise is a promise. "I drove back to the campus later and she was there. We just got our wires crossed."

"Thank God! That girl worries me so.

She's headed for trouble — I can smell it a mile away."

"She's an adult. It's her life to ruin."

"But she's so pretty and she could amount to something, but she just hates everything. It's her mother's fault."

"It usually is. That's also my excuse."

"Eddie! You be nice to me!"

"I'm kidding! Mead seems like a good guy."

She beams up at me. "You think so?"

"Yes. But I really want to take shower."

"Go, go. I'll finish up in the kitchen."

I run down to my basement lair and each step of descent brings me closer to my true home, Hell, which isn't hot at all but surprisingly cool and refreshing. I turn no lights on so that it remains dark, almost perfectly so, meaning Hell has no raging fires or molten pits of lava. The Talking Heads say that heaven is a place where nothing ever happens, but in Hell no one makes small talk. I can think of no better spot than Hell to give Lola a call, futile as it may be.

She said she's coming here, arriving by ten, when the darkness of night thickens into a black soup. And that obviously can't happen. Lola in the city of Richmond? Talk about an unstable compound! She has to understand that she can't toy with my life the way a puppy might devour a pair of old shoes.

I call my beloved . . . and in my head I can hear her phone buzzing away. A contemptuous look at the screen. Incoming call from Edwin? I imagine her smirking and shrugging and maybe cackling in delight with Dahlia and Thor as the three youths mock the pathetic professor who's nearing forty with not much to show for it. Is it possible she's not coming down here alone? That she's taken the circus on the road for my amusement? No, please no!

I don't bother to leave a message because it would be pointless. Texting is her preferred medium, and so it is to the written word I must turn if I'm ever to escape her clutches. You'd think a writing professor could craft a missive of substance without batting an eye, but writing has never come easily to me. So why then did I pursue it as a career? Fame and fortune, mostly. And the groupies.

Those bastard little buttons on my phone, how they mock me . . . the letter I want is never the letter that pops up on the screen, and thus I must retype almost each word two or three times, before finally producing this:

You're really coming? You don't need to. We can talk about this when I get back home.

Right as I hit the Send button, I hear noises coming from the storage portion of the garage, where Mead has his collection of weapons. I want to make sure that the noises are of a legitimate origin and not part of a burglary, and so I poke my head through the door that separates the man cave/laundry room from the workshop (now weapons depot). I see that Mead is rummaging through the boxes. Once he spots me, he waves me over. Inwardly my heart sinks. I just need to shower and have a little quiet in my subterranean room, but now I have to paste that fake smile back on and pretend to care about what he wants to say.

"You might want to see this," he says proudly, holding up a square wooden box decorated with lotus blossoms and red stars. "It's pretty special. One of a kind, really."

He unlatches the box and pulls out a pistol that like all guns looks toyish at first glance but then takes on a more ominous form the longer you look at it. I can almost hear Bev's piercing cry of disgust, given her absolute hatred of all guns, handguns in particular, which is why when I killed her, I refrained from using a firearm and instead opted for a sharp blade. I always tried to treat her with courtesy. All my victims, actually.

"This is a Tokarev TT-33," he continues. "Feel how heavy it is. Over two pounds."

Mead carefully places the grip in my right palm and I clasp it, though because of its heft I nearly drop it. "How could you even aim this thing?" I lift the gun up and point it at a bare concrete wall.

"The person this belonged to never had to fire it very often. He was a general, a tactician of the highest order, one of the greatest warriors the world has ever known, Vo Nguyen Giap."

The name sounds vaguely familiar, but I'm no expert on the Vietnam War or much of anything, except for various execrations in which I'm constantly embroiled. "I can't say that I know much about him."

"He was the architect of our defeat in Southeast Asia. But before that, he ousted the French at the crucial battle of Dien Bien Phu."

"I think I had that for dinner last night."

My lame joke goes through Mead like an X-ray. Frowning, he takes the pistol back from me and somehow ends up pointing it directly at my temple. At least that's what it seems like. "Giap had this very gun with him on the battlefield as he watched the

French troops get cut down in a barrage of mortar shells."

I step away to avoid the barrel in the remote chance the gun is loaded, but I'm also wondering if Mead isn't sending me a signal of some kind. Or he's just a clueless idiot. Whatever, he's pissing me off. "If it's so valuable, maybe you should put it away before something happens to it."

He blinks uncomprehendingly at this statement and lowers the gun to his side. "He's still alive, you know."

"Who?"

"Giap. He's over a hundred years old. The bastard might live forever and keep rubbing our noses in it. But we could've won the war, and there's one good reason why it never happened."

"Because of Jane Fonda?" There's a sharp edge to my voice that he either ignores or enjoys, being something of a loose cannon himself.

"Because LBJ didn't have the guts to bomb Hanoi, the enemy capital. I'm not aware of any theory of war that allows the victor to triumph without cutting out the heart of the vanquished. Instead we bombed the jungles, the Mekong River, little thatch huts, Cambodia, Laos, ourselves — everything except the one city that would've made the North Vietnamese surrender in about two seconds." He pauses this disquisition and stares glumly at Giap's pistol, caressing the trigger with a curled index finger, in an effort to retrieve the last vestiges of whatever totemistic power remains in it. It's obvious that his emotional involvement with Nam runs deep, even though he never fought there or anywhere since he was never in the armed forces, according to Graves. But he still doesn't have the right to point a gun at me, even inadvertently.

"When the French surrendered at Dien Bien Phu," he resumes, putting the pistol back in its special box, "the fate of hundreds of thousands of American soldiers was sealed. One of them was my father, who died during the Tet Offensive."

He gazes at me with glossy eyes, reminding me of an earnest student who genuinely has no idea what a thesis statement is. And my response is the same: "That's terrible. I'm so sorry."

He stacks the box atop the others like it and lets his hand linger there. "I never knew him. I was just a baby when he died. But I suppose it explains my fascination with the war. And the truth is, Edwin, all that you see here, all of this, if my plan works out, will allow your mother and me to live comfortably for a long, long time."

"So you're selling this stuff off?"

"Most of it, yes. And that's an interesting story. There's a potential buyer who wants to stage a reenactment of the battle of Khe Sanh next January in the jungles of Honduras, and what this person most craves is authenticity, which I can supply in spades. My collection is all legit. No replicas, the real deal from the time period. I have pieces no one else in the world has."

"There are Vietnam War reenactors? I know people are into the Civil War . . ."

"The subculture is small but fanatical. No one has ever attempted to stage the battle of Khe Sanh, because of its epic scale. Gettysburg took what? Three days? Operation Charlie took sixteen."

I hear a door above creak open, followed by footsteps on the stairs. "Lunch is ready!" my mother calls down to us.

"Be right there, honey!" Mead responds, and I recoil at the term of endearment he employs so casually, because it seems obscene coming from his mouth. Bev instructed me never to call her "baby," "doll," "sugar," or any other cliché that she likened to termite rot, as such words concealed the damage being done beneath the surface.

She hated holding hands in public. Whenever I asked for oral sex, her reply was the same: *Would you ever put one of those in your mouth?* Case closed. Which is why the one and only blow job she ever gave me, when I think back on it, still sends chills down my spine — because it was done out of pity, after she'd told me she wanted out, and I was waylaid with anger and self-loathing, intensified by a fortnight of sleeping on the sofa — and then she came to me, after getting out of the shower, hair still wet and wrapped in a towel, her robe pulled tight, and I hated the very sight of her. Her confidence, her self-assurance. She never said one word. Jon Stewart was mocking Rush Limbaugh on the telly. Bev used the remote to turn it off, and then she walked over to me and leaned down between my legs. No explanation, no warning shots. Just a sally toward my groin. I wanted to push her away! By then sex had become utterly humiliating to me, and here she was again, forcing me to endure one more failure because she felt sorry for me. But the things she whispered that night, holding my penis like a microphone! Never before had I ever heard her use such foul language, in a voice throaty and raw — before I knew it, without really understanding why, I was fully erect and strangely elated. Maybe our marriage wasn't over. Maybe my sexual issues had been solved by the magic elixir of her uttering her gratitude for my engorgement. It was a miracle, victory snatched from the jaws of defeat. But then she stopped mid-fellate. "So you can get it up if I act like a whore," she said scornfully before pushing herself up, shaking her head in disappointment, and pulling her robe tight. I deflated in seconds, and she never touched me again.

My intention isn't to justify what I did, assuming I've done anything. Soon enough we'll know, won't we? Either the cops will come for me or they won't. The coy teasing will stop, and all will be revealed. But first, something else has gone awry. Mead is dumbstruck. I assume we're going to go up and eat, but instead he's staring at the boxes as if he's been put into a deep trance. Then he pounces like a cat and begins counting them, tapping each one and becoming increasingly agitated while doing so.

"Something wrong?" I ask, trying to be helpful.

"There's an RPG missing. A Chicom Type 69. I'm only counting five but I know I have six. I promised Fyodor Ublyudok six. He's paying for six." He sinks down to one knee, a prayerful gesture of supplication in his time of need. "Someone took it from here."

RPG stands for "rocket-propelled grenade," which wounded or killed thousands of Americans during the Iraq War, which Bev and I both protested in 2005 by holding homemade signs on a sidewalk by the Ithaca Mall. So an RPG is a seriously lethal piece of equipment, and having one unaccounted for is not only a financial blow to Mead but also a public safety hazard to our city and suburb. Not to mention the legal ramifications that my mother, the homeowner, would face if God forbid this heinous shoulder-mounted cannon is ever used in a crime — by whom? When? I think of that kid who was visiting Graves last night, the one I promised not to speak of. But I never promised to help cover up a felony — I have my own crimes to worry about, after all — and thus I find myself in an awkward position, which is usually how I end up.

Mead blows by me and bounds up the steps with surprising agility for someone so flabby. He nimbly avoids barging into my mother, who nonetheless seems shell-shocked by this silent outburst.

"What happened?" she asks with extreme caution, fearing my answer. Her lower lip is actually trembling, the way a toddler struggles not to cry. Any second I expect her to burst into tears. Her lunch teeters on the verge of ruin.

"One of the boxes is missing apparently."

This news makes my mother raise her eyes toward the heavens, only for a second so that she can compose herself. Gibson has drifted into the basement as well, and we form a trio of confused bystanders at the foot of the stairs.

"Why is Dad upstairs yelling at Graves?" she ventures to ask, with a bemused expression that incites my mother to frown in disapproval, further dampening the mood for what was supposed to be a festive luncheon.

"I don't know," she snaps churlishly, in what I can only imagine is an ongoing saga between these two. Gibson keeps on smiling, further fanning the flames. "What is so funny?"

"Nothing."

"Why are you smiling?"

"It's just so stupid."

"I'm sure there's a reasonable explanation," I interject, the peacemaker at war with himself, eager to soothe the troubled waters and rescue the day from the familial discord that threatens to undermine the joy and togetherness of the weekend. A weapon is missing, and Graves most likely stole it —

right? Or is it in the trunk of my Honda? Pay attention! I also had the opportunity to steal whatever my heart desired between the hours of four and ten this morning, but for what purpose? So that when I drive home to Ithaca, I can blow up Igor's studio and finish what I've started? That doesn't qualify as a "reasonable explanation," but it would solve the Mystery of the Missing RPG.

"I just want us all to sit down and eat," my mother laments, her soulful eyes gazing up the stairs. She is a fervent believer in fairy tales, voracious reader of romances, and devout worshiper of the Cavalier, that mythic Virginia demigod whose breeding and manners come straight from the teachings of Sir Walter Scott. Then the door swings open and down comes her Knight in Shining Armor, trailed by his chagrined son. Their arrival has the feel of an imperial inquisition, and we the jury watch in stunned silence.

"Show me," he orders Graves. Then he notices us and reaches out and clasps my mother on the shoulder, tenderly I suppose, but not lovingly. "I'm sorry, honey. This just came up and I have to figure it out because the guy is coming today."

"Today?"

"Just for a second."

"It's a Bazalt box, right?" asks Graves, his posture openly defiant, hands on hips like he's spoiling for the showdown, a boxer standing in his corner waiting for the bell.

"Do you need to be so rude?"

"Yes, when I'm getting falsely accused."

"No one is accusing you of anything."

My mother skips up the stairs to escape the mounting tension. Graves and Mead dive into the storage area. I'd really like to shower but for some reason Gibson remains on the stairs, perched like a pigeon, and so I stay with her out of politesse. The scent of delicious hot food wafts down to the basement. The basics of existence beckon me — cleanliness, food and drink, sleep. And sex . . . theoretically speaking, with Gibson's ripe body hovering a few feet away.

"I never touched it!" Graves shouts, and then seconds later he comes storming out, with Mead in pursuit.

"Did that box just get up and walk away?"

"I think we should go upstairs and eat," I say with more resolve than I intended. Both of them glance over at me at the same time as they come to a dead stop. Maybe I've shamed them into behaving and waiting until after lunch to begin the official inquest into the missing box. Gibson, bless her, stands up and heads upstairs, and it's hard

192

for me not to stare at her heart-shaped ass, since on a college campus that's one of the occupational hazards that come with being a professor — until you make the mistake of crossing the line — not once, not twice, but six or seven times — there's so much I need to disclose. I'm sure my dean knows all, has amassed a sizable dossier, with a battery of lawyers to condemn me, which is actually quite unnecessary because I'll confess. We'll meet in a conference room deep in the bowels of Robespierre Hall. The Committee of Community Standards will sit across from me. I will be offered water. Then the questions will begin. Did you or did you not ask Veronica Freninggen about the details of her relationship with a male student known to all as Rowdy? Did you or did you not get Emily Kramer to describe the anatomy of a diminutive ex-Marine named Leon, present whereabouts unknown, and did she or did she not claim that Leon was "surprisingly huge for a little guy"? Did you or did you not speak with Brittany Bohannon about her tormented fling with a hipster named Nick, who was self-centered, egotistical, controlling, and by far her biggest? Professor Stith, we're starting to see a pattern emerge here, and what's curious is that given your current incapacity, you seem overly preoccupied with the sex lives of your students, almost as if the very idea of an erection captivates you and thus you force these young women to tell you of private, intimate, and consensual sex acts that you drool over in a way that is an affront to critical thinking and complex analysis.

I'm guilty, Dean, except I never forced them. Not once! They all willingly, gleefully, proudly answered each of my pathetic questions . . . and then there was Lola.

"Eddie's right," says Mead, frowning and scratching his chin. "We need to go sit down and eat the delicious meal that's been prepared for us."

"I'd never steal anything from you," Graves pleads, standing next to me, emitting hellacious body odor that is strikingly at odds with his bland looks. "If I took something, I'd tell you. I'm not a liar."

"The food is ready," I repeat, moving away from Graves as quickly as possible and then taking the stairs two at a time to escape the tension and the stench. The welcoming smells of the kitchen come as a relief, though my mother stands at the stove, staring vacantly at a covered dish with oven mitts on her hands. She glances over at me while unsteadily reaching for the casserole.

The table isn't set and Gibson is nowhere to be seen.

"Are they coming?" she asks wearily.

"I hope so. Let me help you."

"I don't need help."

"I'll set the table."

"That's supposed to be Gibson's job."

"I was the best table setter around these here parts, as I recall."

This quip causes my mother to chuckle. Not laugh, as she's too upset for that. I can't imagine the stress this poor woman is under, so much so that she reaches out and slips her arms around me like she's clinging to a life preserver while being dragged out to sea. "I'm glad you came," she tells me, pulling me tight the way she once did when she was proud of her little genius. "I know it was a long drive and you've been very busy."

"Mom! Come on, I wouldn't miss this for the world."

She lets me go with a reproving curl of her lips. "You think I'm making a mistake, don't you?"

But before I can answer, we hear Mead and Graves approaching from the basement, meaning I'll have to keep my opinion to myself for now. Perhaps I'll never tell her what I think, but I'm also getting the vibe that she wants me to put my foot down and set her straight, although if I miscalculate her willingness for candor, she might never speak to me again. Honesty always entails risk and hence carries with it a premium most are unwilling to pay. What has honesty ever gotten me? All my friends in college, every single one, cheated on just about every test or assignment they could, and today most of them earn good money, have families, coach Little League, while I, upholder of the Honor Code, model student, underpaid college instructor, currently possess no wife, no children, probably no job, and soon no freedom once my crimes become known.

"You lose accuracy from five hundred yards," Mead says to Graves, who is hanging on his every word. From the looks of it, the storm may have passed.

"Even with the 69?"

"No doubt! That's the max range."

"You all sit down!" my mother sings cheerfully. They comply and I grab silverware from the drawer. Just like that, the tension has eased considerably.

"Where's Gib?" Mead asks, noticing his daughter's absence.

"She's probably in her room," Graves concludes. "I'll go get her." He pops up from his chair and dashes off, boots clomping like a stampede of stallions. Mead uses the downtime to get back on his phone, elbows propped on the round table my mother has brightened with a setting of vividly colored wildflowers. I act as a dutiful footman while Mead indulges himself, not once asking my mother if he can help. I glare at him as I set utensils down in front of him, and my quiet ire must've knocked some sense into him, because he suddenly puts away his phone and offers to help.

"I've got it under control," my mother squeals in delight. Her fiancé isn't a wastrel after all, but a living and breathing Virginia gentleman. The fairy tale lives on.

Graves returns with Gibson, and somehow all five of us sit down together. The road here wasn't easy to traverse, but a delicious casserole is our reward. Gibson barely nibbles at her plate whereas her brother wolfs his chow down with ferocity, making a queer sucking sound that could be caused by the fishlike shape of his lips. Nonetheless my mother beams proudly at all of us, this slapdash family that may or not may make it to Monday. As silence descends, I grow uncomfortable because I watch Graves chug back an entire can of Coke in two swallows and then head to the fridge for another.

"That's a lot of sugar," my mother rightly observes.

"I need to wake up" is his excuse.

"How late did you stay up?"

"Late. I was working on some stuff."

Mead rolls his eyes, disapproval that Graves seems to bask in. I sense that within seconds another spat will ensue, and so I pipe up to change the dynamics before father and son resume their feud. Pleasant is what my mother wants, and pleasant is what I must give her. I need to rescue the tenor of this meal, and I think I know just the topic. "Guess who I ran into today?" I blurt out like an eager-beaver middle school student.

"Who's that?" my mother quickly rejoins, looking very glad to have my help.

"Leigh Rose Wardell. Do you remember her? We used to date some in high school."

"Wardell? Is she related to Luther Wardell?" Mead asks with a trace of self-satisfaction. The name does carry a lot of weight in Richmond, certain parts of which cling to a Colonial notion of aristocracy.

"That's her father."

"He's one of the richest men in Richmond. And politically connected."

"You never told me you dated her!" my mother croons in a joyous falsetto. We're having a pleasant time now! Edwin the Champion is describing his brilliant social life to an adoring crowd. "I would've remembered that."

"It was no big deal, just a couple of months of casual high school dating. We broke up before we went off to separate colleges."

"You should've married her," Graves chimes in, that devilish little brother of mine, always poking fun.

"Well, she's not married now, so maybe I have a fighting chance."

"So she's single," my mother muses gleefully. "Are you going to see her again while you're in town?"

"I might."

"That's wonderful news!"

"You should definitely marry her!" Much polite giggling ensues, but the sugar is causing Graves to rock in his chair like he's being electrocuted in Oklahoma. These George men, they seem to share a similar mating strategy — go for the wealthy widow. My mother is enabling it, of course, but she's also delighted that finally we're settling in for a normal repast. As my father was fond of telling me, nothing good ever lasts.

"Can I be excused?" asks a glum Gibson,

her casserole still largely untouched.

"But you haven't eaten anything," my mother objects.

"I don't feel so good."

Mead regards his daughter with a fatherly look of concern, because her face does appear drained of color and her movements are listless. She's using again. Fresh from rehab, with a penchant for disappearing, and sleeping with a drug dealer, Gibson has shown nothing to indicate that she's working at her recovery. She offered to get me high, from weed she bought with money she borrowed from me.

"Go get some rest," Mead counsels her. "We need you at full strength tonight at the rehearsal. Aunt Paula is coming down and I know you'll want to see her."

"Aunt Paula!" Graves erupts, staring at me with the intensity of a new convert. "She is the funniest person in the world! One time she drove out to San Francisco just so she could go swimming in the Pacific Ocean and then she drove right back home. Didn't she, Dad?"

"There's more to the story than that," Mead demurs. Wordlessly Gibson stands up and carries her full bowl over to the counter, and with her shoulders stooped and slow gait it seems as if she might not have the strength to make it. Poor kid! It's not enough that she's an addict, but now her dreams of stardom have faded too. The guy who was going to get her booked at a great venue, the lover who'd launch her career, turned out to be a liar. Don't give up, Gibson! My loves have come to ruin, too. "Women have great power," Kafka tells us, and we'd better believe him. If not him, then who? Me? No, you can't put your faith in me.

Run, Gibson, run! Look at your future if you stay on your current path. You'll go back to rehab, sober up, be sent to a halfway house where they'll make you get a job and adhere to a strict curfew, and your best-case scenario is spending nine to five at a Bed Bath & Beyond, the tedium of which is relieved by attending NA meetings in a church community room. If you're lucky, you might start dating a guy in recovery who's as messed up as you are. So go back to your band and make music, write songs, burn every stick of wood in your soul — there's nothing for you here, nothing at all.

"Do you think she's really sick?" my mother asks after Gibson sulks away.

"I don't know what's wrong with her," Mead groans. "Is she doped up again? Is that it?"

Mead and my mother are both gawking at me as if I have some special insight into the torments of young adulthood, not knowing that my own torments with young adults have pushed me to the brink of sanity. "What do you think, Eddie? How did she seem today?"

But I don't get a chance to respond, as Mead chimes in with another hypothesis. "I'm worried that she took an RPG and sold it so she could buy drugs," he asserts, before checking his phone with an impatient flip. "I hate to accuse her, but she's always complaining about not having any money. If she's using again, anything's possible."

Why does no one ever suspect me of being a criminal? Is it my baby face and impeccable manners? Or is it the fact that I'm innocent? I might as well be invisible, because I leave no impression.

"Her problem is that she hates everything," Graves confides, tapping his fingers on the table with the impatience of a hungry diner waiting for a server to take his order. "She's just really down on Richmond and wants out, and I can't blame her. This place is pretty terrible."

"Richmond is a great place to live," counters my mother rather defensively and not altogether convincingly.

202

"If you're a racist, yeah."

"Graves, now come on," Mead gallantly intercedes. "That's ridiculous. Richmond is no worse than most places. Better than most, actually."

I feel that my mother's honor also needs defending, even though I largely concur with the kid's crude analysis. Like most young thinkers, he's prone to gross generalizations. Only adults can discern distinctions between bad and worse, because ultimately those are the choices we face as the years tumble by. "The suburbs of Richmond aren't the same as downtown Richmond," I sermonize with the bland self-assurance of a Rotary Club vice president. "The two are very different places, two different universes in fact. One is stuck in the past, and the other has always embraced the future."

Graves considers his options now that I've joined the opposition. He's staked out an unpopular redoubt but I don't sense retreat in him. He seems like the kind of person whose heels are perpetually dug in. "I never asked to live here and neither did Gibson. We were taken here against our will, like hostages. I liked it better in Fredericksburg."

Mead takes umbrage at this dig and lays down a marker. "Hey, no one's got a gun to your head. You're free to go at any time." The unintended irony that this family traffics in! It's precious, honestly. A gun to your head! Don't skip ahead, though. That is the one demand I have of you. Let this story unspool.

"No! Let's not do this! Not in front of Eddie." My mother reaches across and grabs my hand, a tender gesture I appreciate. "I'm not saying Richmond is perfect, but I never heard you complain too much until recently. I thought this city was growing on you."

"Yeah, like mold."

A fork pointing at his son, Mead offers a stern rebuke. "When I was your age, your mother was pregnant with you and I was working eighty-hour weeks to pay the bills." He pauses to stab at the casserole. "No one asked me how I felt about where I was living or whether I was happy. I just had to get up and go work at RadioShack, which I hated. But I had a family to support."

Graves rocks back in his chair so violently that I fear he's going to topple over, before lurching forward with his chin out-thrust and eyes ablaze. "I'm not as lazy as you think I am. Stuff is happening in my life. I've decided I want to make a difference in this world, and I will."

"That's great, Graves," my mother enthuses. "Eddie, you talk to young people all the time about what they want to major in, right?"

"Sure, it's a big part of my job."

"I'm not talking about my major," counters Graves, wryly smiling at me in the cocksure manner of the young who need no advice but are subjected to some in spite of their indifference. "This is way bigger than a major, way bigger than college. I'm not going to be a passive observer, let's put it that way."

"Eddie, what do you think?"

Here I lapse into my omniscient purveyor of wisdom, arms crossed. Just need a pipe and tweed jacket. "Passion is in short supply. If you feel some, embrace it. Follow your heart."

"Oh, I plan on it — trust me."

The doorbell rings. It startles me because it's the same tinny chime that tethers me to my childhood. "He's here already?" Mead asks, more to himself than any of us.

"Who?"

"The buyer. He's supposed to come at three."

My mother sighs in disconsolation while Mead pushes back from the table and goes to answer the door. Seconds later he returns with a hulking man trailing behind, someone obviously suffering from the heat. His stricken face reminds me of Chagall's "Self-Portrait with Seven Fingers," mostly because of the scarlet tones that seem to be emanating from the man's stone-edifice jaw. His eyes beam like lasers, and his white hair tightly curls into craggy spires. But upon closer inspection, the buyer also looks a lot like my urologist, Dr. Koretsky, himself of Slavic parentage and a man deeply committed to the resurrection of my erection, but whose pronunciation of the word "vascular" always cracks me up because it sounds like "Dracula."

Introductions are hastily made, with Fyodor Ublyudok wiping away sweat with an elegant handkerchief, stitched with gold lace.

"You look awfully hot!" my mother offers. "Would you like a cold drink?"

"Yes, please."

"It's cooler in the basement," Mead assures him. Fyodor Ublyudok reveals nothing with his blank expression, an Old World stoicism wrought from millennia of despair, which only goads Mead to try harder at pleasing. "It's like a fridge down there."

"Hardly!" Graves blurts, earning a glare from his father. But Fyodor Ublyudok isn't paying attention, having taken a glass of water from my mother. He eagerly gulps it down and hands the empty highball back without thanking her.

"You were thirsty!" she exclaims.

"Shall we?" He nods to Mead. "My plane leaves at three."

"Sure, sure," Mead stammers, ushering Fyodor Ublyudok out of the kitchen. "It's all down here."

Not all, of course, because one piece is presumably missing. Will the unaccounted-for RPG be a deal breaker? Hard to say. What is for certain is that the mere presence of Fyodor Ublyudok in her house has caused my mother much consternation, as it's an unwelcome intrusion that disturbs her dream of bliss. Graves and I help her clear the table and begin doing the dishes, but she seems very distracted and agitated.

8

Because I actually do feel pity, I've volunteered to help out with the laundry. My mother's nerves seem frayed to the point where she might blow a fuse. It makes sense for me to step in and do this chore since I'm staying in the basement next to the washer and dryer, and I've always found the purgation of laundry to be spiritually healthy. Clean clothes, clean soul, clean man.

Except . . .

Lola hasn't responded to my last text and her silence has become a thousand scalpels that are carving me into tiny pieces of agony. At this stage I just want clarity. No: I want to hear her voice, her laugh, and most of all her advice. She'd know exactly how I should deal with my stepfather and equally perplexing step-siblings. Though she's young in age, her old soul is full of ancient wisdom, except when it comes to her sex life, which borders on youthful chaos. But the larger point is, Lola and I have shared much more than her vast collection of dick pics.

For example, just a few weeks ago, we went for our first hike to Buttermilk Falls, one of the most breathtaking spots in the Finger Lakes region. It was just the two of us, no Dahlia, no Thor, the first day of summer, the most hopeful time of year, and we chatted about books and movies and bands. She didn't show me pictures of her conquests, I didn't complain about Bev, and we soaked up the sun along with other like-minded nature lovers. Lola stripped down to an itsy-bitsy bikini while I left my shirt on, and for an hour my life felt normal. The power of the waterfall diminished me, reduced me to a mere encasement of protoplasm, and its roar blotted out the running monologue in my head, the constant chastisement of my shortcomings.

Other hikes to the falls followed, but none ever bestowed upon me the insight of being free in nature like that first one. To live without complications! Two people holding hands, spray from falling water glistening in the clean air, happiness . . . but now Lola has declared war and is invading from the North, giving me scant time to construct ramparts secure enough to stop her. Once again Richmond waits for an attack . . .

Mead and Fyodor Ublyudok are conducting business in the makeshift armory, but the door is closed and I can hear nothing of this transaction. A modicum of privacy! I carry a hamper of Graves's clothes back to the little laundry room where my mother still keeps the same ironing board folded up in its usual place next to the dryer, and although I never much used the thing, seeing it somehow reassures me. Not all has changed.

Since the washing machine is a top loader, I just have to pick up the hamper and dump it, whites mixed with darks. The clothes tumble in, and so does a piece of paper. A clue? Pay attention here, because clues such as these are few and far between. Obviously in his haste to clean his (and my old) room, Graves scooped up more than just his dirty underpants. The paper in question is standard letter size, bright red, and boldly designed. In the center is a cartoon likeness of General Robert E. Lee sitting on a horse, but rendered as if he were African American, and grotesquely so, with thick lips and eating watermelon. The text above, written in twenty-four-point font, explains:

The Bastard Sons are rising! The Dirty

South will get clean once and for all. Nowhere to run, nowhere to hide. Bring da funk, Richmond. I didn't own no slaves!!!!

It reminds me of the kind of gonzo advertising a band might unleash, stapling such flyers to telephone poles and bulletin boards around the VCU campus. Gibson had mentioned the name of her group was Hazzie Mattie, but this obviously is the work of the Bastard Sons, which might be a funk band, but there's an ominous, violent quality to this that doesn't seem musical. After I get the washing machine going, using the max amount of detergent, I pull out the trusty smartphone to google the above-referenced organization, using the search term "bastard sons richmond." Not that I'm expecting to find much. But an idle browse on the Internet beats the torment of waiting for Lola.

The first results don't seem promising. Henry VIII apparently had a bastard son named Henry FitzRoy, who was the Duke of Richmond, and so I refine the search to include "Virginia," which coaxes the search engine to relinquish its secrets. The first hit refers to a punk band called Commercial Smell, who back in 1999 put out an eponymous CD with the song "Bastard Sons of Richmond" as the lead track. A link takes me to the Smell's Facebook page, which has twelve followers and no posts. While this obscure group might have some connection to the flyer, I can't determine it, though I'd love to hear some of the song for my own edification.

Then while the phone is in my hands, it rings. The incoming call is from my area code, 607, but from a number I don't recognize or have stored in my contacts.

The police? Checking on the whereabouts of their prime suspect? Would answering it make me appear more guilty or less? Nature loves to hide, Heraclitus told us long ago, and so I decide not to answer but will call back if this person is legitimate or unthreatening or if I feel it's in my best interests to do so. Because it very well could be my dean, ready to confront me with a new allegation, to join up with the others, the charges forming a kind of hunting party of depravity.

But this caller does leave a message, and here it is in its entirety:

Edwin, this is Carter LaSalle, I don't think we've met, but I'm in the theater department at Notting and here's the thing. My daughter Lola has taken several classes with you and she really likes and respects you, and I'm just wondering if she's ever spoken to you of troubles she's having — or if you know where she is because she hasn't been seen for a few days and she's stopped replying to our texts. We haven't called the police yet because we want to respect her space but we're starting to get worried. Any help you can provide, I'd greatly appreciate it. Call me back when you get the chance.

We have met, however. Professor LaSalle surely would have no memory of speaking briefly to me at a faculty workshop on — get this! — sexual harassment, but this training session was two years ago, before his daughter and I fell into the abyss together. As a classically trained Shakespearean, Carter LaSalle always makes a big impression, with his booming melodic voice, precise diction, and Charlie Chaplin features, that boundless, expressive energy that animates each of his disjointed mannerisms. Luckily Lola takes after her mother, in that they both share an ethereal Stevie Nicks quality, the pretty, bookish girl who didn't get asked to the prom, the late bloomer who always will remember the sting of being unpopular even as her beauty increases in inverse proportion to years away from high school. Would you believe that Lola never once was kissed during her mostly unhappy years at Ithaca High School, where she starred on the Quiz Bowl team? This lovely, mercurial, sexually rapacious maenad came to college a virgin.

I stare at my phone as if inside it Carter LaSalle is hiding so that he can catch me in the act. But I can't fault him for being worried about Lola. Given that he's my colleague, I must return his call, but before doing so I must formulate a plan so that my explanation will blur the line between true and false.

I sink onto the sofa where I'd wasted many hours of my life. "I was sick — sick unto death with that long agony," so Poe begins "The Pit and the Pendulum," and I won't claim that the walls are closing in because that is a hackneyed, overused phrase, but in this case the walls *are* closing in. Lola has now alerted her parents of her attachment to me, and once they confront her, she has only to divulge a few choice details and down will come the swinging blade to slice me in half.

Unless . . .

The idea is ridiculous, but I'll admit to harboring the ultimate Hail Mary. I'm doomed at Notting College, professionally, personally, and legally, and I'd never have to return to Ithaca (the opposite of Odysseus) if Leigh Rose and I were to set off for, say, Paris. She in effect would become my

Circe whose palace I'd never leave.

No! A thousand times no! I curse myself for even thinking that her money can save me. But what other choice do I have? Once I get fired from the college, no one will hire me — not even a preschool. And I'm qualified to do nothing else.

The shower washes off none of the guilt. As I stand dripping with a towel hitched around my waist, I realize only one person can deliver me from my current torment, and so I call her.

Of course Lola doesn't answer, and again I can't help but hear that infernal tone as I imagine her staring at her phone and letting my call slip by. Why should she answer? She has nothing to lose and everything to gain by my downfall. A good attorney can procure her millions, and rightfully so. I've really done her wrong. She was my student and I took advantage of her. Go directly to jail, Dr. Stith. The end.

My message is pleading and probably too self-pitying, but it's what I do best: "Your father called me and he's freaking out. This is bad, do you understand that? This can ruin me! Is that what you want? I know it's what I deserve. But call me anyway! I need to talk to you!"

Whenever I tell Lola that I "need" her,

she sneers because in her mind need equals weakness. For that reason, I don't expect I'll hear from her again, except perhaps if we sit across from each other at my trial as she testifies for the prosecution. Even then, she'll probably wink at me once or twice just to make sure the knife is in to the hilt. I don't want our last communication to be me whimpering for her on voice mail, but in some ways it's the perfect ending. A hushed courtroom will listen enrapt at the urgency in my voice as I plead for her to spare me. I'll squirm next to my court-appointed attorney, no juror will look me in the eye, and hopefully the judge will throw the book at me.

Then the unthinkable happens. My phone buzzes. A text from Lola, whose compassion my plea moved. I take a deep breath, ready to face this issue head-on and reach a resolution. Surely she must know what's at stake for both of us. She can't actually believe that we have a future together. But this text is the worst one she's ever sent me. It consists of three words that when strung together become perfectly clear and lucid, capturing an honesty more terrible than the human heart can endure:

I hate you

I reply in a hurry. *Don't even say that. Not funny!!!*

Of course there's no response. The phone feels like it weighs a ton and I want to throw it against the wall and watch it smash to a million little pieces. She hates me? After all I've suffered for her? The career I sacrificed? The ridicule I've endured? I should hate her, but of course I don't. More than ever, I want her to come to Richmond . . . she must come, so that we can hash this all out. Clear the air, start over, explain . . . to her parents, to my dean . . . though I don't know what this mea culpa would sound like.

I could start by returning the call of Carter LaSalle. And I could be honest, and honesty goes something like this:

Your daughter and I care a great deal for each other, but we make each other sick and it needs to end, which I've tried to do, but she won't take no for an answer and so she's driving down to Richmond to have it out with me in person. More than likely I'll probably cave because I can't live without her reducing me to servile groveling, and she has a need to humiliate me and at the same time worship me. I know what I've done is wrong and I'm trying to make it right. We've never had sexual intercourse if that's any consolation.

Push the Dial button, Eddie. Carter La-

217

Salle deserves an explanation. The phone is in my hand and requires little investment from me beyond pressing my index finger down with a minimal amount of force. But I can't do it! I can't lie to this man about his daughter. False hope is worse than uncertainty, and in today's world I can claim a broken phone or poor service as an excuse why I failed to return his call. Besides, there is a good chance that Lola has turned her car around and now is headed home, and so in due time Carter LaSalle will come to glean what's transpired.

I find the energy to get dressed, though soon I'll be attired in an orange prison jumpsuit. Going through the motions is exhausting. My clothes seem ridiculous. Cargo shorts? So many pockets, so little use for them. On the bright side, I could carry six or seven cell phones without bulging, plus a few ounces of cocaine. Bev thought cargo shorts on grown men bordered on infantile . . . but the secrets they can stow away!

Almost clothed, just need a trucker's hat . . . but "I Have Issues" got left behind at Leigh Rose's house.

Leigh Rose, Leigh Rose, where art thou? When I was with her, I was happy. I was myself again. Is there any possibility of seeing her? One text, perhaps? I left my hat there, but if I use that as a pretext to contact her, then she'll accuse me of stealing my ideas from a *Seinfeld* episode. But I didn't leave it on purpose. It was truly an accident. Does it even matter? She's rid of me, Lola hates me, I hate my cargo shorts . . . but upstairs I hear strange noises.

People are laughing.

Actual laughter! I go to investigate. In the kitchen are my mother, Mead, and Graves. Oh, and a bottle of wine.

"Glass of vino?" Mead calls out to me, hoisting the bottle. "I'm buying!"

Even my mother is indulging. The Russian has left. Deductive reasoning tells me that a major purchase was made. "What's the occasion?" I ask.

"Mead sold his collection," my mother announces with pride, beaming at her betrothed, who lords over the table with manly virtue.

"About time!" jabs Graves, lips puckered into a squishy smile.

"Stop! These deals are hard to work out."

"He's kidding," Mead intercedes, filling a glass for me. How I long to be drunk! Intoxication is my last refuge. The hooch in prison is good, I hear. "I can take some ribbing, I don't mind. And anyway, Graves is right. That took way too long!"

"Better late than never!" my mother sings in delight.

The wine isn't anything special, an average Pinot Grigio that's too fruity for my taste, but it'll do the trick and possibly soothe my frayed nerves. "Here's to real business acumen," I toast, clinking glasses with everyone. "I'd sell everything I owned, too, if I could find a willing buyer."

"Mead has worked very hard to pull this together." My mother slips an arm around Mead's shoulders, and this harmless gesture is striking because he seems startled by her embrace, but maybe I'm imagining that he recoiled ever so slightly.

"And it turns out, the RPG wasn't missing after all!" Mead bellows, slapping the table for emphasis. "The original manifest I sent him showed five, not six."

"I accept your apology," says Graves, who instead of wine is chugging down another Coke. The last thing he needs is to become more hyper, but he's well on the way.

"I never offered one."

"Don't blame me because you can't count."

"When is he picking everything up?" asks my mother, a perfectly reasonable question from a nervous homeowner. The sooner Fyodor Ublyudok takes possession, the better. But here Mead waffles, and doubt creeps into our little afternoon soiree.

"Soon," he replies vaguely. Not good enough for an office manager who thrives on logistical precision.

"Next week? Next month?"

"We haven't worked out all the details yet. He needs to hire a moving crew and coordinate with his staff. Don't worry, it'll work out."

"Did he pay you cash?" Graves cuts in, earning a sidewise glance from Mead, who tries to maintain a happy face despite the carping from his son.

"That's none of your business."

"I'm sure everything's going to work out just fine!" insists my mother, with no evidence to support her claim other than blind faith.

"He'd better not be ripping you off!" Graves snorts. The radiant smile vanishes from Mead's gnarled face.

"He isn't. You know nothing of this man's background or how the game is played. It's a delicate process, but he's agreed to my price, he's shown me good faith, and the rest is just logistical stuff that takes time to sort out."

I feel my mother's eyes on me and so I muster a smile, but too late.

"Eddie, are you okay?" she asks.

My cargo shorts feel very heavy, like they've been weighted down with bricks, and I keep tugging on them so they don't fall to my knees.

"Just a little tired, is all," I reply.

"You should rest. We've got nothing to do until the rehearsal at six. Lie down and take a nap!"

Good night, sweet prince . . . I'm pretty sure I'm "not to be," but not even Hamlet could answer that question. "No, I'll be fine," I assure her. "Where's the rehearsal?"

"Tredegar Iron Works."

This was an important cannon foundry that the Confederacy relied on for manufacturing during the war, and now it's part of a sprawling riverfront park. An unconventional choice for a wedding location.

"I didn't know Tredegar hosted weddings," I airily muse.

"A lawyer from the firm got married there last year and it was lovely."

"Maybe I will rest." To sleep . . . perchance to dream, of being in Paris with Leigh Rose. Or running off with Lola to the far reaches of the unknown.

"Save your strength," Mead counsels me.

"It's going to be a long night."

I check the time. Almost two o'clock. Lola should be arriving . . . in a few hours? A few minutes? Never? Whatever the case, I won't be ready or rested.

9

The dryer buzzes and my eyes blink open. Once alert, I grab my phone like a grizzly swatting at salmon. Nothing from Lola. But the door creaks open and I hear footsteps descending. For some reason I start to worry that she's already arrived, though it's just three o'clock. Not possible, even for her.

It's my mother. "Did the dryer wake you?" she asks, peering down at me.

"Was I asleep?" I chuckle.

"Were you?"

"I don't know." My body aches in a very strange way, stiff and clumsy, maybe from the mattress, maybe from the position I maintained as I stared at the ceiling. "I'm not sure I ever sleep anymore."

As she gets closer, I can smell the wine on her breath. Not the world's biggest drinker, my mother is partying with gusto in an apparent effort to socially lubricate the marriage. "Eddie, you seem off. What's wrong? Did something happen?"

"Nothing unusual. I mean, very little happens in my life. That's one of the perks of being a tortured intellectual."

"What's that?" my mother asks, pointing to the bed.

"What's what?" I reply in confusion, afraid that I've misplaced a piece of incriminating evidence.

"That sheet of paper next to you. Isn't that the statue of Robert E. Lee?"

"Oh." I laugh nervously, handing her the Bastard Sons flyer. "I found this in the laundry basket. I'm guessing it belongs to Graves."

"Oh my." She sighs sadly and shakes her head in disappointment as she reads it. Once done, she lets it drop to the bed. "What has Graves gotten himself mixed up with?"

"I'm not sure, to be honest. I checked online and nothing much turned up." I go and fetch the clothes out of the dryer so I can fold them and be useful as promised.

"He is falling apart. We don't know what to do with him. Nothing seems to work. Have you tried talking to him?"

"A little. He's young. He'll grow out of it, I promise. Even I at his age harbored dreams of revolution."

"You did not," she corrects me. "You were a good boy. Oh, Eddie! You don't have to fold his laundry. He should do it."

"I don't mind."

These are the moments that scald me the most. She might as well be dumping a pot of boiling water over my head. She continues to think that I'll amount to something! If she only knew what torment rages inside — as surely she does.

"I wasn't nearly as good as you assumed I was," I insist, smoothing out one of Graves's T-shirts, of the Clash, 1979. Paul Simonon smashing a guitar, an iconic image that adorns posters in countless dorm rooms, including one belonging to a coed at Notting College in Ithaca, New York. It was my first gift to Lola, who dutifully hung it over her bed, and if you look carefully at the picture of Thor she sent me, you can see a sliver of this poster in the background behind his dong.

Her dorm room! That fabled space into which I vowed never to step foot, and yet . . . there have been moments when I made my way across campus to the library that I magically ended up in front of Mather House, where in Room 220 Lola and Dahlia romped through a field of young adult lust.

Actually going inside would amount to a suicide mission, and yet . . . one night in May, during what the college called Reading Days, when no classes were held so that the students could study for final exams, a sultry night when again I was alone and thinking of Lola and her protestations that she loved me — loved me! Her words! I walked into Mather House and felt my chest grow tight as a drum. A rotund girl looked at me from a sofa and waved. She was reading *The Scarlet Letter* and I nearly vomited. I turned and ran out, just like I want to now, right now, because I can't take much more . . . I never should have come home.

"Why would you say that?" my mother presses me. But I don't answer, because the basement door swings open and heavy feet come plodding down. It's Graves. My mother waves the Bastard Sons flyer in his face.

"Is this yours?" she cries. Graves takes it from her and studies the paper with a chagrined smirk.

"Nope. Never saw it before in my life. I wish it was mine. It's pretty cool."

"What is so cool about it? Can you please explain?"

But he ignores her plea. "Can someone give me a ride to the store? I need a tie for tonight."

"A tie?" my mother groans. "I thought you had a tie."

"I thought I did, too, but I don't."

"I can't take you."

"Can I borrow your car?"

Clearly she doesn't want him to, and so I jump in here to defuse the situation. I could use an outing, if only to get out of my head that is stuffed full of Lola anxiety. "I'll give you a ride," I offer. "If you promise to help with the laundry."

"Sure. I suck at laundry, but I'll try," Graves says with a shrug. My mother issues some last-minute instructions.

"Hurry back. We need to leave here no later than five thirty and Graves needs to shower."

"It won't take long, I swear."

So I get to take a ride with my other new sibling. The first one ended up with Gibson almost getting us both killed, but this one must serve a different purpose. I know he's lying about the Bastard Sons, just like he got me to cover for him and keep Avery's visit a secret. Suddenly I've become very protective of my mother, who doesn't need to contend with Graves and his antics on her special weekend, especially considering that her firstborn son is losing it, big time.

Here's what bugs me the most about Graves. He's just the sort of misanthropic Romeo that Lola would entice into Room 220 of Mather House — and there's a remote chance that they might actually meet. Yes, she might get the opportunity to take Graves to bed . . . the angst! The tragic worldview! He's perfect for Lola, who also likes to pretend that she cares about the deeper issues of social justice. What was it, last March when she went on a service trip to Jamaica? Judging from her trove of photos, I surmised that Lola's main goal was fellating as many of the locals as she could, her charitable blow jobs temporarily relieving the downtrodden of misery while they smoked huge blunts and sucked down bottles of Red Stripe. Okay, she also painted the exterior wall of a preschool, which took a few hours, leaving her plenty of time to hang out on the beach in Negril and meet the dreadlocked natives. As she later wrote in a reflection paper, "The people of the village were all so friendly and really opened my mind to a different way of living." Especially on her last night there, when she hooked up with two long-limbed parasail operators, her first threesome in the MMF configuration (Dahlia had gone skiing with her family during spring break).

"Thanks for taking me," Graves tells me as we walk to the Honda. I say nothing. But once we get inside the car, I make an opening move.

"You know what band I'm really into these days?" I ask innocently. "Commercial Smell. Have you ever heard them?"

"No. Who are they?"

"Punk rockers from Richmond."

"Cool. I hate most everything about Richmond, including every stupid band that plays here."

He's really good at lying. I have to tip my hat to him, because he's capable of giving a convincing performance. I'm sure one of the central tenets of the Bastard Sons is to deny that the group even exists, which Graves is doing with stunning vehemence. So I decide to ditch the indirect route and just level with him, in the name of defending my mother.

"I don't know what you're up to," I tell him bluntly, "but I don't like it. That kid Avery was at the house last night when he wasn't supposed to be, and I held my tongue. Now you're lying to my mother about the Bastard Sons."

"I'm telling the truth! I've never seen that flyer before she showed it to me."

"It was in your clothes hamper. Did it

230

jump in there on its own?"

"Maybe it's Gibson's. She likes to pretend she's in a band. And Avery knows he can't come to the house anymore, ever."

"Good. He'd better not."

I step hard on the accelerator and we go rocketing off down Traylor Drive. I'm pissed off at Graves but not enough to hurt him. There's only one person I've ever wanted to kill . . . Igor, Bev's ceramicist boyfriend. Many were the nights when I'd actually scribble down notes on how one might go about killing him. A bomb in his kiln? Poison in his clay? He taught sculpting classes at a local rec center, and I went as far as filling out the application to take the six-week course. I imagined making a huge clay hammer for my final project and then, after glazing it with one last coat, I'd bash his skull in with it. But I never actually turned in the paperwork to join the class, though once or twice I parked in the lot by the art building and just sat there, waiting for a glimpse of this fraud. But that was my life before Lola, before love re-nourished me, before the warm rays of hope thawed my frozen soul.

No, I don't want to kill Graves, but I do want to teach him a lesson. After all, that is my profession.

"Can you take me to Goodwill?" he asks blandly. "It's by the Chesterfield Towne Center."

"You're getting your tie at Goodwill?"

"I'm not going to the mall."

"Fine. Goodwill it is."

What lesson should I teach him? I could leave him at Goodwill, for example, and force him to walk back home, while I drive deeper into the wilds of the old Confederacy, heading for Appomattox Court House, which lies barely eighty miles to the west on this very road, Route 60, on which we now travel. There I'll surrender, because all good Southerners know that Appomattox Court House is where we must lay down our arms.

And the wedding will be ruined. This I can't do to my mother.

"I don't belong to the Bastard Sons," he emphasizes as I pull into the parking lot, thronged with late-model sedans in various states of disrepair.

"I don't care if you do or don't, just so you don't mess up the weekend."

"I'm not a member. Just so we're clear on that point."

"Fine, I'll take your word on that. So it's a group of what? Anarchists? Jugglers? Who are they?"

"I don't know what they are."

"Is Avery a member?"

"He's an idiot."

He gets out and I decide to wait in the car so I can check my phone. There's a chance Lola has contacted me but probably not because she's out for blood now. This is what it feels like to sink to the very bottom. You're at a Goodwill with the others who've been battered by life, and you're stuck. You're trapped. You have no options. All that remains is pointless ceremony. A sham wedding, a holiday that long ago lost meaning, and a dean closing in . . .

Then my phone buzzes and I get a text. Not from Lola. From Leigh Rose. I inhale sharply, my fingers trembling . . .

Can you meet me at the Hotel Jefferson in an hour? I'll bring your hat!

I glance at the clock on the Honda's dashboard: 3:22 p.m. And just then I see Graves leaving the store and heading back toward the car, a white plastic bag dangling from his fingertip.

I reply:

Sure, c u there

10

Back home, I don't have much time to get ready. And I want to look and smell my best, to give myself a fighting chance with Leigh Rose because I might not get another. I hope I don't blow it . . . there's so much pressure on me I feel like I'm being crushed by *peine forte et dure,* a form of punishment reserved for those who'd plead neither innocent nor guilty . . . rocks were placed on the body, one heavier than the last, until the prisoner confesses or dies . . .

The house is quiet, the dishwasher is humming away, and all have scattered to bedrooms behind closed doors. I hurry down to the basement to begin my beautification. If only I could get a tan and lose ten pounds in the next fifteen minutes!

Even before I reach the bottom of the stairs, I hear the shower running, which strikes me as odd, and so I proceed carefully so I don't barge in on anybody. I knock on the door to the room I'm staying in before I enter it, and from where I'm standing I can see that the bathroom door is ajar and I can hear music playing from a smartphone — a song I recognize as belonging to Led Zeppelin, meaning that Gibson most likely is using my bathroom. I decide I should probably head back upstairs to give her some privacy, but then the shower shuts off. I don't want to startle her and so I call out with a friendly "Hey!"

"Who's that?" she cries fearfully.

"It's Edwin."

"You scared me to death!"

"I'm sorry!" Inexplicably, my face turns red from shame. Now she's going to think I was peeking at her, which I wasn't. You saw me. I was trying to be polite and avoid this exact situation. "I'll wait upstairs until you're done."

"I'll be out in a second."

Growing up as an only child, I never had to share my living space with anyone, and it never bothered me that I had no siblings. In college I'd lived with enough men to approximate what life with a brother might have been like, but until I moved in with Bev, the only woman I'd ever played house with was my mother. Hanging out with Gibson comes as a novelty — we're strangers thrown into an intimate setting, and yet somehow we seem to understand each other. Not to say I trust her, because I don't — but there is fascination as I await her next move.

"I'm dreading this," she tells me as she steps out of the bathroom with a towel wrapped around her hair and another that barely covers her sleek and slippery body, smooth skin accented by white strap lines at her shoulders. "I feel like crap and they're forcing me to go, and it's going to suck."

The towel starts to sag down in front but she doesn't seem to care.

"They've both been married before," she continues scornfully. "Why all of the pomp and fuss? Just elope or something. Why drag us through it? What point are they trying to prove?"

"That they love each other?"

"Yeah, whatever. Good for them. They're both drunk, you know. Tonight ought to be a riot."

"My mother isn't a drinker." I shake my head in disappointment, trying not to stare at Gibson, who continues to reveal more of herself to me with an air of complete indifference that only adds to my confusion. She obviously feels comfortable around me, too comfortable, and thus she displays not just her flesh but her own problems with boundaries.

"I'm going to get so stoned for this, it's the only way I'll survive."

"Maybe dinner will be fun. Aunt Paula sounds like an interesting person."

"She'll come on to you. That's how she is."

I laugh and wave her off. If only Gibson knew the truth! If Aunt Paula stripped her clothes off, got on her hands and knees, and begged me to give it to her, I could only politely applaud and offer her a cold drink. But what would Gibson know of erectile dysfunction? She's at the stage in her life when she encounters the opposite problem, a plethora of erections, such as the one that nearly got us killed earlier today.

"I'm serious," she insists, finally repositioning the towel to completely cover up her breasts. "She is a huge partyer. She got married when I was like ten or eleven, and there were like a hundred naked people running around at her wedding. I'm pretty sure one of them was my mom."

"She lives in Richmond, right?" I'm still a bit hazy on the details of Mead's prior life, and still unexplained is why my mother was having a panic attack in front of the restaurant where Mead's ex-wife works.

"Yeah. That's why we moved here. At least that's the story I got anyway, which doesn't make sense because we barely see her. She works and drinks and pretends she's fifteen. She's got a new boyfriend every month, it's hard to keep up."

"So why move here then if you never see her?"

"I have no clue, dude. My dad does some crazy shit. Ask him and tell me what he says."

"No thanks. I'm staying out of it." I slap my hands on my knees like a judge banging down his gavel. "Anyway, I need to get ready. I'm meeting an old friend for drinks."

"Oh, you're not coming to the rehearsal?" Gibson sounds sorry about that, and it's touching, as it shows that she too recognizes that I'm a kindred spirit, even a part of her family now, a safe port in the storm of her crazy life.

"Wouldn't miss it for the world. And then I hear we're having dinner at the Tobacco Company."

"Oh my God, I used to date a waiter who works there. He was a fool. He was only good for one thing. Not that! Dude, get a grip. He got us free drinks everywhere. He wasn't my type, trust me."

"What is your type?"

"You saw him. That's my type. Except the married part."

Footsteps above, and then on the steps coming down. I can tell by the pacing that my mother is descending. A stricken look appears on Gibson's face and she hurries back to the bathroom and shuts the door.

"Edwin! Are you down there?"

"Right here!"

She reaches the basement and then is transfixed instead by little puddles where Gibson had been standing. "Why is there water all over the floor?"

"Because Gibson took a shower."

"These kids are so messy! They think this is a hotel or something and I'll just clean up after them like I'm the maid. Is she in there?"

"I believe so, yes."

My mother charges the bathroom door and pounds on it with wine-fueled irritation. I need to get out of here, this basement, this house, this life. And maybe Leigh Rose is just the person who can deliver me from evil . . .

"Can you please wipe up the water on the floor?" my mother shouts, in an annoyed and agitated voice that once was directed at me for my own sloth. Why doesn't she kick them out on the street, these two miscreant wastrels who deserve the boot? Is it perhaps that my mother enjoys at some level the challenge of parenting her stepchildren? She's told me repeatedly how much she hates living alone, and while she's had various man-friends since the divorce, none had worked out. Now she's getting an entire family to fill up the loneliness she abhors. Her protests, while genuinely expressed, are muted by the fact that she is very much emotionally invested in Gibson and Graves, warts and all. Once a mother, always a mother.

"And didn't I tell you not to come down here and use our shower instead?"

"I don't mind," I interject, sounding at once gallant and perverse. Of course I don't mind, not with Gibson's penchant for too-small towels.

My mother turns and walks back down the narrow hallway, and in horror I watch as she slips on the very same wet spots that she's just instructed Gibson to wipe up. She falls like an ice skater who trips on a crack in the ice, and so she doesn't tumble backward as much as lunges forward and sideways. Had the pullout sofa not been extended, she would have landed awkwardly on the hard floor, breaking an elbow or hip, but since I am staying in the basement, she crashes into the mattress instead, her knee buckling into the metal frame.

I rush to her and, dazed, she looks up at me with a weird smile. "Are you okay?" I ask, clutching her hand to lift her up.

"I think so," she answers unsteadily, sitting up. "That was stupid of me."

I conduct a quick inspection and see a line of blood snaking down the front of her shin. "You're bleeding," I announce calmly. She bends down to look.

"I cut my knee."

It's more of a gash, and fairly deep at that. She won't like hearing this, but I think she needs a few stitches, which means a trip to the ER, which means the dinner reservation could be in jeopardy — as is my date with Leigh Rose. "We should clean that up."

Gibson emerges from the bathroom, still wrapped up in towels, and wordlessly she drops to a knee and begins to sop up the water from the floor with a colorful hand towel. My mother doesn't curse her or blame, but remains pacific and serene, a study in measured poise.

"Thank you," she says pleasantly. When Gibson looks over, her petulant expression quickly turns to concern when she sees the blood. I get up and go to find a washcloth and bandages. Maybe my initial assessment

of the wound was overblown and no doctor's visit will be required. The best-case
scenario is that my mother will limp stiff-
jointed down the aisle on her wedding day,
and the worst is that she'll spend it in the
hospital with a severed ligament. But this
won't be the last of the blood we'll see this
weekend, rest assured of that.

There's no first-aid kit in the basement
bathroom, but I do bring a washcloth back.
Gibson is crying, sitting next to my mother
with her head slumped on her shoulder. My
mother is cooing into her ear and comforting her the best she can.

"I'll be fine," she insists over Gibson's
muffled sobs and breathless apologies. I
bend down and begin to wipe away the
blood on her leg, and though the wound
isn't long, it does look deep.

"You might need stitches," I finally inform
her, holding the washcloth in place and applying gentle pressure, the failed Boy Scout
using what little he knows of wound management.

"Nonsense. It's your basic cut. You always
assume the worst, Eddie."

"Can I see?" Gibson asks, sniffling back
her tears.

"Only if you don't freak out."

Gibson slides down and together we

examine my mother's knee. In many ways my future hinges on that bloodied hinge. We encounter many forks in the road and the paths we choose to take all veer off in wildly different directions. An ill-conceived crush becomes a spouse and a miserable marriage or a great one; a trip to the store for toilet paper leads to buying a lucky lottery ticket or getting crashed into by a drunk driver. The son of the Chinese farmer breaks his leg and avoids war, but then maybe gangrene sets in, the kid loses the leg, and he ends up begging on the streets of Peking. Or he stays in the village and discovers fireworks and the abacus. What if I never get to meet with Leigh Rose? I want to, very much, thinking I'll be happier with her than without — and likewise the prospect of seeing Lola terrifies me. But what proof do I have to support my hunches? None. Just blind faith.

Gibson and I both think the cut is too deep to avoid seeing a doctor, but it makes no difference. My mother won't budge. She has the right bandages in the upstairs bathroom, and tonight she'll wear a dress long enough to cover up her knee. The show will go on.

11

It's ten minutes after five, and I'm sitting near a gaunt bald man playing a Steinway grand piano, one of Chopin's *Nocturnes,* and around me in large, comfortable chairs, beneath a breathtaking skylight that causes the sun's rays to dance in miraculous ways, men in elegant suits toss back bourbon and converse in hushed tones. The lobby of the Jefferson Hotel throngs with plutocrats, and in my frayed khakis and generic blue blazer I feel like a fish out of water against the august backdrop of tailored refinement. Leigh Rose couldn't have picked a more alien place for us to meet.

Interesting fact: until the 1940s, the Jefferson Hotel kept full-grown alligators in its fountains, and now these saurians are memorialized by a slew of clever bronze replicas placed in various spots around the capacious lobby of what is arguably Richmond's most luxurious setting. Not atypically, the grandeur of the hotel was the brainchild of a tobacco magnate, who considered the alligators to be a clever complement to the Beaux Arts refinement, punctuated by the enormous staircase of red carpet falsely rumored to be the model for the one Scarlett O'Hara tumbles down.

The alligators, though, serve as a potent metaphor for what awaits me. Just getting to the hotel proved to be arduous enough, requiring me to slog through rush-hour traffic on a Friday to penetrate the heart of downtown, 101 West Franklin Street, and then to circle around looking for a place to park, which I did, near the venerable Commonwealth Club, a bastion of old Richmond money where Leigh Rose's father surely has his own wing. Talk about a collection of dangerous reptiles! And yet, not six blocks away, some of the greatest punk rock bands in history thrashed on stages long since demolished, and it's that quarter of the city that I long for. But Leigh Rose must have her reasons for picking the Jefferson.

But where is she? I've sent her a text announcing my arrival but haven't gotten a reply. She might be driving and thus prevented from checking her phone. Whatever, I won't have much time to spend with her if I plan on being punctual for the rehearsal.

I'm nursing a glass of house red, overpriced but robust, and anxiously studying the faces of everyone who passes by, much like the sickly narrator of Poe's "The Man of the Crowd," who imagines a life story for each person he sees. But since almost all these faces in this hotel are white, with the same haircuts and attire, there's not much in the way of fanciful diversion, just a parade of homogeneity. Given what Leigh Rose knows of me, why would she ever think I'd be comfortable here? Even if she has her logic for selecting this monument to Crassus, just a few blocks away are funky watering holes — we could walk to them from here. Maybe I have no real shot with Leigh Rose — I don't deserve her anyway, but regardless, could we really click as a couple?

But what other choice do I have? If this doesn't work out . . . I really don't know what I'll do or what will become of me. My phone rings, instantly drawing me out of my nest of self-pity. Because it's Lola. Lola!

"Hey there," I answer sweetly. "Where are you?"

"I'm sitting in traffic outside Washington, D.C."

Lola is calling me? Hell has frozen over after all, because Lola hardly ever calls me. I can't remember the last phone conversation we had. Three days ago? Four? She wanted to tell me about some guy whose nickname was Horse . . . my face grows flush and I begin to gulp for air, caught unaware by this surprise interruption.

"Oh. I'm sorry to hear that."

"It sucks. I don't know how people live like this. I'd go crazy."

"Isn't it too late for that?"

"Very funny, but the last time I checked, you were a certified pervert."

"Not certified. Aspiring."

"You know you're a complete creep and I love that about you."

Love, hate: makes no difference to Lola, who can vacillate between these two emotions like a quantum particle. Do we love each other? Let's put it this way: can love bloom in a sewer? Maybe between two rats, but Lola is more like a swan, while I'm a decomposer, a bottom-feeder, which might actually give me too much credit because decomposers play an important role in a healthy world. Yet there are moments I think I love her, though now isn't one of them. The real problem is that she is about three hours away from Richmond, placing her here well in advance of her estimated ten o'clock arrival.

"I thought you hated me," I remind her

coolly, still struggling to figure out what to do. I can't set up a blockade of the city, although some of the breastworks remain from 1862, when Richmond prepared for a Yankee invasion of a different kind.

"I do hate you, with all my heart."

"Can you call your parents please? They're worried and your dad called me, which really freaked me out."

"Oh, I talked to them already. They know everything."

She places erotic emphasis on the last word, twisting it like a dagger in my back. "You told them about me?" I whisper as the piano player switches to a jazzier number, Gershwin's "Summertime," but the living ain't easy right now, not with Lola cackling in delight just as Leigh Rose emerges from behind a large marble column and waves at me with a big smile, holding up my "I Have Issues" hat.

"No, but I should tell them!" Lola erupts. "You're being such a d-bag. What the hell is wrong with you anyway? It's because of Thor, isn't it?"

"No, it's because of Horse."

"Whatever, dude! I'm sick of talking about him."

"Do you think I enjoy this? I don't. Not even a little. Thor, Horse, I can't keep them straight anymore. But the worst thing you did was tell Dahlia about us."

"You're such a loser."

And then she hangs up on me, promptly exiting on Leigh Rose's entrance, the way characters randomly come and go in one of Beckett's absurdist plays. I stand up to greet my old sweetheart, and we embrace, not like lovers whose bodies have become one, but the way survivors cling to each other to weather a storm.

"I have your hat," she tells me in a soft voice that sounds faintly hoarse, either from overuse or crying or both. She's dressed not in casual wear but a prim and proper gingham dress with a string of pearls, like she's going to a country-club cocktail party. She's got makeup on, too, and it unsettles me to see her rendered thus, just another well-appointed woman of ample means displaying her wealth and privilege while hiding any trace of irony. I barely recognize her.

"Thank you," I say, taking it from her and shoving it into a pocket. "Would you care for something to drink?"

"Um, sure. I don't have much time. I'm meeting my father at six." This declaration seems to force her down into a chair, as if the words themselves weighed too much for her to withstand. Then she falls silent, offering no further clarification, though she need not provide me with any. I get the waiter's attention and he quickly comes to us. Leigh Rose orders a house white and asks for the check. I don't bother to complain.

"I got married here," she says after the waiter leaves.

"You did?"

"I did. It was my mother's dream wedding."

"Not yours?"

"I don't have any dreams, Eddie."

I lean forward and take her hand, which feels cold and lifeless. "What's wrong? You seem very down and depressed. Did things not go well with Norris? Isn't that his name? Norris Mumford?"

"Things never go well with Norris." She emits a nervous giggle that lacks all mirth, removing her hand from mine. "I'm sorry, it's just I'm in a horrible mood. The worst mood ever."

"I can imagine."

"You really can't. No one can." The wine comes but she doesn't even touch the glass. The waiter places it in front of her but Leigh Rose is somewhere else, far from here. How to get her back before she disappears forever? When we dated, we were always honest with each other. Shouldn't I just fill her in on what I'm going through? What do I have to lose?

"I've had an interesting day, too. The girl I've been seeing back in Ithaca is driving down here to see me, uninvited."

She perks up, even lifts up the glass of wine to her painted lips. "The young 'un?"

"She's impetuous."

"Oh, Eddie. You're a bigger fool than me."

"It gets better. She's one of my students."

Her eyes grow wide, but she's animated again. Even smiling. "Isn't that, like, illegal?"

"No. Just highly unethical."

Laughter! We clink glasses in a gregarious toast, and color has returned to her once-pallid face. "Why is she coming down here?"

"Because I told her we couldn't keep this up. She hopped in her car and started driving. I expect her around ten. Unless she's lying, which is entirely possible. She enjoys toying with me. That's an understatement. She lives to toy with me. It gives her untold pleasure."

"And you, too?"

I cock my head back and gulp down some air. "I derive some satisfaction from her cruelty, yes. Mostly I feel disgust."

"Cruelty? Does she hurt you?"

"Not physically. Nothing like that. We've never actually consummated our relationship, in case you're keeping score."

Leigh Rose nearly leaps out of her chair, and her hands go to her gaping mouth. Her reaction is akin to that of an Amazonian explorer who encounters a truly unique culture based on unusual practices. Eating the brains of the deceased, brothers mating with sisters — the sort of depravity long since considered taboo in our world but very much alive in the isolated jungle of my id. "I don't get it. Why is she coming here?"

"Exactly. Why indeed? You've summed up the situation perfectly. There's no logical explanation."

"But she might not be coming?"

"I long ago stopped trying to understand any of it. She's a lovely person, a very talented poet, but highly flammable. I should've known better. I'll blame my ex-wife. Isn't that how divorce operates?"

"But you guys don't actually . . . ?" Her voice trails off, and I can tell that she is utterly fascinated by my indiscretion and wants to know more — and there is so much more to tell. Yet divulging all too quickly won't work to my advantage, and so I shake my head and slurp down the rest of my wine.

"It's hard to explain the mechanics of this relationship," I demur with a devilish smirk.

"I guess it's none of my business."

"No, I just wanted you to know that you aren't the only person today who's been placed in an awkward situation — not that I equate my problems with yours. Mine are trifling compared with what you've been going through."

She sighs and checks the time. "My father is mad at me. My brother is furious, obviously. My mother won't talk to me."

"Just because you won't marry Norris?"

"There's more to it than that."

She seems unwilling to expound, and so I stick to what I do know. "So you've been summoned?"

"Yes, I've been summoned. I'm going to be read the riot act, I suppose. For the hundredth time. They can yell and scream all they want to, but it won't change anything. It won't make me love that prick."

The word "prick" momentarily stymies me, but I push on. "Why do they care who you marry or who you don't marry?"

"There's a few million reasons why, Eddie."

"Of course. Everyone wants to live where the streets are paved with gold. El Dorado, the ultimate gated community."

"But not you, huh?"

Suspicions regarding my motives? Or just the kind of verbal jousting that has come to define our repartee? "When I joined the ranks of academia, I took a vow of poverty."

"Is that why colleges are so cheap to attend?"

"Very funny. Faculty salaries aren't why tuition has risen. It doesn't matter anyway, because I'm going to jail."

"Wait a sec! You said you weren't doing anything illegal."

"My lawyer told me to say that."

We're chuckling again, mocking the very troubles that hound us, but what isn't clear is a path forward. A way out. Life doesn't come with an escape plan. Spending time with Leigh Rose doesn't leave me confused or full of self-loathing. I don't feel fake around her, or like a bore. We share a natural rapport, but logistics argue against us making it anywhere together. I'm the comic relief in her saga of emotional blackmail, a weekend diversion she can count on being gone by Monday.

"Thanks for bringing me the hat," I say with mounting regret, approaching the inevitable good-bye that'll forever separate us. "It really means a lot to me. It was a gift from my therapist."

"I'm glad you two lovebirds are reunited."

"It's a heartwarming story of persever-
ance and loyalty."

"You should write a book about it."

"Will you come visit me in jail?"

"Eddie, stop it. You're not going to jail." A
pregnant pause. "Are you?"

"No! But will you come visit me anyway?"

"In jail?"

"In Ithaca. Where I live."

"I can't visit you, Eddie. And you can't
visit me."

She wipes a tear that rolls down a cheek,
just as the pianist strikes up a strange rendition of "All Along the Watchtower." I use
this musical anomaly to deflect her proclamation from puncturing my heart. "Dylan?
Am I hearing that right? Is that guy drunk
or something?"

But she doesn't seem to understand what
I'm getting at. She blinks at me uncomprehendingly and leans forward, eyes watery
like she's been chopping an onion. "My
father is making me sign a legal document
stipulating that I can't marry anyone who
isn't from my economic status or I'll be
disowned. He'll cut me out of the will."

At first I'm flummoxed and struggle for a
response. But around Leigh Rose, I can
respond in only one way: sarcastically. "I'm

very wealthy. Did you know that about me? I hide it well with trucker's hats."

"I'm serious, Eddie. This sucks. They're such horrible people."

"So you feel it, too? We have something here between us?"

Note how she doesn't directly answer. "They seem to think so and they don't like it one bit. They think you're after my money, which is hilarious because Norris is after my money but the difference is they want him to have it."

"I want you for your body, not your money. They need to get that straight."

She bursts into laughter once more and reaches out to grab my hand. "Oh, Eddie. You're so funny. I know I should tell them to go to hell, but I've got my kids to think of. I'd never do anything to hurt them."

"But seriously, sparks are flying between us, right? It's not just my overwrought imagination?"

"Sparks have been sighted, yes. But I'm in a bad place right now and not very good company."

"I wouldn't want you any other way, Leigh Rose."

"I need to get going. Can't keep Daddy waiting." She opens her handbag and fishes out a purse that itself looks to be made of money.

"Okay then. When I wear those white shoes, I'll always think of you."

Her brow furrows in confusion. "White shoes?"

"For my mother's wedding?"

Her entire body sinks from the sorrow that presses down on her. "See, I can't think right now. My head is so screwed up. These people are wearing me down." She offers me a meek smile as she drops a twenty on the table to pay for the drinks. "Have fun at the wedding. I hope it goes well."

"Yeah, I'll survive."

She can tell my feelings are hurt because she didn't even remember us buying the shoes at Macy's. I don't want her pity or her money or really anything other than a prison cell. I stand to leave, and she hops up as well. "Hey," she says softly, once again taking my hand like she's leading a lost child through the darkness. "Thanks for cheering me up today. I really needed that in the worst way. You're in my thoughts, Eddie. I just have too many thoughts right now, my brain is so crowded and cluttered."

"I know. They're putting the screws to you."

She rises up, clutching my arms, and

plants a sweet kiss on my cheek. Then she leaves.

I'm angry. Resentful, wounded, and frankly numb. Once again I've allowed myself to be duped and placed in a position where I look ridiculous. Did I actually think she'd fall in love with me after confessing to my crimes? I'm an idiot full of bile and bitterness. But here's the strange part, the part you really can't make up, as it comes directly from the department of Truth Is Stranger Than Fiction — whom do I see lurking in the background, biding time beneath a white marble statue of Thomas Jefferson, but Jeb Wardell himself! The rotund walrus has come to supervise his sister and ferry her across the River Styx to the promised land of her riches.

You can't believe what madness takes hold of me, the mild-mannered writing instructor who has been accused of lacking passion and ardor, as I stride purposefully across the high-domed lobby of a prestigious hotel to confront my tormentor. I overtake even Leigh Rose herself, who doesn't know I'm coming up behind her, and glare at Jeb, whose back stiffens at my approach. We say nothing to each other. Leigh Rose grabs an arm to prevent any further advance.

"Come on, Eddie," she pleads with me.

The index finger of my free hand becomes a knife and I slice it across my throat in a dramatic if not tawdry gesture of violent retribution at which Jeb scoffs in one belching wheeze.

"Eddie! Please!" Leigh Rose squeals in a whisper.

I break free of her grip and backpedal away, my eyes still fixed on the bulbous girth of my nemesis, who has only contempt for me and assumes that I'm idly threatening him, which is likely true. But it goes well past that. What I've done is sign my own death warrant. You can't just make a deadly gesture to someone like Jeb Wardell and not pay the ultimate price. I've never threatened anyone before. Not even Igor, who didn't know me and one presumes never lost a night's sleep worrying whether Bev would go back to me. Sure, I imagined killing him, but he was blissfully unaware of that.

What have I done now? Why can't I control myself?

Moments after the showdown, I'm sitting at the bar inside the Jefferson Hotel, the Lemaire, sipping on a glass of wine, and contemplating the end of existence. Socrates wasn't scared of death, but I am. Not just death . . . but my mother's mortification when she learns the truth about me, which strikes me as worse than death.

Happy Hour, and my thoughts have turned to mayhem. Then someone taps me on the shoulder.

"You aren't Eddie Stith, are you?" asks a man around my age, wearing a blue blazer but no tie. I recognize him at once: John Graziano, aka the Graz, my boyhood friend and neighbor, a certified legend in high school for his prodigious appetite for drugs and sex, which he then parlayed into a career as a high-end dealer of narcotics, if the rumors are true.

"Graz?"

"I thought it was you! Hey, man, how's it going?" We engage in a vigorous handshake as a willowy blonde looks on with a whimsical smile. Whether she's with Graz or not, I can't tell.

"Not bad. How about you?"

"The same." He holds up a half-finished highball of some potent decoction. "Just gettin' my crunk on. Haven't seen you in a while, huh? Where you been hiding out, you big wuss?"

"I live in upstate New York. I'm a college professor."

"Yeah? You nailing some hotties or what? I know I damn sure would be."

A fake snicker escapes my trembling lips. Having confessed once, I'm in no mood to come clean again. Some secrets should remain hidden forever. "Yeah, you'd last about ten minutes before you got slapped with a sexual harassment lawsuit."

"Tell me about it. Hey, you remember Mrs. Lambert from high school? The one with the huge cans? I was banging the crap out of her senior year."

"I knew it! She was always smiling at you and waving, and she never once looked at me, never. You bastard."

"It was sweet. She was a freak. She still hits me up from time to time, but she got fat, bro. I don't do fat chicks."

The blonde rolls her eyes at us, grabs her drink, and slips away. The Graz isn't subtle. He's pretty much lived his life in capital letters, and he would certainly know how to kill Jeb Wardell. He probably could do it with his eyes closed. But you can't just come out and ask someone that kind of candid question. There is much finesse involved, not that I know how to steer a conversation toward the topic of murder. But seeing the Graz after so many years fills me with bravado and I suddenly feel glad that I confronted Jeb Wardell like I did, childish as it was — at least I can say I didn't let him kick sand in my face. I stood up for myself, perhaps looking foolish while doing so. Therefore I'm completely unprepared for what he says next.

"I heard you're in town for your mother's wedding." A casual remark, and one I immediately laugh off. It takes a few seconds for me to deduce the tangled logic of his statement. Heard from whom?

"You did? Who told you that?"

"I have my sources." He's still smiling and seems genial enough. Screwing with people has long been one of his favorite hobbies, but the fact is, precious few people in Richmond know I'm in town, one of them being, of course, Leigh Rose. Another is Jeb. Why would he have spoken to them about me? He didn't go to their high school or move in their circles — at least he didn't used to.

"Well, it's true." I sound peevish because I'm flustered by his cryptic behavior that borders on rudeness.

"Funny what life calls on you to do sometimes, the positions we get put into. You came back home and ran into a bunch of old friends, and you don't know the whole story — you can't know the whole story."

Now he's starting to scare me in addition to pissing me off. "What are you talking about? You sound like a Zen master on acid."

"Fair enough. Here's the deal. Leigh Rose Wardell is going through a hard time right now. She's very fragile, you know. Very delicate. Her family's been trying to help her, but she won't take her pills or whatever and no one wants to see her go back to the hospital."

It takes a few agonizing seconds to shake off the stunned silence that engulfs me. "Did Jeb put you up to this? Why are you butting into my business?"

"Dude, chill out for one second and listen to me. Leigh Rose needs help, okay? Do you understand what I'm saying?"

"You followed me here? Do you work for them?"

"Eddie, wait a second. Hold up. You're not hearing me. Leigh Rose is a danger to herself and others, including you. She's been in institutions because of her issues or whatever the fuck you call it. She had a nervous breakdown. She lost her mind."

"I don't believe you."

"That's what her shrink is saying."

"You've spoken to her psychiatrist?"

"Don't get cute like that, Eddie. I'm not yanking your chain, so don't yank mine."

A threat, one I take seriously due to the

one making it. I can't say that John Graziano was my best friend, but we went to
school together starting in kindergarten,
played youth sports together, smoked joints
at parties, snorted his coke, and generally
moved in the same orbit until I stopped
coming home as much. So this exchange is
extremely unsettling and hurtful. And it's
also based on a complete fabrication. Leigh
Rose isn't crazy — she displayed no symptoms of disassociation, no hallucinations,
no self-harming behaviors — just someone
whose family was placing her under ungodly
stress, evidenced by the fact that one of
them, probably Jeb, sent John Graziano to
warn me off.

"Listen, I have no idea what you're trying
to tell me," I say in a voice that I hope
reminds him of Chuck Norris. "If you're
saying Leigh Rose is mentally unstable, well,
I don't see it. And why do you care anyway?
She's an old friend of mine and I'm concerned about her. Why is that wrong?"

"It's not! Dude, no one is saying you're
wrong. You just don't know the whole story."

"Which means what?"

"It means be careful because you wouldn't
want to set her off. She's done things in the
past that are pretty screwed up."

"Such as?"

264

"She's tried to hurt herself, know what I'm saying? For real. This is no joke."

I nod and notice that Graz is sweating like he's just finished running a 5K. He's not enjoying this parley, but he's been sent here for the express purpose of keeping me away from Leigh Rose. He's Jeb Wardell's flunkie, or business partner, or some combination of the two.

"So obviously if she has feelings for me," I say through gritted teeth, "that's evidence of her being crazy."

"No, what I'm saying is, she might say she has feelings for you, and then you look at her wrong, and she slits her wrists. That's what I'm saying."

"Thanks for the heads-up." I turn away from him and stare straight ahead, but I know Graz remains standing behind me. The bar is crowded and there's no stool for him to sit on, and anyway I'm done talking to him. I need to get going if I plan on making it to the rehearsal on time, but I also don't want to slink away from this fight. If Jeb Wardell would go to this extreme to keep me away from his sister, then he must be in big financial trouble. Or something.

"Eddie, don't get mad at me."

I ignore him and instead count the bottles

of booze arrayed on the shelves opposite me.

"Seriously, dude," he tries again, "I'm giving you friendly advice and you're acting like I'm a punk. I thought you had more brains than that. Why would I lie to you?"

"Money."

"Can you talk to me man-to-man? There's a table over in back."

"I'm leaving now. Follow me if you want to, I don't care. See, that's what you don't understand and Jeb doesn't understand — I don't care. I'm not scared. You can't scare me." My voice is louder than it needs to be and draws more attention than Graz prefers.

"No one is trying to scare you, Eddie," he whispers. "Settle down."

We're facing each other again, and I stand up, brushing into Graz's chest while doing so. He stiffens and glares at me, and I burst out laughing like I just heard the funniest joke in the world. "You wanna kill me? Go ahead. Right here, right now."

Those who can hear us gaze on, aghast and appalled. I don't know what's come over me, a kind of liberating death wish that has loosened the fetters of my usual cowardice. Nothing matters anymore anyway. The noose is already around my neck and all I need is a shove from the hangman, then

266

gravity will do the rest.

"Cut the crap, Eddie."

"Is there a problem, Mr. Graziano?" the bartender calls out, which is my cue to exit. With one last cluck of disappointment, I skip out, head held high and feeling stronger than ever. I pull out the "I Have Issues" hat and proudly doff it, winking at a pretty woman who looks to be endlessly bored by the company of aging frat boys she's with. I've just kicked the hornet's nest, and soon enough they'll be coming at me. Unless I go at them first. I spin around to see if Graz is following me and see no sign of him. His betrayal certainly stings, but he's lived in Richmond too long and lost his way. Yet has he really changed all that much? He was a me-first sort of guy and still is, just on a much bigger scale. I hope he's on the phone right now with Jeb Wardell telling him that the target evaded capture.

12

I'm being followed. I hear footsteps behind me as I head for my car, and I turn around to see a tubby little man with bushy eyebrows and a bad comb-over. Harmless buffoon? Or cold-blooded assassin? I can't let my guard down, not even for one second, because trailing him is a middle-aged woman whose stern face exudes homicidal rage. She's got a phone pressed to a cheek and she's barking out orders . . . to Jeb Wardell? John Graziano? If not her, how about the louche hipster across the street . . . is there a pistol hidden in the folds of his vintage cardigan sweater?

Just to be safe I stand aside, pretending to check my phone, while the tubby man and angry woman pass by. But on the crowded sidewalks of downtown Richmond throng countless office workers who might moonlight as contract killers.

Then I focus on my phone — for real this

time — and I see that I do have a message. It is a missed call from my mother, at precisely 5:53 p.m. Her voice mail is simple: "Eddie, please be on time. We're here now and waiting for you."

The rehearsal! If anything ever deserved a walk-through, it's marriage. But the only part that gets rehearsed is the actual ceremony, which is the easiest part in some ways, whereas the performances that require much practice must take place in improv, a two-character show without a script. If only Bev and I could've rehearsed, say, a weekend seduction, or a captivating dinner . . . instead we tanked. We missed cues, stepped on each other's lines, screwed up the sex scenes, and then came the cancellation notice.

I'm late, and I hate being late to things. College professors are slaves to the clock and the calendar, and so I begin to panic. Luckily for me, the location of the rehearsal, Tredegar Iron Works, is close by, and the worst-case scenario is I'll be just a few minutes late, which still makes me slightly nauseous. I hop into my Honda and take off, speeding not just to rehearse a wedding ceremony but also to go back in time, to a factory on which the Confederate States of America pinned its aspirations to begin a country dedicated to the preservation of slavery. A thousand cannons were produced at Tredegar, and those cannons killed tens of thousands of Yankees — and were produced by the very slaves those Northerners were fighting to free. When I was growing up in Richmond, the big brick buildings of Tredegar sat empty and forlorn, a vast testament to defeat. Driving past it, I always looked down from the Manchester Bridge and could almost hear the groans of lamentation rising up from the ruins. In the emptiness lay the residue of secession, which even into the 1980s remained a palpable entity and not some schoolbook abstraction.

Now the buildings of Tredegar have been restored, a park opened, and instead of the stain of surrender, loving couples can come together as man and wife and celebrate the wonders of monogamy. I find a place to park, next to a huge cannon that is pointing out at the James River, resplendent in the first kiss of dusk that has turned the brown water into a luscious shade of chocolate. I'm not sure in which building the rehearsal is being held, but then I see an older man and woman carrying matching guitar cases and I recognize them as Sylvia and Dan (whose last name I can't recall), dear friends of my mother who must've agreed to play music during the wedding. Sylvia and my mother work together at the law firm, and Dan is a pediatrician, but why I remember them is due to the fact that they have a son my age, DJ (Daniel Junior), who has become everything I'm not. Oncologist, father of two boys, champion tennis player, philanthropist . . . for the past fifteen years my mother has dropped subtle hints about how I fall short of DJ's accomplishments . . . but soon enough I'll have feathers to stick in my hat, too.

They stop and wave, smiling broadly, genuinely glad to see me, as neither is capable of expressing a negative emotion or thought. "Hey there, stranger!" Sylvia sings out in a voice that reminds me of preanorexia Karen Carpenter.

"Well, hello to you guys!"

I shake Dan's hand and give Sylvia a hug. They both radiate the healthy glow that comes from a good diet, regular exercise, and a clean soul. "We're the band!" Dan laughs, holding up a guitar case. "Now where are the groupies?"

"Stop it!" Sylvia chuckles, rolling her eyes, which are still bright and kindly. Supposedly she had cancer a few years ago, but she looks younger than I do. Dan is so muscular that he could probably pick up a cannon and twist it into a pretzel. "This is going to be a blast! Your mom is so happy. And Mead seems like a very nice man."

"I just met him today. And his kids."

"We're looking for the Pattern Building," Dan says, leading us to a smaller brick building about twenty yards from the cannon.

"How's DJ?" I dutifully ask, bracing myself for the litany of excellence that'll surely follow.

But there's a slight pause before Sylvia answers, as if in this interstitial silence dwells some unspeakable calamity that has befallen DJ. My nostrils flare and my eyes seek out solace somewhere on Sylvia's placid face, but she avoids looking at me. Is her son dead? Dying? In prison, where I'll soon be?

"He's doing better," she finally asserts with her usual chirrup.

"Has he been sick?"

"No, nothing like that."

"His wife left him and took the kids to Maine," Dan says wearily, standing by the entrance. "It's been awful. He's got custody now, but it wasn't easy or pleasant. We should go in. We're late."

I allow Sylvia and Dan to enter first, and I

linger at the heavy wooden door, contemplating DJ's bumpy ride through the wilds of divorce. If someone like that can't stay married, then what chance did I ever have? Suddenly I don't feel like such a failure — and I glance at the phone with a new surge of confidence. Right on cue, my phone buzzes with another incoming text from Lola, another nail in my coffin . . . and another picture of Thor, this time a side view, his protruding cannon very conspicuous.

My reply: *Nice spatial composition*

How did it even begin, this sickness that courses between us? How did we ever broach the subject? How did we go from a discussion of Elizabeth Barrett Browning to the endowment of her past lovers — a descent to madness that we called love? Love! She doesn't love me, but the idea that I'm a tortured intellectual, a modern-day Kierkegaard, and she's my Regina . . .

Enough! Time to plaster a smile on my face and head in.

I follow Sylvia and Dan through a small gift shop and reception area and back into a small conference room (the Stonewall Jackson, but in fairness another is called the George McClellan), where I find my mother talking to a frail old woman in a wheelchair that's being pushed around by a very large African American CNA with a bursting Afro and nails painted red, white, and blue in honor of the holiday weekend. Folding chairs have been set up in two sections of twenty seats each, and a trellis of confederate jasmine forms the altar where bride and groom will wed. Along with a reed-thin minister, Mead, Graves, Gibson, and a woman I don't know — Aunt Paula? — stand at the impromptu altar, while Sylvia and Dan sit just offstage and begin strumming their acoustic guitars to warm up.

"There you are!" my mother shouts at me, wagging a finger in playful rebuke. "You're late! But better late than never! This is my prodigal son, Eddie. Eddie, this is Mead's mother, Dahlia Simmons, and her nurse Beatrice."

Dahlia! Of all the names in the world, I must confront another with that toxic appellation. A chill spreads across my skin as though I'd slipped into an ice-fishing hole. Dahlia is the real problem in my life, the one I trust least, Lola's roommate who's also in love with her and views me as a rival and a pervert and a fraud. She's probably the one who turned me in to the dean, if anyone did . . . why did Lola have to drag Dahlia into our secret love nest? I don't know that I'll ever get a satisfactory answer to that question.

"Hello," I say, sounding like an idiot, complete with idiotic wave. The old woman stares up at me, lips quivering, folds of skin drooping down from her chin, thinning white hair still neatly combed, and then she bursts out laughing. At what, I've got no clue. Beatrice reaches down and gently touches the crone's shoulder but she continues to guffaw, until my mother takes me by the arm and leads me away.

"She does that," my mother explains in a whisper. "I think it's the heart medicine she takes. Anyway, you stand over there next to Graves."

I take my place as instructed, looking across at Gibson and the woman to whom I haven't been introduced and who I'm guessing is Aunt Paula, Mead's sister. She looks to be in her mid-forties, a fit and trim professional with strawberry blond hair that just touches her shoulders and whose sleeveless black dress reveals toned arms and muscular legs. In short, a juggernaut, very attractive and sturdily constructed . . . but I feel nothing for her and not just because my penis has become a phantom limb. As unlikely as it seems, despite all that is happening in my life, including the possibility that I'm a killer, I've fallen in love with Leigh Rose. It has to be love, when you think about a person nonstop and long to be with them . . . if only we'd been left alone to allow our affection to blossom, but instead the seedling was trampled by the jackboots of a fascist brother.

"I'm Paula," the woman opposite me calls out.

"I'm Eddie."

That's as far as we get before my mother begins barking out stage directions, revealing her theatrical acumen as board member of a community theater. The woman takes charge as if she's putting on a show. Gibson and Paula are ordered to stand closer to the minister, and Graves and I must come closer to the chairs. Mead is told to take a half step back. Then my mother studies the configuration, nods in satisfaction, and cues the music. I recognize the tune as one of my mother's favorite songs, "Just My Imagination" from the Temptations, which is an unusual choice for the processional since my mother is a traditionalist and more likely to pick the "Bridal Chorus" than Motown. But I applaud the deviation from the tried-and-true, and Sylvia and Dan sound great together. I actually start to think that this

276

wedding won't be as offensive as I initially feared.

Then Mead gets a phone call, one that he must take, and he speeds away from the altar and out of the room, scooting past my stricken mother, who was just about to begin her walk down the aisle. She tries to put on a brave face and cracks a joke that sounds more like a barb: "I guess everything is an emergency today."

Paula and I again make eye contact, but she quickly looks away and I do the same. For two years I meet nobody and then today women are tumbling into my life, just as I verge on total ruin.

"He'd better have a good excuse," Paula quips. "I've gotten rid of men for doing far less."

My mother nervously looks around the room, and then turns and marches out to the hall to retrieve the groom. Graves brushes past me and sinks down into a chair, obviously upset about the delay. But seconds later Mead and my mother come bursting back into the room, waving his phone like a white flag of surrender.

"I'm turning it off!" he cries. "I'm so sorry! Won't happen again."

"You're rude," Gibson sneers at him. "It's your wedding rehearsal."

"I had to take it, it was a business call. Now where were we?"

"Go back up there and stand still." My mother gives Mead a playful push to propel him forward. He stops, though, when he notices that Graves is still sitting in silent protest. The music starts again, but father and son are locked in mortal combat and oblivious to its charms.

"You ready?" Mead asks.

Graves slowly stands and slowly steps forward and slowly retakes his position by me, all under the aghast gaze of the minister, who clutches his Bible like a shield. "Easy now," I whisper in Graves's ear, words of wisdom he shakes off as if they were flies buzzing around his head.

Soon my mother begins to walk slowly down the aisle, noticeably limping but still beaming in delight and unfazed by the lingering tension created by the interruption. Look at us all, tossed together like castaways on a desert isle! Mead's mother continues to emit a barrage of jarring ululations, while Mead himself has launched a hundred shady schemes of varying legality, and caught in the collateral damage are his two children, who don't seem able to stand on their own two feet. How did my poor mother end up here, joyous despite the obstacles that remain? Look at how bright her smile is, in stark contrast to the visage of indifference of her future husband . . . who really seems pained or perhaps bored . . . when my mother reaches him, he holds out his hand like a footman helping a dowager down from a carriage. A perfunctory gesture, a kindly one, but not loving in the way I imagine love to be. Which is what, exactly? What right do I have to pass judgment on a relationship, having botched all of mine? Not with Leigh Rose! That one I was getting right.

My mother stops suddenly and spins around.

"How does this look?" she asks, and the only people in the crowd with a clear view are Mead's mother (Dahlia!) and Beatrice. They don't answer, and so Sylvia stands up and goes over to get a better view of the dramaturgical elements of the ceremony. Ever the thorough critic, she stands at two different vantage points before rendering her verdict.

"It's beautiful," she declares with her hands clasped beneath her chin. This appraisal seems to appease my mother, who gazes beatifically at Mead, who in turn continues to stand as stiff as a corpse, more fly caught in a spider's web than man about to take a wife.

"Do you have your own vows or do you want me to use something more traditional?" the minister asks.

"The vows! We have our own."

My mother hurries over to her big shoulder bag that's perched on a chair and begins to paw through it. Why isn't Mead helping her? She's having trouble walking, and yet he keeps his distance from her. I wonder who called him on the phone . . . his ex-wife, whose existence is never spoken of but who hovers over these proceedings like an apparition? I never did ask my mother why she was having a panic attack in the parking lot of the restaurant where the woman works.

"I think I left them at home," she says, dejectedly tossing her bag onto the floor.

"Are you sure?" Mead asks.

"Did you bring a copy?"

"Was I supposed to?"

"It's no big deal," the minister gently interjects. "You can always e-mail them to me tonight or tomorrow morning, just to be on the safe side. But just to be clear, the vows are what comes next, right after the procession?"

"Maybe we should just use the traditional vows." My mother frowns. "You know, 'to have and to hold' and all that. It might be easier. The more I think about it, our vows were a little hippie-dippie. We were trying too hard to be different."

"Whatever you want," Mead quickly agrees.

"Can we try it once the traditional way, just so I can hear it?"

The minister is a seasoned pro and walks them through a very vanilla rendition that is quite familiar but still strangely moving. During high school my mother dated a few men, got her heart broken by one, but I never entertained the idea that she'd get married. But here she is, with-this-ring-I-thee-wed. Even though the traditional vows are hackneyed to the point of meaningless-ness, two people can become one; a loving spouse can ease life's burdens and fill in the empty spaces. Only a person who's been cast into the wilderness alone can fully appreciate the calming succor of a real partner, a soul mate who can soothe the savage beast.

"What do you think?" my mother asks Mead after the first read-through.

"Sounded fine to me. But I'll defer to you."

"It was flat. Something was missing. We should use our vows even if they're too over-the-top. Second weddings are all about tak-ing chances, huh?" She turns and faces her musicians. "Start the recessional right as we're turning to walk out. Let's try that one time."

At that very moment, a park ranger enters the room. The music stops, silence falls.

"Pardon the interruption," he says firmly but calmly, "but this building is being evacuated. If you'd all follow me, we'll make our way outside."

Mead's mother begins screeching like a barn owl as we gather our things. Turns out, someone has phoned in a bomb threat. Oh, and the choice for the recessional song: "The Long and Winding Road" by the Fab Four.

13

Only later at dinner we do learn that similar threats were simultaneously phoned into Chimborazo Park and the Museum of the Confederacy. Gibson discovers this unhappy news flash via Instagram while a waiter clears our table of dirty plates.

"What's Chimborazo Park?" she asks, for once joining in on the conversation instead of keeping her eyes fixed on a small screen.

"It was a big Confederate hospital," replies Dan. "It was actually very well organized and successful from a medical standpoint. In high school DJ volunteered there as a docent at the museum."

Oh yes, I remember that being thrown into my face, as I skipped from crappy job to crappy job. But who's laughing now? That's cruel of me. DJ never asked to be my yardstick and rival. Like his parents, he's never said a bad thing about another person, even when it was deserved.

"Who on earth would want to blow it up?" my mother blurts out, nearly knocking over her glass of wine as she wildly gestures her incredulity. "What's the world coming to? What if Tredegar is closed tomorrow, too? What are we supposed to do? We booked the site eight months ago."

"We'll have the wedding at our house," Mead claims in a deadpan. Serious proposal? Mock suggestion? Impossible to tell with him. No matter, my mother isn't buying it.

"We can't fit forty people in the living room!"

"Sure, we can. Second weddings are about taking chances."

"I don't want to clean the house on my wedding day. Oh my God, I think I'm going to faint."

My mother is drunk. Normally no son would divulge an unsavory detail about his mommy, but in this case her inebriation will have consequences, and will change the course of my story. I don't control these events . . . clearly the reverse is true. I'm the one being manipulated, followed, stalked, and threatened. Were it up to me, Leigh Rose and I would be on a plane bound for Paris and her lawyers would have already drawn up a prenup. As it is, I'm sitting at a big round table at the Tobacco Company, the bastion of Shockoe Slip, Richmond's oldest hip area ushered in during the initial phase of yuppie gentrification in the late 1970s. Before becoming a restaurant and bar, the building was a tobacco warehouse and still retains the rough brick walls to prove it.

"Is your mom okay?" Paula whispers to me.

"I've never seen her drink so much," I sheepishly admit, idly waving a fork at my steak, the first one I've ordered in about twelve years. The return of the carnivore perhaps heralds the arrival of a new version of self — one tough enough to take on Jeb Wardell and John Graziano. But the steak tastes horrible and I feel stupid for ordering it. I want to crawl under a rock and die. I'm grateful when the waiter removes the plate from my sight.

"It's from all the stress. I can relate."

"She's going to be hungover on her wedding day. The something-blue will be her gills if she doesn't slow down."

"I was so burnt out for both of mine! I think I was wheeled down the aisle in a gurney, with a saline IV to fight off the dehydration. Not a great way to begin a marriage."

"I eloped."

"Oh, how romantic . . . and simple. No muss, no fuss."

"My ex-wife wasn't big on ceremony."

"I almost flew to Vegas with a man to elope. He chickened out at the last minute. We were in a cab almost all the way to Dulles, and he just looked at me and said, 'This has all the makings of a bad idea.' And he was right. He was sleeping with about twenty different women at the time."

Normally a woman this candid and open would be someone I peppered with questions, eager to gobble up every overlooked detail. Instead I nod like a bobblehead figurine and try not to belch. Paula and I were expected to hit it off, since we're both single and well educated. I want to stress that there's nothing in the world wrong with Paula; it's just that I can withstand no more. Acute observers might accuse me of waiting a bit too long before applying the brakes. There's good reason to fault me for lacking self-reflection. I feel remorse, some might say, only because I've been caught. But that's a complete misunderstanding of my situation. Guilt has been with me every step of the way, not as a chide but as a coach, urging me on to new lows. Why can't I dismiss the confrontation at the Jefferson

Hotel? I had no future with Leigh Rose even before I "ran into" John Graziano . . . right? Or was our burgeoning love sabotaged by greedy hucksters out to gobble down her money?

"I hear you write books," Paula tries again, shrugging off my placid exterior and inability to chitchat. "Novels, correct?"

"Yes, guilty as charged."

"That takes some serious courage. I know I didn't have it. Law school was the only place for a bitch like me."

"Whereas law school would've eaten me alive."

"Are you writing anything now?"

She's interested in my writing career! Do you know how many nights since the divorce I longed for a woman I could just talk to about what's dearest to me? Now here she is in the flesh, taking great pains to include me in the conversation when she could just very well chatter on with Graves or Gibson or her brother or Sylvia, anyone else at the table . . . and yet I feel nothing. Just emptiness. "Not really," I mumble. "I'm between projects."

"It must be so hard to find the time and the energy. And the discipline it must take!"

I'd love to tell her all about my ironclad intestinal fortitude that consists mostly of

287

me wringing my hands in defeat, but before I can, Graves stands up to address us. At first I surmise that he's giving a toast, but apparently not.

"I just want to say good-bye to everyone," he announces with as much gaiety as he can muster, "but I need to go meet some friends who need my help. I'll see you guys tomorrow."

"You're leaving?" my mother cries in a voice rendered shrill with wine. In Graves's defense, it is almost nine o'clock and he didn't order dessert. Gibson is also looking a little bored as well. It's a miracle that the "kids" lasted this long.

"I've got somewhere to be. Don't worry, I'll be fine."

"No one's worried, Graves," Mead chimes in, cheeks puffed out in manly confidence and legs crossed at a jaunty angle. "We're just sorry to see you go. Who is it you're meeting up with?"

"Some people."

"Nameless people, I get it. One isn't Avery, is it?"

Graves recoils defensively, and then stiffens, jutting out his chin as if daring his father to take a swing. "Not just him. He might be there, I won't lie."

"Where are you going, exactly? What kind

of help do your friends need?"

"Don't interrogate the boy!" Aunt Paula intercedes, every inch the older-sister-cum-lawyer. "He's an adult and can make his own decisions."

Not wanting to stifle the buoyant mood of the dinner, or perhaps plied by an excess of wine as well, Mead relents and waves his progeny off with a dismissive flick of his wrist. Graves bows and then takes his leave, hurrying out before his father changes his mind. In his wake, Gibson's mouth drops, stung by the unfairness of her brother's escape while she remains chained to the grown-ups table, sitting across from Dan and Sylvia, who've been ladling out friendly advice by the gallon. She looks to have had her fill.

"I need to go, too," she says with a decided lack of specificity.

"No dessert?" my mother brays. She is officially hammered. Her eyes have become cross-eyed and she seems to be listing in her seat, about to topple over any minute.

"Excuse me," I say to Paula, hopping to my feet and going over to my mother, who takes my hand and kisses it.

"I'm so glad you came! Isn't this fun? Isn't it?"

"Are you getting tired?"

"Isn't Paula pretty? She's so pretty. So, so pretty."

"Maybe I can take you home? Do you think that's a good idea?"

"Leave?" my mother sighs in exasperation. "We haven't had dessert. What's wrong with everyone tonight? Did you talk to Graves? How did he seem to you? He really isn't the same kid. He's always so angry. You were never angry. You were such a sweet boy. Are you dating anyone? Oh, Eddie, have you ever thought about moving back to Richmond? You seem so unhappy up there in Ithaca. Maybe I'm wrong but I think you could use a change of scenery."

I don't have the heart to tell her that indeed changes are looming for me. "I'm getting tired," I tell her, faking a yawn. "Yesterday just about did me in. We should go soon."

"Why did they call in those bomb threats? Who's behind it? Do we know yet?"

"No. Chances are, it's just a group of radicals who want attention." The acolytes of Gramsci, out to foment revolution among a somnambulant populace — I should be attempting to link up with them, not dismissing their subversion.

"They're cowards, is what. They'd better not ruin my wedding day! Or they'll have real trouble on their hands."

I step over and tap Mead lightly on the shoulder. He spins around and seems stunned to see me, and I halfway expect him to raise his hands in surrender. I quickly explain the situation and we quickly formulate a plan. I'll take Gibson and my mother home, and he'll get his sister and mother (and her nurse) to their hotel. I volunteer to go get my car, which is parked several blocks away, so that my mother won't have to stagger over the cobblestones with her bum knee.

Before leaving, I say good-bye to Dan and Sylvia, two decent people who've held on to the moral center of the universe while the rest of us long ago let go. I'm sorry I didn't get a chance to speak more with them, but we promise to catch up tomorrow at the reception. "DJ's coming and he's bringing the boys," Sylvia announces excitedly.

"Great. I look forward to seeing him."

"He's always asking about you, you know, whether you've published a book yet."

"Not yet. Not in this universe anyway." Politely Sylvia chuckles, but we both understand all too well that disappointment chokes me like kudzu.

"We just got back from a mission to Haiti," Dan jumps in, and I know that he can spend hours describing the incredible work he does there, but my mother is literally about to put a lampshade on her head.

"I really need to go," I cut in, before Dan begins his heroic narration. I give Paula a wave, and then she bounds up from her chair to catch up with me. My heart leaps into my throat. When females pursue me, I usually find a way to screw it up. Once in Prague, where I spent a semester on a Fulbright, I was walking across the Charles Bridge on a moonlit night, the River Vltava sparkling in dreamy iridescence, when I ran into another American scholar, a specialist on Czech birth control issues — talk about getting served on a silver platter! She invited me back to her flat just off Wenceslas Square, and all I had to do was play it cool and let her research interests act as an aphrodisiac — but we ended up having an argument about Lacan's notion of Otherness — there was a time when I never, ever considered the possibility that I could be wrong! Such heady times! To be so in love with yourself!

"Is anything going on later?" Paula asks me hopefully.

"I'm not sure. I've got to take my mother home." And then deal with my sort-of girlfriend who's out to destroy me. Or try to find the woman I fell in love with buying shoes. Or flee from the police who must be minutes away. One thing I cannot do is make love to you, Paula. The arrogant boy-king of Prague is long dead. Or is he? Because I really can't help myself . . . "But I might want to see some music later if you're up for it."

"Yeah! For sure! Let me know if you're headed out. I'll give you my number. I could really use a fun night."

"Cool." I fish out my phone and input the numbers she rattles off. Then I finally head for the exit. But a hand on my shoulder detains me.

"Hey, what are you doing?"

It's Gibson, who looks like the spitting image of Scarlett Johansson in a strapless white dress that displays the ample curves of her shapely form. Every man in the restaurant is gawking at her as we walk toward the exit. Many must think I'm the luckiest dude in Richmond tonight — if they only knew the truth.

"I'm going to get the car," I tartly explain.

"I want out, too."

"Come on. There's not a second to spare."

We leave, my head filled with bile and bad premonitions. Gibson must sense my ill humor and tries to cheer me up the only way she knows how.

"We can get really stoned," she sings once we're outside.

"I'm not in a very festive mood, I'm afraid."

"Why not? What's bugging you? You can tell me."

"It's hard to explain."

"Is it Paula? You didn't like her?"

"I liked her, she seems incredible."

"So what is it then?"

My car is parked at the bottom of Main Street, in a pay lot staffed by a hooligan who looked like he just got out of prison. For all I know, my Honda is at a chop shop in Mechanicsville. My mind will give me no rest tonight. "I told you, it's kind of difficult to put into words."

"Your mom thinks you're in some kind of trouble."

"What?"

"That's what she was saying on the drive over to the restaurant. She's really worried about you. She thinks you've really changed."

"Everyone changes. It's inevitable."

"She thinks your wife is messing with you."

"Ex-wife. And she isn't."

"I think you should get really, really

stoned with me. That's what I think."

"Well, when you're eighteen, that fixes every problem."

"Duh. Because it does."

"Said the person who just got out of rehab."

"It was court-ordered."

"Meaning what? It didn't count?"

"It was total horse shit! Oh my God, those people in rehab made me want to get high every day I was there."

The capital city is raucous tonight, even as the stifling heat saps every last drop of moisture from our bodies. Night doesn't bring relief but a darker complexion of aridity. I couldn't cry if I wanted to. My mouth is already parched from the short downhill stroll to the parking lot beneath the interstate overpass. Drunken revelers shout at Gibson, and she shoots the finger at one obnoxious kid cruising by in an old Mazda. Brake lights flash on and the car abruptly stops. The kid leaning out of the window jumps out and with arms extended glares menacingly and advances toward us.

"Why you got to be so mean, baby?" he says. He's thin and wiry, not tall, a shirtless rack of ribs. It looks like a gun is sticking out of the front of his drooping shorts. Horns blare as the traffic grinds to a halt.

"Go away," Gibson hisses at him.

He grabs his crotch. "Come get some."

"There's nothing to get."

This random scuffle has all the makings for a senseless slaughter. She's questioned his manhood, and he's got a gun. Any second he'll start firing away. I leap in front of Gibson, more than happy to take a bullet for her. But it turns out my valor was unnecessary as the kid spews more venomous insults and then jumps back into the car, which speeds off toward the Poe Museum.

"That was fun," I quip once the danger has passed. "I guess you get that a lot."

"What?"

"Guys hassling you."

"I guess so. Especially from the idiots who come down here."

Even the parking lot attendant gets into the act and tells Gibson how pretty she looks tonight, his voice dripping with lascivious intent. I admit to feeling protective of her, since she possesses the kind of ineffable beauty that makes men behave like beasts. I want to whisk her into the Honda and shield her from this unfeeling world. Together with my drunken mother, I'll ferry these vulnerable women to safety. But there are still two more I worry about, their whereabouts unknown — Leigh Rose and

Lola, one trapped, the other in hot pursuit — and both symptoms of a deeper problem I can't fix.

Mead is waiting with my mother outside the restaurant. I pull up, Gibson hops into the back, and my mother wobbles into the passenger's seat. Mead gives her a peck on the top of the head like he's seeing a toddler off to preschool, and then we depart.

"Wasn't Paula pretty?" my mother asks, as if she can formulate only one thought, that of setting me up with a woman.

"I already agreed she was."

"Smart too. Beauty and brains. Oh, why did I drink so much? I never drink this much! Now Mead's mad at me."

"He's always mad," Gibson chimes in from the rear.

The voice startles my mother, who whips her head around and then back again like her skull is rotating on a broken axle. "Why is she here?" my mother asks as though Gibson can't hear her.

"I was bored," she huffs.

"You're always bored."

"That's not true," I interject, earning a guffaw of rebuke.

"She says she is, all the time!"

"I do not!"

I put the radio on and expect my old

favorite, XL102, to come on, but my settings are for Ithaca stations and so static fills the car. We crawl along Main Street, thronged with motorists and pedestrians. At one point I knew all the navigational shortcuts to avoid the traffic, but now I'm stuck like the rubes from the sticks who seldom venture into the big, bad city. Once I find the radio station, some crappy "alternative" song comes on (Papa Roach, I think), but it seems to quiet everyone down. Gibson tells me to take a right and then a left, and soon we're on Franklin Street and in the clear. My mother falls to sleep with the profundity of a heroin addict, and I can tell by the ghoulish glow emanating behind me that Gibson is on her phone. All is well, so it seems.

"Can you drop me off somewhere?" Gibson suddenly asks, as we approach the intersection at Lombardy Street. "Please, please, please! We've got a gig tonight!"

"Seriously?" I don't want to accuse her of lying, especially about anything relating to music, which she knows I consider sacred. My mother actually stirs a little, as if trying to send me a message from the depths of her alcohol-induced stupor. Maybe I should wake her up and ask if Gibson has permission. But she seems out of it, so I'll have to make the call. Looks like another episode of *Pervert Knows Best.*

"Where are you playing? What time do you go onstage?"

"At the Dungeon. It's on Broad Street. Like in an hour we can get onstage."

"Broad and what cross street?" The light turns green and I accelerate, once again confronted by a half-baked entreaty from this mercurial young woman whose plans change by the minute. My resolve, however, has worn thin, and I don't feel much fight left in me. If Gibson wants to ruin the weekend by traipsing off with whatever coterie of lowlife she desires, I can't stop her. Hell, maybe I'll go check out her band myself . . . with Paula. Oh my God, make it stop . . .

"Broad and Allen. I think it's near here."

"How will you get home?"

"I can get a ride. Oh, thank you, thank you, thank you! You just made me the happiest person in the world."

"Don't mention it." The truth is, I live to make young women joyous, whether through grade inflation, harmless flirting, or sordid decrepitude (if they're so inclined).

"Graves just texted me. He is so weird."

"What did he say?"

"He said I need to be careful tonight."

"That's pretty good advice, especially for you."

"I've got more common sense than he does. There's Allen, take a right."

I put on my blinker and ease over to the turn lane. As soon as we round the corner, a huge statue comes into view — that of General Robert E. Lee, towering sixty feet over us like a backlit god, regal in the night, still offering the hope of victory to a defeated people. In an interesting twist, I actually find the Lee statue somewhat noble, even elegant, which is hilarious because I know that these impressions spring from my contrarian mood and are intended to counteract Bev's heated dislike of all things Confederate, especially the statues on Monument Avenue.

A huge traffic circle takes me around the fenced-off statue that sits on a parklike enclosure, and at that moment it's crystal clear that I'm no longer myself. Something fundamental has changed within me, a gear has shifted and is now stuck, and I'm speeding along a highway the destination of which remains hidden from me. I shouldn't be dropping Gibson off at some sleaze bar but I am, acting against my better judgment.

"It's around here somewhere," Gibson says once we reach Broad Street, at one time Richmond's grand avenue but parts of it remain mired in urban decay, such as this block appears to be. I understand that this is the kind of downtrodden environs where subaltern music blooms, but letting Gibson out here, attired in that dress, near a small deployment of winos and street detritus, strikes me as unduly dangerous. But I do so anyway.

"There it is!" she calls out, too loudly.

I pull over in front of the Lucky 13 Tattoo Parlor. The Dungeon looks like it's situated in the basement, hence its name, and a burly bouncer is perched on a bar stool though no one waits in line to enter. When the car stops, my mother awakens for a brief second but then falls back into slumber. Gibson hops out and promises to be home "at a decent hour." Luckily the wedding isn't until the late afternoon, and so she has plenty of wiggle room.

"Maybe I'll come down and catch your set," I tell her, earning a quizzical look.

"Okay, if you want to."

"If you don't mind."

"No, that's cool. They said an hour but who knows. The owners aren't very organized."

Some wraithlike guys carry musical instruments into the club, and I can tell Gibson is eager to join them. I wave her off and then drive away, speeding down Broad Street, eventually passing the old train station, an enormous building that resembles a Greek temple but now is home to a science museum. The only Amtrak station I ever used was located in a tiny little hut next to nowhere in Henrico County, a place without grandeur or romance. During college I would hop on a train bound for Gotham to go see music and generally bop around the Village, where I'd pick out my future apartment. But it never came to pass, did it? Never did make it to NYC after all. But I've got no regrets . . .

Liar, liar, pants on fire!

How many regrets can one man possibly have? I'd need a large suitcase to lug them all around. Or cargo shorts from the Gap.

"Where's Mead?" my mother groggily asks.

"He's driving his mother to the hotel."

"Is he mad at me?"

"He didn't seem mad."

"He gets so mad and I try so hard."

"Maybe you should think twice about what you're doing. You could be rushing things. I don't see why you need to be in such a hurry. If you have doubts, now is the time to question. Don't you think? I don't mean to be such a jerk — because I want you to be happy — that's all I care about."

I nervously wait for her reply, hands trembling as I grip the steering wheel — there, I've done it. I've spoken. I've officially butted in and now she'll weep and I've ruined the entire weekend. How could I be so thoughtless? What is wrong with me?

At the next red light I glance over at her and see that her eyes are closed. She's got a beatific smile on her sleeping face, indicating inner harmony. I'm guessing my words fell on deaf ears. She literally didn't hear me. A reprieve of sorts. It would prove to be my last.

14

We arrive home fifteen minutes later, with my mother awakening at the sound of my tires rolling over the gravel in the driveway. She blinks a few times to orient herself and then remains still even after I park.

"Did I make a fool of myself?"

"No, don't be ridiculous. You were bubbly and cute and a gracious hostess."

"I drank too much," she chides herself in misery. "I never do but I did tonight. I'm so stupid."

"You're home now, and it's still early. You can take a shower, have some green tea, and you'll be fit as a fiddle by the morning's first light." Edwin the Optimist, always looking on the bright side! Making lemons out of lemonade!

"Why is the garage door open?"

I focus my gaze on the house and notice that indeed the garage door hasn't been closed all the way, leaving a foot-wide gap from the concrete floor. Instantly I'm re-minded of the first of the times we were robbed, the crime being detected in the same manner, except my mother had been driving and I sat in the passenger's seat. The thieves had smashed a window in the side door and let themselves in. They stole some jewelry and a gun my mother had purchased for protection.

History might be repeating itself, as there are guns galore in the basement.

"Stay here," I tell her, adrenaline flowing like lava as my brain responds to the percep-tion of danger, a biochemical reaction older than humanity and thus one of the most authentic experiences a mammal undergoes. Too often I get confused and never know what is or isn't real, a common problem for academics. Not now.

"I told him this would happen!" she cries in anguish, already fearing the worst, which is another trait we share, along with our love of hats. The one I need to doff now is a Sherlock Holmes deerstalker. The intrepid detective must use his powers of reasoning to crack the case.

"Let me go scope out the situation. Stay here until the coast is clear."

"We should call the police."

"Just hold on a minute. I'll be right back."

"Eddie, don't do anything stupid. These people Mead deals with, they're bad. I don't trust them. Especially that Russian man. He was so rude!"

"You don't want the cops sniffing around here with all the stuff Mead's stored in the basement. Some of it might not be entirely legal. So one step at a time. Let me go check it out and then we'll plan our next step."

For some odd reason, more along the lines of a hunch, I suspect that Lola has had a hand in this devilment. She doesn't know my Richmond address, but she is a skilled online data collector who'll stop at nothing to gather all the dirt on someone she thinks has wronged her. At any one time she might be holding six or seven different grudges, and assembling a dossier of damnation if she should ever need the ammo to retaliate. After one spat, for example, she'd unearthed the restraining order Bev had taken out against me — that's something I haven't yet mentioned, for the simple reason that I'm deeply ashamed of it. Not that Lola found it off-putting. No, no: in her febrile post-adolescent brain she thought my inexcusable behavior was romantic, even sexy. *I didn't know you could get so passionate! I'd love to see that side of you, Edwin. You don't seem to care about anything or anyone like you cared about your ex-wife.* Lola enjoyed saying the phrase "ex-wife" because it made her feel all grown-up. But she was also correct in her analysis: only Bev could generate enough electricity to power my lifeless soul. Only Bev could cause me to pick up a lamp, her favorite lamp, the lamp I'd brought back from Prague for her, and smash it into a million little pieces at her feet, resulting in a well-deserved restraining order. And should Bev ever turn up dead, that restraining order will be exhibit A in the case of *The State of New York v. Edwin Stith.*

Slowly, like a two-toed sloth, I walk down the driveway to the garage. The fact is, no strange cars are parked in the driveway or nearby that I've noticed, though Lola knows better than to tip her hand. Whoever was here is probably gone, but the question is: what did they take? All of it? Some? Did Fyodor Ublyudok come to claim his purchase — or was the phone call Mead had to take during the rehearsal a vow to collect, no matter what?

Once I get close enough so that I can see through the gap, I sink down to my knees and use my cell phone as a flashlight. Right off I can discern that the boxes and crates remain. I don't know if they've been emptied of their contents, but the weapons would be hard to move otherwise.

So will Lola hop out now and shout *Boo!*? I wait, expecting her to attack. Crickets chirp nearby, and a dog howls in the distance. Maybe I'm giving her too much credit. It's also possible that someone forgot to close the garage door all the way and lock it. If you don't lock it, it will slide up.

I stand back up, sweating profusely but somewhat relieved that this situation didn't call for an emergency response. Still, I want to check out the house before I allow my mother to go inside. I walk over to tell her this, and I find her on the phone and speaking in a hushed tone.

"It's Mead," she tells me anxiously, now a sober drunk who hangs suspended between the two worlds, alert but not quite. "He wants you to go check on something."

"Sure. I was going to go through the whole house."

"He said you know what he means by the Giap pistol?"

"Right. He showed me that earlier."

"Can you go check if it's still there?"

I have no problem doing that, but I do immediately question why Mead would harbor suspicions about that particular gun. He must have a suspect in mind, an entire scenario, and I'd love to ask him who or why, but there isn't time. So for now Lola appears to be off the hook, though her arrival is imminent . . . so many meteors hurdling toward us!

Back at the garage door, I'm about to lift it up and duck in when I stop to consider a salient question — how did anyone gain entrance without breaking in? The side door appears to be locked — it is, I quickly check — meaning I'll need to run upstairs and do the same for the front and back doors — because as of now, this is looking like an inside job, perpetrated by someone with a key. Or who knows where the spare is hidden (beneath a rock in the front garden).

The garage door furls up, automatically turning on an overhead light. Before taking a step in, I wait for any strange sounds or movements. An arresting stillness greets me, the calm after the storm. I make my way directly to the box where the Giap pistol is kept, and I find it opened, with the gun missing. Mead was right. This in no way solves the mystery, but deepens it further. Before reporting this news, however, I gallop upstairs to determine the question of a forced versus unforced entry, and not surprisingly I ascertain that both front and back doors are locked at the dead bolt, all the windows are shut and latched, and the house shows no other signs of robbery. Whoever came in knew exactly what they wanted and took only that, leaving a host of expensive and easily pawned items behind.

Graves George, come on down!

There's no reason to sugarcoat it. At this point he's the most likely culprit, but I've taken great pains to show you that I'm suffering from various mental lapses, that I'm an inveterate liar, and that I have my own secrets to keep . . . so don't hold your breath waiting for some neat ending that will tie up all the loose threads. At some point I'll just stop, when I run out of lies and am left with only the truth, which is usually too terrible for most of us to confront.

I hurry back down to the driveway so that I can deliver the grim news to my mother. She relates my intelligence to her almost-hubby and then listens to a lengthy disquisition back from him, nodding and repeating "Okay" in a halting voice. Finally she gets off the phone, which she drops in her lap as if it weighs a few tons. "He said he'll be home soon and take care of it," she says quietly, perhaps because she's as confused as I am.

"Take care of what? Who does he think took it?"

"He didn't say. I'm tired, Eddie."

I help her out of the car and walk with her into the house, entering through the basement because the garage door is still wide open. I close and lock it after we get inside, which is itself curious. Graves must know by now that the garage door will rise up if not locked, and so whoever exited through it didn't lock it, not knowing about this flaw. Meaning? I don't know . . . someone had a key? A door was left unlocked?

My mother trudges up the stairs and I follow behind, determined again to be Mr. Bright Side, but it's hard to see how lemonade will get produced from this crop of lemons. She has imbibed not only too much wine tonight, but also too much whine, from Mead, his children, herself. The person who broke in tonight took more than a vintage gun; my mother's happiness also has gone missing. She stands at the kitchen sink and lets the water run, staring at it uncomprehendingly, and I offer to make her some tea.

"Where's Gibson?" she asks instead of answering. I pick up the kettle and fill it, then turn off the faucet.

"I dropped her off at a club because her band is going to perform tonight."

"She's using drugs again. She'll never learn."

I turn a burner to high and place the kettle on it. "Music can be a very therapeutic outlet. In case you haven't noticed, Gibson is quite pretty and I can see her making it. She also seems very determined."

"It's her mother's fault. She never set any boundaries for those children and by the time Mead got them, it was too late."

"The mom, his ex-wife, she lives in Richmond?"

"I suppose."

"And she works at O'Bloom's?"

She turns away from me rather guiltily, but it wasn't my intention to get all Perry Mason on her. I'm the last person who'd ever cast aspersions at someone for odd behavior, such as showing up at places where the ex might be. I know she's ashamed, and shame is like bleach: it can cleanse or it can deface, depending on the amount. "That's not the only reason I was there," she admits, sinking down into a chair at the table. "I happened to be in the area, and I thought I saw his car. It's hard to miss that car. Then I couldn't breathe, and so I called you."

"Which explains why you couldn't call him."

"I wasn't snooping on him. I trust him. He's very honest and he's never lied to me about anything."

Honest people scare me. Honest people like to tell the truth, even if it means crushing someone's heart. Honest people disdain guilt and feel so much better after they've confessed, leaving the rest of us to clean up the mess. How long would the world last if everyone tried to be honest? Ten seconds? Does this dress make my ass look big? Are you having an affair? Did you kill your ex-wife? If the human species evolved to be an honest one, then why is our frontal cortex so immense and capable of inventing entire landscapes that are utterly false? Why do we dream? Unreality is as crucial to us as oxygen. "I'll defer to your wisdom," I say, getting down two mugs from a cabinet.

"She's very pretty. She looks just like Gibson."

The green-eyed monster, rearing its ugly head. How did you deal with your own jealousy, Edwin? In a healthy way? How many hours did you spend googling "Igor Nemsky" in the hopes of finding something incriminating or revealing or even better titillating, perhaps a testimonial from an old girlfriend describing his prowess in bed? "She isn't his wife anymore, but after tomorrow you will be."

"Unless Tredegar gets blown up first."

The water begins to boil, causing the kettle to hiss ever so slightly. I turn off the burner and fill the mugs. I locate two bags of green tea and let them steep. Of course I've been thinking of that strange flyer I found among Graves's laundry, the one vowing to bring "da funk" to Richmond, courtesy of the Bastard Sons. Is "da funk" they had in mind akin to a neo–Weather Underground communiqué? The Weathermen bombed multiple buildings and blew themselves up as well, but I don't know that the Bastard Sons even exist. Still, maybe it's time to take a harder look at Graves, now that the gun is missing and landmarks are being evacuated.

"Do you think Graves took that gun?" I ask, careful not to sound overly hostile. My mother needs no more weight added to her burden.

"No. I think the Russian did. There were problems, apparently, with the money and the freight costs."

"How did he get inside? There's no sign of a break-in."

"I don't know. I still think the police should be involved but apparently I'm the only one who does." This strikes me as perfectly reasonable, but we both know the authorities won't be called in, which leads me to consider the problem from a different angle.

"Why can't Graves associate with Avery?"

This question sends a jolt through my mother's slumped body. But secrets revealed carry a potency strong enough to raise the dead. "Why do you ask that? Was he here?"

"Can you tell me why first?"

"If he was here, we must know that. Avery is a very disturbed person who really needs to be monitored. Was he here at the house?"

"When I arrived last night, I saw Graves saying good-bye to somebody and he asked me not to mention it."

"Eddie! How could you do that?"

That is a great question that could apply to any number of episodes in my life. In many ways, it's the ultimate question that defies easy analysis . . . or does it? Perhaps the explanation is straightforward: I'm a creep. But my mother won't accept that verdict, and so I must grope for causation because reasons must exist for everything. She deserves better, though. I've failed her like I have everyone else.

"I was exhausted from the trip, and we'd just met. Graves seemed like a normal person, whatever that means. So did Avery, for that matter. And the next thing I know, Graves asked me not to say anything about

315

his friend stopping by. I didn't want to bring everyone down — remember when the RPG was supposed to be missing? I was going to mention it then, but the RPG was found and I took Graves shopping. It was stupid and wrong, but I just wanted the weekend to go off without a hitch. Who was I to jump into the middle of a family squabble? It had been years since I stepped foot inside this house. I didn't think I had the right."

My mother refrains from jumping on me and instead takes her mug of tea and sips it. My hands are shaking too much for me to lift mine. I need to calm down, gather myself, forge ahead . . .

"So now we know where Graves is and why he left," she offers stoically. "Maybe I'm overreacting. It's just Graves used to be a very sweet kid who wanted to make the world a better place — but then something in him snapped and people like Avery started hanging around, spewing all kinds of garbage about revolution. We decided that someone like Avery wasn't welcome in our home."

"Graves seems to be in a very apocalyptic phase right now."

"I think Mead's home."

She jumps up from the kitchen table and strides over to a window in the dining room just in time for headlights from an approaching car to shine through the sheer curtains. I'm in no mood to see my future stepfather, and I've pretty much reached my limit for the evening as far as recriminations go. This mess isn't entirely of my making — others are, but this one belongs mostly to my mother, who's making a disastrous choice with her life. I don't need Mead grilling me about Graves or Avery or Gibson, and so I hurry down to the basement under the pretense of having to use the bathroom. The dark cool is a welcome tonic to combat the relentless heat that not even air-conditioning can combat.

Then my phone rings. The caller ID reveals that it's . . . Lola. She always seems to find me in my most desperate hour, displaying an uncanny knack of exploiting my wounds for her amusement. She'd better appreciate the hell she's put me through. But instead she drops the biggest bomb of all.

"I'm here," she announces. "What a pain-in-the-ass drive that was."

"Here? Where's here?"

"In your stupid hometown."

"You're in Richmond? Lola, this is madness. You shouldn't have come here." I pause, though, because the truth is much

317

more nuanced. "I'm glad you did. Where are you?"

"In a crappy hotel."

"Which crappy hotel?"

"Why do you care?"

"Because we need to talk."

Silence, perhaps the most deafening sound I've ever heard in my life. Its maddening cacophony burns my ears and I wince in pain, wishing she would speak. In an act of mercy, she clears her throat, ending the torment. "About what?"

"About us."

"Us? There's an us? Since when was there ever an us?"

I wish I could record her making that same declaration in case I need it for the coming deposition. Not that my defense would ever stand up in a court of law. No us, Dear One? You deny even that? You've already drained the swamp and allowed the muck to bake beneath the sun?

"Okay, we just need to talk about what's going on. That's why you drove down here, right?"

"I drove down here because I was bored out of my mind."

"Oh, is that so? Judging from the photos you sent me, you didn't seem bored."

"Oh, him. Seen one, seen 'em all. How

many times do I have to tell you that?"

"Where are you?"

"Oh my God, this bed feels like it's made out of concrete."

"What's the name of the hotel?"

"Do you even care that I love you?"

"You don't love me."

"That's true. How could I ever love someone like you? You're basically a pervert pretending to be a college professor. How gross is that?"

"Just tell me where you are and I'll be there before you find the ice machine."

"Let's meet somewhere. This place sucks. It smells like bleach mixed with urine."

"Why did you pick some dump? We have decent hotels in the capital city of Virginia."

"It was cheap and a girl has to mind her budget. So tell me where you'll be tonight and I'll find you when you least expect it."

Ah, one of her favorite games, Hide-and-Go-Seek, culminating in the Surprise Attack. Showing up unannounced at my apartment gave her untold delight, and even when I protested that these rash intrusions were risky, even dangerous, she laughed with the delirium of a lunatic. The converse also seemed to thrill her — not being where she said she'd be, causing me to wait in vain or roam the lonely streets of Ithaca looking for her. Anything that caused me duress excited her ganglia.

I get an idea. How about going to Gibson's gig? With Lola? That's probably one I should jettison, but the words come tumbling out anyway.

"I was probably going to check out a band at this club called the Dungeon. It's on Broad Street."

"Like I know what Broad Street is."

"It's a major road, Route 250, runs right through downtown. You can't miss it. The cross street is Allen, I think."

"I hooked up with a guy named Allen once. He was slightly above average, but pretty thick. Good stamina."

"Thanks for the update."

"No problem. I'll meet you there. The Dungeon. I like the sound of that. Is it a swingers' club?"

"No, it's not. Are you sure you don't want to talk first? It'll be loud in there and hard to hear each other."

"I love loud places, you know that."

"Yeah, but I'm confused. Why did you come down here? That's a long drive just to hang out with a perverted professor roughly twice your age."

Here she pauses. I can picture the naughty smile she likes to flash. "I've got a surprise for you."

"A surprise?"

"A big surprise."

Mucus thickens in my throat like brown gravy and I worry that I'll choke on my own disgust. She knows she holds all the cards in this "relationship" and can foist upon me any humiliation that springs from her feverish imagination. I don't want a big surprise or any surprise; I just want her to leave me alone to live out my days in quiet obscurity.

"I hate surprises."

"You'll love this one."

"I seriously doubt it."

"It's what you've always wanted."

"A clean conscience?"

"You can't find one of those on craigslist! Which is where I found my gift to you. And he is special."

So Lola has gone online to search out a new lover, apparently for my benefit, and I want to vomit. I really do. I never intended to put myself or her in this situation, and I'm trying to do all I can to make it right. I never asked her to come here. She did so on her own volition, but now she's upped the ante. She found a guy on craigslist? On the weekend of my mother's wedding? "Lola, honestly, I feel sick to my stomach right now."

"I'll send you his picture. That'll cure you."

"No! Please don't! Lola, we really need to talk. Where are you staying?"

"You're no fun. You used to be so fun but now you're a huge downer. You're getting old, ya know. You have gray pubic hair, in case you haven't noticed."

"I don't look in that area of my body anymore. Just tell me the name of the hotel. We really need to sort this out."

She sighs in fake resignation. "This craphole is called the Chicory. It's next to a TGI Fridays." Well well well . . . I've heard of the Chicory Motel, though I can't remember quite where it is. And another TGI Fridays beckons me. The Gettysburg police must be dolts, because I haven't heard one peep from them.

"I'll find it. See you soon."

She ends the call with no good-bye. She never offers parting words but just dashes off to whatever stimulus happens to catch her eye. It's quite odd, how she's handling this spontaneous visit. I still don't know if she's actually here. None of her texts include her current location, and so the possibility remains that she's playing some elaborate game with me while still ensconced in Dahlia's dorm room back in

322

Ithaca and is sending me on a wild-goose
chase. I wouldn't put it past her.

15

I quickly type "Chicory Motel Richmond" into my search engine and up it pops, located on Robin Hood Road in the city's northern quarter along I-95. It would be a likely stop for a college student who would just pull over once they got close to the destination.

Chicory also happens to be Lola's favorite flower.

We saw one lovely blue clump along our first walk to Buttermilk Falls — we were normal then — at least as normal as I could be with anyone her age. Lola knew so much about these plants, such as how well they grow in nutrient-poor soils and how they bloom just once per day. *Kind of like me,* was her attempt at self-reflection. According to Lola, chicory proves that something beautiful can emerge from ugliness, and even cracked sidewalks can house a natural wonder.

We held hands, we kissed, we lounged on rocks like lizards, snacking on pita chips and gurgling back cheap wine. If I could freeze any moment of my life, that would be the one.

Maybe we can settle things between us. All might not be lost, unless Dahlia has reported me to the dean. In which case it's over for me. At that point I don't know, I really don't.

What to wear? Lola likes it when I dress up — if I wear a jacket and tie around her, she is liable to turn into a tigress. The more professorial my appearance, the more aroused she becomes. Colleagues have noticed that during the past semester my attire has matured. Gone are the frayed cargo shorts and ripped T-shirts, replaced by tweed or cardigan, often selected by Lola herself. Dressing me in the morning was a hobby for her. Not that she slept over much, because Dahlia would get suspicious, Dahlia the infidel, Lola's corrupter . . . it was, after all, Dahlia who set up Lola's first three-some, with the starting power forward on the basketball team (which had a losing record, I might add), and it was Dahlia who procured all subsequent partners for their amorous entanglements. Not to say Lola didn't conduct her own recon missions, starting with frat boys from Cornell before moving on to our own campus, eventually targeting students from classes I was teaching, such as Thor . . . but by now she has to realize that we can't continue. Surely she's more reasonable than that. I'll let her down gently, blame myself, beg her not to ruin my career . . .

I guess the clothes I have on will suffice, though she likes my blue blazer least of all, as it reminds her of her father, a domineering sort under whose thumb Lola lived in a tightly circumscribed world. He didn't allow her to date boys in high school and kept her to an eleven o'clock curfew, thereby unleashing a very embittered and naïve maiden upon the sybaritic excess that is today's private liberal arts college. Carter LaSalle should have known better, but perhaps his own peccadilloes motivated him to clamp down on his daughter — after all, years before I ever encountered Lola, I'd heard rumors coming from the theater department that Professor LaSalle had turned Preston Hall into a brothel in which he was the sole client, all under the nose of his adoring wife. Tsk-tsk. At one point Bev asked if any students had ever thrown themselves at me, and I told her that only a fool would risk so much for so little. While we were married, I ignored at least five lusty females, all graduating seniors, who basically issued me a blank slate to ravish them at my leisure. Not once — do you hear me, Bev? — not once did I indulge. And still she divorced me, virtuous Eddie.

I must tell my mother of my plans so that she won't worry if she learns I'm gone, and so I dutifully troop upstairs and find her and Mead conversing in the kitchen. By the sound of their voices, things have settled down somewhat.

"There he is," says Mead. "Sorry you got dragged into all of this nonsense. I swear things aren't usually this nuts around here."

I doubt that, but hold my tongue. "No word from Graves?"

"Nothing. First thing in the morning, all the stuff in the basement is going into storage. I'm renting a U-Haul truck and I'm hoping you can lend me a hand if you're not busy."

"Sure thing." I'd rather get a root canal than abet his quasi-criminal enterprise. Saying no isn't an option, however.

"Thanks, Eddie! You're the best!" My mother beams with pride.

"It shouldn't take long," Mead continues. "An hour, tops. I should've done it a long time ago but I had my own selfish reasons

not to. You live and you learn, right? Hey —
my sister really liked you. She thought you
were a total hoot."

"Oh, great. She was a cool chick, no
doubt."

"Are you going back out?" my mother asks
hopefully. "Maybe you should call her and
invite her along. She just got out of a bad
relationship."

"The worst!" Mead adds. "The guy
treated her horribly."

"He was very full of himself."

This is a hard sell. It's like I'm buying a
used car with lots of mileage but with a
good maintenance record. What the heck,
I'll take Paula for a test drive. Lola loves
complications. Makes the game that much
more interesting for her.

"I was thinking of seeing Gibson's band.
Paula is welcome to join me if she's into
that kind of thing."

"Gibson's band, huh?" Mead shakes his
head warily. "You're a braver man than me,
Eddie. You can't pay me to watch that. I
don't know about Paula. She tends to be a
bit more adventurous than the rest of the
family."

"Even the Beatles had to start somewhere."

"I'm sure Paula will think it's sweet of you

to ask her," my mother gushes. Somehow, despite the odds, we've become one big happy family. Not even David Copperfield could've pulled off that illusion, and ours promises to be just as fake as one of his schmaltzy Vegas shows.

"I love to support live music and local bands, and since Gibson is family . . . why not?"

"Be careful," my mother cautions as I take my leave. "Things seem crazy tonight and I just want everyone home safe and sound."

"I won't be too late."

"That's right!" Mead chuckles. "We'll be up at the crack of dawn and ready to move some cargo."

My mother rushes over and gives me a hug with the lachrymose intensity of someone whose son is about to hang from the gallows. "Thanks again, Eddie. I'm sure everything's going to work out."

"Good night!" I call out before making haste to the Honda. I don't want to keep Lola waiting, because her idle hands will do the devil's work. Robin Hood Road is a good twenty minutes away, so I need to rush. My route to the Chicory Motel and Lola takes me first to Cherokee Road, meaning I'll drive directly past John Graziano's house — or to be more precise, the one he grew up in. There's no way he still lives with his parents. It takes me five minutes to reach this unremarkable residence, and I'm disappointed that there's no sign of life within — no cars in the driveway, no lights on. Leigh Rose, where are you? She admitted there were sparks flying between us. I didn't imagine it. We had something . . . I step hard on the accelerator and rocket around the curves that bend with the river . . .

I race to the hotel, ready once and for all to have it out with Lola — and to hold her in my arms if she'll let me. Red lights mean nothing to me and I burst through intersections with reckless abandon, crossing just as yellow turns to red, which Bev liked to tell me was technically a moving violation. But she's not here, is she? The faster the Honda zips along, the further I plunge back into the familiar darkness that Lola cultivates. Yet there are times when we do just "hang out" and watch movies, hinting at a future that she really doesn't want with me, but now, on this night, in my fragile state, I crave her not because of the sexual energy she radiates but because she is the one person, the only person, who knows me for who I truly am. Around everyone else I put on a not-quite-convincing show, a tiresome act that drains me each day, but Lola demands nothing, expects even less, and carves out space for me to breathe. I really hope that she's lying about her "big" gift for me. I'm not in the mood at all. I literally want to put my head in her lap and have her stroke my thinning hair, which she claims is cute. I kid you not! The thing that disheartens me most, my receding hairline, visual evidence of my inevitable decline, is something she finds attractive. Maybe I do love her.

But Lola's car isn't in the parking lot of the Chicory Motel, a very modest, bland building of around twenty rooms, and it takes me about fifteen seconds to ascertain that one of two scenarios is playing out: 1) she's stepped out on a quick errand; or 2) she is toying with me and remains in Ithaca. After a moment's reflection, a third possibility comes to mind, that she's run off to find the guy from craigslist.

My heart sinks as I idle in my car, parked at an angle so that I face Richmond's new minor league baseball stadium, called the Diamond, which replaced beloved Parker Field, one of the last of the old-fashioned grandstand venues with rickety wooden seats and urinals that were cattle troughs. Once home to the venerable Richmond

Braves, now Parker Field has become a bulldozed park, the R-Braves play in Gwinnett County, Georgia, and the current team is called the Flying Squirrels. We can't step in the same river twice, can we, Heraclitus? The one constant in life is change. How clever, how insightful! No, I won't bore you with mundane insights that have the complexity of a Britney Spears ballad. Lola is up to her old tricks, it would seem.

I send her a text: *where r u?*

I wait a reasonable amount of time, thirty seconds, for a reply but receive none. So I call her and wait until I get kicked to her voice mail, but leave no message because there's really nothing to say. I'm not going to just drive away; Lola is a spontaneous creature with many impulses that course through her, and so I can't rule out an errand and a hasty return.

A minute passes, a minute during which my tenderness and longing get replaced with anger and bitterness. I told her I was coming! That's the frustrating part of this misbegotten affair, how I suffer for her amusement. It took me about fifteen minutes to drive from my home, up the Boulevard, to Robin Hood Road, a street name steeped in irony because as I sit, I begin to sympathize with the Sheriff of Nottingham, who was forever outwitted by his nimble foe. Lola doesn't steal from the rich and give to the poor; she sleeps with the well endowed and describes it in detail to the impotent, staying one step ahead of my suspicious dean. I should sell the film rights of my story to Larry Flint.

The Chicory contains no real amenities beyond a roof and a bed, and its ordinariness must've offended Lola, who has an eye for the eclectic. In Ithaca she loved checking out weird stores like Jabberwock or Angry Mom Records, not to mention Headdies Pipe & Vape Shop because she liked to pretend to be one of the junkies who called DeWitt Park home. As such, she often wore her hair with frosted tips, which, combined with black lipstick, created an aura of danger she thought all poets should have.

Peering into the reception/office, I can see a chubby schlub clerk behind the front desk, and even though he probably won't tell me anything, I decide to go ask if he doesn't have a Lola LaSalle registered.

The sound of the nearby interstate traffic reminds me of the roar of an angry sea, which would make me a sort of ancient mariner in search of his long-lost albatross. I pull open the heavy glass door and step inside a frigidly cold lobby that is only slightly larger than my kitchen. The rack for brochures of local attractions looks like it might be from the administration of Jefferson Davis, and I shudder to think of how old that pot of coffee must be.

"Can I help you?" the clerk asks, reading glasses perched on the end of his stout nose. He's perusing an actual newspaper and when he folds it over, I see that it's the *Wall Street Journal*.

"I need to get a message to a guest who's staying here," I lie with utter sincerity.

The clerk cocks his head in surprise, caught off guard by an ordinary request that at a place like this is anything but. "What's the guest's name?"

"Lola LaSalle."

He swivels in a chair, causing it to squeak in agony, and then starts typing on a keyboard connected to a computer, the same model we owned about fifteen years ago. After a few fruitless moments of waiting for the antique processor to execute a search, he shrugs in defeat. "No one here by that name," he says equivocally, perhaps unsure that his computer could spit out a correct answer.

"No one?" I gently press.

"Believe it or not, the people who stay here sometimes provide me with false IDs."

"Sounds like her." I drum my fingers against the counter. "Thanks anyway. Have a good night."

Lola has a fake driver's license because she isn't yet of legal drinking age, but I don't have a clue what her alias is. She might have used it to check in, but why would she need to conceal her identity? If I had to guess, I'd go with my second hypothesis, that of Remaining in Ithaca in Order to Screw with Me . . . which begs the question, why did I even bother to come here? What is wrong with me? What did I think I'd accomplish by driving to this fleabag motel where I had to converse with the illegitimate son of Norman Bates?

"Sorry, I hope you find her."

I note a tone of contrition, of genuine emotion, and so I linger a moment.

"Chicory was her favorite flower."

"Most people don't have a clue what the name means. They stay here because it's cheap."

"That's perfectly rational."

A few nods indicate that the small talk has reached its limit. He lifts the newspaper back up to his face and begins again to pore over the stock tables. After one last glance around the lobby, pretending that Lola is hiding beneath the coffee table, I leave. Will

I ever see Lola again? Just an hour ago, it disgusted me to think that she possessed the power to destroy me — and she still can. Can a man truly love a woman who is destined to ruin him? But will she actually drive a stake through my heart and turn me in? Or did Dahlia beat her to the punch?

I call Lola yet again, and yet again she doesn't pick up. Leave a message this time? Why not? What do I have to lose at this point? The words begin gushing out.

Hey, why aren't you here? I really want to talk to you. I know how much you despise the maudlin side of my personality, but I'm really confused. This entire situation, it baffles me. How did we end up here? Didn't we have other options? Did it have to become so confrontational? You're trying to hurt me and guess what? It's working.

But I'm not alone. On the stairwell nearest my Honda, there's a woman sitting on the bottom step. No, it's not Lola, but she looks very young and vulnerable, and she's crying. Not balling, but more like a very lonely sniffle, plaintively elegiac. Our eyes meet for a brief moment, and I hesitate out of habit and compassion. After all, Lola's tears had brought us together, that first fateful step toward my undoing.

"Are you okay?" I ask in a funereal tone

to match her lamentation.

She emits a sardonic laugh before sharply inhaling. Light from the office casts a ghoulish glow on her narrow, chiseled face, youthful though careworn as if constant sadness has shrunken her skin, revealing the skeleton beneath. "I'm doing great. My boyfriend just stole my car and all my money."

A fellow bottom dweller. "Have you called the police?"

"Hell no. It's worse when he's locked up."

"Worse than this?"

She doesn't answer because she has no reason to explain the emotional calculus of her life, and in the ensuing silence I resist the temptation to put my hands around her neck — but I'm no killer! I want to help this helpless creature, but how? Should I give her money that I don't have? Offer her a ride to nowhere? Is there a limit to compassion, a point at which empathy must dissolve into indifference lest we all empty our bank accounts to make the world a better place? I'm standing there like a mute idiot whose feet are stuck to the pavement and whose hands can't remain still — fidgety fingers finding no peace on this dark night.

"Just leave me alone," she mutters. I wince at the sharp pain this admonition brings. She considers me a creep, which is quite perceptive of her, showing tremendous critical thinking skills. There's really only one parry I can execute to deflect her thrust. My impure hands reach for my wallet, and from it I take out the last of my cash, around sixty bucks — this is madness, because I can't stop myself — my hands can sometimes ignore the commands sent to them from my atrophying brain and they act as they please, often in order to spite me — they deserve to be severed from my body and replaced with obedient prosthetics.

"Here," I say to her, holding out the money as a burnt offering. "Maybe this will help."

"No way."

"No, take it. Please."

"I'm not a hooker, dude."

"This is a gift, from one human being to another."

She stands up, turns her back on me, and bolts up the steps with the speed of a gazelle outrunning a lion. If only the dean of faculty could see me now! I've been accused of numerous professorial failings, including a lack of service to the larger community (in addition to a dearth of scholarship and mediocre teaching evaluations), but here I am, offering alms to the downtrodden while not once making an inappropriate advance toward her. This is professional productivity in its purest form, because I'm engaged in good works without expecting any reward in return.

My phone rings. It's Lola. Third time today, a new record. Or a new low.

"Got your message," she sings sweetly. "You're in a mood, aren't you?"

"Where are you? Are you even in Richmond?"

"Duh! No, I'm orbiting Saturn. Where else would I be?"

"I said I was coming to see you and to sit tight, but now you're gone. Again."

"Mr. Big wants to host, and so I'm headed to his place now."

"Seriously? That sounds like a horrible idea. You don't know the first thing about this guy."

"Well, I know he might just be the all-time record."

"This is what I'm talking about. We can't go on like this. This is nuts. You're finding guys online! How do you know he won't slit your throat?"

"You can meet me there. He doesn't care if you watch us."

"No! Then he'll kill both of us. I don't like this one bit. You shouldn't go to some stranger's house, especially if you think I want you to, because I don't."

"Then why do you care so much about the dudes I sleep with?"

"I never asked you to do anything!"

"Is that the lie you're telling yourself these days?"

"It's not a lie. I don't want you meeting strangers on my behalf. I never asked you to and I don't want you to. It's dangerous. You can't trust people these days. You really can't. We have to stop this, Lola. Right here, right now. It's gone too far. Someone's going to get hurt."

I pause so that she might respond, but instead I get only dull silence because at some point the call was dropped. In other words, she hung up on me yet again. I know better than to call back. She won't answer, and now my angst has compounded. I gaze up at the night sky for distant solace. The distraught woman whose boyfriend robbed her stands at the railing of the balcony above me, staring down with a quizzical expression of disapproval. She doesn't know the first thing about my troubles but she passes judgment on me anyway.

Shaken, I stagger to the Honda, the bills I was going to give away crumpled in my fist. I get into the car and start the engine. Just when it seemed like things couldn't get worse with Lola, somehow she always finds a way to add fuel to the fire. She's got me all wrong. If I'm really a morally bankrupt creep, as she implies, would a smart and attractive woman meet me for a drink? Let's see, shall we? A little experiment will clear this right up.

I call Paula, who sounds delighted to hear from me. "I was starting to think you were staying in for the night," she says gregariously. So far so good. "I hate to drink alone. I do it far too much these days."

"I'm going to see Gibson's band if you want to join me."

"Gibson has a band? How awesome is that? I'd love to see that girl rock a crowd. I bet she's badass."

"It's at this dive called the Dungeon, which is on Broad Street near Allen. I make no promises that it'll be refined."

"I like dive bars every now and then. I'm game for just about anything."

Proof! And beyond a reasonable doubt! Ladies and gentlemen of the jury, I'm not a creep.

I put the car in drive. And I drive.

16

I park on Marshall Street by an abandoned warehouse and walk two blocks back to Broad Street. Hookers loiter beneath streetlights, and some even whistle at me. If they only knew how futile these solicitations are! Yet futility best sums up the age we live in. Never have so many labored so hard to fix the world's problems with so little to show for it. Ours will be the "too little, too late" generation. My life can serve as a perfect microcosm for what ails humanity: I've known for years that I'm headed for oblivion but haven't lifted one finger to stop the slide. If anything, I've gotten worse.

Broad Street pulses with a manic energy. Six lanes of traffic, rampant jaywalking, a street performer banging on five-gallon buckets: the drifters and grifters of Richmond have long congregated in this seedy underbelly, and that certainly hasn't changed. The Dungeon fits into a continuum of antiestablishment clubs that have come and gone in this section of town. Twenty years ago I was trying to sneak into New Horizons and Casablanca, where ten years before the Dead Kennedys once played an epic set. Again I ask: how can I possibly be a creep?

I smile and wave at the prostitutes, bidding them a fair evening. Still, I've heard nothing from Lola, which is a tad strange and giving me pause. Paula, on the other hand, has sent me a message to say that she's running a little late but she's still planning on "hooking up" with me.

A burly bouncer guards the entrance to the Dungeon, but there's no line to get in and so I shouldn't have a problem. Except that I'm dressed like a complete square, in my rehearsal dinner attire, and the bouncer stops me.

"This is a private club," he grumbles.

"Is there a cover?" I reach into a pocket and pull out the crumpled greenbacks I was going to give to the forlorn woman at Lola's hotel, which luckily she'd refused as otherwise I'd be broke. Downstairs I hear a loud, thumping bass clearly inspired by early Primus. If that's Hazzie Mattie, I'm already impressed. Not many bands can replicate the Primus sound or should even try.

"Ten bucks."

I give him one of the bills and head on down. Apparently money still talks around these parts, and even a well-dressed deviant can get into a down-and-dirty punk rock club for the right price. On the stairs I pass by two girls who look like they're around fifteen, dolled up in matching Marilyn Manson accoutrement, the familiar goth decorations of black lipstick and white pancake face mask, but each with bright purple hair that they've managed to braid together so that they're united like Siamese twins. Inside, the club is sparsely attended, maybe thirty people tops, with the mean age around 20.4, but the lead singer of the band stands out because she's onstage prowling on all fours in a leopard-skin leotard that clings to her bodacious curves — Gibson is aflame, microphone in hand, leaping up as the drummer bangs away on the snare. Throwing her head back, Gibson roars inaudible lyrics, earning a few shouts of support from the audience who thrash in front of her, bodies gyrating and crashing into each other, a small mosh pit but a frenetic one. Gibson owns the stage, claims every inch of it with a raw, brash sexuality, but no one else in the band can keep up with her. The drummer is slow, the bassist knows how to do only a fraction of Primus-inspired riffs, and the lead guitarist looks like he had heroin for breakfast, lunch, and dinner, which for some musicians would help them reach new heights of expression but for this stiff junkie brings only torpid fingerpicking.

Gibson is holding nothing back. She reminds me of a combination of Janis Joplin and Brigitte Bardot, a gravelly, whiskey-soaked voice with the body of a sex kitten. It's captivating to watch her, even if I can't make out the words of the songs. What she has can't be taught, the visceral, seething performance that comes from a dark place yet is suffused with blazing light. She can become a star. Maybe nobody but me in this crapulous venue can see it, but Gibson has the wow factor. It's impossible not to watch her and she seems to know that she possesses the power to command attention.

The song abruptly ends. Gibson wanders around the small stage as the drummer taps on the rim of his kettle as if to keep the beat for the next number. Then the lead guitarist starts shouting at someone in the audience, and the heckler then takes it upon himself to spring up on the stage, where he assumes a karate stance to threaten the guitarist. The crowd starts booing and hissing, and suddenly the guitarist takes a swing at the guy using his instrument as a baseball bat. But he misses when his nimble target jumps backward, causing him to knock into Gibson, who because of the unforeseen collision then tumbles off the stage and lands more or less in the mosh pit. Bedlam quickly erupts and fights break out in about six different locations at once. I rush over to check on Gibson, who's supine on the beer-splattered floor and in danger of getting trampled by panicked punks whose heavy boots could crush her. I have to shove several of the marauding wastrels away, but when she sees it's me coming to her rescue, she smiles thinly as she yells choice curse words at the people knocking into her.

"You okay?" I ask, after I've hoisted her up.

"Yeah, I guess. My ankle hurts. Asshole!" She shoves a small banshee with gusto, sending him sprawling. Bouncers and bartenders struggle to regain control of the melee. Someone grabs the mike and begs for everyone to "chill the fuck out," which actually does help calm down the situation. But confusion still lurks as Hazzie Mattie attempts to regroup in front of the stage. The lead guitarist has a bloody nose and his guitar has a broken neck, which he waves around as he vows vengeance.

"I'll kill that little piece of shit! He won't live to see tomorrow!"

The drummer takes umbrage at his mate's bravado. "You didn't need to get into it with him during our set, man. Now look. It's all fucked up. Gibson was killing it, too."

"Fuck you, man. Fuck this band."

With that last imprecation, the lead guitarist storms off, possibly heralding the breakup of Hazzie Mattie. The bassist gives chase but then gives up and returns with a defeated shrug.

"Let him go," the drummer counsels. "He was way too into smack for me. And he sucked."

"Now we need to find somebody else," Gibson says resolutely, already thinking of a solution to the problem. No quit in her, a very admirable trait and one I don't share.

A man around my age with spiked salt-and-pepper hair and a huge looping earring comes up to the remnants of the band. He's probably the club's owner and he's most likely going to banish them forever, given the fracas that broke out.

"That was awesome, guys!" he gushes. "That was smoking hot. Loved the look, the energy." He's staring right at Gibson when he says this, showing that he's no fool. "I want you guys to come back for another set."

"Really? When?" Gibson knows an opportunity when she sees one, and it's smart of her to nail him down on the details.

"Next Friday? Does that work? Can you find a replacement for Dog?" Gibson had mentioned him, the lead guitarist and founder of Hazzie Mattie.

"It's his band. We'll need a new name."

"Whatever, you'll think of something. We can pay you a hundred bucks. That's what the opening act gets. We booked a group from Norfolk to play here, I Stole This. Heard of them? They just signed with Rummage Records. They kick ass."

"Hell yes!" the drummer yells and gives Gibson a hug, but she's not interested in him. She's flirting with the owner, the decision-maker, displaying again a toughness that'll take her far in this sexist world. She's giggling and flipping her hair and touching his arm, just like Lola did when she first tried to seduce me. Who can resist these blandishments?

But after the owner is gone, general euphoria sets in among the band members, who've just tasted their first portion of success. They kick around ideas for the name of their new band, including such gems as

Barney Fife and Snirtle. They're all shouting at each other like they're trading hog futures, and something tells me they won't come together tonight. Still, it's uplifting to see Gibson standing on the cusp, with her future beckoning, while my past lumbers on. I really don't know what to do with myself, since Paula hasn't arrived. I stand a respectable distance from the ebullient group, on the lookout for a woman who will be the oldest person in here once she arrives. Maybe I should call Paula and tell her not to bother, since the show was aborted. I could meet her elsewhere for a drink.

Then, out of the corner of my eye, I think I see Lola. Just a fleeting glimpse of a young woman bounding up the stairs. No way, impossible, and yet I find myself moving, legs churning, heart pounding, fear gripping me around the throat . . . it's happening, the sure-loser gambit she's forced me to take to counter her own bold opening . . . and now I blindly pursue quarry with no firm grasp of the endgame. Yes, I'll admit I'm thrilled she's apparently stood up her online lover to seek my company, if in fact it is her.

Which it isn't. Once I reach the top of the stairs, and the light grows brighter, I can plainly see that the woman in question isn't

Lola and isn't a woman, but a very ef-
feminate and tall transvestite. Disappointed,
crushed even, I lope back down the stairs
just in time to run into Gibson and her
cohort.

"I think we're going out," she tells me
sweetly. "You're more than welcome to join
us."

"No, go, go! I'm going to meet up with
Paula for a drink."

"Cool! She's a super cool woman. She's
always telling me to go for it and have no
regrets."

"She's a smart person then."

"It's so awesome that you came! Sorry
about how screwed up things got."

"You were amazing. Seriously. You're going to be a star."

"Shut up!"

"I'm not kidding! You guys got a paid gig
out of this and it's all because of you. Not
them."

"I'm sorry I was such a bitch to you
earlier. There's only so much I can put up
with when it comes to my family and I was
at my limit."

I nod in commiseration. "Promise me you
won't stay out late tonight. Tomorrow's a
big day and we need to be functional.
Maybe even cheerful."

"I'm tight."

She hugs me in a daughterly way, and I feel very protective of her. Since I'll never have kids, this is as close to fatherhood as I'll ever get. Right on cue, as she's about to leave, I see a familiar face hovering nearby, that of the man whose wife is a cop with a service revolver and a bad attitude. I recognize his strong jawline and chiseled features. "Wait a second," I say in a hushed tone. "Isn't that the married guy who lied to you and almost got us killed?"

"He just showed up! Yell at him, not me."

"I'm not yelling at anyone. Don't you think you should stay away from him?"

"Probably."

"Are you going to stay away?"

"Probably not."

"There you have it, ladies and gentlemen, poor decision-making! He's a liar. The worst kind of liar. Some liars are sort of entertaining, but he's toxic."

"I got nothing better to do. You're the one I'm worried about."

"Me? I've never been better."

"Yeah, right. If you say so."

With that last salvo, she spins around and catches up to her group of friends and fans and lovers who've misled her, while I loiter in a darkened club where no one knows me.

351

Another band is setting up onstage, and I allow myself to study them. Chances are, they won't make it any farther than this stage, and yet they carefully set up their equipment as if they're getting ready to play a sold-out stadium. Some might call that courage, others vanity. I cross my arms in grudging admiration. Why did I never follow through with my music? Why did the idea of joining a band strike me as ridiculous? Was it the fear of failure? The fact that I lacked talent? Since when did lack of talent ever stop anyone from pursuing a dream? Lola thinks that I can write a very great book. She's told me so many times and seems to mean it, but it's hard to tell with her.

Paula! I need to call her and save her a trip to this decrepit part of town. I lug out my phone and see that Lola has texted me. It's beyond uncanny how she manages to insinuate herself into my life during my darkest moments, when I feel completely lost and adrift, when I despise myself for missing her.

Her message is simple:

O M G

Then appears a picture. Of a man. Of a man's penis. Of a man's penis that looks like it was made in a rubber factory in Liberia. The pigmentation of his appendage suggests African origin but I don't want to perpetuate racial stereotypes. I will say that he is no larger than Thor, who was white (and insufferable). But there is something poignant about Lola being with this person of color, especially as I stand in the city of Richmond, Virginia, on a hot, dry night in July. In many ways, the Confederate States of America was based on one noxious concept: the fear of miscegenation, the outlandish idea that a white woman would commingle with a black man, who, once freed from the civilized bonds of slavery, would rampage through his master's house raping and pillaging. The election of Lincoln, the fire-eaters argued, would unleash the beast within these hypersexual subhumans, and once the votes were counted in 1860, fear gripped the South and secession soon followed. It was a form of pornography, really, this morbid fascination with black men befouling white women, though few Southerners would ever admit to it. Hence, the myth of the Lost Cause, the noble fight for states' rights, replaced the prurient vitriol of race-mixing and led to the erection of statues along Monument Avenue, the most famous of which, of General Lee, stands not two blocks away

353

from me.

"Hey!"

I look up and see Paula, who's managed to change into attire more befitting the urban landscape than my J. Crew ensemble.

"I was just getting ready to call you! Gibson's night ended early and that's a funny story."

"I know, I just ran into her. She said it went great, though. I'm so proud of her. She's a tough chick, like her mama."

"We don't have to stay here."

"It might get loud."

I don't know Richmond like I once did, but I guess that if we walk back toward Grace Street we'll find a little watering hole or bistro more to our liking. "I'm sure there's something nearby," I say as I gently place my hand on the small of her back to indicate that we should leave.

Back outside, even more street urchins have gathered near a barbershop on Broad Street, where a rap battle is in full throat. We steer clear of the commotion and instead stroll toward a bank, which for some reason seems safer. "My cabdriver didn't believe me when I told him where to go," Paula mirthfully explains. "He kept asking me if I was sure."

"Just wait. In one block, you'll feel as

though you've gone back in time. In Richmond the contrasts are very stark."

"That's very perceptive. Most of the men I know couldn't provide half that level of insight."

"I don't like to brag, but I'm an intellectual."

"I can tell."

We both dissolve into an easy laugh, turning right on Allen Avenue, where as I predicted within a block, on Grace Street, sit enormous brick mansions that harken back to a stately prominence not found in the tattoo parlors and boarded-up shops we just left. "Wow!" Paula gasps, admiring the lovely streetscape. "You were right. Look at these places. It reminds me of parts of London, almost like Belgravia."

"I've heard that before. These are beautiful homes, and the ones on Monument Avenue are even better, and of course there's that showpiece, too."

She stops dead in her tracks.

"Is that . . . Robert E. Lee?" She points at the statue illuminated by spotlights below. It rises a block to our south, with the general astride his horse, both of them hovering in the darkness like ghostly forms. Paula picks up the pace, a moth drawn to the flame of History. "We have to go check that out. I had no idea it was so ginormous."

"You've never seen it?"

"This is my first trip to Richmond. Hard to believe, but true."

"Well, it's our city's most famous landmark, and a real must-see. Shall we?" We zip past a restored school, called Orchard House, and it's absolutely charming, with big arched windows and neo-Gothic finials to add a Normal Rockwell flair. Ah, the simpler times of Jim Crow segregation! I can imagine all the little white boys and girls at recess marveling at the nearby heroic monument and thinking that they were in proximity to the godhead in the same way that Athenian children would gaze up at the Parthenon marching to Plato's Academy. "We are nearing hallowed ground, you know. You might want to remove your shoes and bow your head. If you look directly into General Lee's eyes, your pupils might melt."

"Very funny. Are you always this droll?"

"No. Weddings bring out the best in me."

Another flirtatious giggle. What's this feeling bubbling inside me? Could it be the nascent embryo of attraction? Of course, makes perfect sense! The one woman in the world I really should steer clear of is someone around whom I feel very comfortable, who is single, has no kids, is educated, and thinks I'm droll, which is a wonderful adjective to be called by a lover — but she's also going to be my step-aunt. I can literally address her as Aunt Paula, in bed and out. How down and dirty is that? Enough to kickstart my groin? Could be, could be. Will miracles never cease?

We come up to the traffic circle that surrounds the Lee monument, which is situated in the middle of a grassy lawn. From our vantage on Allen Avenue, we see the general's back and the horse's tail, as General Lee faces south, and so we must go around for a better view.

"I need to get a selfie with this. It'll be a scream."

"My ex-wife hated this statue with a passion. She acted like it was my fault it was ever built. I had to keep reminding her that I had nothing to do with it."

"I know the type. Married one of them myself."

Monument Avenue is thick with traffic and so we must wait to cross at the light. There is a definite European atmosphere to this part of Richmond. While not the Arc de Triomphe, the Lee monument is no less impressive and erected for an equally spurious reason; one celebrates the nobility of the Lost Cause, the other speaks to the glory of Napoleon Bonaparte. Interestingly, the Lee statue was fabricated in Paris, at the atelier of Marius Jean Antonin Mercié, described as a "short, thick-set, squarely built man, with dark hair and eyes, and short black beard." Miss Sarah Randolph of the Lee Monument Commission traveled to Paris in the summer of 1887 with Lee's daughter Mary, who brought to the artist the general's frock and spurs in the name of verisimilitude . . . and it was there, amid the charming gardens just off the Avenue de L'Observatorie, that Miss Randolph began a torrid affair with Mercié, whose selection had outraged the locals who'd vied for the commission only to lose out to a Frenchman, albeit one who'd been trained at the Academy des Beaux Arts and who enjoyed an international reputation. Scandal quickly erupted, staining Miss Randolph's spotless name.

"You know quite a bit about this, huh?" Paula observes as we head over to the wide median that runs down the center of Monument Avenue.

"I guess my wife's loathing of it caused me to surf online for some historical context." I pause here, the stand-up comic never far away. "I know how to waste time. It's maybe my greatest skill."

"Why is his hat off?"

Indeed, Lee's hat rests on his thigh, and in the other hand he holds the reins. The horse beneath him has all four of its legs on the ground, indicating that the pace is a slow walk, not a triumphant gallop. "The artist apparently was adamant that Lee's brow be visible, because he wanted to capture the depth of the man's character. Lee is inspecting the troops after the defeat of Gettysburg, a very elegiac moment in the history of our people, for which he took full blame."

"His expression is somewhat pained. Okay, I need a picture. Where should I stand?"

So now we configure a quick photo shoot, with me as cameraman. She hands me her phone and I place her on top of a park bench, so that in the shot her head appears to be holding up the statue, serving as the plinth, as it were. The lighting isn't great, but it'll do. Anyway, I prefer a hard-edged patina to my selfies. Nothing too pretty.

"Say *fromage*!" I call out.

Paula gives me a wry grin and I snap off two shots. She leaps down and together we check out the results. Her verdict: perfect. "That's hilarious! It's like sitting on top of my head. What an eye for proportion you have, Professor Stith."

I detect a playful tone in the way she pronounces the word "professor," indicating that she might harbor the remnants of a schoolgirl fantasy, which isn't uncommon. "How about that drink?" I laugh nervously, fighting back the impulse to tell her everything, and I mean everything.

17

During his last visit to Richmond, Edgar Allan Poe became convinced that the people he cared the most about in the world were dead when in fact they were very much alive. Many scholars have mistakenly attributed these delusional episodes to rampant alcoholism, but Poe no longer was drinking in the summer of 1849. What possibly could have driven the great Poe to fits of psychosis? We know he was broke, constantly badgering editors for money they owed him, and yet hopeful that he could start his own literary magazine, to be called *Stylus,* if only he could find a benefactor. He gave the last public lecture of his life at the Exchange Hotel on Franklin Street, and charged admission of twenty-five cents. People hung from the rafters to hear the famed author speak on "The Poetic Principle," hoping that he'd read "The Raven." Instead Poe delivered a manifesto on beauty that envisioned a poetry unshackled from the "theory-mad" desire for morals or instruction. Here was Poe, facing ruin on many fronts, extolling art for art's sake, while dismissing as lightweight the busybodies who think poets should capture the Truth. No, said Poe, we should all be striving for something just beyond our reach, that which is floating in clouds, babbling in brooks, rising with mountaintops to the cerulean sky. In the audience was a woman named Mrs. A. B. Shelton, with whom Poe had been in love as a young man. Then called Elmira Royster, she was now a widow, and a wealthy one, and Poe himself was a widower, having lost his child bride two years before. Would his old flame rescue him from financial morass? He'd courted others in New York and Boston, but had never remarried. But by the time he reached Richmond, his situation was deteriorating. In the last letter Poe would ever write, he told his former mother-in-law, "My clothes are so horrible and I am so ill."

Do you see the obvious parallels? Although my clothes are reasonably fashionable, I too need to be rescued. At first I thought that Leigh Rose might have been my Elmira, but now that I'm getting to know Paula better, I'm beginning to see things in a different light. We're really hitting it off. Not to say that we're a perfect match. She is loud and at times abrasive, and physically my superior, as evidenced by her hobby of marathon running. "I only run from the cops," I crack, and to her credit she laughs at my lack of rigorous exercise.

"Then how do you stay in shape?"

"I like to take long hikes when I can. We have some pretty cool trails around Ithaca, to waterfalls and such, and I guess if you brood enough, you can cover ten miles in an afternoon." I fail to mention that Lola also enjoyed these excursions and sometimes came with me, but I don't need to divulge all my secrets over a glass of wine. We're sitting in Siam, a newish Asian place off Lombardy and the only thing open in our general vicinity.

"I'd like to climb Everest one day," she muses, not really vociferously enough to indicate a true passion. "Who knows? Maybe I'll quit my job and move to Nepal."

"I dream of leaving the country all the time." Yes, and going to countries that don't have extradition treaties with the U.S. I hear Russia is nice in the winter.

"Where would you go?"

I pretend to mull over her question, stumped for an answer, because I honestly don't spend time envisioning myself in far-off lands. Airplanes terrify me. Driving long distances is even worse. If I could walk to Russia, cross the Bering Strait on snowshoe . . . "I spent some time in the Czech Republic on a Fulbright."

"Would you go back?"

"No, I've been ordered by the U.S. consulate never to go back. Plus, I struck out with every woman in Prague."

"I find it hard to believe you have trouble meeting women. You're very charming and debonair."

"It's an act. I'm actually quite creepy."

She giggles with her brown eyes shining at me, strong chin jutting out, veins in her neck bulging — why do I find athletic women so intimidating? There's nothing soft about her, which is a very sexist way to esteem women, but I do prefer my lovers to have a certain vulnerability. Not only can Paula scale Mt. Everest, she can probably rip it from the earth and throw it across the Great Wall of China. She needs a man as dedicated to physical fitness as she is. My passions, alas, tend toward the unspeakable.

"Give me an example," she challenges me in a mirthful tone. "I'm a lawyer, and I like corroborating evidence. Tell me one way you're creepy."

"Just one?"

"How many are there?"

"Let me ask you this. Are you more interested in felonies or misdemeanors?"

"What?" She sounds alarmed now, and her smile vanishes.

"I'm kidding! I'm not a creep. Ask any of the students I'm sleeping with."

She bursts into a hearty guffaw, but inside I'm getting tense and nervous and I can't relax . . . okay, I'm no psycho killer, though Lola's unknown whereabouts are making me quite uncomfortable. Here I am, enjoying myself, having fun with a mature woman who has no children and no husband, dead or alive, while somewhere in the city of Richmond Lola is meeting up with a complete stranger because she thinks I want her to. Afraid of losing me, she's upping the ante, and it seems like I should do something, anything, to figure out how to defuse the situation. Yet I do nothing but sip mediocre wine.

"Back in law school, I slept with one of my professors, but it was only because I had to get an A in Contracts and the rumor was if you slept with him, you got the A. I got the A. My guy friends were so pissed! I laughed in their faces. Sucks when we turn the tables, doesn't it? Some of my more feminist friends were appalled, but again, I didn't care what anybody thought. Now, would I want my daughter doing that? No way. That professor today couldn't get away with that."

"He couldn't?"

"He could? I thought there were policies in place to prevent it."

"Those policies only make things worse. The temptations are even greater now, which means the atmosphere is turbo-charged, sexually."

"Interesting. So it still happens?"

"Maybe not as blatantly, but there are il-licit affairs on every college campus in this country."

Her face is flushed, turning a roseate shade. My stomach really can't handle this topic. Because what I want to do, more than anything, is confide in someone. It's hard being this alone in the world, lugging around the onerous weight Lola has dropped on my narrow shoulders. My legs are starting to wobble, but I don't know if I can trust Paula . . . or anyone.

"But you've never done it?" she asks clini-cally, as if checking off a list of symptoms.

"Once." I can't believe the sound of my own voice, disembodied and hovering above me.

"Oh, really? Not that I'm surprised. I'm sure all kinds of girls have a crush on you."

"It was the biggest mistake I've ever made in my life and I deeply regret it."

She doesn't know what to make of my unprovoked admission and studies me with abashed curiosity, obviously needing more of the story but too polite to ask for additional details. She offers condolences instead, heartfelt and genuine. "I'm sorry to hear that."

"It just ended and I'm still a little freaked out by it. I'm sorry to be telling you this — you probably think I'm some heinous sexual predator, but it really wasn't like that. She initiated it and I wasn't strong enough to resist."

"I wouldn't beat myself up over it. Chalk it up to the frailty of human nature. We've all done stupid things. It's not like you killed her, for crying out loud."

Something in me gets dislodged, and a boulder comes tumbling out of my mouth. "She's here."

"Where?" Paula begins looking around the small interior of the restaurant. There are maybe ten other patrons, none of whom seem to be likely candidates for a college-aged femme fatale.

"No, she's here in Richmond."

"She lives here?"

"No. She drove down from Ithaca because she was so upset when I ended things."

Paula laughs empathetically. "Listen, the only reason I'm not sleeping with hot young guys is because I can't. They no longer give me the time of day." She pretends to wipe tears from her eyes. "How did we get on this subject? I think I could use another glass of wine."

She looks around for our waiter, a portly gent who spoke broken English and wore an apron that looked to have the innards of a slaughtered animal smeared all over it.

Can I get away with dating Paula, who'll become my step-aunt tomorrow? I do need a good lawyer, and she's very easy to talk to. Not sure how she'll take my perpetual flaccidity, but true love can conquer all. Not that I can love anyone. Isn't that Dostoyevsky's famous definition of hell? The inability to love? If so, I've reached the penthouse suite — er, basement grotto.

Paula spies the waiter, who seemed to be hiding behind a soda cooler, and waves him over. Then my phone rings. I assume that Lola is calling to tell me that she's rendezvoused with her online lover, and I'm actually considering not speaking with her. She can't spoil everything in my life. Let me have one last night out with a classy woman. Is that too much to ask? With a stern look on my face, I check the caller ID, only to be completely blindsided by who it is.

Leigh Rose Wardell.

"I have to take this," I tell Paula, pushing back from the table. I'm shaking from a sudden onset of nerves, and my trembling index finger has trouble pushing the red Answer icon to engage. "Hey," I say sweetly once I get outside into the hot night air. Dreams never die, as long as you never let go of them.

"I told you to stay out of this."

A man's voice, gruff and angry. My head snaps back as though I'd been jabbed on the chin with a savage punch. "Who is this?"

"You don't know what's going down and now you've really screwed up."

It sounds like John Graziano's voice, but why would he use Leigh Rose's phone to call me? I look up and down Lombardy mistakenly thinking that I'm being watched. But I see only the usual human flotsam milling around. More to the point, why in the world am I being hauled back into this drama at all? Graziano already told me to stay away and I haven't done anything in the interim to meddle. It might behoove me to point out this fact. "Graz, hold on. What the hell are you talking about?"

"Dude, you're messing with the wrong people for the wrong reasons. I don't know if I can fix this."

"Fix what? I haven't done anything! Where's Leigh Rose? She'll tell you."

"Very funny, Eddie. You always had a great sense of humor."

"I'm not kidding!"

"Eddie, I like you. I got no heat with you. Think of this as a courtesy call. You need to be very careful. If you're telling the truth, then she's lying, and I already told you that she's crazy and you can't trust her. She just might get you killed."

"What did she say? I haven't talked to her since the hotel and so I really don't know what to tell you. What's going on? Be straight with me, Graz. I deserve that much."

But he doesn't answer. The call goes dead and I'm left with a phone in my hand and a hole in my heart with the diameter of a bottle of scotch. My own safety matters little; if Jeb Wardell wants to take me out, he's welcome to try and I might just help him finish the job. But Leigh Rose is in danger. They have taken her phone, but since they called me, they must not know where she is. She's made a run for it, apparently. But why would she even need to go to such an extreme and abscond without her phone? Unless she's already dead and they're setting me up to take the fall . . . echoes of Poe again, who imagined his loved ones were dead, in his tattered clothes and poor health . . .

Shaken, I try to gird myself before going back inside. My head is pounding riotously, however, and so I pace back and forth on the sidewalk until a modicum of composure settles in. But that's proving to be difficult with the welter of emotions bursting inside. Did Leigh Rose claim her undying love for me — and did that get her killed? Or has she bolted out of her gilded cage in order to seek me out, which without a phone will prove to be a daunting task? Should I go look for her? I wouldn't even know where to start.

Paula must think I'm insane. I have to go back before she calls 911, but I'm not much in the way of company at the moment. Who would be, after getting threatened for no reason? They think they can push me around. Graz called to intimidate me, but guess what? They're reading me all wrong. They think I care! Ha! They assume that I have the same aspirations as a normal person, when in fact my entire moral axis

371

has rotated dramatically in the past twenty-four hours. I press the Redial button on my phone, not even sure what I'm going to say, standing beneath a streetlight with a hand jauntily placed on a hip, jaw set in stone . . . but no one answers. Leigh Rose's voice mail kicks on but I don't leave a message.

I take a deep breath and exhale through my nose, mimicking an exercise Bev taught me from her days as a yoga instructor. She didn't like it when I took her class, though, because I wasn't flexible enough to keep up. I never understood why she married me. Even on our wedding night I was confused. I always knew she'd snap me in half, that I was too brittle for her. Ithaca was crawling with pseudo-intellectuals who could maintain a downward dog pose for more than six seconds, and one day Bev would replace me with a more limber model. The thing is, I don't even know if Igor can touch his toes.

One last cleansing breath . . . Bev would be so proud. And appalled. But not surprised. I can already hear her at the press conference: *I could have predicted this years ago.*

"Sorry that took so long," I tell Paula once I'm back inside the restaurant. The festive mood has been spoiled, and I can tell she's both worried and annoyed. She had to have seen me prowling around like a caged lion. There's really no plausible explanation for that, other than the truth. Oh, what a concept! I can just be honest with everyone.

"I hope it wasn't bad news," she offers coolly.

"Actually, no. Just more of the same. The last few days have been . . ." I laugh like an asthmatic lunatic, devoid of mirth, just a bitter caterwaul from someone befuddled by events.

"Was it the student?"

At first I'm not sure to whom she's referring, and my mouth gapes in temporary confusion. She's talking about Lola, duh. Lola who listened to me, who hated tedium as I did, who didn't care about my erection — we fell in love without ever making it, at least in the normative sense. To think I was going to ignore her if she'd called! Why won't she call now? Because she's risking life and limb for me, the stupid kid. I'm seized, absolutely gripped, by an overwhelming desire to hold her. I really can't explain these jarring vicissitudes that overtake me, these mad alterations of my feelings for her. Why didn't we just get married? We actually discussed it back in May, during Finals Week. Lola was studying for an interesting class on the history of the family as a social construct. We were in my apartment on North Plain Street, and I'd just volunteered to go get a burrito because she was famished. I noticed her face was buried in a book called *The Way We Never Were* by Stephanie Coontz, and Lola quickly explained the central argument, that at no time in American history was there ever such a thing as a "normal" family with mom, dad, and the kiddies. "Kind of like us," she tossed out with a sly grin.

"We're a family?"

"Why not? We could be."

I have to admit that the entire concept enchanted me, at least during the walk to the Mexican place, where I envisioned the bliss of spending the rest of my days with Lola and her harem of oversized peckers. This same notion also sickened me, but not quite as much as it allured me — close to equilibrium, though not enough to repel me. And so over bean burritos and bottles of Sol we talked matrimony. She was eager to show the world her undying love for me, which I begged her not to do — so instead she just let Dahlia in on our little secret, thereby razing our private Idaho.

"No," I tell Paula, suspended somewhere between a dream state and a brutal realization. "I won't be hearing from her again."

"Why do you say that?"

"I just know her. No, that call was another disaster. Normally so very little happens to me, that this parade of misfortune is most unusual."

"If you need to go . . ."

"I need something. A new job. A new car. A clean conscience."

"Let me pay for the wine. My treat." She reaches for her purse, and I stare glumly at her hands, her fingers long and slender, skin leathery and tough from her constant exertions. My hands? Soft as throw pillows.

"We haven't even gossiped about the wedding," I protest listlessly.

"Oh, that. I like your mother. She's a sweet lady."

"But?"

"But nothing. My brother is old enough to make his own choices and like I said, I don't judge people."

"You agree that the arrangement is a bit odd."

"Oh, for sure. But all married couples are odd in my opinion." A hearty laugh, a credit card produced, and an evening draws to a whimpering close because that's how the world will end, not with a bang, but with a . . . except that we both hear a bang. A very loud noise that sounds like an explosion.

"What was that?" she asks me, voice tremulous as she rises up from her seat.

"That sounded like a bomb going off." I jump to my feet. The other customers stand up, too, and we all gravitate to the street. The local residents join us, streaming out onto Monument Avenue, and en masse we head toward the Robert E. Lee statue a block away because that was the direction of the loud noise. The first sirens wail in the distance, horns blare, and the air reeks of smoke, though I see no fire. We hurry our pace, and the gathering crowd grows in silent increments. Soon we are at Allen.

"Oh my God," Paula cries. She points a trembling finger. My eyes trail over to the statue. The marble plinth remains, but the bronze figures that had once stood on it are now missing. No, not missing: just toppled over, mangled on the turf below in a smoldering heap.

"They blew it up," Paula sniffles. "I can't believe that just happened."

She struggles to fight back tears, wiping at her eyes that continue to stare in disbelief at the empty space still lit up by the spotlights below. But now they seem more like searchlights combing the night sky for another bomb to drop. I put an arm around her shoulders and she leans her head against my chest, and we cling to each other as more sirens scream in the distance.

18

So now we have our first murder victim, and indeed the dead have died again. Robert E. Lee, who passed away in 1870, has been killed in battle. Having dodged cannonballs in real life, he couldn't escape an insidious high explosive in his bronzed life. But don't let your guard down for one second, because this is the major motif of my story and I'd be remiss to stop here, with one dead person dying again. There will be more.

But this one! So epic in scale, grandiose in ambition! If the intent was to excise the heart of this city, no target would have had the same impact. Richmonders projected their best selves onto this statue, as Lee didn't take secession lightly and agonized over the decision to fight against the nation he'd spent his career defending. He was no fire-eater eager for brother to slay brother, but a thoughtful, decent public servant, a hero from a sullied age, someone who acted upon deeply held principles. Now his iconic likeness lies smoldering on the ground. It feels like a political assassination.

I can't relate the overwhelming sadness that descends from the inky night onto the shocked crowd that gathers at the circle where the statue once reigned over the city. The first responders come in hordes: I count seven hook-and-ladders, six ambulances, and twelve police cruisers, all of which arrive in less than two minutes. The authorities quickly cordon off the scene, not that anyone has made any attempt to disturb the remains of the fallen hero. We stand muted by shock, too numb to move, to speak. The hundreds who come to catch a glimpse do so in complete silence that doesn't last long. Behind us I can hear some angry voices, plotting revenge.

"I say we knock down the Ashe monument," someone growls. "They wanted his black ass, they got it, and now look what they did."

"Hell yes. Somebody should do something."

"This is bullshit."

Paula shoots me a glance, and I shrug in commiseration. The rabble has been roused, but the mob seldom picks the right target to rip apart. And that someone could be the Bastard Sons. It's not hard to connect the flyer I found in the hamper to what just happened. This was a blow at the very heart and soul of old Richmond, and someone will pay dearly for it. If Graves had a hand in this . . . if he took an RPG . . . then Mead, and my mother, will also face possible legal ramifications, not to mention endure the calumny of an entire city. The scope of the ramifications staggers me.

"Let's get out of here," I say, taking Paula by the arm. I have to get home and help the family confront the enormity of the potential problems this act of terror has created. I'll tell them what I know and let them decide how to proceed from there. What do I know? That Graves had a suspicious-looking flyer that assailed Robert E. Lee? That he hated everything about Richmond? Not exactly a mountain of evidence. Through the years the Lee statue has been defaced multiple times, mostly with spray paint . . . but this is of a far greater magnitude.

Helicopters flutter overhead, and the news trucks have descended. One has parked in front of the brick school, and a cherry picker lifts up to position a camera for a

Hitchcockian view of the carnage from above.

"Your poor mother!" Paula exclaims. "She's spent months planning the big event and now all hell has broken loose. First the bomb threat, and now this. What's next? The plague?"

"This won't end well," I offer solemnly. "The city can't handle something like this. You heard those people back there. This could get very ugly in a hurry."

"Nowadays there are cameras everywhere, and I bet they'll get to the bottom of it sooner rather than later. Somebody saw something. Witnesses will come forward. They always do."

We're at Broad Street again, which is utterly deserted, almost as if aliens had swooped in and scooped up all the street life. "Where are we headed?" she asks.

"Oh, I should get home. I can give you a ride back to your hotel. I'm parked over there, a couple of blocks away."

"Yeah, the night has taken a turn for the worse."

But we're not out of the woods yet . . . the dead will continue to die. I wish I could say that the mystery has been solved, but we're not even close to the finish line.

"I hope Mead isn't mixed up in any of

this," she says gravely, catching me by surprise.

"Why would you say that?"

"Because of his business. The only thing that could have done the damage we saw to that statue was a rocket-propelled grenade, and I know Mead buys and sells weapons like that, without a license. And he buys and sells these kinds of weapons to and from seriously flawed people."

An image of the Russian forms in my mindscape, a hulking reddish figure with cold blood and insatiable appetites. Should Paula know this? She's family, right? And blood is thicker than water. "I met one of those flawed people today," I say, trying not to sound like a TV reporter breaking a big story. "A Russian."

"No surprise there."

"But wait. Right before I came downtown, when I took my mother home, we saw that the garage door was open. Some of the stuff was missing. Mead suspected it was the Russian who wasn't happy with the pace of negotiations, and so he wants to move all of it into a storage facility first thing in the morning. I'm going to help him."

She cries in anguish as we near my Honda. "I knew this was going to come back to haunt him. He has to let Vietnam go. It won't bring Dad back. He promised me this was the last shipment and after this he was going straight. He wants to make high-end brass beds. But he needs some capital to start it. He won't borrow money. He's got this hang-up about owing people money."

"We shouldn't jump to conclusions," I say as I unlock the car. "We don't know what happened. I'm going to look on the bright side for once in my life."

She grins at me with a shake of the head. "I tried that once and I ended up married to a drunk. No, it's safer to assume the worst and let life disappoint you from the opposite direction."

"I usually get disappointed from all directions. What hotel are you staying at?"

The Radisson, on Franklin. She rattles off the address and we depart, careful to stay clear of Allen and Monument, an area that by now must resemble a war zone. It still feels surreal, yet all crime tears open the soul — crimes you commit or crimes you witness, both become landmarks that add permanency to life's aimless wandering. I can see why someone would want to eradicate the Lee statue and at the same time I appreciate its enduring legacy to those who see in General Lee magnanimity and grace under pressure. "Will this city survive?" I ask rhetorically, feeling in my heart the terrible passion of both sides. This is the curse of all Southerners who think — the past is never past, as Faulkner tells us, but more than that — the past haunts the future in Dixie, because the original sin of slavery, the greatest crime of all, continues to shred the soul to smithereens.

"You never know," offers Paula, as she gazes out at the desultory streets, "it might just heal some old wounds and bring everyone closer together."

"Are you always a contrarian?"

"Pretty much."

I like Paula. I'm not ashamed to admit that. She has some of Bev's best qualities without the sanctimony that sometimes came with them. Most lawyers end up jaded and broken, having long since given up all hope of finding justice in this world — whereas Bev never quit thinking she could change things for the better, despite overwhelming evidence to the contrary. Then all of a sudden I became the embodiment of all that was wrong with society, and she turned against me . . . isn't that what happened?

Paula continues talking as I steer through the Fan, whose restored brownstones never cease to enthrall. "Contrarians are misunderstood. People think we like to argue just to argue, but I see it differently. I like to keep things fresh. Ideas get stale, just like lettuce, crackers, and marriages."

"And bread."

"So you're a quibbler?"

"I've never been accused of that. I do like details and exactitude." Just ask Lola! She'll tell you all about my desire for precision and nuance. Strange I haven't heard from her in a while. Maybe she's grown tired of the tiresome game we've been playing. Oh, if only that were true. Her silences are usually followed by eruptions that blister me.

"It's too bad our night got cut short," Paula says as we reach the hotel. I pull into the drive that allows me to deposit her at the entrance to the lobby. "I think I'll take your advice, though, and just wait until more facts emerge before I worry too much about Mead."

"You probably shouldn't take advice from me."

She gives me a come-hither look, and I half expect her to invite me up to her room. And I'd probably go, if only because I enjoy failure. "I focus on the message, not the messenger. You seem like you have a good head on your shoulders. Why shouldn't I listen to you? Are you hiding something, Eddie?"

I don't even bat an eye. "I'm hiding a lot of things. So many things."

She beams at me, radiating delight. "I can't read you. I usually read everyone, but you're a tough case. You're unreliable. In an endearing way."

Unreliable? Me? I like to think of myself as precise as a Swiss watch. Paula is basically calling me a liar as a compliment, but I'm finished with lying, which itself is probably a lie. Still, I try the truth on for size, to see if it fits. "What if I'm being honest? Have you considered that?"

She almost says something but stops herself. Maybe she was ready to accuse me of being a fraud, or maybe she was going to invite me up. We'll never know.

"Good night, Eddie. See you tomorrow." We shake hands, and hers lingers in mine — or at least I perceive it to be so. How horrible of us, if we were to engage in some incestuous hanky-panky before the wedding, no strings attached — Lola employed that phrase too casually, without really pondering what a string is or how attachments can be formed without a string — and usually those bonds are the ones that are the hardest to sunder.

"Bye!" I say, waving once my hand is free. Paula hops out and I'm alone again, alone with my thoughts, with my hands, with my life that rests in them. I don't know why I want to drive my Honda straight into the James River. Is it because I'm fighting back the demonic urge to kill Paula? No, I don't want to kill anyone. I know it looks bad, that unexplainable things keep happening to me, that a student inundates me with texts, that my old friend from high school has threatened me, that my stepfather or stepbrother or some combination of the two might have had a hand in destroying Richmond's most cherished monument. All I can say in my own defense is that I'm trying my best. I really am.

But look at how I'm trapped! I'm driving home to see if I can help out, wheeling down Cary Street, obeying the speed limit, when Lola texts me. It's impossible for me to get away from her. I don't even want to know what she has for me this time — or do I? What if she needs my help? This craigslist guy might have trapped her inside his crappy apartment and I have to go rescue her . . . which admittedly is one of my ultimate fantasies . . . Bev never needed me, whereas Lola ached for my approval, my feedback, my support. And now perhaps my derring-do. Unless she's just screwing with me again.

I pull over into the parking lot of a small public library, steeling myself for any number of possibilities. Lola is the ultimate wildcard, as unpredictable as the weather and just as severe under the right conditions . . . but also full of sunny days, languid and peaceful, like when we hiked to the gorge to lounge by the waterfall.

Waterfall. Uncanny.

Lola has texted me a photograph of the very same waterfall I was just thinking about, with this caption:

I wish I was there right now. I hate this guy.

My throat constricts as though I'd just gargled with drain cleaner. In two sentences Lola has managed to summon a welter of conflicting emotions, showing the promise of a young poet mastering the craft. There is fond remembrance and longing for the golden age of June, followed immediately by a jarring shift in perspective from the plaintive to the annoyed. Yet even in this declaration of hatred, gaps remain and the unexplained surges to the foreground . . . why does she hate him? What's he doing to her?

I reply: *Are you ok?*

No poetry, but a simple plea from a man

whose muse long ago fled him. Here in miniature is the fundamental dynamic of our relationship: I struggle to ascertain basic facts, while she floats in and out of comprehension, forever eluding me, jumping from bed to bed, but always ending up in mine, where we read books by candlelight like a middle-aged couple . . . yet she claims to adore just those moments, knowing my hands will never stray and I'll remain faithful. If I can find her, I'll smuggle her into my basement abode so that we can fall again into the comfort of the quotidian, books perched on chests, she smelling of jasmine bath wash, skin luminous, eyes equally shiny, and all mine . . .

She responds: *He's a moron.*

So leave.

I don't want to be rude. He'll think I'm a racist.

Where are you?

I wait two minutes to hear back from her, agonizing minutes, each second another pinprick until my arms and legs have turned numb. But I also have to remind myself that Lola still has refused to show herself to me in Richmond, and until she actually appears before me in person, I have to remain skeptical. At the same time, she could be in grave danger.

Three more times within thirty seconds I implore her: *Tell me where you are and I'll come get you.*

Now what? I'm sitting in the parking lot of a library that used to be one of my favorites in the city. The Belmont branch. I'd retreat here during times of academic stress in high school and find a table in the back where I could work in seclusion. Before that, during the worst of the divorce proceedings, my grandmother would drive me here so I could check out books and then we'd get little bowls of ice cream at Stanley Stegmeyer's . . . she was the one who encouraged me to follow my heart and become a writer. And I did, for many years, try to make her proud. But she moved on to the Underworld, and one day I'll join her there. Maybe even tonight.

I try Lola one last time: *Are you ok??????*

Why does she derive pleasure from torturing me? Especially now, with all that's happened, all that I must take care of, my family in extremis, depending on me to help out, Lola decides to pile on. I really can't deal with her childish antics. If she's out to exact revenge because I want to end it, I'd say she's succeeded tenfold. My brain has become infested with the spiders she's released. A new resolution: I'm going to ignore her. I'm not going to play along anymore. If she's in trouble and needs my help, then she should simply ask me. If she does, of course I'll drop everything and go to her. But she must ask directly, or otherwise I'm taking the vow of silence, which Lola hates more than anything in the world. One Saturday afternoon we accidentally-on-purpose met up at a farmers' market — our trysts were straight out of *Madame Bovary* — and she made the mistake of remarking on how cute she thought the harpist was (this market usually featured a band of co-op yokels). For some reason her quip irritated me. Now mull over that! By then she'd fornicated with around twelve different guys for my viewing pleasure, but this one time I got jealous because indeed the harpist was handsome and probably smart and well-adjusted and all that I wasn't. I stopped speaking to Lola and it drove her nuts. She almost hit me in the mouth with an organic eggplant. One thing Lola will never tolerate is being ignored.

Finally composed enough to drive, I head down Main Street. Once I get home, I'll need to tell my mother everything I know about Graves. What she and Mead decide to do with my debriefing will be up to them. At this point they need to know the facts so that they can respond appropriately. But given that there was a bomb threat against Tredegar earlier today, when Graves was at the wedding rehearsal, there's a chance that Graves has nothing to do with the Lee statue getting blown up. At least, no direct involvement.

At the intersection with Thompson, my phone rings. Ha, my first chance to ignore Lola! Let's see how well she takes to my shunning her. Except it's my mother calling.

"Eddie?" She sounds shaken, distraught, unsteady.

"What's wrong? Are you okay?"

"I don't know."

"I saw it like two seconds after it happened. It was so sad and just overwhelming on a spiritual level."

"What do you mean?"

"The big statue of Robert E. Lee on Monument Avenue? Somebody blew it up tonight. It's got to be all over the news."

"Oh my gosh. No, I hadn't heard. Eddie?"

Her voice is growing fainter, like she's about to lapse into a coma. "I'm here, Mom."

"The police stopped by looking for you."

19

I'm speeding south on Powhite, getting ready to cross over the river. All looks black below me, a vast abyss that has no bottom. "The police? What are you talking about? What police?"

"Two men came here for you."

"Did they say why?"

"No. They just asked if you were here and when we last saw you. Eddie, are you in trouble?"

"No! Why would I be in trouble? I'm sure it's something to do with Leigh Rose Wardell and her crazy brother. They've been going at it hammer-and-tongs and somehow I'm mixed up in it. I'm so sorry you had to deal with that! I'm sure it'll all get straightened out."

"You're not in trouble?"

"Not that I know of."

"I have the detective's number. He wants you to contact him immediately."

She gives me the name of this public servant, Burt Voss, who sounds like he could chew up a diesel engine, and the number I'm to call, which I try to scrawl down on an old bank deposit slip, but it's hard to write and drive at the same time. Somehow the Honda has gotten up to eighty-five miles an hour and it starts shaking from the excessive speed. My foot, however, continues to press on the accelerator against my wishes. How did I lose control of my appendages? My feet, my hands, my dong — none do as instructed anymore.

"I'll call him," I assure her. "First chance I get."

"I'm worried, Eddie. Why do the police want to talk to you?"

"As soon as I know something, I'll tell you. I'll call him right now and clear this all up."

"You can tell me, Eddie! If you need help, we'll get you the best lawyer!"

I hate upsetting my mother. Her approval was something I always sought growing up, and whenever she expressed even mild disappointment, I'd feel horrible shame, which is the psychological motive for murdering Bev if in fact she's dead, which she isn't. Still, my mommy issues do sound plausible and could explain away most of my transgressions. Maybe I'll drop by a local police precinct and confess, thereby saving Detective Voss the trouble of having to find me and employing CIA-approved interrogation techniques to coax the truth out of me. As I've stated many times already, no one wants to come clean more than I do, even though I doubt someone named Burt Voss possesses a nimble-enough mind to fathom all to which I'll confess.

"Mom, I don't need a lawyer. If I ever thought you could help me, you know I wouldn't hesitate to ask."

"You're in trouble now and this is the first I've heard of it. Why would Leigh Rose Wardell call the police on you?"

"It was probably her brother, Jeb, who hates me because he doesn't think I'm good enough for his sister or her money."

"That isn't a crime. Eddie, you're not telling me something. The police just don't show up in the middle of the night because of a family squabble."

"He's setting me up! He's out to ruin me. John Graziano is his henchman and he keeps calling me and threatening me."

"John Graziano?"

"The one and the same."

"But you two are friends and have been your whole life."

"I know, but it's all true and I can prove it." Actually, I can't, because the Graz called me from Leigh Rose's cell phone. Foiled again! Detective Voss won't believe one word I tell him without some corroboration.

"Prove what? What's this all about anyway?"

"Let me call the detective and I promise I'll tell you everything he says. I'm sure it's a misunderstanding of some sort, just another ploy to keep me away from Leigh Rose. But it won't work, because we're in love."

My mother sighs and not from joy, but because perhaps for the first time in her life, she's given up on me. Never having been a parent, I can only guess at the emotional devastation that comes with seeing your child with eyes wide open, the rose-colored glasses having been shattered by reality. The police have come looking for me and I profess my love for a woman she's never met; I haven't been home in two years, and months have gone by without us speaking; she's sent me texts I've ignored, birthday cards I've barely glanced at; the only semblance of a relationship I've maintained with her is the flowers I send to her on Mother's Day, which I've done without fail. And no one was more upset with me than Lola — she's the one who shamed me into repairing things, into reaching out, and finally into coming home. She's the one who told me that I was being a selfish brat and to get over myself. She's the one who insisted my mother has the right to fall in love with whomever she wants, just as Lola herself did. Lola's mantra was simple: stop judging other people and start judging yourself.

"I'll take care of it," I promise again, the little boy who vows to make his bed each and every morning. "Nothing makes sense now but it will once I figure out what's going on."

"Please do. I'll be here waiting for your call."

"Thanks, Mom. And I'm sorry about all of this. The last thing I ever intended was to ruin your wedding."

"It's not ruined yet. But call me as soon as you know something."

We hang up just in time for me to take the exit for Chippenham Parkway, which will ferry me back toward the river at Stony Point and finally home. But if I stay on Chippenham and cross the river, Route 150 becomes Parham Road in Henrico County, and I won't be far from the austere McMansion of Leigh Rose Wardell, where I might finally extract answers to intractable questions. The Honda cruises along the smoothly paved highway, blowing past a pickup truck with a Confederate flag bumper sticker. When will the reprisals begin? When will Robert E. Lee be avenged, even though the man himself sought peace and reconciliation following the war? This city will be tested like it hasn't been since it burned to the ground in 1865. It very well might reignite. I can feel dark forces alive in the air.

I need to call Detective Voss. One solution would be to take the Stony Point exit and pull into the parking lot of the mall so that I could dial the number, provided I can read my own handwriting. But for the sake of argument, let's assume that I can decipher the chicken scratch and I reach Burt Voss, wizened investigator with a failed marriage and a drinking problem — a past that haunts him still — to be played by Christopher Walken in the film version — add any cop cliché here for dramatic effect — anyway, let's say I talk to him. I already know what he wants to talk about, meaning I don't need to talk to Burt Voss in the same sense that you can't step in the same river twice. In other words, life is boring and we must not say so. You shouldn't talk about people behind their back. I'm no tattletale. Or turncoat.

So I zip right past the Stony Point off-ramp, experiencing another out-of-body moment wherein I become an observer of myself. It seems as if I'm headed for Leigh Rose's house, not knowing who or what I'll find there. Something tells me, though, that all the principals are hunkered down on Cragmont Drive, keeping an eye on her. John Graziano warned me not to get involved and then accused me of butting in when I didn't. Since he already thinks I'm meddling, why not meddle? See, people need to know one thing about me: I can't be pushed around. If they want to get rough, well, in the backseat, there is a gun, a very famous pistol, that once belonged to General Giap of the North Vietnamese Army.

20

Here's a true-false quiz. Try your best and no cheating.

1. I took the gun for protection.
2. I took the gun because of the perverse pleasure one derives from transgressing established norms.
3. I took the gun knowing all along that I'd be forced to kill someone, possibly myself, or others, or all of us.
4. I took the gun because I liked how it felt in my hand, the power it conferred, its long and rigid barrel a fine replacement for my deflated phallus.
5. I took the gun because I haven't been thinking clearly of late.
6. I took the gun without knowing whether it had bullets loaded in its chambers.

7. I took the gun thinking I could pawn it if I ever needed quick cash.
8. I didn't take the gun.

One or more of the above statements is true. But wait! Wasn't the gun already missing when I went to check the garage after arriving home and suspecting we'd been burgled? I said it was missing, but I didn't confess to pilfering it at that moment because I couldn't own up to the simulacrum that I've become. Or I was conveying the truth then and am lying now purely for the joy of it, because I'm on the way to Leigh Rose's house for a possible showdown-hoedown with my antagonists.

As I cross the Harry F. Byrd Segregationist Bridge yet again, my mother calls me, frantic for an update.

"Did you speak to the detective?" she gasps.

"I just got off the phone with him."

"What did he say?"

Here I need to be convincing and believable, two qualities that Bev claimed the characters in my novels often lacked. Had I known then how talented a liar she was, maybe I would've taken her critique more to heart. If what she claimed is true, then I have a daunting task before me. But I feel bold and inspired, and inside my head bursts a chorus of bugles to urge me on.

"Well, not much. It's basically what I thought. Jeb Wardell is accusing me of trying to steal Leigh Rose's money."

"Really? You mean like fraud? But that detective said he worked homicides."

Something she failed to mention the first time! How quickly the ground shifts beneath the feet of a fabulist, who by dint of sheer imagination attempts to conjure a universe out of whole cloth. It's not easy to populate a dreamscape, and those authors who can seem to have direct access to the Hindu concept of *svatantrya,* a darkly creative force I grope for but mostly miss. I can almost hear one of Bev's disapproving grunts as she marked up a manuscript, because here again my efforts appear to have come up short. I can't lie my way out of a paper bag. Those who can, do; those who can't, teach; and those who can't teach, teach composition classes (and sleep with their students).

"No, he just asked me questions about Leigh Rose, like when was the last time I'd seen her, that kind of thing."

"How do you know she's not dead?"

"What's that?"

"How do you know she hasn't been murdered? That detective works homicides, and so maybe he's working a homicide. Did he say anything about that? You aren't a suspect, right?"

The bugles in my head have given way to a dirge, the strumming of a Portuguese guitar, with a sad woman wailing. Is Leigh Rose dead? I never considered the possibility, showing again the limits of my creative talent. Criticism, correction, emendation — these are my dubious gifts to the world. I find fault with immature writing, which is like shooting fish in a barrel.

Did Leigh Rose become one such fish?

But how? When? What motive did I have? Settle down, I didn't kill her. But someone else might have, which makes my trip to her house even more poignant. "No, he didn't say anything about that." A logical inference leaps to mind, one so unexpectedly powerful that my shoulders arch back against the seat. "Maybe she's the suspect. Oh my God, I can't believe I just said that."

"What? Do you think she killed somebody?"

"I don't know." I take the exit for River Road, suddenly remembering how John Graziano had told me that Leigh Rose wasn't mentally stable, an assertion I dismissed as ludicrous. Is it possible that she lashed out and killed her brother or Norris

Mumford? Is that why Graz called me on her phone and told me to watch out, that she could get me killed? Now I actually feel like contacting this Detective Voss, except for the fact that it's entirely possible that Voss was looking for me on an unrelated matter. But how much longer can I avoid him?

"Eddie, I don't have a good feeling about this. You should never have gotten mixed up with these people."

"I'm not mixed up in anything. I don't know what's happening, but you shouldn't worry about me." I don't know that I come across as totally convincing, since I'm very worried myself. I need some guidance, a piece of good advice, a sign — yes, a sign from above to lead me in the right direction! But River Road seems devoid of any manifestation of the divine, unless the godhead resides in a big sterile mansion set a hundred yards off the street.

"Are you coming home? Mead is very worried and wants everyone to get off the streets. There have been reports of looting and vandalism downtown. Graves won't answer the phone, and neither will Gibson. The cops have been by already, looking for you of all people! Not Graves, not Gibson, but you! This is not the night I'd planned on, believe me."

"Is there anything I can do to help?"

"Gibson's band played tonight? You saw her?"

"Yeah, she was great. Then she went out with people to celebrate and she promised me she could get a ride home."

My mother inhales sharply and then blurts out a question. "Do you think I should cancel the wedding?"

"No! You need to soldier on, pardon the pun. Normal life must continue."

"They might impose a curfew or even send out a riot squad if things get too bad."

"Let's not jump to conclusions. We don't know what's going to happen."

Her voice lowers to a conspiratorial whisper. "I don't think Mead can do it. He's very upset. I've never seen him this way. He's down in the basement now on the phone with someone. Are you coming home, Eddie? This has been one of the worst nights of my life and I feel so alone. I didn't think I'd ever be alone again by marrying a man with two children, but I am."

"Yeah, it won't be long. You should relax, though."

"I can't relax! I'm getting married tomorrow and someone blew up Robert E. Lee! How am I supposed to relax?"

Have a glass of wine? She's already imbibed too much. No, she needs the sleep of a blushing bride, carried off to slumber with a pill if possible. "Do you have an Ambien?"

"No, I don't. I wish I did. Maybe Gibson has some in her drug stash."

I'm about a minute away from Leigh Rose's house, still unsure what I'll do once I get there. "I'll be home soon, Mom. You should get to bed and just turn out the lights."

"Where are you?"

Can I keep lying to my mother? For the past fifteen minutes I've done nothing but spew total garbage, which she's unconditionally soaked up because she trusts me or at least wants to. Whereas Faulkner could tell people he was in the Royal Canadian Air Force and Salinger could claim he was a goalie for the Montreal Canadiens, lying doesn't come easily to me — and neither does book writing, as it did for those two. So why bother trying to invent? Haven't I proven I'm incapable of conjuring? Fooling people takes a devious talent I lack. "I'm stopping by Leigh Rose's house," I assert. She gasps in horror.

"Why on earth are you there? Get away from her, Eddie! Are you crazy?"

"Yes, I am."

"Eddie, please come home right now. You're scaring me again."

"I just want to check something first."

"What?"

"It's hard to explain."

I pull into the semicircular drive. Her car is parked in front, and I see no others. She must be home alone and thus soon enough I'll know why Detective Voss stopped by. Right? Won't the truth leap out like a tiger from behind a bush? One look from Leigh Rose will be enough for me to calculate the permutations, unless of course there is no look from Leigh Rose because she's in the city morgue.

"Eddie!"

"I'll have to call you back."

I hang up on my mother and then reach for the pistol. It is damn heavy and cumbersome, and loaded with bullets I found in Mead's collection. As I get out of the Honda, I shove it into position at the small of my back, where my blazer will hide it and my taut belt will keep it in place. A gun! It still seems very strange to be in possession of one, but I was correct to take it because the situation has grown more complex. Someone has set me up — or not! That's the maddening part of life, the endless not-knowing, the blindness through which we stagger, the struggle to ascertain basic facts. Who's dead? Didn't we begin our journey with this very issue? Somebody dead will die again? Leigh Rose? Bev? Norris Mumford?

Lola.

No. It can't be Lola, because she texted me not long ago. But here's yet another possibility: Dahlia, the feral roommate. Talk about motive! She knew everything about my twisted relationship with Lola that was actually quite loving and intimate, but Dahlia was unequivocal. I was a creep. A super-creep.

Ya! Look at me now, creeping up to the front door of Leigh Rose's house with a gun wedged in my pants because I want to know why a homicide detective has been snooping around — and why she doesn't love me enough to run away to Paris, tonight.

I ring the doorbell, and the chime thunders ponderously. My chest puffs out as I stake my ground, unafraid of what will come next. Which is precisely nothing, even after I push the button once more. I step back to examine the house and see that lights are on upstairs. Is she avoiding me? On the phone with Norris Mumford to alert him of my intrusion? If so, then soon enough the posse will arrive to claim my scalp, led by no less than the Graz, John Graziano, child-hood chum turned ice-ice-baby slayer.

Which is what happens, only much faster than I expected.

There is a curve in the road in front of Leigh Rose's manse that allows me to see the approach of headlights from the west before anyone in the car can spot me. As soon as I detect the high beams, I dive behind a bushy sedge just in case the car belongs to one of my adversaries. Not that I'm shielded much, and my Honda in the drive is a dead giveaway (pun intended).

The lights track around the curve, and the engine purrs, a testament to the excellence of German engineering. A big Mercedes swings into the drive and rolls to a stop, almost suggesting a bit of hesitancy on the part of the driver. I can't see much from my vantage, such as faces, but I can clearly hear voices.

"Whose car is that?"

"I dunno."

"It's Edwin Stith's."

"What is he doing here?"

"Probably banging the crap out of your sister."

"Shut the hell up."

"She digs his whole bohemian thing."

"I said shut up."

Three voices, one belonging to the Graz, another to Jeb Wardell, and the third presumably to Norris Mumford, whom I've never met. Their shoes scuff along the fresh skim of black asphalt and then quicken up the stairs. The security system is disabled with a series of beeps and squeaks. The front door opens and closes. Then silence.

Should I leave? Now would be the time, when the coast is clear outside as they look for me inside. Staying would accomplish what? What point am I here to prove again? That's right: they can't push me around.

But she digs me! Didn't the Graz just confirm my suspicions? Leigh Rose does have feelings for me, but they're keeping us apart.

So do I perform a frontal assault? My own version of Pickett's Charge, that fateful sally across the cornfield on the last day of Gettysburg? Didn't it end in slaughter, with the South hopelessly outnumbered? Let's see, three of them, one of me . . . those odds didn't seem to bother Robert E. Lee, who ordered the suicide mission, one last-ditch effort to save the Confederacy.

The gun now rests in my sweaty palm.

But then the front door swings open. "Eddie!" someone calls out for me. A woman. Leigh Rose. I can see her bare feet and ankles through the thorny branches. So she's alive . . . meaning Detective Voss came to question me about another homicide, but whose? Does it even matter?

"Get back inside!" someone barks, probably Jeb, but Leigh Rose ignores him.

"Eddie! Talk to me, please!"

My opponents must have guns, too. It's a safe assumption in a nation of two hundred million pistols and rifles. This could get ugly if I come out brandishing a weapon, but then again, who'd ever suspect me of being armed and dangerous? A wanted man, even!

"Eddie, if you can hear me," Jeb cautions, "leave right now before someone gets hurt."

The NRA would be very proud of what happens next. I begin to revel in the power of the gun in my hand, as it seems imbued with sinister forces that connect me to warlords and gangsters. I rise up from my crouch, my head poking through the bush that conceals me.

"Eddie, what are you doing?" Leigh Rose squeals, delight mixed with dread, yet another complication in a night full of them.

"Go inside, Jeb," I say firmly, as we eye each other in a macho showdown. His walrus face creases into a surprised grimace, hands resting on his wide hips.

"I'm not going anywhere," he counters.

"I want to talk to her in private."

"Just go already," Leigh Rose retorts, giving her brother a slight shove that doesn't budge him. "You're so annoying."

"Why are you even here?" he challenges me. Before I can respond, Graz comes out and does a double take when he spots me in the bushes.

"Eddie?"

"Can I talk to Leigh Rose for five minutes, please? Alone?"

"You should go," Graz intercedes as he looks around for helicopters or drones that might drop down from the sky.

"He doesn't have to go anywhere," Leigh Rose sniffs, before jumping down off the stoop and joining me in the bushes. Norris Mumford has apparently merged with the group as well. I can't make out his features too clearly because he remains in the shadows, but my first impression is: bland and regular. Nothing remarkable, just another well-bred sybarite from the burbs of Henrico. "It's my house and I say he stays."

She slips her hand into mine. Her skin feels clammy and cold, despite the oppressive heat that presses down on us from all sides. Sweat literally drips from every pore of my body, and dehydration is making me dizzy. It was a mistake to come here. I belong with Lola, my love. She must be back at the hotel by now. How do I get away, with Leigh Rose clutching onto me like I'm a life preserver?

"I have to get out of here," I mutter under my breath.

"Me too," she whispers, reeking of booze.

Graz takes center stage, determined to play Brutus to the hilt. A good man driven to treachery for a noble cause: my demise. "Eddie, don't make this hard on yourself. You don't know the whole story —"

"He knows plenty! He knows you guys all want my money and you can't have it." But in Leigh Rose's voice now I can detect traces of instability that were lacking earlier. Is it just that she's drunk? But what if Graz is right about her mental condition? Leigh Rose squeezes my hand even tighter, so that blood can't circulate to my fingers. Is she crazy? Or have these idiots driven her around the bend?

"Eddie, get in your car and drive away. That's the smart move here. We've all had a long day and Leigh Rose could use a good night's sleep."

"They think I'm suicidal! It's all crap! Just leave me alone, okay? I'll be fine."

"She tried three weeks ago," Graz says solemnly.

"That's a lie! You all hate me because I won't marry Norris, and I won't marry Norris no matter what lies you tell about me. I'd never kill myself."

"Her daughter found her facedown in the bathroom. That's why the kids aren't here."

"They're at camp. Listen to this crap! Eddie, let's go. Take me anywhere. Just get me away from these people."

"I don't know what's going on," I announce forcefully, summoning courage from the gun perhaps, or just from the last drops of humanity left in me. "If Leigh Rose needs mental health services, you should get a professional to help her, because this little intervention isn't working. You three get inside so I can talk to her."

"We're not going anywhere without her," Jeb informs me.

I want to shoot him. How happily I'd blow his face off with a single shot. But I just can't bring myself to lift the pistol.

"Five minutes, okay? I just want to ask her a few questions." For several seconds all quiets down and it seems as though they're going to comply with my request. Having dealt for years with students on the verge of a nervous breakdown, I'll quickly ascertain whether Leigh Rose is mentally sound. But then Jeb notices something and his mouth drops open like he's about to devour an entire ham.

"Is that a gun?" he asks in horror, pointing at me, his index finger wagging in front of his beer-swollen belly.

I don't bother to reply as it's pretty obvious what's in my hand. A rollicking spasm of ire seizes Jeb and nearly lifts him off the ground, and I lean back in case he jumps on top of me.

"You've got a gun? Were you planning on shooting all of us? You gutless prick! You probably blew up General Lee's statue, too, I bet. A gun. Fuck your gun, Edwin. You don't have the balls to use it."

A cooler head prevails, in the form of the even-tempered John Graziano, who manages to come between Jeb and me. "Eddie, put the gun away," he counsels, his body serving as a human shield of sorts. Flying under the radar, though, is Norris Mumford, who ducks inside the house, presumably to get a weapon of his own. Or to call the cops. Or take Leigh Rose's credit cards.

"I brought it to protect myself," I say emphatically, not about to unilaterally disarm while facing down a ravening lunatic in Sperry topsiders and an ill-fitting Hollister T-shirt. Jeb doesn't have the body to pull off a slim fit. "There's some crazy stuff happening tonight, as you're well aware of. I didn't come here looking for trouble, let's be clear about that."

"Why did you come here then?" Graz asks, sounding sincere in his confusion.

"To check on her."

"You suck!" Jeb thunders at me, not persuaded by my concern for his sister. "You're fucking everything up and you think you're so smart, but you're stupid and a coward. You stuck your dumb nose in it now, nerd. There's gonna be hell to pay, promise you. Might as well shoot me. Come on, tough guy. Put a bullet in me."

"Just hold on." Graz sighs, revealing a weariness with his master's antics. "Nobody is shooting anyone. Eddie, drop the gun and walk away."

"No way."

"Then just leave."

"Fine."

"Eddie's staying with me tonight," Leigh Rose shouts with the gusto of a carnival barker, grabbing me around the waist.

"That can't happen," Graz parries. "We both know that and so just drop it. Eddie's leaving, aren't you, Eddie?"

Norris has finally returned, and if he has a gun, he's concealed it. He does whisper in Jeb's ear, however, sharing some pearl of wisdom that causes Jeb to grin callously.

"Eddie? You're leaving, right?" Graz tries again.

Leigh Rose pulls her body against mine, which causes me to tense up. On an intellectual level, I understand her embrace to be an act of defiance, and there's a slight chance she has feelings for me. But besides that, the more pressing issue is what if she is in the midst of a breakdown and needs help that she won't get from this gang of miscreants. Should I stay to assist her, to save her even — yet I might be completely wrong about everything and getting played by Leigh Rose for a fool, and not for the first time. I never signed up for this heroic role, but I'm the one who came here, only because the police are looking for me . . . the police. Hmmmm.

What I say next surprises me because I honestly didn't think that I could outwit anyone . . . but I suppose self-preservation takes over at some point, and I need to know why the cops want to speak with me. "Well, sure thing, I'll go," I reply, brazenly staring down Jeb, gun still in my hand. "But let me tell you something. The cops have been to my house already. Whatever little scheme you morons are pulling off here, it's already too late."

"What cops? What the hell are you talking about?" Graz's nasal monotone has given way to worried snarl, which is music to my ears, amplified when Leigh Rose begins laughing hysterically. So these washed-out frat boys are up to no good, though I don't know what precisely they're doing.

"He's a lying piece of crap!" Jeb growls, but Graz ignores him. It isn't hard for me to be convincing, because I'm merely telling (some of) the truth.

"Eddie, what are you talking about?"

"Don't listen to him," Jeb brays once more. I decide to be coy, knowing I've struck a nerve. I pat a pocket with a cock-sure grin.

"I got the number right here. Think I'll give the detective a call and tell him everything I know."

"He's bluffing!"

But Graz knows me better than Jeb, and he can tell I'm being sincere. "Hold on. Eddie, there's no reason the police would come question you about anything we're connected to."

"Right!" Leigh Rose squeals in delight, undercutting Graziano's humble entreaty.

"That isn't for me to decide," I mutter, trying to maintain a poker face devoid of emotion, when inside I'm bursting with doubt. "All I know is my mother said the police want to talk to me. I figured it was about you all." Or about a homicide in Ithaca. Maybe one in Gettysburg. There are always competing scenarios.

"You can say that again," Leigh Rose chants, a welcome if not deranged chorus of support.

It proves too much for Graz to withstand. "Wait! Just wait. What do you want? You want to sleep here tonight? Is that it?"

I remain stoic, not from choice but due to the fact that I'm speechless, which only fuels his angst. So Graz sweetens the pot as only a frightened plutocrat can.

"Is it about money? Just come clean, okay? I don't have time for any games. What the hell do you want, Eddie? Name your price."

"Maybe he's not a prick like you guys are," Leigh Rose erupts, shaking the bush in rebuke like a jungle goddess as she waves her arms. "You wouldn't understand that because you only think about yourselves. But Eddie here is a college professor, he's a scholar, and you can't just buy his integrity."

"Yeah?" Jeb sneers, eyes burning at me. "Okay, would you stay quiet for a hundred thousand bucks? Would that take care of your integrity?"

"Go to hell," Leigh Rose answers for me,

and a good thing, too, because I probably would've taken the money, what with all the legal bills staring me in the face.

"Eddie, what do you want?" Graz asks point-blank.

"For what?"

"For turning the other cheek."

A little humility goes a long way. I tell him the absolute truth, the very reason I came here at all. But would they really hand over a hundred g's? Guess we'll never know . . .

"I want to talk to Leigh Rose alone for five minutes."

Next to me I hear Leigh Rose gasp, not in surprise, but more like she almost tripped and caught herself at the last second. Her hand finds mine and she squeezes tight. The gun now feels like it weighs a ton. If I'm not careful, I might literally shoot myself in the foot, provided this weapon functions.

"Sure, no problem." Graz tries to herd his comrades inside but Jeb is unwilling to leave, Stonewall Jackson reincarnated.

"That's it? He can threaten us and we do nothing?"

"Come inside, dude."

Until now Norris Mumford has been a complete nullity, the typical amiable dunce whose natural habitat is the background. But for some reason, acquiescence brings out the tiger in him. Retreat proves liberating, and thus free from being a mere follower, he produces a revolver and points it at my face.

"Get the fuck out of here, loser," he growls.

His voice is deeper than I expected, resonant even, cowboy in texture, and I have no doubt he'll blow me away if given the chance. Leigh Rose shrieks and covers her mouth, while I marvel at the sheer brilliance of this nonentity, who is calling my bluff against the wishes of his compatriots.

"Don't be an idiot!" Graz remonstrates, slapping at the gun like it's a nuisance.

"He doesn't need to be up in our business."

"I hate all of you!" Leigh Rose screams, and even among the far-off McMansions, neighbors could probably hear her. Graz of course realizes the potential pitfalls involved in an unseemly public outburst, but Norris, perhaps impelled by stupid masculine jealousy, continues to take aim at me. Even by now Jeb wants the standoff to end, and puts his arm around Norris's shoulders the way a coach might console a losing player. It's a tense moment to endure, two men with guns in the middle of the night, both vying for the same woman (not really), one of us an outlaw, a desperado, a pervert . . .

"This is ridiculous," Graz fumes. "Get inside. Let them talk. Eddie, five minutes."

Norris Mumford wavers, seemingly caught between two poles — giving in to me, the embodiment of all that is wrong in the world, according to RushHannity, or standing up for his bedrock principles, which might land them all in prison. Thankfully he comes to his senses, more or less. "He's the reason she's acting all crazy," he fumes, the gun dropping down in surrender, Jeb Wardell by his side, the moon above in a waning crescent phase, meaning that tomorrow night there'll be even less of it revealed to us below, until finally in a week it'll disappear altogether, thereby mirroring my own lapse into obscurity.

Now I'm alone with Leigh Rose, and we're still ensconced in the bushes. First we must crawl out before we're devoured by annoying gnats and ants that seek out our moist flesh. We emerge from the primeval forest and walk over to my car, reminding me once more of being with her in high school. At the end of the night she'd always walk with me out to the driveway and kiss me good night, where we'd laugh some more and mock the serious, never doubting that our youth would last forever. Now, however, I must assess her mental stability and decide whether to intervene in a meaningful way. But if I were to leave with her, the three amigos would give chase. And where would we go? Surely not to the Chicory. My phone has been blowing up, as they say, but I can't bring myself to check it. For now, Leigh Rose gets my full attention, since we'll probably never see each other again.

"Are you okay?" I ask gently, still holding the gun, which I'm loath to put aside. But she's fascinated by it and tries to take it from me. But she's the last person who needs a pistol.

"Where did you get this thing, Eddie? It's huge."

"It belongs to the man my mother is going to marry."

"Can I hold it?"

"Seriously, are you okay?"

But she continues to ignore this crucial question and instead grips the gun by the barrel and pulls it away from me. It takes a sustained effort to thwart her, which only makes her snappy. "You don't trust me? You think I'll shoot myself right here? Come on, Eddie. Don't believe the lies they told you about me. I just want everyone to leave me alone. I have two children to raise."

"And they're at camp?"

"Sort of. They're with their grandparents, whose estate is like a camp." Sometimes all it takes is one pebble of truth to begin the rock slide of admission. She finally releases the gun and stares down at her bare feet. "Okay, things haven't been great with me. My daughter can be a pain in the ass. My son is lost. It's my fault." She sniffles and I find myself reaching for her. But she remains frozen in place, a block of ice in this torment of heat. "I'm the worst mother in the world. I don't deserve any of this. I really feel like I'm losing it. No, I've lost it, Eddie. I'm totally crazy. They're right. I'm a horrible person." Then she giggles girlishly, even as tears stream down her face. "Did the cops really come talk to you?"

"According to my mother."

"That figures. Those idiots, they're always looking for easy money. Silver mines in Kenya, uranium deposits in Bolivia, I can't keep up with it all. Oh, and bullets. They're buying like thousands of rounds of ammunition because they think the government will ban bullets."

"Do you want me to get you out of here? Because I will. I'll take you wherever you want to go so you can get help, if that's what you want."

She searches the night sky for guidance, but sometimes the stars don't align the way we want them to. "I'm going to marry Norris."

"What?"

"I said yes. I accepted his proposal. We're going to fly to Las Vegas tomorrow and get married." She cackles bitterly, brushing perspiration from her eyes. At night this part of Henrico County grows deathly quiet, and buried deep within the bosom of the land, beneath these monstrous houses of red brick, are the decayed roots of tobacco plants and the white bones of black slaves who toiled here. Generations of women have roamed these gentle hills and dreamt of escape, from drudgery, servitude, war, poverty, boredom, insanity . . . maybe standing right on the same spot Leigh Rose now occupies, laughing at life, and crying, too.

"That explains why he wanted to shoot me," I observe, ever the logician in search of a priori causes.

"He's a prick."

"Then why are you marrying him?"

"Because I can't marry you."

"No, you really can't."

"But how did the cops get your name, I wonder? That part scares the crap out of me. Those three inside, they need to chill

425

out with their little plan of world domination before it's too late."

"I can take you away from all of this! Seriously! We can leave right now!"

"Oh, Eddie. I want to, I really do. But I can't leave Richmond, now or ever." She melts into my arms one last time, and it feels as if the credits should roll. But nothing is more illusory than an ending.

21

It's after eleven p.m. Lola has summoned me. She claims that she's at the Chicory Motel (again), that her tryst has ended, and that she might now grant me an audience. My mother has also called and wants to know when I'm coming home. There is also the matter of returning the call of Detective Voss, though I really don't want to and I'm very bad at forcing myself to do unpleasant jobs like publishing academic papers no one will ever read. If I call Voss, my life will be ruined. If I don't call Voss, my life will be ruined. Either way, I'm ruined. Good times were had by all!

Unless Lola can figure out a way for me to move forward. She's got a devious mind and knows how to work an angle . . . so to the Chicory I must now go, for a consultation with the queen of the quick fix, who routinely forced her professors to change her grade, and who never paid a traffic or parking ticket in her life. I have to admit that I'm running out of energy. I can picture myself reclining on a brick-hard hotel bed, with my head nestled in Lola's warm lap, her long fingers caressing my hair, while listening to her concoct a foolproof plan to elude the pursuit of my tormentor, the relentless Detective Voss, who seeks nothing more than my total destruction. In the background the TV will be on, at a low volume, because Lola finds the chatter to be soothing, a habit of hers I'd love to break. She hates silence, and being alone is hell for her.

River Road winds me back toward Richmond, and when I reach the sprawling River Road Baptist Church, I decide to let my mother know of my plans. I want to relieve her of worry on the eve of her wedding, but instead, when she doesn't answer the phone, my own concern for her grows exponentially. I leave a harried and half-baked message, promising I'll return after I run a few more errands. But what's going on back at Traylor Estates? I picture several scenarios: the SWAT team surrounding the house in full riot gear or else the Russian weapons dealer and a gang of marauding Slavs with vengeance on their vodka-smelling breaths, out for a pound of Mead's flesh. Panic seizes me around the throat and begins choking the life out of me. Driving becomes impossible and so I pull over into the driveway of an older and stately home, built back when River Road slithered into the countryside. I call my mother again and get kicked to voice mail, and I yell at the phone for being so stupidly obtuse at this perilous moment in my life. What hath I wrought? Not even Lola can help me now if the situation has devolved to that point . . . Lola . . . I can't even bring myself to call her! I want her, I need her, I love her — and yet I can't tell her what I've done. She'll laugh in my face, and rightly so. She has her whole life in front of her, and what of me? Will conjugal visits to prison sate her?

I can't go back to Leigh Rose's house, either. All avenues of escape have been cut off. Defeat is something that Richmonders know well, but if General Lee could lay down his sword with grace, I can, too. I fish out Detective Voss's phone number, ready to join the ranks of the dead who haunt our city. I can't allow my mother to suffer due to my own perfidy. You break it, you own it.

I dial with my hands trembling in fear, nerves shot, brain fried . . . I'll confess to everything they want me to. I killed Kennedy and I killed Jim Morrison. I sold heroin to John Belushi. Let's get this over with.

"This is Voss."

I almost hang up, but I've crossed the Rubicon now and there's no turning back. "Hi, this is Edwin Stith returning your call."

"Edwin Stith, yes, thanks for calling me back. I was hoping you could help me with something. I got a call from a colleague in the Ithaca PD and they're looking for a missing girl, by the name of, let's see, it's here somewhere, Lola LaSalle? Have you had any contact with her?"

"I have, as a matter of fact."

"You have?"

"She's called me a few times today but left messages. I haven't spoken to her directly because it's been a little crazy here, with my mother's wedding. Her father called me as well. She's missing?" I have to admit to these contacts because her cell phone records are easily obtained. Anyway, I've got no reason to lie about her whereabouts.

"No one's heard from her in a few days, which I understand isn't that unusual from what they tell me, but her parents are worried. But you've heard from her today? Did she say where she was?"

"No, she just told me about some guy she

was trying to find that she met online. She's a very adventurous young woman, one of my favorite students, but if her parents are worried, that is a different story."

"But you never spoke to her in person? She just left you messages, but didn't say where she was?"

"No."

"Here's the confusing part, Professor Stith. When the Ithaca PD checked her cell phone records, it turns out she's making calls from Richmond."

"From Richmond? Are you serious?"

"She never said she was in Richmond?"

"No. Never. She is crazy, I swear. Maybe she wants to surprise me." I laugh like an amused uncle who gets a gag gift on Christmas. But Lola has screwed up royally now. Voss doesn't believe my genial lies — he's no fool, he knows she came down to see me but that I can't admit to that, given today's policies against amorous relations on campus.

"Why would she want to surprise you?"

"That's how she is. A merry prankster."

"You two are close, I take it?"

"I work at a small college. I'm close to many of my current and former students."

"Well, Professor Stith, thanks for clearing that up for me. I'll let everyone up in Ithaca know what you've just told me. This is your cell number? I can reach you on this in case there are follow-up questions?"

Of which there'll be a million, because now the entire world knows about Lola and me! Oh, happiness! The end is nigh! Edwin Stith, kaput. The king is dead, long live the king. Her little escapade, her telling of Dahlia . . . these are trifles, sure, except in the world of academia, where she's accused me of high treason. The nymphs aren't to be touched. No touching! It's worse than kindergarten. Yet many want to be touched by a mature man . . . Here's a fun fact about Lola. No one but me has ever brought her to orgasm. Yes, all those prodigiously endowed stallions have swung and missed, because they know nothing about how to make love, how to reach a woman's innermost parts, which don't reside between the legs. Only I, the eternally flaccid, can make Lola climax because I'm patient and attentive and focused on her enjoyment. Does Detective Voss, or my fussy dean, or any of our moralizers in cap-and-gown, understand what true love even is?

I put the car in drive, resigned to my fate. One last trip to the Chicory, where Lola will greet me with a smile, but it's the smile of the Cheshire cat. Her claw marks are all over my career. Poor kid! Her desire to be rebellious has led to my undoing . . . I should've seen it coming.

As I continue on down River Road, I scan the radio stations of Richmond to find news, any news, of the destruction of the Lee statue. A part of me still wonders when the names of my stepfather and stepbrother will get mentioned, but on the AM dial, a sedate DJ intones that no arrests have been made, no suspects have been identified — and no group has taken responsibility. I might have expected that the Bastard Sons would have owned it by now, by issuing a proclamation of some kind. Usually that's how such shadowy groups operate, not that I'm a domestic terrorism expert or any kind of expert.

As I reach the River Road Shopping Center, anchored by Ukrop's Supermarket, famous in Richmond for clean-cut baggers and never being open on Sunday, I debate whether to call Lola. I don't know that I'm composed enough to speak with her, but I also want to alert her of my impending arrival so that she doesn't fly the coop again. I have the phone in my hand as I wait at a red light where River Road merges with Cary Street. But then it rings, the tone jarring me from a Lola-induced reverie of conciliation. The caller ID reads Gibson.

Whoa. This can't be good news.

"Hello?" I answer cautiously.

"Hey, it's me, Gibson. Where are you?"

"Um, just heading up Cary Street. Why?"

"There's a problem."

"What kind of problem?"

"Graves is in trouble and he needs our help. I'm at this dive bar in Oregon Hill, and you have to come get me and then we'll go get him."

"Where is he?"

"He won't tell me."

"Then how are we supposed to get him?"

Gibson sighs at my lack of imagination. "Just get over here and pick me up. He's really in trouble. I'm at Bazooka Joe's on Pine Street. Hurry, okay? I'm serious."

The other shoe has dropped, as it usually does. Though Gibson didn't say, I'm pretty sure I know the cause of the trouble Graves finds himself in. Just when I thought I'd never need a gun again! But on such a restive night, with legends tumbling and the dead dying again, it's a good thing to have a very heavy sidearm. Will it actually discharge a bullet? We'll see . . .

What of Lola? She has summoned me and yet again we appear destined to miss each other. She can't stand being alone, I get that, but maybe this once she can curl up on the bed and watch one of her stupid TV shows until I get there. As I speed along Cary and approach the front edge of Windsor Farms I call her, and what do you know? She doesn't answer. This is getting annoying. We live in an age of advanced technology and global communication, and I can't even complete a simple phone call with my beloved. I leave a message informing her that an unexpected family emergency has detained me, but that I badly want to see her and that we have much, so much, to discuss. I'd rate my performance as acceptable. I don't think I came across as panicked or angry, just efficient and concerned. Lola doesn't react well to stress, and if she thinks I'm upset with her or in trouble, she can fly off the handle. It's already an open question why she won't pick up her phone.

I head toward Oregon Hill, a working-class neighborhood located near where the state penitentiary used to be. Like much of downtown Richmond, it has experienced a revival of sorts. I took Bev to a Vietnamese place there on our last visit home, and the signs of gentrification were evident even then. The little row houses were being renovated and painted bright colors, and the state pen had become a chemical plant.

Some might call this progress, compared to the drug-infested blight of the area when I was in high school.

For what seems like the hundredth time today, I cruise down Cary Street, through the fashionable districts of the Fan, until fifteen anxious minutes later I reach the sprawling urban campus of VCU. I know I'm getting close to the turnoff for Oregon Hill, and for some reason Laurel Street rings a bell. I hang a quick right and pass over the Downtown Expressway. It takes me a few minutes to realize that I'm just minutes away from Tredegar Iron Works, where tomorrow my mother will be married and today a group threatened to blow it up. Is that the next target tonight?

And if Graves has committed criminal acts, and I were to help him evade capture, then I'd be an accomplice after the fact and guilty of obstruction of justice. In the larger scheme of things, these charges are more akin to mosquito bites than real wounds. Still, I hope Gibson understands that we can't harbor a fugitive.

The streets of Oregon Hill narrow considerably, and I can tell that parking is a real challenge in this congested little plot nestled against the river. At a stop sign I quickly consult my phone to get a grip on where

Bazooka Joe's is. Pine Street is a block over, and so I turn left and then slowly glide a few blocks south, on the lookout for an open space. In addition to Bazooka Joe's, there are other small, eclectic establishments that doubtlessly Lola would love, as she delights in frequenting cramped retail spaces and packed cafés where the tables are pressed together and the menus are handed out on clipboards . . . this is her kind of mojo, very Ithaca in feel. Bev too liked off-the-beaten-path curiosities, but not even Oregon Hill made her warm up to Richmond.

A parking spot! In front of a record store. I deftly swing the Honda into position, showing off my unsurpassed parallel-parking skills. Now, onward. But my legs have suddenly grown wobbly, just as I've reached the home stretch. If I were a jockey, I'd be lashing my flanks with a riding crop. To little avail. My body has begun to cramp up in weird ways, indicating that I need water. This night is starting to take its toll on me. My head literally starts to spin as I step down the brick sidewalk, uneven in places, causing my balance to be thrown off. Another metaphor! The ground is shifting beneath my feet, and nausea creeps into my upper GI tract.

Bazooka Joe's, dead ahead. I forge on, hoping I can make it. I'd sometimes experience these strange blackout episodes during a two-year trial of painkiller addiction, which more or less has ended, at Lola's urging . . . yet another way she cares for me! It's been a month since my last "poppage," as I came to term my pill usage. I bought them from my neighbor, a woman who'd been in four car accidents in four years, and whose spinal fluid leaked everywhere, or something, and her pain management consisted of selling her prescriptions so she could buy food and bourbon. In a sense, I was conducting civic engagement, building bridges between academia and the surrounding community . . . without me, she would have starved. Without her, I would've actually felt the pain of Bev leaving me.

Bazooka Joe's is crowded, and I don't have the body strength to seek out Gibson. Instead, I slump into an empty bar stool that became vacated right as I was going to crumple to the floor. I hold up my hand and feebly wave it. The bartender, a raven-haired waif adorned with fierce tattoos, comes over.

"Water," I croak. "Thank you."

Wordlessly she fulfills my request and within seconds I have a big Solo cup of ice water to chug down. If only guilt could be quenched like thirst! There needs to be an elixir that can wash away the lingering pangs of regret that only your hometown can elicit. I need to be with Lola now, right this second, but yet again affairs of state interfere. I check my phone; no call back from her. She's in Richmond, that much we know. How this will play out is anyone's guess.

I leave the bartender a dollar tip and begin my search for Gibson, which takes only a minute because Bazooka Joe's is very small. And loud. And smelly. My stomach is barely hanging on. Gibson, thankfully, is ready to leave at once.

"We have to go," she says, pulling me by the arm. I enjoy it when women take over. Only then can I truly relax. Nothing about manhood pleases me anymore. I could have made an excellent court eunuch in ancient China and given my verbal skills risen to a high rank, having won the confidence of the emperor that his concubines were safe around me.

"Where is he?"

"It's a long story."

"Condense it."

"What?"

"Make it short and sweet. I don't have

time to go on a wild-goose chase."

She ignores me, pushing through the bar. Outside, she wheels to face me, deadly serious in her kittenish way. "Graves is like freaking out," she intones, rubbing her temples with her hands like a long-suffering housewife confronting a doltish husband. "He texted me that he was going to die unless someone could get him out of there."

"Hold on. Where is he right now?"

She consults her phone with expert dexterity. "St. John's Church. Never heard of it. Do you think it's a bar?"

I stifle a laugh, long ago having learned that the young might lack certain knowledge but still possess a purity that ignorance only emboldens. "No, it's not a bar. St. John's? Really? It's like the oldest church in Richmond. It's where Patrick Henry delivered his 'Give Me Liberty or Give Me Death' speech during the Revolutionary War."

"Oh, that makes sense. Graves is always rattling on about that."

"It's not far. Should we go get him?"

"No. Let's stand here like a pair of morons."

For some reason I snap at her. "I don't have to do this, you know. Stop acting like I'm the hired help."

"Fine. Get the fuck out of here then!"

Gibson never backs down, always stays in attack mode.

"I don't mind helping, but don't get in my face."

"Grow a pair. Graves is probably dead by now anyway. Those jerk-offs he's been hanging with, they're nuts."

"I'm parked over here."

She still walks in front of me, the indomitable one, eighteen going on thirty, exuding a raw energy that can bend metal. At least she trusted me enough to call me in her time of need, a marked improvement from her running out of the 7-Eleven this morning . . . was it this morning that I first met Gibson? It seems like a lifetime ago. We've managed to pack in quite an assortment of excitement during our brief relationship — hitchhiking, a sexual romp that nearly got us both killed, a killer set at the Dungeon, and now this, a rescue mission of sorts, that will take us to the ideological birthplace of our nation.

"You heard about the Lee statue, right?" I ask after we both get into the Honda.

"Yeah." Her shoes come off, and bare feet go to the dash.

"Do you think Graves had anything to do with it?"

She inhales sharply and shakes her head

441

almost in disgust. "I hope not. But you shouldn't even talk about it. Never. You could jinx him."

"Come on, that's ridiculous." I start the sickly sounding engine, noticing that I need gas. "We need to stop for gas. There's got to be a station on Broad Street, don't you think?"

"Can we stop after we get him?"

I quickly calculate the distance involved with the amount of gas in my tank. "Sure. As long as we find a station right after. Get on your phone and sleuth out a place near St. John's Church."

She begins the assigned task at once, and the glow from her touch screen casts an angelic light on her face. But my heart sinks, thinking of Lola . . . she's at that fleabag hotel, waiting for me. Now that we've been outed, there's no reason for us to hide . . . I can take her to the wedding tomorrow and proclaim my love for her in public. No more lies, no more hiding! Give me liberty or give me death!

But traffic in Oregon Hill is snarled and we crawl along Pine Street. Gibson bounces in her seat, yelling at the cars ahead of us to move. I share in her frustration, because the longer this takes, the longer my reunification with Lola will be delayed. They say good things come to those who wait, but not when you're dealing with an impetuous young woman with a bottomless appetite for the macabre.

"What the hell is going on?" fumes Gibson. "No one in this city can drive! Graves just texted me and he's really scared. He thinks they're going to find him."

"Who's going to find him?"

She falls silent, unwilling to betray her brother's confidence. But noncompliance right now isn't an option, and so I press harder. "Listen, I need to know what I'm getting into here. If Graves is mixed up in the Lee statue getting blown up and we help him in any way, then guess what? We become accomplices after the fact and we'll go down with him. Do you want to get dragged into the Bastard Sons?"

"How do you know about them?"

"That doesn't matter. The point is, you have to tell me what you know. I'm not willing to go to jail because of suburban revolutionaries who don't have a clue. And you already might know too much, by the way, so you need to be extra careful."

She sighs bitterly, smart enough to realize I'm right but too stubborn to give me any credit. She takes the only legal avenue that makes sense, which is also infuriating. "In that case, I don't know anything."

"Is that so? You seem to know something about what's going on."

"I don't."

"What about the Bastard Sons?"

"I've never heard of the Bastard Sons."

It's a virtuoso performance of plausible deniability on par with the Reagan administration. I get the impression that not even waterboarding could make her spill the beans on Graves. Again, from a legal standpoint, she's on solid ground. But from my perspective, I still know next to nothing. But soon one of my secrets is revealed. Her feet plop down from the dash and fall to the floorboard, where she bumps into something. She reaches down and picks up Giap's pistol and holds it gingerly, with her fingertips, like it's been dipped in battery acid. I'd neglected to move it to a more secure location.

"Oh my God!" she cries. "Is this yours?"

"Put it down! Gently, please."

She complies, my heart pounding away in terror. "It's like the biggest one I've ever seen. Where'd you get it?"

"From the basement."

She smirks in apparent appreciation. "Good. We might just need it."

Suddenly the traffic clears and we start to

gather speed as we head toward the river. Why is it that I can conceal nothing while Gibson is able to remain enshrouded in mystery? Once more she's leading me on a fool's errand to do her bidding against my better judgment. But I press on, in the name of saving the wedding, which by now might be irredeemable.

When we reach Belvedere, where I put on my left-turn blinker, I think: it's funny my mother hasn't called me back.

22

The venerable St. John's sits atop Church Hill, a district that in my childhood was known for being the epicenter of urban blight. But no longer. Like Oregon Hill, Church Hill has undergone profound changes that have brought in bistros, art galleries, and boutiques. Evidence of the eighteenth century remains very much at the fore, but now with a veneer of twenty-first-century cool. As Gibson and I approach the wooden church by ascending the steep embankment at 24th Street, I ask her where we should look for Graves, as the grounds of St. John's take up an entire city block.

"I'll text him," she replies. As we wait at a traffic light, I notice a familiar car parked on Grace Street opposite from us: it's the same Isuzu pickup truck that I'd seen in the driveway when I'd first arrived home, owned by Avery, if that's his name. The kid

Graves wasn't supposed to be hanging out with.

"Hey, isn't that Avery's truck?" I ask, and Gibson looks up, spooked by words.

"Where?"

"Right there." I point, and she responds by ducking down low in the front seat.

"If he sees me, we're dead."

"What?"

The light turns green and I freeze. "What should I do?"

Gibson is texting away in her defensive posture, which would tax a yoga instructor. "Take a left."

There isn't much traffic now and unimpeded we proceed west on Grace Street for two blocks, where she then tells me to take a right. I keep looking in the rearview mirror to see if Avery is following, but as far as I can tell, the truck is still parked in the same place. We're now slowly rolling down a narrow lane, past an ordinary building that houses something called ChildSavers. Irony abounds at all times, even if we mostly ignore it.

"Graves is not replying," Gibson moans in agony. "I wonder if they already found him."

"Who, Avery? I thought Avery was his friend."

"Avery has no friends, dude. Take a right."

447

I do what I'm told and we now climb up East Broad Street and pass Patrick Henry's Pub & Grille. The stately if not pugnacious church again comes into view, as fittingly Gibson leans over and picks up the gun from her feet. My eyes bug out of my head at the sight. What brash plan is cooking inside her pulchritudinous skull? What has my pilfering unleashed?

"Whoa, hold on," I say in my most paternal tone, omniscient and annoyed. But Gibson brushes me off with a shrug.

"Just drive, okay. That asshole isn't winning this time."

"There's another time? Why can't we just call the cops? This is madness."

"Park there." She means on the street beneath a leafy maple tree.

"Why?"

"Just do it. And keep the car running."

The needle on the gas tank is pushing E. I follow her instructions, and as soon as we're parked, she jumps out before she can explain even the rudiments of her scheme. I watch as Gibson goes hurrying off toward the backside of the white church, whose spire rises gracefully over the old city. She's stuffed the gun into a shoulder bag, and soon she rounds a corner and is gone. Still no word from my mother, not to mention

Lola . . . all of this feels so wrong. I'd call 911 myself, except for the obvious reason that my own crimes prevent me from reporting this outrageous showdown in the shadow of a hallowed ground. Any second I expect to hear gunfire, which, back in the day, when Richmond was the murder capital of the country, a shoot-out on Church Hill was a regular happening. I don't have much time left as a free man, and spending it this way, filled with dread instead of in Lola's arms, strikes me as unfairly absurd. The powerlessness of waiting . . . all day I've been chasing down ghosts in a city surfeited with them . . . maybe Bev was right after all . . . there was no reason to return here, to come to Dixie . . . my mother could visit us in Ithaca, which she refused to do because she knew Bev hated Richmond . . . the two women in my life, constantly sparring, at war, with me the collateral damage.

Minutes slice by, chopped by the savage knife of Time. How much more can I endure? I should call Detective Voss back and beg him to come arrest me, though he'd be the most surprised homicide flatfoot in history since there are no charges pending against me. But he could also bail us out of this mess before it's too late and I have to tell Mead his children are dead . . .

There they are! Finally something has gone right tonight! Gibson and Graves come sprinting down the sidewalk, and on Graves's face is a grin that can only be described as joyous, while Gibson remains stoic as usual, unreadable, because she gives the world nothing for free. If only I could be as strong as she is for one minute of my miserable life! One second! To be aloof and untouchable! I crawled up into an ivory tower thinking I'd find solace in scholarship, in seeking the truth . . . but pleasures of the flesh proved more powerful.

They pile into the car, with Gibson shouting at me to step on it.

"Come on, we need to haul ass!"

I try to accelerate but, like me, the Honda's best days are behind it. This is most likely her last road trip before she is turned out to pasture in a junkyard. So many memories in this interior. Bev gave me a hand job in this very car, on our third date, after we saw a Billy Corgan solo set — Bev had a thing for Billy Corgan, which in retrospect was a dead giveaway that she lacked discernment in men. Because guess what? Igor looked just like Billy C of the Smashing Pumpkins! How had I failed to make that connection until now, when it's too late?

"Floor it!" Gibson exhorts in frustration, as the Honda struggles to make it up Church Hill.

"I am! This car is old, okay? And it's almost out of gas."

"Duck!" she snaps at her brother, reaching into the backseat to squish him down. Once Graves is hidden from plain sight, Gibson too crouches into a semi-erotic position, with her face inches from my groin, not unlike the posture Bev assumed during the aforementioned hand job. And the first time Lola took a ride with me in this car, it was to see *Magic Mike* at the Ithaca Mall . . . no, bad joke. The truth? Sure, why not. Here's the truth. On our very first car trip together, Lola and I went to the drugstore and I watched her buy Trojan Magnum XL condoms, while pretending to look at hearing aids near the cash register. The clerk was a young woman, pudgy and pimply, and I swear she handled that box of condoms with a heartrending tenderness. Or maybe she was spooked by my proximity. Or I wanted her to react, for Lola to giggle, anything, but it was just a plain cash transaction (I'd paid, of course), a simple transfer of funds in the sputtering engine of Capitalism. Later, Lola would put an XL condom on some chemistry major named Derrick and snap off a series of photos for our sordid amusement . . .

"What's happening?" I ask, a poignant question that has multiple applications. I might be referring to the present moment that involves the three of us, but I also could be speaking just about myself and my own existence, or that of every living thing on the planet.

"Don't say anything, Graves. Not a word, ever, to anyone." Gibson would make a great Mob lawyer. The ice water in her veins could cool the atmosphere and reverse global warming. Graves is panting like a golden retriever in the backseat, as though he's just come from a romp at the doggie park.

"You should turn around," he tells me between gasps for air. "In a few blocks you're going to enter Chimborazo and if they're following us, we'll be trapped." He's referring to a hilltop Civil War battlefield that is now a park and medical museum. That part I know; the "if they're following us" is what I don't get.

"Avery? That's who you're talking about?"

"Don't answer that question!" Gibson orders. I almost refute her with an "Objection, Your Honor," but I just take a right to circle back around to Main Street. We fall into an awkward silence, not unusual when a family takes a car trip. I'd seen Avery's oddball truck, and so there was no getting around the fact that the kid is here somewhere, possibly out for blood. Why would he have turned on Graves? The simplest explanation is that Graves somehow has become expendable or a danger — perhaps he wanted out of the plot, a charitable interpretation that invests Graves with a moral center. At the opposite end of the spectrum is that Graves wanted to blow up more stuff in Richmond and Avery was the one who vowed to stop him. Obviously these two views are antithetical and it really matters which is correct, unlike most academic arguments, which focus on splitting hairs no one cares about.

"If you want out," I say humbly, with avuncular concern, "you can get out. Nothing is impossible."

"We can't talk about this," Gibson rebuffs me.

"I'm just offering the wisdom of someone who's been in and out of hot water," I tartly reply. "If Avery is coming at you because you know this entire plan is ridiculous, then you can simply call the police and make a deal to save your hide."

"I'll never do that," he says calmly. But to

which moral system is he adhering? The one of honor or the one of revolution? The honorable man never snitches, and the revolutionary never quits.

"So what do you want me to do? Take you home? What?" I don't hide the anger in my voice, because they need to know that they are pissing me off. I never asked to be dragged into this maelstrom of misguided mayhem, and apropos of Poe, at that very moment we drive by the great writer's house, on the 1900 block of East Main Street, now a museum where during high school I'd drop in just to feel his spirit. "Just tell me and I'll do it. But if you had anything to do with blowing up the Lee statue, I'll call the police right now because that was total horseshit."

"He didn't," Gibson answers for him.

"How do you know that?" I challenge her, but she retreats into her inscrutable silence.

"I can't go home," says Graves nervously. "They'll look for me there. That's the first place they'll go."

My mother hasn't called me back yet — because she's being held at gunpoint? The image of that horror explodes in my mind with the ferocity of a rocket-propelled grenade. "They might be there already!" I yell in exasperation, stepping hard on the accelerator. "Are you that stupid? What did you expect them to do, send an Uber car for you?"

"Cool out!" Gibson chides me.

"No, I won't cool out. My mother hasn't called me back in an hour and she won't answer the phone, even though we said we'd talk again in minutes. Do you see the problem here? Don't tell me to cool out. We have to get back there right now."

"If I'm not there, they'll leave," Graves assures me. But his voice catches, indicating that he doesn't completely believe himself.

"Can you hear yourself? You sound like an idiot. Shut up, both of you, and let me handle this."

"I didn't blow up the statue," Graves pleads, gripping the headrest and pulling it back so that my body inches toward him. "I was never down with that, never. A pointless gesture that wouldn't bring us closer to taking this entire system apart."

"What system?"

"The one where the rich get to steal and the poor get to starve."

I don't know that I believe his protestation of innocence, but now isn't the time for a doctrinal dispute about the revolutionary vanguard. "I hope you're telling the truth. So who did it then? Do you have firsthand knowledge?"

"I think Avery is following us," Gibson blurts out, gazing into the side-view mirror. I check the rearview, and she's right. The battered truck is on our tail. But he might not know that Gibson and Graves are in this vehicle, as Main Street is a major road that connects east and west and courses through downtown and the Fan. I need to conduct a little experiment to test the hypothesis.

"Hold on, I'm turning up here." At Shockoe Bottom I hang a quick right at 13th Street and continue on up toward the State Capitol building, designed by Mr. Jefferson himself. The truck must've moved on, because now it's nowhere in sight. At Broad Street we wait at a light for a left-hand turn.

"Good job," Gibson offers, giving me a high five.

"That was just like *The Fast and the Furious,* huh?" I chuckle, enjoying this brief triumph. I try calling my mother again but get no answer. If Avery's here, he can't be there at the house . . . unless there are other coconspirators.

"He won't give up that easy," sighs Graves in dejection. "He thinks I'm going to rat him out, but I hate the cops as much as he does. Maybe more. Honestly, he just likes to destroy things, including people's lives. It's a game to him."

"Is there someone else who might be looking for you?" I ask pointedly, as we pass by the Dungeon of all places, scene of Gibson's earlier musical apotheosis. We keep coming full circle and retracing our footsteps, as though we're trapped in an ungodly Möbius strip.

"I guess. I doubt it, though. Avery's the one to worry about."

"You need to tell the police what you know." I slap the steering wheel for emphasis, but the manly gesture seems not to move the needle.

"That's not happening."

"You can't endanger my mother's life like that! If anything happens to her . . ."

"Nothing will happen!" they both shout at me in tandem, voices shrill in abnegation, despite the fact that evidence to the contrary is staring us in the face.

"Eddie, I promise you, your mother is fine. Don't forget our dad is at the same house, you know, and so it's not just you with a dog in this fight."

"Stop acting like Graves did something wrong," Gibson protests while lighting up a cigarette. "He's the one who flexed. This is all on Avery."

"I don't know that the cops would agree. Where did the bomb come from? It wasn't an RPG?"

"It was, but I didn't get it for them. They got it on their own."

"It didn't come from the basement?"

"Hell no. See, that's where it all started, when I wouldn't hook them up. Then Avery started acting like I was a traitor. I thought he was going to kill me last night when he stopped by. Then you showed up. Probably saved my skin."

"See?" Gibson pounces. "Graves isn't the bad guy."

But I'm not easily swayed by simplistic explanations, and if I had a red marker in my hand, I'd be gashing this essay to shreds. "I never said he was, but you have knowledge of a crime and you're bound by law to report it."

"What law? The law that lets billionaires buy elections? Whatever. I'm following Thoreau's advice on this. The only place for a just man is prison."

"I think that might be a misunderstanding of his philosophy."

"Man, I'm not telling the cops anything, but if you want to call them, be my guest."

I pull into a gas station at the corner of Broad and Thompson. Neither Graves nor

Gibson offers me any gas money. Again, I have to remind myself that these two aren't my problem. By some miracle I'm actually returning them home, safe and sound, where they can wake up tomorrow and ready themselves for the wedding. My mother will have no clue of what I endured to deliver these two hellions to her doorstep, and she doesn't need to know. I owe her that much. And anyway, Lola has never strayed far from my thoughts, and the sooner I can deposit Mead's children in Traylor Estates, the sooner I can resume my search for my bride — yes, bride! I intend to pop the question! I want to make her my wife, now that we have nothing to hide and our love can bloom in the July sunshine. Dahlia's disgust means nothing anymore, and her disapproval of me will wither on the vine.

As the gas pumps out of the hose, I try calling my mother once more, to alert her of our imminent arrival, but she doesn't answer. Gibson's window is down and she notices my wince after I put my phone away.

"She still won't answer?" asks Gibson, a trace of worry in her otherwise flat monotone.

"No. I don't know what's going on. We were talking like every five minutes and now nothing. Try your dad."

Gibson rolls her eyes. "Graves, you do it. I hate calling him."

But he punts, too. "I don't want to call him."

The tank full, I reset the nozzle and take my receipt. Then I get back in and try again to get some help. "Somebody please call him, okay? I want to know what's going on and why my mother isn't answering the phone." The young these days! So petty about the small stuff.

"Fine, I'll do it," Gibson huffs, yanking out her phone. "Anything to shut you up."

Some gratitude! She has zero appreciation for all I've done on her behalf. I reach over and grab the phone from her. "I'll do it myself, thank you."

"Give me my phone, asshole!"

She begins clawing at me and I quickly relent before she gouges my eyes out with her nail-polished talons. Maybe Marx was right about the bourgeois family — it's just a collection of strangers configured to consume as many goods and services as possible. I'd ask Graves whether he agrees but I don't really want to hear his exegesis on Marx or anything else, and so I start the engine and fall into a brooding silence.

"He didn't answer," Gibson mumbles,

gazing down at her phone.

I say nothing. In a few minutes we'll be home and all that is unknown will drop away and bare, cold reality will be revealed. My mother deserves far, far better. Assuming it'll take place, should I even bother going to the wedding tomorrow? Do I want to see these people again? Another life beckons . . . once I find Lola, we can talk about our plans. Starting over seems like the best route to take, especially for a pair of newlyweds. Writing instruction is a miserable job and colleges are always seeking failures to fill the slots no sane person wants. We could basically select any city and move there. As a faculty spouse Lola can resume her studies tuition-free . . . just as she is now at Notting College as a faculty child. How many make that transition within the span of an academic year? Few, I'll bet.

A big dollop of water lands on my windshield, followed by another. We're crossing the Huguenot Bridge, and I wonder if somehow the river hasn't splashed up from below, which seems highly unlikely.

"It's raining?" Gibson asks excitedly.

"Is it? It's not supposed to." I gaze up at the sky. It does seem suddenly more overcast.

"Weather forecasting is pure guesswork,"

461

Graves chimes in from the backseat, as a few more drops fall down.

"It's been like a month!" Gibson gushes, putting her hand on a window. "I wish I could run around in it."

Now that would be a spectacle, Gibson soaking wet! I almost stop the car to indulge her, and me. But I can't betray Lola, and so I drive on. A torrent then batters us for around forty seconds, and I really can't see the road. Our spirits lift, however, because the rain is an omen, despite the fact that it ends as mysteriously as it began. Just a passing shower, a stray bit of moisture in an otherwise parched land, proving that we can't know the future. At least I hope that's true, because I'll need more than a weird weather pattern to alter my present trajectory.

23

Both cars, Corvette and Acura, are in the driveway like normal, and the garage door is shut tight as a drum. Standing outside my house, I don't notice even a leaf out of place. Still, until I know my mother is safe and sound, I won't rest, which is why I have the gun stuck in my pants again, just in case. Gibson and Graves push on ahead of me toward the front door, but I linger back, inspecting the lawn, making sure there aren't midget rebels behind the trees. Maybe the worst has passed and Avery has relented in his pursuit of Graves, but I doubt it. He really shouldn't stay here tonight, unless Avery has been arrested. Otherwise Graves is putting us all at risk. Perhaps he knows this and is making plans to evacuate . . . I could take him with me to the Chicory Motel, maybe get him his own room. But then he'll become my responsibility. No thanks.

When I get inside, I hear voices coming from the kitchen. One belongs to Mead, the other to Graves, and I decide to duck down to the basement and avoid what could be a confrontation. I loop around to the stairs by taking the main hallway, and then dart for the door, hoping no one will notice me.

Too late.

"Eddie?" Mead calls out. I have a hand on the knob and I'm just a few feet from my sanctuary. "You got a second?"

"Sure thing." I step back, nervous about the gun, Mead's prized possession, that's poking me in the backside. I make sure that I face Mead at all times, which shouldn't be hard since he's sitting down at the kitchen table, with Graves perched next to him. A bottle of scotch stands at his elbows, along with an empty tumbler.

"Everything okay?" he asks innocently.

"Yeah. As far as I know. Is my mom asleep? She wasn't answering the phone."

"Yes, she went to bed. Tonight was a bit much for her. Hopefully tomorrow goes better. Pour you a drink?"

"No, thanks. I'm a little worn-out myself."

"She's worried sick about you. I just want you to know that if you need my help — I know a lot of people in city government, and the state, too — but if you ever need something, just ask me."

"What did he do?" Graves asks, amused by my plight. It is ironic, Mead offering me assistance while his subversive son has plotted an overthrow of the same government in which he boasts having many important contacts. Just another reason I long to join Lola at the Chicory.

"Nothing," Mead replies, glancing at me with a soulful expression. "Right, Eddie? You don't need my help with anything?"

"Do you need mine?" I coyly turn the tables. He chuckles and pours a drink.

"Probably. Definitely, you and Graves both. First thing in the morning, we're getting those boxes out of here. Luckily the wedding is in the afternoon and we'll have time to get it done."

"The Russian bailed?" Graves asks.

"I guess so. He's a strange fellow, he really is. He wants the collection, but he doesn't want to pay the freight charge to Central America. He thinks the seller should, which is nuts."

"Are you scared of him?" I inquire, earning a smirk of rebuke from Mead.

"I'm not scared of anybody, especially him. He thinks that because he's got money, he can just walk all over people. Usually he can. But money has never impressed me much."

It takes all my strength not to laugh in this man's face, because I can tell by the way his lips are pressed smugly together that he *actually believes his own lies.* He then shoots me a self-satisfied wink, and that's enough to send me running. Enough! Basta!

"Well, good night," I offer with a dauntless wave. But Mead ushers me back by leaping out of his chair.

"Hold on, Eddie. Wait up."

I stop. Mead pats Graves on the shoulder. "Can you give Eddie and me a minute alone? Thanks, buddy. You should turn in anyway. It's getting to be that time."

Wordlessly Graves leaves, eyes fixed on the floor. Mead and I are both standing. His smile vanishes, and his arms fold across his broad chest. His eyes narrow the way a hawk might scan the ground below for a scurrying squirrel.

"Why did you take the gun?" he slowly says, emphasizing each word, the separate syllables of which prick me like jabs of a needle. I blink a few times to gather myself. My inability to lie once again waylays me, and all I can conjure is the truth.

"I needed it, but I don't anymore. Here, take it."

466

I reach around to grab the pistol, but Mead raises his arms in the air like I'm robbing him. "Whoa, whoa! I don't want it! It's yours now. My gift."

"That's utterly absurd. Take your gun. I was wrong. I apologize. Honestly, take the gun." I hold it out toward him by gripping the thick barrel, but he refuses it.

"Why did you need it? That's the real issue. Why? What's going on? Why did the cops come here? Your mother cried herself to sleep on the eve of our wedding, and I think we both deserve an explanation."

I feel my face growing flush with shame. At least, it should be shame. In a perfect world I'd be aghast. But there's more anger than shame. Much more. "Stop trying to prove a point and just take the gun."

"Why are you mad at me, Eddie? Shouldn't I be the one who's mad?"

"You are mad, and that's why you're humiliating me."

"Is somebody after you?"

"No, but given your nefarious dealings and those of your children, I thought I needed protection."

"The cops didn't come here to question me or my kids. They came for you."

"And I took care of it. Now, I'm sorry I took this without asking first — that was wrong. Sometimes I do things without thinking. But I'm returning it to you, safe and sound. Just like I did your children."

I place the gun on the table and it makes a dull thud when it lands. Mead nods in sorrow and meets my gaze, which causes me to avert my eyes. "I can't help you if you won't let me. What's the Wardell family have to do with this? Are they after you? Because if they are, you have to understand that they play for keeps."

"I told you, it's all been taken care of."

"Let's hope so, for your sake. They own the cops in this city. They could make trouble for all of us."

"I've got nothing to hide."

"I know you don't approve of me, and that's fine. I'm not stupid. You think I'm out for your mother's money, the half-million dollars. Eddie, I don't need it. So you can stop making assumptions about me. But I do want you to consider your mother's feelings in all of this."

"I don't need a lecture from you on filial piety. My mother's happiness is really my only concern."

"So you're taking the Wardells on by yourself? That's your plan?"

O ye of little faith — I already slayed the dragon solo, with my hands tied behind my back. But I won't boast of my exploits. "No, my plan is to go downstairs and get some sleep."

Mead lifts the gun up and proffers it to me. "You can have the gun. It doesn't fire, you know."

"I don't want the gun."

"If you need protection, the Glocks all work. I think there are fifteen of them in various boxes. Not sure about the ammo. I'm sure I can dig some up."

"It's fine, thank you. I don't need a gun. We should just forget this ever happened, okay? I'm sorry about taking the gun and being a bit standoffish toward you. This entire experience has been overwhelming." I hold out my hand and we shake, letting bygones be bygones. I debate whether I should tell Mead about Graves's possible involvement or noninvolvement with the Bastard Sons, and decide to say nothing. If Graves is guilty of anything, he'll be found out. If he's not, all the better. At this point, given that Graves is unwilling to disclose what he knows, there's not much anyone can do about his legal status. And anyway, Graves is an adult and presumably capable of handling his own affairs. I got the children home; my job is complete.

After one last nicety with Mead, I finally

get to retreat to the basement and recover a measure of peace. The dark cool entrances me and instantly calms my frayed nerves. All quickly becomes clear to me. I must go to Lola tonight, right now. I call her but I know she won't answer because she's pissed at me, having run out of patience as I crisscrossed the city on various important missions that kept us apart. But no more. I leave her a message, telling her I'm on the way, and then gather my things, which doesn't take long because I never really unpacked. It's funny to think that it took a trip to Richmond for me to appreciate what I have with Lola back in Ithaca. Distance provides perspective, a corrective for when the tree is directly in front of our face and the forest eludes us. The world seems small when your life consists of about ten square blocks. Even when Lola and I hiked to Buttermilk Falls two weeks ago, just that excursion alone taught me much about her and us. Tomorrow, before the wedding, I'll show her all of Richmond — Poe, Patrick Henry, the Confederate generals (minus one) — and my personal favorite, Maymont Park, whose sloping hills and serpentine paths ease the pain and heartache and regret — and we can eat lunch in Carytown, and I'll take her to Plan 9 Records . . . and she won't dismiss this city like Bev did. No way. Lola loves life too much. And me.

At least I hope she still does.

I let myself out through the basement, meaning one last time I need to scoot through the boxes of Vietnam, the rifles, machine guns, uniforms, helmets, and yes, rocket-propelled grenades of America's dumbest war. Before I leave, I take in the tableau so that the details sink in. The slight odor of gunpowder, the Cyrillic lettering, and the wooden box where Giap's pistol should go, still sitting open where I'd left it. Perverseness at work again: the motivation of human behavior Poe explored with grace and confidence, his narrators mostly explaining what really has no logic, trying to make the irrational and the impulsive comprehensible. For example, just beyond the boxes of weapons, on the bare concrete-block wall, if you look closely enough, you will see the very faint outline of some old graffiti, consisting of a single word, "FUCK," I'd scrawled with a crayon when I was twelve. What had possessed me to do it? Some dark urge, yes, but I was also sure that I could erase my handiwork, and yet the harder I rubbed against the crayon marks, the more lasting the letters became. Straight out of Poe, I tell you! And it remains there to this day, a monument to the struggles of the soul divided against itself. Because I confessed. I told my mother when she got home from work and I wanted to be punished. She laughed it off and promised me that in time the word would fade to oblivion, but she was wrong. It's still there, barely, hardly at all, but alive. My sickness.

I rush out, hauling my luggage like a harried footman, and jump into the Honda, my trusted steed, my Traveller. The engine sounds even more strained, exhausted from the long drive from New York and the endless trips to and fro across the river today, but this will be it. We'll reach our final resting place, the Chicory Motel, and there we'll both retire. The end brings such sweet melancholy and time to reflect. Lola won't believe the stories I have to tell her, but will she treat me as Penelope did Odysseus, with initial contempt from the years of neglect, the mistrust of his very identity? Lola knows who I am. I won't have to show her any battle scars, since she put many of them there herself. Each of her lovers has left a mark on me, diminished me in some way . . . we'll have to figure out what to do because I don't want to share her anymore. Will she agree to that arrangement? Because here's the truth, which I hate to admit. The fact is, Lola and I have made love. And we didn't need any dick pics or dirty stories because our souls interlocked and my performance issues vanished. It was during our last hike to the falls, where we found ourselves sunning on a rocky outcrop surrounded with clumps of chicory — it just happened. For once I took control of the situation and we truly in every sense of the word became lovers.

I drive fast and furiously, AM radio blasting . . . still no arrests, no suspects . . . witnesses describe seeing a green truck (the color of Avery's vehicle) near the intersection of Allen and Monument . . . the black neighborhoods remain quiet . . . the white neighborhoods also remain quiet . . . is that a joke? Do the white neighborhoods of Richmond even make a noise? A slight clearing of the throat, the sound of ice cubes clinking into highballs . . . I reach the Boulevard and then head north. Not long now.

Robin Hood Road. The Chicory Motel.

I pull into the parking lot and reclaim the same spot I'd parked in earlier. The same cars look to be in the same spaces. Has anything changed? Time can stand still in Richmond if you're not careful and years can pass before you realize it's too late. Like Leigh Rose. Happened to her.

Lola's car isn't evident to the naked eye, which doesn't mean she isn't here. Or isn't coming back. I must pay for my crimes and she'll exact a toll by making me wait. I hop out and look hopefully around at everything. The air seems freer, less burdened. I don't know her room number and so I'll have to get one of my own because I can't just sit in my car. It'll attract unwanted attention.

My phone rings. It's her! It's Lola! I want her like I've never wanted another woman in my life. I'll show her that my problems are solved and she's the reason I can love her like a normal man.

■ ■ ■ ■ ■

DAY TWO —
JULY 2

■ ■ ■ ■ ■

I wake up alone at 7:14 a.m. I can smell Lola, a faint hint of lavender, and in bed next to me is her favorite scarf, of regal purple silk. I reach for her but her side of the bed is empty. I sit up, shivering from the ancient air conditioner that has no thermostat — it continues to crank out frigid air as if cooling down a morgue. My eyes survey the room, a small square consisting of particleboard desk, brass lamp, and wobbly dresser. The TV is circa 1983 and must weigh a ton. On a wall hangs a garish print of a watercolor featuring the bearded visage of Stonewall Jackson. Another is of a male cardinal, the state bird of Virginia, which is for lovers, according to a highly successful ad campaign from the 1970s that was surprisingly titillating.

I bolt out of bed, throw open the door, and step out onto the balustrade that overlooks the parking lot. Where has Lola gone?

There's no sign of her car. Has she left again without saying a word to me? Without leaving a note? The morning sun glares at me as it shines bright in a cloudless sky. It's going to be another scorcher because it's already stifling hot for early morning. But I don't mind the heat, which allows me to warm up for a second before heading back into the arctic freeze in room 212. The rays are so strong that my innermost recesses might actually feel the solar burn, but I doubt it. With Lola gone again, nothing can melt the desolate ice in the center of my heart. We promised each other never to become the kind of couple who lapses into estrangement and silences.

I rush back inside to check my phone, and there I make a disturbing discovery. Staggering, actually, and completely unexpected. Lola's phone is sitting right next to mine on the water-stained bedside table. The two devices are paired up, in fact, in a highly staged way, the edge of hers touching mine, a suggestive pose that I interpret as Lola's attempt to convey consanguinity with me — yet I also find it unlikely that Lola would purposefully leave her phone behind, which points to a dreadful possibility.

She's been abducted.

The horrible force of that idea pushes me

down onto the bed, my head shaking in disbelief. It's simply not possible. I was here and would have heard something, unless I'd been drugged. Again, that would have been impossible, since I'd only sipped water from the tap in the bathroom.

Then for reasons I don't really understand, I pick up my phone and collect yet another mystifying clue. Three hours ago, at 4:32 a.m., I received a text from Lola.

Bye, Eddie. I need something more in my life and I think you know what I'm talking about. I'm going dark for a while. Off the grid — no phone, no contact. Into the wild! No one will find me, so don't bother looking.

I am stunned. It appears that she left on her own accord. She's ending it with me. It's over between us. She's run off with that guy she met online (which might explain the "going dark" phrase), but her phone is right in my hand. I could easily retrace her footsteps and figure out where this guy lives and then . . . what?

I drop her phone on the mattress and instead stare glumly at mine. There's no point in calling or texting her anymore, so how do I propose to get in touch with her?

Lola's phone rings, and the tone startles me because it's a shrill clang like from an old-fashioned rotary model and it reminds me of being a child. I look down to see who is calling.

Mom.

Her mom, my colleague, Nora Hicock, an ethereal woman with long black hair and sad eyes who headed up the college's Women's Resource Center and who at faculty meetings always had the same suggestion for the president: *We should make the arts a vital part of the undergraduate experience,* which no one disagreed with but no one knew how to fund. Still, I admired her doggedness as only a quitter can. Her beauty was on the wane, no doubt, but in her I could still detect the last gasps of her youthful bloom. I'd love to answer the phone and ask her questions about her daughter, as she must possess motherly insight into Lola's impetuosity, the sting of which hurts mightily right now. Forsaken for another! For a stranger she barely knows, whose only redeeming attribute was a prodigious dong, but whose personality she described as "stupid," whose company she didn't enjoy — no, there's no way she left me for Mr. Craigslist.

I reread her text, trying to be as objective as possible. The "something more" might mean a relationship with someone from her generation, a guy who has an Instagram account, for example, or a gamer tag, neither of which I possess. But the references to "into the wild" and "off the grid" suggest a retreat into obscurity, an abnegation of the life we were going to spend together. She was going to be my wife and now she's gone!

I don't know what to do. Minutes tumble past as I sit motionless on the bed, in my J. Crew boxers, staring down at her iPhone 5C, the security code to which I happen to know because I've watched her input it around six million times, but I can't bring myself to plunge into her hidden world. It feels wrong, prying into her personal space, and at some point I've got to start respecting boundaries. I can't just hack into her phone whenever I want to and peruse her correspondence, flip through her photos, scroll down her list of recent calls, and invade her social media accounts like a rogue marauder. No! It's a complete and utter violation of her trust — but she's missing. The phone might contain a clue of her whereabouts.

I agonize, staring at her phone's background screenshot, a group photo of kids from her dorm, including two guys she slept with . . . that's it! That's it right there! She got sick of my sickness . . . at one time she rather enjoyed showing me the dick pics of her hookups but she tired of it, resentment growing in increments indiscernible to the naked eye — and when I didn't show much appreciation for her latest conquest, Mr. Craigslist, for whom she drove all the way down to Richmond, she turned on me and my perversion. I wasn't grateful enough, or at all. Worse, I'd tried to end it! Yes, I did! I wanted out, but then somehow during the madness of yesterday I realized that I loved her more than life itself.

I type in the code and unlock her privacy. A quick check reveals that the only person she's texted or called since yesterday has been me, and she hasn't replied to the texts from others like her mother or Dahlia. She's sent no e-mails that I can discern unless she has a different account somewhere, which is entirely possible because I see no record of her communicating with anyone from craigslist. But she might have relegated that exchange to a Yahoo account . . . unless there never was a guy from craigslist and she'd invented him just to rub my face in it, to draw some blood . . . it feels too creepy to be examining her life in this manner. Damn her! Things were perfect until she started telling people like Dahlia, and now I've got nothing. Just her phone.

The thing is, she didn't simply forget or

misplace her phone. She abandoned it, which means she isn't coming back. She's off on some great adventure to the nether reaches of the unreachable world — Alaska? An island near Vancouver? I would've gone with her! But she chose to forego my companionship. This conclusion sends me rushing outside again in a desperate search of the parking lot. The cold air has caused condensation to cling to the glass that resembles a sheen of winter frost . . . Lola left at 4:32 a.m. or shortly thereafter, more than three hours ago, and by now she's either on a plane or crossing into Tennessee or Maryland or North Carolina, grinning from ear to ear to be rid of me. Repudiation! Negation! Disavowal!

Just so she's alone. I can abide by her picking solitude over me, but if she's with that dipshit from craigslist . . . or somebody else . . .

I stagger to the bed and fall face-first into it, my nose landing on her phone, cracking the screen Lola protected with the ferocity of a lioness. There's a cut/abrasion now on the hard bridge of my ugly nose, the nose I long dreamt of having surgically removed — I look terrible, taking stock of myself in a motel bathroom. Flabby middle, no muscle tone, and skin a sickly shade of white: Herman Munster looks healthier and more robust than I do. My body would serve a fitness club well, as the perfect "Before" model in an advertising campaign.

I slink away from the mirror, engulfed by desperation. Should I sign up for an Instagram account? Would that win her back? Or just alienate her further? Let's put it this way: did the soul patch I grew win me any affection from Bev? (Igor also sported such facial hair.) No! It turned her off even more, my opaque attempts to curry favor. Lola would react similarly, perhaps with less exasperation and more ridicule . . . she's gone and I have to accept that.

Except that . . .

My phone rings! And because hope is a weed that no pesticide can kill, I rush over to it thinking Lola has come to her senses and is standing at a pay phone, maybe for the first time in her young life. She might not even know how one of those artifacts works.

But it's my mother. My mother!

"Good morning," I sing out sweetly, with my teeth suddenly chattering. Christmas in July! Soon I'll be a snowman.

"Eddie, where are you? Where did you go?"

"I had to take care of something and it

was all the way across town, and so I got a hotel room instead of driving home. No biggie. What's up?"

"I have been worried sick! You could have left a note or something."

"I thought I was coming back first thing this morning. I'm sorry, I know I screwed up. I'll never do that to you again."

"Mead needs your help with the boxes. Graves won't get up, the little punk, I swear."

"I'm on my way. I can be there in fifteen minutes."

"What were you doing in the middle of the night across town?"

"It's hard to explain. I'm coming home right now."

"Can you please tell me what's going on?"

"There's nothing to worry about."

"Why did you take one of Mead's guns last night?"

I cringe at her soft voice, velveteen and gentle, careful to spare my feelings when she should be letting me have it with all she's got, the fury of a mother whose only son has squandered his many gifts. "I was spooked about Leigh Rose . . . listen, let me get going and I promise we'll talk later, but I don't want you to worry because this is your big day."

"Okay." She pauses, wheels spinning as she mulls over my specious explanation. "But you hate guns, though."

"I still do, more than ever. I'll see you in a few minutes."

"Mead really needs your help. He hurt his back playing football in high school and he shouldn't be lifting anything heavy."

None of us should, Mother, not a single one of us should try to pick up the weight of the world that consists mostly of misery. Nothing heftier than a feather! Look at the strain I'm under, saddled with a burden of my own packing. "I'm glad to help," I say, "and tell him to wait for me. I'm literally walking out the door."

Not literally. I have to get dressed and gather my things first. I shove mine and Lola's phone into a front pocket, the closest we'll ever be again in all likelihood. The "I Have Issues" hat is pulled firmly down to shield my eyes from the sun. Now I'm ready to depart and blast off to the Great Beyond.

It takes no time before I encounter my first obstacle, a police car in the parking lot. The sound track here should jump to an ominous bleating of bassoon, if only to stir up the notion of danger. Perhaps the film director might next cut to a close-up of me, mouth grimly set, stubble barely visible, before pulling back to an overhead shot of me descending the stairs, luggage in hand. In the office I can see that the cop is speaking with the manager, and they both clearly look over at me and my luggage. Have I finally reached the end? Is this it, my long-awaited and well-deserved doom? I won't put up a fight. When have I ever? I'll hold out my hands and let the cuffs get clapped on. I'll confess right here and now, just ask me.

The cop turns back around and continues his conversation. I soldier on, curious why I'm not being detained for questioning. Could it be for the simple reason that I've broken no laws in the Commonwealth of Virginia? Catch me if you can, copper! I feel like Edward G. Robinson right now, but also strangely deflated. The show must go on even when the actors have tired of their roles.

Once inside the Honda, I lack the energy to put my key into the ignition. After doing so, I find that shifting the gear stick into reverse takes sustained effort. Did I even sleep last night? I must have, given that Lola was able to slip away, right through my fingertips, without me stirring. Therefore, I had to have drifted into a deep slumber, but one that wasn't restful, because I don't recall ever being this exhausted. Even during the worst of the divorce proceedings with Bev, whose lawyer went for my jugular, while my "hired gun" fumbled around to string two sentences together, when it seemed like I never slept, I still felt the "life force" of Swedenborg animating me to endure the spiritual pain. But now, I can't lift my hand to change the radio station from AM to FM or to plug in my phone so I can queue up some morning tunes. Not even music moves me! That's never happened before. Silence falls like netting, and the more I struggle to free myself of it, the more entangled in the mesh of solitude I become.

At some point Lola will contact me using someone else's phone, so I should expect a call or text from an area code that I don't recognize . . . assuming Lola has memorized my cell number, which I tend to doubt. Hence, e-mail will become her only means of reaching me, e-mail that I haven't checked recently, since I was contacted by the dean, but now I have to peruse it or else I won't hear from Lola again until . . . when? Will she ever return to Ithaca? Or will she hide out in Richmond, the city I fled? That would be a hoot, as my mother likes to say.

As I drive south on the Boulevard, a little voice inside my frazzled head tells me, in an innocuous whisper: "Go to her, go to her."

Meaning Leigh Rose.

I actually begin to laugh like a madman, gripping the steering wheel like it's a carnival ride whirling me about. My fellow motorists must regard me as an accident waiting to happen, and that's not far from the truth. Why would I go back to Leigh Rose's house? What good could possibly come from that? What would I even say to her? This urge, this drive, this compulsion, makes no sense at all, yet few irrational acts do. Without question I seek solace from Leigh Rose to salve the wound inflicted on me by Lola, but I've barked up that tree already.

There's no one I can turn to now. Ergo, I must go home.

A U-Haul truck is parked in the driveway, its orange snout pointed at Traylor Drive like a vigilant watchdog. Mead is nowhere in sight. The garage door is open, exposing the innards of the basement, the boxes that must get safely stowed. It seems somewhat negligent to expose these weapons without adult supervision, but Mead has yet to convince me of his competence.

I park in my usual spot, in the ditch, leaving my luggage in the car as I don't know where I'll hang my hat tonight. Lola still might come to her senses. Stranger things have happened and one can't preclude any remote possibilities. Call me desperate and deluded, but I maintain that Lola will return. On what do I base this prediction? Certainly not evidence, all of which points to the contrary. My feet shuffle along the gravel drive, kicking up little clouds of dust with each step. Our land is parched and withers in agony. Next will come a plague, and then the end of days . . .

Mead emerges from the basement, wearing a heavy-duty back brace that belongs on a cyborg. Already he is drenched in sweat, face reddened, hair matted down. He waves and I nod, not exactly détente but more cordiality under duress.

"Your mother was worried about you," he says bitterly, wiping his brow with a hand towel from my bathroom. Had he been snooping around in my lair, searching for clues of my depravity? Fruitlessly so, as all my secrets are kept under lock and key.

"I spoke to her this morning."

"It didn't help very much."

The blame game has begun . . . when the wedding crashes and burns, I'll become the main culprit of the debacle. I'm guilty of many crimes, but not of being unsupportive of my mother. "I'm very sorry to hear that. You didn't need to tell her about the gun. I'm sure that didn't help her relax very much."

"I'm not going to lie to her, about that or anything else."

"There's no point in arguing. Let's get these boxes out of here before they cause more trouble."

"What trouble have they caused, Eddie? Besides you stealing from me?"

I don't like his tone but decide to ignore him. I just don't have the energy to offer verbal combat. Lola has sapped me of the little strength I had. "What boxes go first? Or does it matter?"

"These are all legal, by the way. Every single item in my collection I have clear provenance of."

"I'm not accusing you of anything, okay? I just want them out of here before, say, your Russian friend stops by again."

"I can handle him."

"Good for you, now let's get started, shall we? I haven't even had coffee yet this morning and I might keel over at any second."

"There's some brewing upstairs. Maybe you can say good morning to your mother."

I bite my lower lip hard enough to feel a dull pain. From his position on the moral high ground, Mead is shelling me with grenades of disapproval. Let him think what he wants. I'm not the one taking advantage of an older woman who's fallen for his dubious vows of love. Like many reprobates, Mead is turning his guns on me as a way of deflecting attention from his own misdeeds. The sooner this wedding takes place, the sooner I can get out of here. Tonight even. Where will I go next? Home to Ithaca, where my enemies await my arrival? Maybe I can hide in one of these crates that will get sent to Central America, where I can slip unnoticed into the jungle.

My mother rushes over to me as soon as she sees me come up from the basement. "Oh, Eddie!" she cries in a voice hoarse from insomnia. "Are you okay? Tell me the truth. What's going on? Where were you last night?"

I hug her, and remorse bubbles up inside me. Hurting her was never my intention, and the only balm I can offer her now is what she most desires, which is the truth. Some of it, anyway. Bite-size morsels of honesty. An entire meal would sicken her. "I went to find someone." I sigh, sinking down into a chair at the table. She sits by me, a comforting hand resting on my stooped shoulder.

"Who? A woman? Leigh Rose Wardell?"

"Not her. Someone else." My head drops in shame. "I don't even want to tell you because you'll think less of me, and I hate the idea of disappointing you even more than you already are."

"I'm not disappointed, Eddie! No, you've never disappointed me!" She pulls me close and kisses me on top of my head.

"I haven't come home in two years. I'm a jerk."

"Not at all. You were just sad and depressed because of the divorce. I don't blame you, for what that awful woman did to you."

"It wasn't just Bev's fault. I share much of the blame, too. Most of it, in fact."

"Please. She's the one who left you for another man."

"I don't blame her one bit."

"Eddie, listen to yourself. So who were you looking for last night?"

"Can I get a cup of coffee? I really could use one."

"I'll get it, you sit." She springs up and in

a flash places a steaming mug of java in front of me. But the acid in my stomach is raging and I suddenly can't imagine drinking or eating anything. So I cradle the warmth of the mug in my cold hands. It's like I'm still in the hotel room, freezing, alone, and afraid.

"I went to find a woman I've been seeing. She's one of my students."

I can't look at my mother, though her eyes poke me in the ribs where my heart used to be. The blackness of the coffee is all my vision can endure, offering me chromatic balance, black turned to black.

"You're dating one of your students? Is that allowed?"

"No, of course it's not. I'll most likely get fired. No, I deserve to get fired."

"Wait a second. But she's here in Richmond?"

"She was. She's gone now. It's over, but it never should have started. Basically my life is a total wreck. I'm a horrible person."

"Don't say that!"

"It's true."

"You just made a mistake, is all. Because of how sad you've been. Bev broke your heart and your spirit, too. You haven't been yourself, not for a long time."

Footsteps tromp up the basement steps.

Mead needs my muscles, flabby though they may be. At least I can be of some use. There's nobility in manual labor. Too bad I know no trade other than scribbling.

The door swings open and Mead comes into the kitchen. My mother's arm rests across my back, as though I might topple over if she lets go. Her support means everything to me and yet only increases my self-loathing. What would it take for her to disown me? A murder charge?

"There's a problem," Mead says sternly. "A big problem."

"What is it?" my mother asks.

"That kid Avery is here and wants to talk to Graves. He claims it's urgent and he won't leave unless Graves comes down."

Avery, yes, the owner of a pickup truck and presumably the destroyer of Robert E. Lee. This isn't a positive development. Graves remains in the crosshairs, and my rescue of him last night has proven to be a temporary fix.

"What should we do?" my mother asks, frightened and perplexed.

"I know what I'd like to do," Mead huffs manfully. "Break his little twerp neck."

"Let me talk to him," I offer, which Mead promptly brushes aside.

"You should stay out of this."

"Too late for that. I'm pretty sure Graves is mixed up in this whole Lee statue thing, and so is Avery."

"They are?" my mother gasps, horrified. "Why would you say that?"

"I don't know. Graves has dropped suggestions to me. Maybe I'm wrong and misreading the signs." A half-truth at best, but I won't confess for the kid.

"Graves would never do something so stupid," Mead flatly states.

"He didn't, but Avery probably did, and Graves knows that."

Mead rubs the back of his neck and flares his nostrils. He doesn't want my help, but Avery won't listen to him because they used to argue and Mead banished Avery . . . and so that leaves me as the only available conduit to talk some sense into the anarchist's head. Together we can begin Gramsci's "permanent revolution" and make the ruling class bend to our demands . . . such are the fervid dreams of the office-bound intellectual. I could tell Avery, my eyes bulging with bloodlust: *Get Stonewall Jackson next.* Or I could advise him to go to college, where for a tidy sum and a lifetime of debt he can get true enlightenment without having to suffer much, certainly nothing like what the Buddha or Jesus endured . . .

"What will you tell him?" my mother asks as I stand up.

"I'll think of something."

Mead smirks, unimpressed but powerless to stop me.

Avery has parked his truck directly in front of the U-Haul, snout to snout, bumpers almost touching, as if he'd wanted to drive his vehicle into the engine block of the larger truck. Typical in such bewildering situations, the man in question is nowhere to be found. Is he going to ambush me? He's already annoying me beyond my limited patience. If he came to threaten Graves, he's barking up the wrong tree, in that he is the one most vulnerable here, considering that Graves is guiltless whereas Avery is knee-deep in this adolescent rebellion. Avery took his best shot at Graves last night and failed. There are no second acts in an American life (just look at me).

"Where's Graves?" I hear a voice behind me, from the boxes in the basement. Mead was probably unwise to leave his cache unguarded even for a minute. I spin around and see the unctuous urchin, attired in a polo shirt and cargo shorts, hair combed, freshly shaven . . . hardly the rugged mien of an enemy of the state.

"You should leave," I say firmly, in my most serious voice, the one I use to conduct hearings on honor code violations.

"I need to talk to him and I know he's here."

"If he wanted to talk, don't you think he would? It's obvious he wants nothing more to do with you. Take the hint and take a hike."

He blinks repeatedly like he's trying to deliver a message in Morse code. Or he's flummoxed, unsure of his next move, not having planned an exit strategy beyond the Act itself, the strike against tyranny that's resulted only in his vilification. This city won't sleep until he's brought to justice . . . stupid kid, he should be in Ohio by now, not hanging around as the rats jump ship.

"I want to help him before things get too heavy," he explains in a burst of disclosure that makes no sense.

"Help him how?"

"You don't get it, bro."

I bristle at the sobriquet of "bro," the usage of which is indication of rank idiocy. "What don't I get, bro?"

"None of it. I need to talk to him. Wake his ass up."

"Why were you after him last night? Huh? Why was he running from you? Don't come slick at me. I know more than you think."

He takes a step at me, teeth exposed like a junkyard dog. But I'm not scared. Far from it. This confrontation is energizing, visceral in intensity, and the perfect remedy to rid me of Lola's betrayal. Obviously I haven't been in many showdowns of this variety, but something has snapped in me — starting last night when I stared down Jeb Wardell and John Graziano. Maybe I can take control of my life and weather the storm. "You got it all wrong," he counters acidly. "He was coming after me. Why do you think I'm here? I'm no punk. I've been trying to talk him out of it."

"Come on, I don't have time for this. Just get out of here or we'll call the cops."

"You won't call the cops." He chuckles in delight, patting one of the boxes. "You can't call the cops. Whatever, I tried. Graves is on his own now."

"We're all on our own, always and forever."

Avery cocks his head in derision, snorting at my armchair existentialism. "After he blows up a couple thousand people, you won't be joking around much anymore."

"He's not going to do that."

He gives me a satirical thumbs-up. "Sounds like you're on top of it. Let's hope you're right. Peace."

Then he breezes by like he's out for a leisurely stroll, cocksure and haughty, hands wedged in his pockets like he's fishing for loose change. At this point I can't claim to know what's going on or whose version of the truth is correct, since each has blamed the other for the vandalism. Most likely, both are lying a little, but I don't want to untangle the knot. At least I've succeeded at one level: Avery is getting into his truck and driving away. To the victor go the spoils.

The U-Haul truck is loaded and I'm going to die. Some of those boxes were bulky and weighted down with heavy artillery, and now I'm the one who needs a back brace, or just a trip to a chiropractor.

A chiropractor!

Bev used to go to one, a Dr. Entasse, of whom she once said, "He's very handsome." An innocent comment made at dinner, delivered dispassionately, with the kind of remove characteristic of a chaste woman. A better man might have laughed it off. But the tailspin I fell into! For months I was sure that she was sleeping with this guy, since until then she'd never complained of her spine being out of alignment. Presto, change-o, she started going to a hunky doctor weekly for treatments I didn't think she needed. One could argue that my jealousy began the decline that ended with flaccidity, divorce, and Igor. How so? Well, because I made my own appointment with Dr. Entasse, without Bev's knowledge, just so I could glean information such as the size of his hands (very large) and his sexual prowess (undetermined). Ridiculous, demented, uncalled for — but there I was in his office, seeking out evidence of Bev's infidelity as if her panties would be stuffed in a drawer of tongue depressors. Not my finest hour, to be sure, but what I didn't know then was how far I still had to go before I touched bottom . . . apparently I've got fathoms left to go . . . but I eventually told Bev of my visit to Dr. Entasse, propelled by my envy, and instead of thinking it a cute but misguided declaration of my undying love, Bev saw the first glimmer of soul sickness. *I can't believe you did that. Why would you ever think that? Because I said he was handsome? I think all kinds of men are handsome and I'm not jumping into bed with them.* I never should have told her. Some events must to the dustbin of history go. Things were literally never the same between us. Even as I tried to live it down, Bev discerned more evidence of my failings. The bright sunshine in our bedroom darkened like the plains before a dust storm, all because of a lumbering, dimpled chiropractor with hands the size of frying pans and presumably a crotch to match . . . which we spoke of one night, with Bev coolly speculating that Dr. Entasse was a stallion because he reminded her of an ex from high school, a basketball player she dated who was "massive" and then, right there, I felt my major organs shrink into raisins, leaving a void that has never been filled . . . my sexual functionality became sporadic and then nonexistent . . . until Lola rescued me . . .

"You follow me to the storage place," Mead instructs as I wipe gallons of sweat from my skin. "Then we'll drop the U-Haul off and I'll drive back. I parked my car there."

"Sounds good. You lead the way."

I jump into the Honda and even before I start the engine I fish Lola's phone out. No one has called. *Throw it out the window,* a voice urges me. Get rid of it. Send it to oblivion. To do so would be to give up on her, but phones can be replaced . . . what of love? Can the Apple Store ease my pain?

Edgar A. Poe again! How many of his characters were driven mad by a possession they just couldn't rid themselves of? Has

502

this iPhone become my oblong box? Never a good sign when you can compare yourself with one of Poe's manic, deranged narrators! There's a wooded lot right across the street . . . as a child I never played in there because once the authorities found a dead body buried in a shallow grave, and my mother was adamant that I refrain from venturing into this bosky grove. But what a fitting cemetery for Lola's phone . . . for our love . . . because once I toss this last artifact of Lola's away, the end will come and we will be no more, my beloved and I.

Can't do it.

The U-Haul slowly pulls away, and for a few seconds it looks like Mead is going to run into the ditch, but then he straightens out and makes it to Traylor Drive. We proceed, after I turn my Honda around and catch up to him. Lola's phone is still in my hand, and I'm driving like a teenager unwilling to let go of the most important inanimate object ever invented. And the worst. In 1985 Lola never could have driven to Richmond to torture me like this. I wouldn't have known she was here, unless she stopped by the house to see me in person. I could've gone through the weekend in relative peace and calm, unaware of her determination to ruin me. Because somehow that

503

became her ultimate goal, and for the life of me I can't figure out why. Why? Why? Why did she turn on me? She said she was sorry for ever telling Dahlia, but she did so only because she thought I'd want to know about the threesome they'd had with Thor. In effect, she claimed that she was going to ruin my life in order to please me, which is the kind of strained logic we used in the Vietnam War, where the village was destroyed in order to save it. Of course I pointed out that Lola could have told me all about the threesome with Thor without alerting Dahlia, but Lola didn't think that was fair to Dahlia. But the truth is, Lola wanted to tell Dahlia about us, she delighted in rehashing the worst of my obsessions, and together the two of them could laugh at my pathetic hang-ups, tittering away as they watched YouTube and admired Thor's boner and mocked me for being what I am, a degenerate who deserves mockery, of that there's no dispute . . . mockery and worse . . . calumny, ridicule, detestation . . . heap all on my head. But she professed to love me. She'd promised never to tell. It was supposed to be our secret.

Her infernal phone continues to sabotage me! I could roll down my window and let it drop out of my hand, where it'll crash against the black pavement of Chippenham Parkway and break into a hundred or so pieces, become unrecognizable, because that's what happens when you fall from grace. Will the healing process begin once I summon the strength to eradicate what's left of Lola from my life? A better question: how long did I keep some of Bev's stuff in the apartment after she'd moved out? Answer: I still have her tennis racket, some swim flippers, a spatula, two nonstick frying pans, and a bathroom scale, which has lost its calibration and makes everything five pounds heavier. I should've moved, too, and found a new place, somewhere to start over, instead of wallowing in the mire of the love nest we once shared. It's a fun game, thinking of all the things you could've and should've done differently . . .

Now we're on Hull Street, also known as Route 360, in the heart of Richmond's blue-collar grit. Mead heads west but not for very far, before turning left into a dusty parking lot, home of Longstreet Storage, which has seen better days. The fencing that surrounds the ramshackle collection of buildings looks strong, however, robust and topped with barbed wire. Mead stops the U-Haul in front of a gate and jumps out to come confer with me.

"I'm going to open this gate, and you follow me inside," he says excitedly. "But be quick about it, because the gate will swing closed in five seconds."

"Sure thing. I hope I make it in time."

"Me too. That gate is pretty unforgiving."

I steady myself as Mead hops back into the truck. Performance under pressure has never been my forte. I've been known to snap. I can lose my cool. Like when Lola told me about Dahlia. She honestly didn't think it was a big deal because Dahlia would never tell anyone. The young are so trusting! So unable to imagine the worst! Even after I described the various ways that Dahlia could harm me — I mean, she signed up for my Advanced Nonfiction class in the fall — and let's say that I were to give one of her essays a B, which in today's collegiate landscape is akin to failing — she could dangle Thor in front of me, batter me with that sausage-like appendage, and hold me hostage until her grade was more to her liking. I can't operate under those conditions, but Lola's attitude remained consistently naïve, dangerously so: *Dahlia is my friend, she's cool, she can keep a secret . . .*

The gate swings open, and Mead slowly lurches forward. Very slowly, eating up precious seconds, so that now I've got to decide whether to risk following him and getting caught in the gate or just holding back for another attempt. Why does everything have to be so hard? Why so much struggle? Throwing caution to the wind, I step on the gas and floor it, hoping the gate doesn't swing into the front grille and smash my headlights. My tires spin against the gravel and then I feel the gathering force of acceleration propel me through the gate that begins its return swing just as I go through the opening, barely escaping a collision by no more than a few inches.

Breathing hard, I continue to trail behind Mead as the U-Haul navigates through a series of turns that takes us finally to building twelve, where Mead rolls to a stop. He seems to know his way around this labyrinthine facility, like he's a frequent visitor; all the more strange that he just didn't put his collection in storage to begin with and spare us all the trouble. Whatever, I'm here to do my part and not question motives.

I park a few yards behind the truck so that we have room to unload. My body already aches from the strain of the loading and I dread dragging myself through another round, especially in this heat. There's no shade in this blasted landscape, just asphalt and sun, a toxic combination in July.

Mead hitches up his trousers as he waits for me to get out of the car, his face as imperious as a pasha surveying his lands. I search hopefully for a dolly or any wheeled conveyance, but find none.

"Let me go open the unit," he says, producing a huge ring of keys that must weigh a ton. We enter building twelve and then walk down a long hallway that is deathly silent, the only noise the click of our shoes against the concrete floor. I don't talk because there's nothing to say. I just want this to end and for me to crawl under a cold shower for the next hundred years. Making it to the wedding seems impossible.

Out of the corner of my eye I spot a dolly. Inwardly I rejoice as I go retrieve it. Mead stands at an imposing door of rivets and steel and tries to unlock it, though this task is impeded by the sheer number of keys he has. Eventually he curses the door and looks around helplessly.

"This is the right one," he mutters but gets no affirmation because we're alone and I have no idea what is right or what is wrong anymore. "Goddamn it, I don't need this in my life. They switched the lock out without telling me."

"Maybe we should ask somebody," I suggest, stating the obvious.

"Oh, that means I have to walk all the way back to the office." His head drops glumly and he tries a few more keys, the last gasps of a foiled plan. "Why would they just switch my lock like that? They probably want more money. It's like a form of extortion. I hate this place. I honestly do. The guy who owns it is a criminal. I kid you not. I'm pretty sure he lets people stow dead bodies in here."

"Have you been paying the rent?"

"Yes, of course, to the best of my knowledge."

Spoken like a true dissembler! Always add a qualifying statement to soften any absolute, something the American political class has mastered. "Then it's probably just a misunderstanding."

"Yeah, or a shakedown."

So our little errand to Longstreet Storage has bathed Mead in a new light, or perhaps revealed cracks in the foundation that my mother has tried to wallpaper over, namely, that he is a regular deadbeat. I'm not buying his conspiratorial explanation of why his lock got replaced; the most likely reason is that he is behind on his payments, meaning now I have indisputable proof that he needs my mother's money, that he doesn't have a pot to piss in, that he's a lout, that she's being taken advantage of . . . none of which matters because love is blind, mute, dumb, stupid, and ultimately self-defeating.

"I'll be right back," he tells me stoutly. "One way or another, they're going to open this door."

Which begs the question: what's behind the door? Why is he keeping this trove in storage while he filled my mother's basement with dangerous weapons? But that's Mead in a nutshell. Each revelation only adds to the confusion, whereas facts tend to clarify and define. Not with him. The knowns create unknowns, variables multiply on their own, and all that's solid melts away under the steady glare of rationality.

I sit and rest against a wall. A storage facility is where secrets go on vacation to unwind. Each locked door stands guard against intrusion, allowing the contents behind the luxury of complete stillness. Like people, most of the units are innocent and harmless. But a few aren't, and it's behind those doors we want most to look . . . and enter . . . and become.

My phone rings. Ithaca, New York, area code. There is no reason on earth I should take this call. But there is a chance, however remote, that it's from Lola. Maybe Dahlia came with her on this excursion and now

Lola is using Dahlia's phone . . . the prank will be revealed, the two girls will howl in ribald laughter, and I'll be left to wonder where it is from here I go.

"Hello?" I answer crisply. My head, though, bobs a little, and my breathing begins to quicken.

"Is this Edwin Stith?" A man's voice, one I'd recognize anywhere, as it belongs to the sonorous Carter LaSalle, Lola's father, theater professor and serial philanderer.

"Yes, it is. May I ask who's calling?" So polite! Manners so refined! Two grandees of academia exchanging pleasantries . . .

"This is Carter LaSalle. I believe you know my daughter, Lola." His usually pleasant tone has grown angry and seethes with resentment. Maybe this was the voice he used when he told Lola she was lazy and unmotivated, average even, which in the La-Salle family is a capital offense. This is how he sounded when he told her that she lacked passion and drive, that her grades were horrible, that she was destined for nothing.

"I do know her and let me stop you right there. I know why you're calling. I haven't seen Lola and I don't know where she is. I told the police that last night, and I wish I knew more. The last time I saw her was in Ithaca."

"At your apartment?"

"No, Lola's never been to my apartment. What are you implying?"

But he leaps right past my fake outrage. "Where was it then, Professor Stith, if you don't mind me asking? You see, we're quite worried about her. No one has seen or heard from her in several days, and we know that she's made calls and sent texts while in Richmond, but only to one number. Your number. She won't return our calls and respond to our texts."

He created her but blames me for her self-destructive tendencies. A daughter needs a father's approval, and he never gave Lola one warm embrace, one reassuring hug, because nothing she did was ever good enough for him. So if she's shunning him, he has only himself to blame.

"I don't know what to tell you. I haven't seen her. I never invited her to join me down here, and she apparently came on her own volition."

"Why would she do that, Professor? Drive down to Richmond to see you?"

"You'll have to ask her that. I can't speak for her."

Then he explodes like Lear on the heath, ravening and wild-eyed. "Don't you play that sanctimonious game with me, Stith!

You'd better clean up your act and pray that no one has laid a finger on her. I've spoken with the dean, and apparently this isn't the first complaint someone's made against you, which I find disturbing."

"I've done nothing wrong."

"Excuse me for not taking your word for it." Then he stops shouting at me and I hear noises in the background, perhaps his wife's voice urging him to show restraint, ever the gentle soul, even when confronting her daughter's defiler.

Or is it the other way around? I haven't been promiscuous, I haven't been snapping photos of my lover's genitalia, and I haven't been cavalier about destroying someone's life and livelihood. I've been nothing but honest and sincere, not to mention supportive and congenial, in all my dealings with Lola.

Carter LaSalle gets back on the line. "Stith, listen to me. I know Lola can be impulsive, but this has gone too far. I'm not accusing you of misconduct per se, but appearances count and this doesn't look good."

"It sounds to me like you are accusing me of the worst kind of violation." And rightly so! How unpersuasive my denials must sound, and as a trained actor, Carter La-

Salle can recognize a winning performance.

"I don't know what's happening between you two. All I know is that she's never done something like this before and we're worried sick. Please, I'm begging you, if you know something, anything at all, tell us! Just tell us! That's all we're asking for, simple decency." His strong voice cracks, again reminding me of Lear, as the old man leans over Cordelia's corpse, holding that tragic mirror to her gaping, dead mouth, hoping to find life within her. But failing.

"I've told you everything I know," I stammer, moved by his raw entreaty. "I'm worried, too. She's a special person I've gotten close to and worked with on a number of issues . . . this is the last thing I ever intended. If she in some way misinterpreted my efforts to reach out to her, I do apologize for that. In the future I'll need to establish firm boundaries."

"Yes, Lola's roommate told us that you two were very close."

I swallow back bitterness and breathe through my nostrils so that I can try to control my own swirling emotions. So Dahlia spilled the beans, just as I feared she would. I hate to be the one who says I told you so, but . . . "I need to go," I curtly explain. "My mother is getting married today, and so we're quite busy getting ready."

A silence descends as I await Carter La-Salle's response. I don't know if he's holding his breath or covering the microphone with his hand, but seconds tick past before he speaks again. "I'm sure we'll be in touch soon, Professor."

"Again, I hope this all works out for the best."

That kindly sentiment probably fell on deaf ears, as Carter LaSalle hung up before I could deliver it. Well, that was productive! I've become Notting College's Public Enemy No. 1 just as I'd predicted. I'm filled with shame, in case you're wondering whether I've debased myself to the point that I no longer experience basic human feelings. Not true. I'm ashamed of myself. Carter LaSalle's denunciations still ring in my ears. It's going to get worse, though. This is just the beginning . . .

Mead returns with a gnarled little man whose face is dotted with brown blotches and who walks with a peg-leg limp. I can tell by Mead's taciturn expression that he's highly distressed. His mouth quivers and his cheeks are pale, and he avoids making eye contact with me, the witness to his unmasking. I can barely hear what the little man is saying . . .

"I tried calling the number we had on file but it was disconnected and the e-mail you gave us didn't work, either. You're lucky I didn't haul this stuff to an auction house."

I stand up but keep my distance, as this really isn't my affair and Mead doesn't seem to want me nearby. The little man unlocks the door and stands back as Mead rushes inside. I can't see what's in there from my vantage, and so I creep forward a little . . . and see boxes, which Mead is pawing through.

"You'll need to settle up with me today, Mr. George, or I'll remove all of it by the close of business." Then the little man limps off, leaving behind a foul odor of mold and cigar. I wait a minute or so before calling out to Mead. I stick my head inside and see him sitting on a box, staring down at his feet.

"It wasn't supposed to be like this," he says softly. "I had it all worked out and then the next thing I know, it all fell apart. But that's life, huh?" He forces a smile and pats his knees but then doesn't move.

"What are in these boxes?" I ask, trying to sound clinical and not nosy. Mead probably will give me a misleading nonanswer, but instead surprises me with moving candor.

"I guess you could call them personal effects. Stuff I really should let go of but can't quite bring myself to. My wife, Graves and Gibson's mother, didn't want any of the kids' baby stuff and when we split up, I hated to throw it out. I mean, how do you throw out a birthday card your daughter wrote for you? Or your son's baseball trophies or collection of Hot Wheels? I know it's stupid and sentimental, but as someone who enjoys holding on to the past, who finds treasure in trash, you know, I couldn't — I can't — I have to keep it."

I want to believe him, I really do, but I also can't help feeling as if he's feeding me a heaping pile of crap. I'd love to look inside these boxes, but so far he doesn't seem inclined to show me an example of his children's handiwork. And there are a plethora of boxes in here, enough to contain the toys and drawings of a dozen kids. With room to spare — almost like the boxes in the basement had once sat in here before he moved them into my mother's basement. No, nothing he's saying adds up. Or some of it is true, some of it not.

"It really looks like you kept every scrap of paper they ever scribbled on," I say in a leading way, just to let him know I'm not a complete rube.

"I did. It's my vice — I hoard. But I'm also ready to make a clean break and start over with a blank slate, so to speak. I've been talking to your mother about downsizing, eliminating the unnecessary, and living spare and purposeful lives. Huh? Why not?"

Some of the boxes are labeled, however. *Marla's Room. Kitchen Stuff. Wedding Shower.* Has he kept the contents of his marriage in here? I can understand not wanting to toss out your daughter's stick-figure drawings of you and her circumscribed by a heart, but why keep your ex-wife's cheese grater? Why keep a box of her things at all? Not just a box, but boxes and boxes . . . and of course I can sympathize, as a spurned husband myself, with the addled thought process that goes into starting over.

"Who's Marla?" I ask, emboldened by these clues that taunt and tantalize.

"My mother, who saved all of my baby stuff. It's sad, really, this save-everything disease."

Oops. Now I need to backpedal. "So it runs in the family."

"Without skipping generations. I guess we should get a move on here. There's still a lot on my plate today."

Slightly chagrined, with a dollop of egg

on my face, I turn and head out, nearly running into a very large person who has been hovering outside the door, who is about the heft of a fat walrus — somehow Jeb Wardell has found his way inside the locked storage facility and now has effectively deployed his own blockade, as his bulk takes up the space we must pass through to get out. I stagger back, arms up in surrender. Mead stands but says nothing.

"What're you doing here?" Jeb asks, annoyed but verging on angry.

"I could ask you the same question" is my stout reply. Even though Jeb is glaring at me with malicious intent, I'm not afraid, because in a flash of recognition, the pieces start falling together. Now it makes sense. Leigh Rose told me last night that the three stooges were engaging in all kinds of misbegotten get-rich-quick schemes, including the mass purchase of "ammunition." Of course Jeb Wardell would do business with someone like my stepdaddy, whose collection of ammunition compares favorably with an armored division.

"What do you want?" Mead responds, not as firmly as I would have hoped. So this might spiral out of control. Perfect! Just what I wanted to have happen to me today. But such is Fate. Perhaps I'll be a murder victim at last and will perish next to the man out to soak my mother's inheritance . . . unless he's the one who pulls the trigger.

"We need to talk, alone." Jeb snorts through his nostrils like a bull about to charge.

"There's nothing to talk about," Mead says, more manfully.

"I really want to deal with you without him here." He means me, of course. The expendable one. The man after Leigh Rose's money. But I'm not going down without one last spike of the football in the end zone.

"How's Leigh Rose?" I ask with a toothy grin.

Jeb Wardell points a finger in my face. "Don't ever talk about her again, do you hear me?"

"It's an honest question!"

"What is it you want, Jeb?" Mead steps in between us to act as a buffer. Not that he could prevent Jeb Wardell from tearing me to shreds. "I'm getting married in a few hours and don't have time for this."

Jeb does back down, at least a little. "We need the merchandise," he says firmly. "I don't know what happened yesterday but I'm just telling you, this is no way to handle the situation."

"Someone is feeding you bogus information," Mead sputters, convincing no one. Hey ho! Have I stumbled upon the "other source" from which the Bastard Sons got an RPG launcher? Is this "other source" glaring at me now with saliva dotting his mustache? Because how did he find us? Sheer luck? He randomly picked a storage facility off Hull Street and managed to locate the one person he was looking for? No, he's been here before, perhaps multiple times. Mead knew plenty about the Wardells and offered me protection from them.

"We shouldn't discuss this in front of him," Jeb groans, pointing at the door in a gesture for me to leave.

"Ah, come on, Jeb!" I laugh in mock bravado. "I know what's up. I loaded the boxes onto the U-Haul. I've met the Russian. Don't pretend like this is some big secret here."

"This isn't a joke, Stith. Not anymore."

Ominous words that echo down the quiet corridors of building twelve. Given all that's happened, I hate to say it but Jeb is right. This has transcended personal vendetta and become something much more dangerous. Mead had better tread very lightly. He's gotten involved with the popular kids at school and right now it seems like they're stealing his lunch money. If he's not careful, he'll

take the fall. This is how this group operates.

"No one said it was a joke," Mead interjects. "But I need my money. All of it."

"The Russian said he paid in full."

"The hell he did! I'm not covering the
shipping costs."

"We need to make the boxes in that
U-Haul go away as soon as possible. I don't
care what you have to do, that's the goal.
Don't be stupid."

"I'm not being stupid, Jeb," Mead retorts.
"I can't vouch for what you and the Russian are up to, but I'm a collector of war
memorabilia and I've got nothing to hide.
Do you? What are you talking about anyway?
Why the rush? Why are you trying to push
me around?"

Does Mead really not know the depths to
which Jeb Wardell would descend in order
to make a buck? He honestly has no idea,
given the terrible events that have rocked
the city since last night? Or is he trying to
convince me of his innocence, me of all
people, from whom guilt hangs like drooping Spanish moss?

"The sooner we wrap it up, the better" is
all Jeb will admit to. Gone are the bluster
and bravado, and now fear is in control.
Maybe he doesn't know himself what he's

done, who might've come into possession of an RPG launcher . . . or what remains in the hands of people he can no longer find.

"Jeb, stop talking in riddles," Mead chides. "If you want this stuff shipped out, pay for the shipping and I'll make the arrangements."

"What's so funny?" Jeb growls at me.

"Nothing! Leave me out of it, Jeb!" I cry, making sure I don't smile, which I often do when nervous. "It's not my fault your paranoid empire is crumbling at your feet."

"We told you to stay away from Leigh Rose but you couldn't do it, and now she's . . ." But he doesn't finish his sentence and her fate remains undefined. Emboldened, I take a step toward him as Mead grabs me by the shoulders.

"Now she's what?" I demand.

"She's spewing nonsense!" he shouts. "You messed with her head, dude! She's saying crazy shit and it's all your fault."

Ah, now it becomes clear to me . . . Leigh Rose has a conscience and Leigh Rose won't keep her mouth shut . . . and the mess must get cleaned up at once. The FBI, ATF, every law enforcement acronym in the country has come to Richmond, and Jeb is in a panic because Leigh Rose not only refuses to drink the Kool-Aid, she's spitting it back in their faces.

"That's enough," Mead barks stoutly, coming between Jeb and me. "I don't know what the hell is going on here, but I don't like it. Until I get paid for shipping, the merchandise stays in storage. Jeb, if you're mixed up in anything nefarious or illegal, you can bet your bottom dollar I'll tell the authorities everything I know."

His words comfort me. Mead could be lying, but Jeb's ashen face tells a different story. Only later do I think that Jeb came to the storage facility to kill my stepfather, but ceased when he encountered me. Why that would've deterred him doesn't add up . . . unless he knew his sister truly loved me and he didn't want that blood on his hands. Wishful thinking?

Is there any other kind? And anyway, my heart will always belong to Lola.

According to my cell phone, someone e-mailed me at 9:01 a.m. The subject line is deceptively clever: "The Cops Are Looking for You!!!!" I don't open the message right away because there's something suspicious about the e-mail account of the sender, *iamhighashell@yahoo.com.* This borders on crass and Lola never would stoop to something as juvenile as an oblique marijuana reference, all of which makes me think this account was set up by Dahlia or someone else Lola might have told about us, such as Thor . . . and what would have stopped her from amusing that vain miscreant who mostly kept his head on his desk while I lectured (brilliantly), as if the sound of my voice caused him utter misery? Nothing, obviously, since she delighted in exposing my frailties to the world.

Against my better judgment, and even as Mead is pulling away from me to exit the storage facility, I open the e-mail. It reads as follows:

Police in Ithaca are looking for the driver of a late model Honda or Toyota that may have been involved with a hit-and-run fatality last night. The accident took place on Mecklenburg Road, near the intersection of Winterhaven at approximately 3 o'clock. Witnesses described a white male between the ages of 30 to 40 years old driving at a high rate of speed before running into Solomon Wright, 53, of Enfield, who sustained internal injuries and was pronounced dead at Cayuga Medical Center.

After this copy-and-pasted snippet from

the *Ithaca Journal,* there's a chilling post-script:

Was this you, Professor? Hahahaha

That's it. A newspaper article and an accusation. One of Lola's practical jokes? Or something more sinister?

I can't fall too far behind Mead, who's already driven off. I put the Honda in gear and drive, having first to turn around, which means winding through the byzantine lanes of the facility. I quickly catch up, but I'm still flummoxed by the e-mail. Let's say it was from Lola. Is she insinuating that I've metaphysically run her over? Isn't it the other way around, though? Am I not the victim of her own wanton assault on my heart? She can't possibly blame me for her hasty, heartless departure from the Chicory. No, I seriously doubt the validity of the e-mail.

So who sent it?

Dahlia, perhaps, though her modus operandi would incline more to open warfare and not this subtle barb . . . which points to yet another person, most likely Thor, as the culprit. Lola insisted that she never told that leering dwarf that I was a tangential party to the threesome, which was staged roughly

526

a month ago at the small summer sublet Lola shared with Dahlia, a few photos of which Lola shared with me, to go along with hours of narration, because ultimately that was how we spent our most intimate moments, lying together on the bed that had grown so cold when Bev slept in it, candles flickering, mood music in the background, usually of my choosing . . . and we were fully clothed! Never question that aspect of our romance. There were times when I did ask her to walk around my apartment and perform mundane tasks in the nude, but never when we did Story Time. Story Time! We even gave this decrepitude a name, as though it merited an official designation. Her idea, by the way. As was the threesome with Dahlia and Thor, which I grew to oppose. It was one thing when Lola would seduce a stray here and there, and then describe to me the nuts and bolts of the coupling (along with photos). But to bring her roommate in, and not any roommate but a roommate who already suspected something was afoul, was to risk exposing me in such a way as I'd never recover.

Lola: She'll never know you'll see the pictures.

Me: But she'll be in the pictures, meaning she'll be involved.

Lola: She won't care.

Me: You'll have to lie to her. You're sure you can do that?

Lola: It's not really lying if she never finds out.

To Lola, lying was a sin worse than death. I knew that about her and implored her not to take chances with generating emotions she couldn't control. The guys she slept with, she couldn't care less about. They meant nothing to her. But Dahlia occupied a different niche in Lola's cosmology. They'd had threesomes in the past, though not for many months, as love blossomed between Lola and me. Here I might take a measure of the blame for what happened. I found the threesomes fascinating, and when Lola asked if I wanted her to engage in one, I replied, without as much as a pause, without envisioning what would unfold, without keeping one eye on the grave, as we all should as we stagger through life, YES.

Yes.

Yes, please.

And then I thought: No.

Please don't.

Too late! Lola really wanted to get Dahlia and Thor together, as Dahlia knew all about Thor's reputation for being blessed in the groin region and so she expressed interest . . . it was a slow-moving train wreck. On the night before, the following exchange more or less took place.

Me: I really think this is a bad idea. I really do.

Lola: But wait till you see this guy! Your jaw will hit the floor. He calls it Thor for a reason.

Me: Then you just go solo.

Lola: Dahlia wants to do it. I can't say no. She'll ask me why and then I'll tell her.

Me: You can't tell her, ever. Right? Never.

Lola: I won't! Chill out. I've had threesomes before. I know what I'm doing.

That night, I didn't sleep a wink. Not that I sleep well on any given night, but that night, when the three of them convened, I was a mess. Though nothing yet had happened to me, I knew that in short order all would unravel. I tossed and turned, checked my phone for any updates, stared out the window, graded a few essays (with no one getting higher than a B minus), and at around 1:42 a.m. started drinking every molecule of alcohol in my apartment: half glass of wine, three shots of tequila, two of rum, and a thimbleful of bad scotch. By 2:34 a.m. I was completely hammered, as drunk as I've ever been in my life. Sleep should've been my final destination, but instead I sent Lola a text, consisting of two words.

Show me.

You see, until then I'd been very careful with digital communication with her. Never had Lola sent me photos of the phalli she'd accumulated, because I didn't want any kind of electronic trail that could link us for eternity and seal my fate. Story Time was when she showed me the dick pics on her phone, along with her riveting description of the sexual acrobatics. We spoke on the phone every so often but seldom texted, again in an effort to reduce my exposure. Plus, we liked the face-to-face encounter of Story Time, and out of those sweetly tender and ultimately demeaning moments our relationship grew and matured, until it became love, until we both knew that we were united in spirit, until we pledged devotion to each other . . . but when I drunkenly texted her on the night of the threesome, she, being dutiful and inebriated herself, replied with a photo of Thor in all his protruding glory.

Ashes to ashes, dust to dust. My goose was cooked.

There was no putting the genie back in the bottle. I hit the Send button, and then she did, and my secret darkness was now part of the permanent record of the history of mankind. And it ate me alive from the inside. Once the floodgate was open, the barrage began and each of her texts was just another nail in my coffin. But my ruin dated back to that besotted night when I broke down and sent an ill-advised text that could never be retracted. How I hated myself! I really can't describe the ferocity of my self-loathing during the merry month of May, usually a time of joy in the life of an academic, spring semester over, summer beckoning in sun-drenched freedom, but not for me. I knew in time that one mistake would cost me and I knew exactly how it would happen. Dahlia would find out because Lola would tell her, which is exactly what happened. I was powerless to halt this ineluctable march to my undoing, even as I couldn't imagine a life without Lola. During the same hour I might find myself deliriously happy and unspeakably sad, emotional matter and antimatter creating and destroying joy and sorrow. There was no one in whom I could confide, except for Lola, and about this turmoil I could say nothing to her because I had to pretend that all was well . . . because all was well at certain moments, like when we hiked to Buttermilk Falls and she collected chicory and made a wreath she wore around her neck. And we made love by the crashing waterfall, and all Lola wore was her purple silk scarf . . . and said she loved me.

Two days ago, Thursday to be exact, I called Bev. Not to confide in her! I'd never give her the satisfaction of cheering me up. Honestly, I don't know why I called. I was sober. I had stopped popping pills for about a month. Lola was supposed to hook up with some guy whose nickname was Horse. Dahlia knew about us. I was alone in the apartment. Of course, after the divorce, being alone became pretty much my default setting and you'd think after two years of practice I'd have perfected the art of solitude. But Lola had disturbed my routines and altered my patterns, and I relied on her companionship. Forget the pictures of her conquered — I enjoyed cooking dinner with her, goofing around with her, waking up next to her — all of which I knew was going to end now that Dahlia was in on it.

So why did I call Bev? Why did I lacerate myself with that particular knife? What did I expect from her? She wasn't happy to hear from me. In her voice I detected the gruff exasperation of a person whose patience had run out long ago. Igor was out of town at a ceramics instructor's conference. Meaning she was alone. Even then she didn't want to make conversation with me. Every answer was terse. She asked me no questions, answered mine only with a parsimony of words that by comparison would make the average pro athlete sound like Cicero as an orator. Finally, after about ten minutes of pointless drivel, I got upset. "Listen, things aren't great for me right now and the least you can do is be my friend and pretend like you care what happens to me. You promised me that we'd stay friends, or was that just another convenient lie?"

She didn't like hearing that from me. "I don't have time for this, Eddie. Or the energy."

And for the first time that I could remember, she hung up on me. I held the phone in my hand like it was the carcass of a dead animal and stared at it for any lingering sign of life.

I didn't go over there.

Not right away and not to kill her. I didn't kill her. I didn't go over there, at least not right away, because first I sent Lola a text asking her about Horse and heard nothing back. Nothing! Not one word. I hadn't wanted her to go. I'd begged her not to. Yet there I was, asking for an update on a tryst I'd attempted to squelch . . . after calling my ex-wife and getting the phone slammed in my face (what a quaint expression!). What I mean by "I didn't go over there" is that I didn't actually enter Bev's new home. I do admit to driving on the street that passed by Igor's studio/ashram, with the Zen rock garden in the front yard, but I was actually on my way to Lola's sublet she shared with Dahlia, and I didn't go in there, either . . . but lingered outside, hoping to catch a glimpse of Horse and my beloved angel . . .

Look at the torrent one bogus e-mail has unleashed! I'm sitting at a red light at the Huguenot Road intersection, still following Mead, and I feel worse now about everything than ever. Should I bother to reply to the e-mail? And say what? To whom? Could it actually be from Lola? There's no way. The sooner I accept her verdict on me, the better. I possess her phone . . . but I still wonder whether I've been living in a dream (or nightmare, take your pick). Here's the absolute last thing I'm positive of when it comes to Lola. On Thursday night she didn't return from her assignation with Horse (real first name Mark, she would later tell me) until well after midnight, hours later than she said she'd be home, and when she got home, she showed me no pictures of Horse because there weren't any. There weren't any? Wasn't that the entire point of her going to meet up with him, so that we could share her devilment together during Story Time? There weren't any? Why not, pray tell?

"I don't know. I just never got around to it."

Did he live up to the billing of Horse?

"I guess so. He was really nice, not what I was expecting at all. His mother is dying of breast cancer and we talked a lot about that."

You talked? You didn't copulate? Did you even see it?

"Not really. It was dark. We sat in the dark and talked about his mother. He wants to go to med school and become an oncologist. Oh, and he plays the saxophone. He's in a jazz band at Cornell. I'm really tired. I just feel like crashing."

So they bared their souls for each other and divulged inmost dreams and hopes, fears and failures, and from the little bit she told me of the night with Horse, I deduced a simple truth: she told him everything, just like she'd divulged all to Dahlia. Who was next on the hit parade? The dean? My kindergarten teacher? A rant on Rate Your Professor?

■ ■ ■ ■

After we dropped the U-Haul off, Mead told me that he had some errands to run and so he sped off in his spiffy Corvette. I return home without him. This news has shaken my mother. She looks at me as if I've just spit tobacco on the kitchen floor while spewing profanities.

"What errands?" she asks excitedly. "Did he say where he was going? I'm supposed to leave in an hour, and he was going to drive downtown and pick up his mother and Paula. I don't know what errands he's talking about. I don't have time to worry about this. I still have to shower and get ready. Now I know why the bride and groom aren't supposed to see each other before the wedding."

But her nervous laugh sounds forced, and her smile is crooked and brief. I don't tell her about Jeb Wardell confronting us at Longstreet Storage. It might kill her.

"What can I do to help?" I offer.

"Just get Graves and Gibson to Tredegar by two. Gibson is up, as you can see, but still no sign of Graves. I'll knock on his door again."

"That's it? You don't need anything else?"

"You've done so much already. Everything else is covered, as long as the caterer doesn't flake on me."

Then she darts away upstairs, talking to herself.

"I know where he went," Gibson announces with a heavy dose of sarcasm. She's eating breakfast — a bowl of dry cereal — and scrolling through her phone. Even a mundane task in her hands seems thrilling. How she's managed to make it through life largely unblemished is a complete mystery. But she's not long for this world. Her pace is unsustainable, and the best part is, she knows that but doesn't care.

"Okay, I'll take the bait. Where is he?"

"Never mind, if you're going to be a prick about it."

"I'm sorry. I don't mean to come across like a prick." I don't like saying the word and it comes out of my mouth in a stilted manner. I clear my throat, wipe my face with a rag . . . "Let's try again. Where do you think he is?"

"Want me to show you?"

"Show me?"

She looks around to make sure we're alone and then speaks in a conspiratorial whisper. "He's at my mother's house, I promise you."

"Why did you tell me that?"

"Because it's true. How much do you want to bet?"

"A million dollars. No, nothing. I don't even care. I really don't." Except I do. Will catching him in the act stop the wedding? Do I have the courage to inform my mother? Highly doubtful . . .

"You don't care that this whole thing is a sham?" she asks.

"No, to be perfectly frank, I care a lot. You have no idea. All day I've been struggling." My voice drops in abjection. "Just forget it. I'm the biggest sham of all."

She rolls her eyes and resumes her thumbing. A part of me wants to go see if Gibson is right, however. Just for my own satisfaction. And doing so would also get us alone in the car together, Gibson and me . . . because the happiest times I've had lately have been with her. If I could just capture a fraction of her fierce spirit! We could also talk about music, and her dreams . . . the future! She actually has one, whereas I . . .

"Okay, let's go," I say quietly. "We have to hurry, though."

Gibson puts her phone down.

"It'll take ten minutes," she says emphatically, because the young are prone to fits of moral outrage . . . and are suckers for sob stories . . . and can't leave well enough alone. Exhibit A: Horse. Totally unnecessary. An unwelcome diversion. But Lola insisted, on my behalf, despite my own disavowals. Horse the Galloping Oncologist, beating cancer off with his meat stick . . .

I'm going to hell.

"That's all the time we have," I tell her, slapping the counter. "You're on. And I bet you five bucks you're dead wrong."

"Oh, so you want to wager real money! Let's roll, Jelly Bean. I have to tell you, though, that I'm never wrong."

She stands up, pushing away from the table, just as Graves comes in. His hair is wild, and he resembles a madman, like he just stepped out of a Russian novel. And the body odor is overwhelming. He smells like a garbage truck that lost a fight with a sewer.

"When was Avery here?" he demands of me.

"This morning."

"He's texting me all kinds of crazy stuff! He's blaming it all on me! He's nuts!" He holds up his phone as a kind of spectral evidence of Avery's cunning duplicity. "I can't deal with this right now. They're setting me up to take the fall. I know they are."

"Then go to the police first," I urge him,

a suggestion that he again brushes aside with a dismissive wave of his hand. There was no talking sense to him last night, either.

"No way."

"Are we going or not?" Gibson asks, impatiently, indifferent to her brother's plight. Maybe she knows something about Avery we don't. Or she just doesn't care.

"What about all of this junk with Avery?" I retort, nodding toward Graves, who's wafted over to the kitchen table and dropped into a chair.

"Avery is a punk and he'll always be a punk," she sneers in defiance. "Graves?"

"What?"

"Did you do anything to that statue?"

"No."

"Then shut up about it." She turns back to me. "Come on, I want to show you and get that five bucks."

I don't want to leave Graves in this condition, but Gibson wants to go and she won't be stopped.

"You need to take a shower," I snap at Graves. "You can't mope around all day. We need to get ready for the wedding and arrive on time as instructed." It pays to be a very punctual deviant. You draw less attention to yourself and avoid conflict.

"I'm not going," he groans in despair.

Gibson raises her arms in outrage. "If he's not, I'm not!"

"You're both going!" I object vociferously, staring them both down. "Now cut the crap. Stop thinking about yourselves and do something for someone else for a change. You'll feel better and help make the world a better place." Bev used similar exhortations with the same result: Graves doesn't seem willing to cede an inch, and I slipped further and further into self-pity . . .

"They'll kill me. You understand that, right?"

"Avery doesn't have the guts," Gibson laughs with a mordant chuckle.

"Not Avery. Stefan."

A name I had yet to hear mentioned in conjunction with the Bastard Sons. "Who's Stefan again?"

"We're running out of time!" Gibson cries, pulling on my arm. Her hands are surprisingly strong, her grip robust. "Come on, it doesn't matter. Stefan is a punk just like Avery and they're both idiots. Graves, you're being a total wuss. Stop being all dramatic so you can skip the wedding."

"This isn't a game, okay? Stefan shot somebody last night. I saw it."

"Who did Stefan shoot?" Gibson remains skeptical but releases my arm to listen to the explanation, which comes in a staccato burst of fear and anger.

"This guy, you don't know him. I don't, either, really. His name was Nick or Dick, but Stefan was going bonkers and screaming about traitors to the cause, and that's when I got out of there. He was going to shoot me next, and he still might, the crazy bastard. I think he's the one who blew up the Lee statue."

"Oh, totally!" Gibson shouts. "I see that!"

"Okay, okay," I jump in, waving my arms as if to signal an incomplete pass in football. "That's enough. This has gone way too far and you can't sit it out, Graves. This guy Stefan sounds like a true menace to society and extremely dangerous, and you can't let him continue to hurt other people, regardless of how you feel about the police. It's wrong, plain and simple."

"I'm not going to the cops."

"Whatever, leave him alone," Gibson says, once again taking my arm and generating a feeling that cuts a little too close to the bone, with my flesh a little too tingly and her body a little too close to mine. "We need to go check on Dad. I think he's at Mom's."

"That's ridiculous," grouses Graves. Gibson flips her brother the bird, which he promptly dismisses with a faint sigh. "I'm serious, just stay out of his business."

"I've caught him cheating before," Gibson assures me.

"Maybe it's not such a great idea," I'm forced to admit, sorry that I ever agreed to her plan of snooping around. It's not like my mother doesn't harbor her own doubts of Mead's fidelity, since she had what she called a "panic attack" in front of the restaurant where the ex-wife works. "What point would we be making? What purpose would it serve?"

"I won't say anything," she pouts. "I just want to know."

All children of divorce dream of the reconciliation that will bring the family back together, that magic bullet of rekindled love capable of healing the rip in the soul. Gibson's desire to ensnare her father in a trap is the obverse of this desire, which doesn't mean it's no less compelling. Given her womanly curves and abundance of sex appeal, it's easy to forget that Gibson is barely out of her childhood, an adult in name alone, and often victim of her own conflicting emotions. For some reason it's important to her to drive by her mother's house, perhaps as a way of saying farewell to the dream forever.

"Okay," I relent, suddenly struck by a

sensation that was once familiar but lately has become alien — that of being a human being, one with compassion. "You promise it won't take long?"

A tear struggles to escape her eye, and she brushes it away as one would slap at a gnat. So many holes become chasms, it's a wonder we all aren't swallowed up in the abyss of our lives. At one time Lola thought she could count on me to support her, offer solace and succor, and never leave her hanging . . . compared to an aspiring oncologist, what could I ever offer her? Or anyone?

Through sniffles, Gibson asks: "Can we stop for smokes, too?"

"Is this yours?"

Gibson is holding Lola's iPhone in her hand, having scooped it up as she got into the Honda. Claiming it as mine won't work because we've already discussed the merits of Android versus Apple, with me firmly on the side of my Google brethren. Being quick on my feet is a strength of mine, yet here the right lie escapes me and I flounder for a response.

"Oh, that?" I snort nervously, struggling to insert key into ignition. "My girlfriend left it in here."

"Girlfriend? You never said you had a

girlfriend. Who is she? What's her name?"

"Doesn't matter because we broke up. Here, let me have it."

But Gibson ignores me and instead starts pawing at the screen, which is the last thing I want her doing. "Hey, someone named Mark called! Twice!"

"Let me have it, please." I reach across and forcefully grab the iPhone from her with more intention than she was perhaps expecting.

"What the hell, dude! I was going to give it back."

"You shouldn't go through her personal stuff."

"I was just looking at it."

"I know what you were doing. Just forget about it. She's not worth the trouble."

"But how did she leave her phone in your car if you guys broke up?"

Driving around town with Gibson has been, except for a few bumps in the road, a mostly pleasurable experience, but not when she's interrogating me about my love life. I was looking forward to listening to music with her, chatting about nothing, instead of this awkward conversation. Anger suffuses my voice, as it bubbles up inside. "I don't know. I found it before I left to drive down here."

"She must be pissed."

"I'm taking good care of it. At least I was until you got your mitts on it."

"Is Mark her new boyfriend?"

Am I even headed in the right direction? We're approaching Cherokee Road, and common sense says we should take a right for access to Chippenham Parkway. I have no clue where her mother lives. "Which way?"

"Oh, yeah. Take a right. My mom lives off Forest Hill, not far from where she works. So is Mark her new flame or what? Is that why you two broke up?"

"You ask a lot of questions."

"I get bored easily."

"Do you mind if we don't talk about this? I hate to get all maudlin, but the wound is still pretty raw."

"I thought you reconnected with one of your old high school sweethearts, the rich one. What happened to her?"

We're passing by John Graziano's house — that of his parents, anyway — when she pops this question, as unlikely as that might appear to be. Yet plain as day, parked in the driveway, is Leigh Rose's SUV, with the distinctive Dancing Bear bumper sticker. The saga continues apparently, just without my participation.

Except I see her emerge from the house. Running.

I hit the brakes hard enough for us to skid to a stop.

"What's wrong?" Gibson asks, startled by my maneuver. Without answering I crane my head to get a good look at the scene, to make sure my eyes weren't playing tricks on me. Indeed, Leigh Rose is sprinting across the lawn where we once played pickup football games and hide-and-go-seek, and then she hops into the SUV. She's running but no one appears to be chasing her. There are no other cars in the driveway, either.

"You know that woman?"

"That's her."

"That's who?"

The Tahoe recklessly backs up and then speeds off down Cherokee Road in the opposite direction as we're headed.

"The old high school girlfriend."

But why is she going that direction? She lives across the river . . . unless she's going to my house. But why would she? No . . . she isn't looking for me, is she? It doesn't matter, I have to find out, and so I execute a hurried and artless three-point turn in the middle of Cherokee Road, nearly backing into a mailbox sturdy enough to have split my car in two, all while Gibson peppers me with questions and asides to which I can't readily respond.

"What are you doing? Are you trying to kill us? You're being a total freak right now! Calm down, dude!"

"I have to catch up to her!"

It's a white-knuckle ride up and down hills and around curves, but something tells me that Leigh Rose has finally made up her mind and now has taken the proverbial bull by the horns by making her break from those sleazeball frat boys. All isn't lost! Just when things couldn't have gotten any bleaker in my life, again the unexpected surges from the morass of defeat. There's still time for us, the clock hasn't run out. Yet, if I'm wrong, yes, that's right: the dead will die again. What was over for good will end once more forever.

My Honda strains against the exertion of making up distance, but I manage to get within sight of Leigh Rose, in time to see her turn left on Traylor Drive! My street! She's turning down my street! She loves me after all! Jeb admitted as much at the storage facility . . .

"See!" I exclaim in triumph, pumping my fist like I just hit a home run, "she's looking for me! She's driving to my house!"

"Why?"

"To find me. We fell in love. I know it sounds stupid, but it's true. We reconnected. It's just one of those amazing things that happen sometimes, against all odds."

Gibson reaches over to honk the horn but I brush her hand away. "Don't jinx it! Just let it happen. Don't get in the way."

"Oh my God, you're such a dumbass! She's probably going to some other dude's house."

"She just ran away from her fiancé, so I highly doubt it."

As we near the Stith homestead, Leigh Rose hits her brakes, just as she should if her destination is my abode. I slow down, too, of course, grinning like one of those idiots who are told they just won the Publishers Clearinghouse Sweepstakes. Because that is a bogus contest where there are no real winners. Just chumps.

"Cops!" cries Gibson, sinking low in her seat. My neck muscles tighten and my throat constricts as if I'd just chugged rat poison. "What the fuck should we do?"

Police cars have surrounded our house and the street is blocked. A line of three cars waits to speak to a patrolman directing traffic. I'm right behind Leigh Rose. But not for long.

"What are you doing?" Gibson screams at me.

"Turning around."

"Why? Graves is in trouble!" Tears flood down her pretty face as I back into a neighbor's paved drive. The Olsens, a couple whose children were quiet, passive, and sickly. Grace was the daughter, a year behind me in school. She was my date to the prom. Our first and last night out together. I asked her because I knew no one would. She barely had any friends and I was sick of the popular girls at my school who were as predictable as a twice-told tale. At first Grace thought I was joking and wouldn't go with me, but I assured her I wasn't. There was a tremulous beauty in her trying to get out of her prolonged adolescence. I turned out to be correct in my assessment: by the end of the summer, Grace Olsen had blossomed into a perfectly lovely young woman.

■ ■ ■ ■

DAY THREE —
JULY 3

■ ■ ■ ■

My attorney is named Cynthia Fox and I'm not kidding. No, never will I kid again, because I find myself in grave legal trouble. Pardon me for sampling from Snoop Dogg, but murder was the charge that they gave me. No one accused of homicide can ever tell another joke or make a pun, but instead the jailed felon must grind onward and ineluctably toward acquittal. Can Ms. Fox, Esquire, lead me to freedom? Can she restore my good name, rescue my reputation, and prove this charge to be baseless? For my sake, I certainly hope so, though I'm not counting on it because I'm guilty as sin.

One salient fact about my legal counsel: she is extremely attractive, in the bookish, professional way of a natural beauty who has worked hard to establish herself in a career demanding that she prove that her brains exceeded her looks.

"Mr. Stith, I just have some basic paper-work you need to complete in order that I can begin to represent you in this matter," she begins, in a voice strong and clear. A jury would fall in love with this woman. When she looks those twelve average Americans in the eyes and tells them I'm not guilty, they'll believe her, especially the menfolk who've been conditioned to accept as fact whatever a beautiful woman says.

"My mother hired you?" The medication has made me feel extremely fatigued and detached. Risperdal is a very potent antipsychotic with dangerous side effects, but mostly it leaves me feeling stupidly drunk.

"She has retained my services, yes, but you need to agree to my representation."

I could give you all the details right now. I could just disgorge my innards for you to poke through and we'd have an answer, a solution to the puzzle of *the dead will die again.* But I don't know that I can do that. My hold on reality, according to the psychiatrist who examined me yesterday following my suicide attempt, is tenuous. So take my "confession" with a grain of salt. The state of Virginia thinks I'm psychotic, but not so psychotic that I can't tell right from wrong, just psychotic enough to require medication.

"I agree," I say gallantly. How I adore staring at her. It's like I'm back in Prague on my Fulbright and I'm walking across the Charles Bridge when I see a fellow American — how like sore thumbs we stick out in the Old World! — a student from Slippery Rock College with the classic features of a *Vogue* model, who got drunk with me on cheap wine and ended up sleeping on the floor of my hovel by the Old Jewish Cemetery. We did not — I repeat — we did not have sex. This wasn't my decision, but hers, and frankly she made a wise choice, given my homicidal propinquity.

"I'll just need your signature on this document."

She slides over a piece of paper that I don't bother to look at. The line where my John Hancock is needed has been highlighted in yellow for me. The pen must weigh a hundred pounds and I struggle to hold it upright.

"Everything okay, Mr. Stith?"

"No. Yes. There, done."

I slide the paper back to her and she deposits it in a manila folder with expert efficiency.

"Tell me you used to be a model," I gush at her, and she registers no emotion as she sits across from me in the city jail's cramped, cold room where lawyers confer with their clients.

"No," she replies crisply, legal pad and pen arrayed before her.

But those cheekbones! That sinewy neck! The trim figure, the long legs, and most of all, the pellucid blue eyes that sparkle with genuine goodness, as if the Creator had hewn her being from the diminishing stock of Righteousness available in the universe.

"Where did they find the body?" I ask crisply.

"Pardon me?"

"The body? Where did they find it?"

"I don't know, Mr. Stith. I'm here just to make sure the extradition hearing is fairly run and that your rights are protected. Do you understand that? I'm not your defense attorney. You'll get one of those after you've been transferred back to New York and have been arraigned." Her voice cracks a little as she explains the nature of our professional relationship, which might best be described as fleeting. She's like a legal one-night stand. And she doesn't seem to relish talking with me about the body of the deceased, and who could blame her.

But it matters to me. It matters only in the sense that I made attempts to bring comfort to the afflicted, the hallmark of a fully developed humanity. She had wounded me. She had given her heart to another, and yet still I gathered pine needles to support her lovely head, fashioned leaf litter into a kind of bower, and in those cold, dead hands, placed a hastily collated arrangement of chicory. It was her favorite flower. I wrapped her scarf around my neck and took her iPhone, which I was going to throw into the crashing waters of the falls but decided at the last minute to keep with me. In case she ever called. Or texted. And I knew she would, because I had to hear from my beloved.

As I hiked out of the park, steeled for the unbearable journey south, I saw that my number was right there on her screen. So I sent myself a text.

Take me with you. She was dead nevermore.

Then I took a selfie.

No . . . then I went mad.

It's currently one p.m. on July 3, and any true Southerner worth a white hood and burning cross knows that right now, 150 years ago, George Pickett ordered his charge across the cornfield at Gettysburg, an act of idiotic bravery and savage heroism that captured, like nothing else ever could, the atomizing forces at work in the courageous hearts of a doomed breed. After the field was littered with dead, and the battle lost, Robert E. Lee surveyed the carnage and uttered the most honest words in all of American history, "It's all my fault."

ABOUT THE AUTHOR

Lee Irby teaches history at Eckerd College and lives in St. Petersburg, Florida. He is the author of the historical mysteries *7,000 Clams* and *The Up and Up*.